The Banting Enigma

The Banting Enigma

THE ASSASSINATION OF SIR FREDERICK BANTING

William R. Callahan

FLANKER PRESS LTD.
ST. JOHN'S, NL
2005

Library and Archives Canada Cataloguing in Publication

Callahan, William R., 1931-
  The Banting enigma : the assassination of Sir Frederick
Banting / William R. Callahan.

ISBN 1-894463-70-6

  1. Banting, F. G. (Frederick Grant), Sir, 1891-1941--Death
and burial--Fiction. I. Title.

PS8605.A45B35 2005   C813'.6   C2005-905404-2

Copyright © 2005 by William R. Callahan

PRINTED IN CANADA

FLANKER PRESS
ST. JOHN'S, NL, CANADA
TOLL FREE: 1-866-739-4420
WWW.FLANKERPRESS.COM

Cover Design: Adam Freake - Consumer Quest

  Canada Council Conseil des Arts
for the Arts du Canada

We acknowledge the financial support of: the Government of Canada through the Book Publishing
Industry Development Program (BPIDP); the Canada Council for the Arts which last year invested $20.3
million in writing and publishing throughout Canada; the Government of Newfoundland and Labrador,
Department of Tourism, Culture and Recreation; the Newfoundland and Labrador Arts Council.

For Roderick B. Goff of Gander, Newfoundland,
probably the last person alive to have spoken
with Sir Frederick Banting.

Enigma:

Something that is inscrutable, mysterious, hard to understand.

Webster's Dictionary

AUTHOR'S NOTE

Inscrutable, mysterious, hard to understand . . . Major Sir Frederick Grant Banting, M.D., unquestionably was all of these in his work and his life – and in the circumstances of his shocking death in the winter of 1941 on the edge of Newfoundland's Bonavista Bay wilderness.

The cause of the fatal airplane crash near the isolated fishing village of Musgrave Harbour remains a mystery more than six decades later. It is true that certain reasons for it have been suggested, principally icing in the carburettors. But there has been far from universal acceptance of this conclusion – now, or when the crash occured.

The salient fact is that five brand new, nearly identical Hudson bombers took off in reasonable weather on a flight from Gander, Newfoundland to Prestwick, Scotland. Four completed the flight without incident. The fifth experienced trouble – catastrophic trouble – and astonishingly, not in one, but in both engines. The aircraft in which Banting was a passenger turned back immediately when the trouble began, but failed in the attempt to complete the short return flight to base.

The reason or reasons for Banting, the renowned physician-scientist and Nobel Prize winner, being where he was on a mid-winter's day in 1941, in the midst of the Second World War, are obscure at best. It is well-known that his superiors were opposed to his going to Britain at the time. A commissioned officer, was he so obsessed by the need to be directly involved in the war as to risk insubordination, to act against orders?

Finally, there is Banting's conviction that germ warfare was inevitable, and his determination to see that Canada and Britain were equipped to fight fire with fire, as it were, in the development and use of biological weapons. Many people would say that this ran diametrically counter to his reputation as the humanitarian co-discoverer of insulin, the life-saving method to offset the effects of diabetes, one of the worst scourges of mankind.

The novel locates this inscrutable Canadian and the tragedy of his untimely passing in the context of twentieth-century wartime history, ranging from the beginnings of the First World War to the middle of the Second. To achieve this, it has been necessary to recall to mind many of the people, institutions, and occurrences that contributed to that context. In particular, the novel recalls events of the last few of those thirty tumultuous years that are largely unknown or have too readily been forgotten.

The Banting Enigma is not a history book; rather, it is a historical or documentary novel. Pains have been taken to authenticate the part real people played in these events. Perceptive readers will have little difficulty discovering instances where "fitting" has taken place.

W. R. C.

PROLOGUE

To German military historian Friedrich von Bernhardi is ascribed the proposition that war is nothing less than a matter of biological necessity – an expression of "the natural law upon which all the laws of Nature rest . . . the struggle for existence." A cavalry officer who had achieved the rank of General in the Kaiser's Army, von Bernhardi concluded that nations are bound either to progress, or else to decay. Applying this principle at the commencement of what would prove to be history's bloodiest, most destructive century, his judgment was unequivocal: The Fatherland must choose "world power or downfall."[1]

Of similar mind was Count Alfred von Schlieffen, who became Chief of Germany's General Staff in 1891. He contributed to the debate over who would, or should, rule Europe, if not the whole world – was there really any doubt about it? And he authored the German military strategy that, long after he himself had gone from the corridors of power, would launch the First World War. That bitter contest endowed human civilization with the dubious legacy of such newly developed tools of mass destruction as aerial bombing and strafing, rapid-fire machine guns, armoured vehicles of enormous portable firepower called tanks, and several varieties of poison gas.

By these and other means the combatants pursued a conflict so terrible as to earn from the leading British historian and novelist Herbert George Wells the all-too-optimistic description "The war to end wars." Of course, it did no such thing.

The Schlieffen Plan, as it became known, was based upon a massive incursion across neutral, independent Belgium in order to invade and conquer France: a bold sweep intended to end only when Paris had been captured. French forces would be encircled and, it was anticipated, easily outflanked – a strategy for a short war of six weeks, a mere summer adventure for the vaunted German forces.

However Britain, having learned her lesson at Waterloo, had been careful to establish a buffer against attack, a land frontier rather than the vulnerability of the English Channel, by guaranteeing Belgian neutrality. Thus when Belgium was invaded, the British did as their commitment required and declared war on Germany.

There was, of course, more, much more: An Austrian ultimatum demanded the ultimate penalty for the assassins of Sarajevo for the murders of Crown Prince Franz Ferdinand, heir to the Hapsburg Empire, and his wife, the Countess Sophie. The response was considered inadequate, so Austria declared war on Serbia.

The Russians, self-styled protectors of all Slavs, mobilized against Austria. They refused to stand down on Germany's demand, so Germany declared war on Russia.

France, committed to come to the aid of the Russians, mobilized against Germany. The Kaiser was thus given the excuse to do precisely as von Schlieffen had proposed two decades earlier. The Schlieffen Plan was frustrated at the Battle of the River Marne. With superior forces in striking distance of Paris, the tide suddenly turned as the faltering French, aided by the formerly reluctant British, took sudden and unexpected advantage of a miscalculation on the part of the invaders and put them quickly into retreat. In just four days in September 1914, Germany lost its chance for a decisive victory over the French and the opportunity to prevail in a wider conflict.

There followed the horrific struggle, a bloody tug-of-war in the trenches, in which millions of lives were sacrificed for uncertain occupancy of a few yards of mud and barbed wire. Scores of cities, towns, and villages were destroyed. Vast stretches of formerly productive farmland were turned into burial grounds for men, horses, and the emergent machinery of modern conflict. Civilian populations were terrorized and decimated, and the economies of nations laid waste.

After four years of bloodletting, on November 11, 1918, a ceasefire was declared, and an armistice signed. By that time, three million German and Austro-Hungarian soldiers had been slaughtered, not to mention huge numbers maimed in mind and body. The war had cost, in addition, the lives of one and three-quarter million Russian soldiers, nearly 1,500,000 Frenchmen, about 1,000,000 British Empire troops, including Newfound-landers and Canadians, and almost 650,000 Italians – the cream of each country's youth.

One hundred and twenty-five thousand Americans were among the dead. The one million soldiers, sailors, and airmen committed to the fray under the Stars and Stripes, the United States formally abandoned its neutral stance in January 1917, tipped the balance against Germany – thus the American myth that the Yanks won the war "over there" virtually single-handed-edly.

Under terms of the punitive settlement imposed by the Versailles Conference, which took place from January to June 1919, the victorious Allies demanded that Germany pay huge sums in war reparations – 132 billion gold marks, or thirty-three billion U.S. dollars. This led to ruinous inflation in the early 1920s. Germany was required to reduce substantially its military strength, and in a wholesale rearrangement of the map of Europe, forced to give up territory in the west, north, and east. The deep resentment thus engendered led to years of violent nationalism, brought to a head by the worldwide Depression in which German unemployment soared from 1,500,000 to 2,500,000 in the first months of 1930. Those lucky enough to keep a job were required to take steep cuts in pay, and what they did receive was becoming worthless.

Increasingly, people blamed the nation's troubles on Jews and foreigners, and to a lesser extent, on the alleged perfidy of the nation's military leaders. The loudest and most insistent voice raised against Jews and foreigners was that of Adolf Hitler, a German Army dispatch runner awarded the Iron Cross, First

Class, for bravery in 1917. Under his rabble-rousing influence, the German Workers Party became the National Socialist German Workers (Nazi) Party. It had fewer than 20,000 adherents in the mid-twenties, but could count 120,000 by 1929. By 1930 elections, it claimed one million members and its seats in the Reichstag jumped from twelve to 107. Two years later, it had the largest bloc with 230 seats.

By force of numbers, Hitler was named Chancellor by a reluctant, aging President Paul von Hindenberg on January 30, 1933 and given dictatorial powers. Ten days later there occurred the mysterious fire that gutted the Reichstag, blamed by Nazis on the Communists. The torching of parliament was, in Hitler's words, "a sign from God" that the Communists must be destroyed.

Hermann Goering, First World War fighter ace who began his service to the Führer as commander of the Nazi Storm Troopers or SA saw it as the start of the revolution against the Communists in Germany, and declared every one of them must be shot. Soon he converted regular police forces into the State Secret Police or *Geheime Staats Polizei* – the Gestapo. The mention of this organization struck fear into the hearts of all, both within Germany itself and in occupied lands, who could not or were suspected not to support the regime. And with good reason. Brutal persecution of Jews and political opponents was carried out. Imprisonment, torture, and mass murder became commonplace. Tens of thousands were rounded up and sent in railway cattle cars to concentration camps where they died or were exterminated.

Opposition political parties were disbanded, strikes outlawed, and all aspects of economic, cultural, and religious life brought under the iron control of the central government and the Nazi Party. It had its own elite squad of Hitler bodyguards, the dreaded, ultra-racist SS (*Schutzstaffel*) that Heinrich Himmler built into a powerful army within the army.

Hitler's expansionist policies resulted in reacquisition of the Saar territory and the Rhineland, annexation of Austria, and occupation of the Sudetenland. In March 1939 he occupied the remainder of Czechoslovakia. Then, in August, the foreign ministers of the Third Reich and of the Union of Soviet Socialist Republics, Joachim von Ribbentrop and Vyacheslav M. Molotov, also premier under Marshal Josef Stalin, suddenly and secretly signed a non-aggression treaty. Having failed to persuade Poland, with which he already had a similar, ten-year agreement, to join in attacking Russia, Hitler reversed his field, and set out to convince Stalin that they would each benefit greatly from mutual occupation of the intervening nation of 35,000,000. Thus they proceeded to divide up Poland, whose population was decimated by massacre, starvation, and imprisonment in concentration camps such as brutally infamous Auschwitz.

Hitler's invasion of Poland on September 1, 1939 brought ultimatums to withdraw from both Britain and France. He did not withdraw, and days later both declared war. Thus was joined the bloody struggle known to history as the Second World War.

Stalin, meanwhile, was not deceived by his erstwhile German ally, any more than Hitler was deterred from his original plan to conquer the U.S.S.R. However, the Polish interlude provided the Soviets with valuable time and opportunity to prepare for the German assault that, sooner or later, was sure to come. Stalin played out a game of wits with Hitler – a deadly serious game from which the Nazi leader would emerge the eventual loser.

In a few days Soviet forces occupied nearly half of all Polish territory, thus pre-empting German capture of rich oil fields and other resources that it coveted. Hitler was blocked from the Ukraine, Finland, and the Baltic states. Ten months later, on June 22, 1941, he attacked the Soviet Union, and when he did, Stalin was waiting.

Meanwhile, the Nazi steamroller had crushed Denmark and Norway, the Low Countries, and France, and in a few weeks drove the British Expeditionary Force from the Continent at Dunkirk.

Hitler and his Fascist ally Mussolini now were unchallenged from the North Sea to the Mediterranean. Only England stood in the way of their achieving complete mastery of all Europe. The next step, therefore, in this plan for total domination consisted of pounding the British into submission from the air and cutting off their supplies by sea. Waves of *Luftwaffe* aircraft roared daily into airspace over their cities, towns, harbours, and military installations to drop thousands of tons of explosive and incendiary bombs, while on the high seas an expanding fleet of U-boats sent to the bottom millions of tons of shipping bringing essential goods from North America.

The decisive Battle of Britain in which, during a four-and-a-half-month period in the summer and early fall of 1940, outnumbered British and Commonwealth airmen fought off the air assault, undoubtedly was the turning point in the war. It was matched by the Battle of the Atlantic in which, slowly but surely, the U-boat menace was defeated and delivery of war supplies both to Britain and to Russia assured. The Roosevelt Lend-Lease Plan, the destroyers-for-bases deal which helped take back command of Atlantic shipping lanes, and the inventive strategy of delivering North American–manufactured planes to the Royal Air Force by air through Gander, Newfoundland, rather than crated on submarine-vulnerable ships, were decisive elements.

In the larger picture, the sudden invasion of the Soviet Union in 1941, and the consequent division of German resources, cannot be discounted as the major flaw in Hitler's grand strategy. At first the Nazis claimed the usual rapid gains, but having lost the initiative in the long siege of Stalingrad, they were driven back and eventually expelled from Soviet soil. In the end, as Stalin's forces became the first of the Allies to march into Berlin itself, on April 30, 1945, the Führer took his own life. A week later all German resistance ceased.

Meanwhile, Germany and Italy had found a new ally in Japan, a nation already well on the way to imposing in Eastern Asia and the western Pacific the total domination Hitler came perilously close to achieving in Europe.

Its war with the United States began when hundreds of Japanese carrier-based aircraft surprised and crippled the U.S.

Pacific Fleet at Pearl Harbor, Hawaii, in a dawn raid on December 7, 1941. In response, the United States declared war on Japan, initially faring badly. Not until mid-1942 could the Americans claim major advances; by mid-1945 Japan had been driven from the Western Pacific.

Then President Harry S. Truman ordered the atomic bomb dropped on the cities of Hiroshima (August 6) and Nagasaki (August 9). On August 15, 1945, the Japanese accepted terms of unconditional surrender.

But what of the war in Western Europe? It had also spread to North Africa; Allied forces succeeded in wresting supremacy from the Axis at El Alamein in late 1942. Sicily fell to Anglo-American forces in July 1943 and Mussolini was driven from power.

The invasion of Normandy on June 6, 1944 – D-Day – signalled the final phase of the war in Europe. By fall the forces of the Third Reich, already driven from Soviet territory, were expelled from most of France and Belgium. The Battle of the Bulge, a final, desperate German counteroffensive aimed at dividing the Allies in the Ardennes, a forested upland in southeast Belgium, by creating a "bulge" or breach in their lines, began in mid-December. However, after a month of heavy fighting, it was clear that the momentum was with the Allies. Suddenly, it was over. Hitler had disappeared from the scene. At 2:41 a.m. on May 7, 1945, in the city of Rheims in northeastern France, General Alfred Jodl signed the instrument of unconditional surrender on orders from Admiral Karl Donitz, who had assumed direction of German affairs.

The tangled fate of conquered Europe would be settled, at least temporarily, by Big Three conferences (the United States, Britain, Russia) at Yalta on the Black Sea in February and Potsdam in eastern Germany in July and August.

In the First World War, sixteen nations were regarded as belligerents (the British Empire, in all its parts, considered as one). The Allied powers counted more than five million dead and missing, the so-called Central Powers somewhat less than

3,500,000. Ten million civilians were classified as "displaced." Fifty nations were considered belligerents in the Second World War. It was estimated that there were more than 15,000,000 battle deaths, 10,500,000 among the Allied powers (including 7,500,000 Soviets) and more than 4,500,000 Axis troops. Civilian deaths were thought to equal, if not exceed, military losses.

The extraordinary thing about the two World Wars was that the Americas largely escaped their physical ravages. Except for a certain, almost insignificant level of sabotage and the effects on civilian ship travellers, and excluding voluntary contribution of personnel and *matériel*, North, Central, and South America and their cities, along with their civilian populations, emerged virtually unscathed.

Newfoundland, with its capital of St. John's, proved a significant exception. As the nearest point in North America to Europe, and the strategic access point to the North American heartland, the Island with its Labrador territory lay as a tempting, undefended target for the Nazis.

As a Nazi-occupied base at the mouth of the St. Lawrence River, Newfoundland would have complemented development of freighter U-boats for the purpose of refuelling and resupplying the German Navy, enabling it to achieve mastery of Atlantic sea lanes. It would have enabled medium- to long-range *Luftwaffe* bombing planes to strike any city in the United States or Canada. It would have increased greatly the overall scope and effectiveness of the Nazi war machine, bringing closer to nightmare reality Hitler's dream of world domination.

Fortunately the Allies, in particular the Americans, got there first – and not by accident. They assigned tens of thousands of troops, as well as warships, bombers, and fighter planes, to major Newfoundland installations – Gander, Fort Pepperrell, Argentia, and Ernest Harmon in Newfoundland, and Goose Bay in Labrador – and dozens of lesser locations. This was the result of a clandestine meeting in 1941 between Roosevelt and Churchill in the tiny

Placentia Bay inlet of Ship Harbour, Newfoundland – the $50,000,000,000 strategy of Lend-Lease, of destroyers-for-bases, that history would ultimately enshrine as the Atlantic Charter.

It did not, however, diminish Nazi efforts to disrupt United States, Canadian, and British wartime operations in Newfoundland. Quite the contrary. And those efforts, for a time at least, enjoyed a troubling measure of success.

Because of his failure to establish a North American foothold, Hitler ordered his head of armaments production, Albert Speer, to begin work on the *amerikabomber* – huge aircraft to ferry fleets of smaller, manned, suicide-bombing planes across the Atlantic, suspended from their superstructures. Released in mid-air, their purpose would be to devastate United States cities. It was said the Führer could easily work himself into a frenzy describing how the Americans would pay for opposing his Third Reich plan to rule the world, how the skyscrapers of New York and San Francisco would be transformed into giant infernos, collapsing upon themselves and carrying thousands of occupants to their deaths.

But before the plan could be carried to fruition, the war was over – with the man mainly responsible for history's bloodiest conflagration dead by his own hand.

EASTERN NEWFOUNDLAND

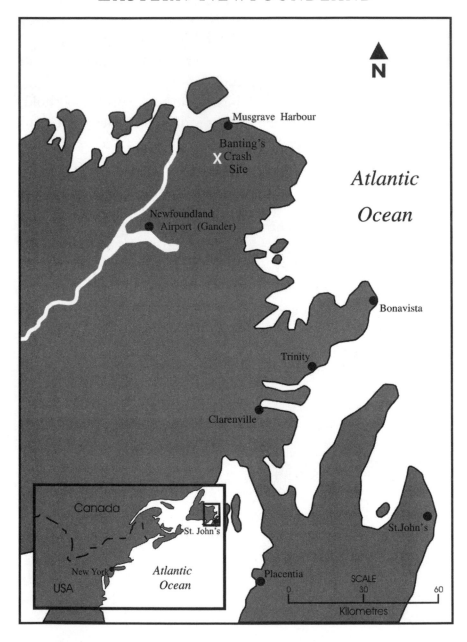

PRINCIPAL CHARACTERS
(in order of appearance)

The First World War Period

Sir Frederick Grant Banting	Medical doctor, co-discoverer of insulin
Lieut.-Col. Cluny MacPherson	Chief medical officer, Newfoundland Regiment
Edward Patrick Morris	Newfoundland Prime Minister, 1909–17
Sir Walter Edward Davidson	Governor of Newfoundland, 1913–18
Lady Margaret Davidson	Wife of the Governor
Karl Otto Stroesser	German spy, *Abwehr* agent
Werner Heinz Schmelling	Stroesser's assistant
Head Const. Isaac W. Bartlett	Constabulary chief, Bay of Islands
Elizabeth Ann Bartlett	Bartlett's wife
Nathan Azariah Kelloway	Bartlett's assistant
Andrew L. Barrett	Managing Editor, *The Western Star*

The Period Between the Wars

Michael Grattan O'Leary	Editor, *The Ottawa Journal*
Lieut.-Gen. A. G. L. McNaughton	Canada's Chief of Defence Staff, head of NRC
William Lyon Mackenzie King	Prime Minister of Canada
Charles Decatur Howe	Canada's "Minister of Everything"

Chalmers Jack Mackenzie	Acting President, NRC
Air Marshal A. A. L. Cuffe	Eastern Command, Royal Canadian Air Force
Adolf Hitler	Chancellor-Dictator of Germany
Wilhelm Hermann Goering	Founder of Gestapo, chief of *Luftwaffe*
Duke of Windsor	Former King of England
Wallis Warfield Simpson	The Duke's wife
Franklin D. Roosevelt	President of the United States
King George VI	King of England, 1937–1952
Queen Elizabeth	The King's wife

The Second World War Period

Sir Thomas Humphrey Walwyn	Governor of Newfoundland, 1936–46
Lewis Edward Emerson	Commissioner for Justice & Defence
M/Sgt. Alvin James Altehouse	U.S. Army Air Force member, saboteur
Capt. William Joensen, U.S.N.	Master, USAT *Edmund B. Alexander*
Col. Maurice D. Welty	Commander, U.S. troops on board ship
Thomas E. Ricketts	Pharmacist, Victoria Cross winner
Admiral Wilhelm Canaris	Hitler's chief of military espionage
Patrick J. O'Neill	Chief, Newfoundland Constabulary
H. A. L. Pattison	Newfoundland Air Policy Advisor

Thomas M. McGrath	Acting Aerodrome Control Officer, Gander
Joseph C. Mackey	Pilot of Banting's plane
Sir Wilfred Woods	Commissioner for Public Utilities
Air Commodore G. V. Walsh	President, Banting Crash Court of Inquiry
Sir John C. Puddester	Commissioner, Public Health & Welfare
Gilbert Hiscock	Constabulary Officer, Carmanville
H. J. Cody	President, University of Toronto
Capt. Benjamin Taverner	Master, SS *Caribou*
Albert Benjamin Perlin	Editor, *The Daily News*
Mr. Justice Brian E. S. Dunfield	Inquiry Commissioner, K. of C. hostel fire

ONE

University of Toronto, Ontario, Canada, 1915

FEW PEOPLE COULD have predicted that a son and heir born to William and Margaret Banting in the Ontario farm belt a few years before the end of the nineteenth century would turn out to be one of history's most important medical benefactors, as a co-discoverer of life-saving insulin, barely two decades into the twentieth. Or that, in the wake of the bloodiest conflict in human history – the First World War – this same, now famous Canadian would also become one of the world's most forceful proponents of chemical and biological weapons, and of germ warfare.

Young Fred Banting rode to school on a mare named Betsy, helped with the chores – at one stage, his special responsibility was cleaning out the chicken house – and perhaps because his steady girlfriend was the local clergyman's daughter, considered submitting himself as a candidate for the Methodist ministry.

He headed off to university, and to this point his world unfolded in the normal, accepted manner that, as a healthy offspring of a reasonably well-off farm family, he had, perhaps, a right to expect.

Then came the Great War, and for Banting, for millions of young men like him, and for people everywhere, everything changed.

One day a physician newly returned from the killing fields of France arrived on campus to lecture students of the University of Toronto on what was really going on "over there." His purpose

1

was to emphasize the pressing need for more medical graduates to work at saving the lives and limbs of wounded Canadian soldiers on the battlefields of Europe.

A graduate of McGill and Scotland's Royal Infirmary, Lieutenant Colonel Cluny MacPherson was chief medical officer of the Newfoundland Regiment; his home was in St. John's, capital of the neighbouring British Crown colony. He recalled for the overflow audience the awful scenes as chlorine gas, unleashed in canisters by forces of the German Kaiser, was employed against Canadian, British, and French troops for the first time at Ypres in the last week of April 1915.

"It is almost too horrible to describe," said MacPherson, who at the time had been on loan to the Canadians to help upgrade their field hospital facilities. "Although the Allies had intelligence that the Germans were planning something new, something very big, the reports were given little credence. The result was that the attack came as a total surprise, devastating to the unsuspecting Allied troops.

"It was early morning. The sun was just becoming visible over the horizon." The students listened in rapt attention as he continued. "The forward lookouts noticed a grey fog spreading silently over the ground on a light breeze, from the direction of the enemy trenches. Suddenly, men were choking and coughing. Many were overcome and died where they fell because the medical people were unable to help them – being afflicted by the gas themselves.

"I think it was the quiet . . . the eerie silence with which the killer gas spread into the Allied lines, that was so shocking. Nobody could quite believe that it was happening."

He noted in passing that the use of toxic chemicals as weapons of war had been foreseen at an international peace conference at The Hague some fifteen years earlier. However, a resolution calling on the nations to "abstain from the use of . . . asphyxiating or deleterious gases" had received little support.

A tall, trim, authoritarian figure in military uniform, MacPherson was most impressive. He described in clipped, clinical tones how, after a few days, Allied troops began to be issued with cotton pads, impregnated with a chemical solution, that could be tied over the nose and mouth. But it was an awkward solution at best, and offered little or no protection against chemical weapons such as the mustard gas that the Germans soon began using. That gas caused severe, slow-healing burns to the skin and irreversible damage to the eyes and respiratory tract.

Had the war continued into 1919, it surely would have become an all-out fight employing chemical weapons on a large scale. The Germans were impressed with their success, which had exceeded expectations; the British realized they could not fail to meet the enemy on his own ground.

Fortunately for thousands of men on both sides who would have been blinded, had their lungs irretrievably damaged, or been permanently disfigured, the war was over in November. An armistice took effect at the eleventh hour of the eleventh day of the eleventh month of 1918.

The tall, gangling Banting was in the forefront of admiring students who crowded around MacPherson at the conclusion of the lecture. They were eager to shake his hand and to make the acquaintance of a man they accepted, without question, as a true battlefield hero.

"It is a great privilege to meet you, sir," Banting addressed the Newfoundland soldier-physician. "May I ask . . . . Aren't you the inventor of the first gas mask for use on the battlefield a few months ago? I realize that it might have seemed immodest for you to mention it in your lecture, but I feel you should be given full credit, if I may say so."

The officer, whose obvious reserve failed to allay the youthful enthusiasm of his questioner, chose not to respond other than to nod slightly.

"I think this business of chemical weapons is not going to go away," Banting continued. "We can expect more of it in future, rather than less. It seems the only way nations can defend themselves is to have the same weapons, or more and better – for defensive purposes, of course – as those who might attack them. Can there be any alternative?"

"Well, young man – what did you say your name was – Banting? Well, Mr. Banting, that is quite perceptive. I'm afraid I can't really disagree with you," MacPherson responded gravely, and as he turned to accompany his host from the assembly room, added "unfortunately."

Like thousands of patriotic young men, and a small cadre of women, throughout the British Empire who were ready to give their all "for King and Country," Banting sought to enlist. Had he been accepted by the Canadian Army, as an ordinary foot soldier he might have been swallowed up by the war and never heard of again. However, fate had determined another course for the aspiring physician.

Rejected by army recruiters for poor eyesight, the following year he was accepted into the Royal Canadian Army Medical Corps. On graduation with a Bachelor of Medicine, the twenty-six-year-old was commissioned a Lieutenant and assigned to duty in Canada, first in Ontario and later New Brunswick, before being ordered overseas.

Yet the MacPherson lecture had left a deep impression. It convinced Banting that only if his country, Canada, and the Empire to which she belonged, were at least as well-prepared to meet an unscrupulous enemy as that enemy was to attack them, could they survive in a world suddenly sunk into the depths of a new barbarism. In the mind of Fred Banting, the absolute need for them to develop and maintain stores of chemical and biological weapons would become an obsession. It was one that would lead, ultimately and inevitably, to his mysterious and untimely death.

TWO

Government House, St. John's, Newfoundland – A Year Earlier

EDWARD PATRICK MORRIS hesitated for a long moment before exiting the horse-drawn Victoria carriage that had delivered him under the portico of Government House. Since the mid-nineteenth century, the massive structure of local stone and English granite had been the official residence of British potentates in St. John's, North America's oldest city and capital of England's first overseas possession. In August 1914 world events were moving with mind-numbing speed, and the Prime Minister of Newfoundland realized that the Island was being swept up in them. The latest was the declaration of war by Great Britain. It carried the inescapable obligation upon the various parts of the Empire to join in – with all that that implied from the provision of troops for overseas, to demands on local governments for home defense and security, to the enormous financial and social costs on their peoples, and for who knew how long.

Morris studied the stiff, formally worded statement issued in London by the United Kingdom Foreign Office, received and placed in his hand by a secretary as he prepared to leave for the meeting to which he had been summoned by the Governor:

> *"Owing to the summary rejection by the German*
> *Government of the request made by His Britannic*
> *Majesty's Government that the neutrality of Belgium*
> *should be respected, His Majesty's Ambassador at*

5

> *Berlin has received his passports, and His Majesty's*
> *Government has declared to the German Government*
> *that a state of war exists between Great Britain and*
> *Germany from 11 o'clock p.m. August 4."*

He shivered involuntarily, notwithstanding the heat of high summer, as he reflected on the words of the declaration. It carried all the force and effect of a death sentence for millions of innocent, unsuspecting people – very likely including numbers of his own countrymen.

We are confronted, Morris thought, *not alone here, but all over the Empire, with a spectacle the seriousness of which we have not yet been able to realize, and the consequences of which are so far-reaching that not one of us, not even the principal actors in the great tragedy which is being enacted in Europe today, can estimate them.* As leader of the government and the King's First Minister he would find himself expanding on this theme in the House of Assembly and elsewhere in the coming days.

He gathered his papers and, as if on signal, the cabbie stepped down to set a retractable step in place, respectfully standing back as his passenger descended. Kit, the heavy, well-groomed mare between the shafts, sensed the shifting weight of the carriage, and turned her head curiously to observe the activity. She chose that moment to defile the Governor's driveway with a steaming memento of the visit which, before leaving, her master would be obliged to recover in a metal box-shovel carried for the purpose.

"Thank you, Sir Edward," the cabbie murmured, bowing slightly over the hand that conveyed the fare together with what he knew would be a substantial gratuity.

Anticipating the precise instant of the Prime Minister's arrival, a servant drew the door smoothly open to admit the leader of His Majesty's government. Hovering near the entranceway was the aide-de-camp, Captain A. C. Goodridge.

"Follow me, please, Sir Edward," Goodridge invited him, and they proceeded along a wide corridor. The meeting between the

King's representative and the head of the Newfoundland government would take place in the Drawing Room, where His Excellency waited, attended by his private secretary.

They were somewhat alike – the same age, both having been born in 1859, early in the third decade of Queen Victoria's long reign on the throne of England, and both of medium stature and substantial girth. But there the similarity ended.

Sir Walter Edward Davidson was an aggressive Irishman who had attended Cambridge University and begun a career in the British civil service in Ceylon, becoming in time chairman of the municipal council and mayor of Colombo. He had a three-year tour of duty in the South African Transvaal from 1901, which included much of the Boer War, before being appointed Governor of the tiny Seychelles Islands in the Indian Ocean. On becoming Governor of Britain's oldest colony in 1913, just as war clouds were gathering for the worst bloodletting in human history, he was no stranger to the reality of armed and total conflict – and appalled by the degree to which Newfoundland was unprepared to meet what was to come.

A St. John's man born and bred, with a laissez-faire bent, Morris had taught school briefly in the isolated Placentia Bay village of Oderin, where his brother Michael was the parish priest, before attending the University of Ottawa. He became a lawyer, and was elected to the Newfoundland House of Assembly in 1885. After two decades as a Liberal, he broke away to form the People's Party, which tied with the Liberal Party in the general election of 1908, and the following year formed the government. Morris was at its head, the first Roman Catholic prime minister in half a century. His second term was dominated by the outbreak of the First World War and the turbulent issues that accompanied it. In 1917 Morris would depart for London to become a member of the Imperial War Cabinet, leaving William S. Lloyd as acting prime minister. Subsequently he would resign altogether on being raised to the peerage as Baron Morris.

"Mr. Prime Minister."

Davidson greeted Morris with a firm, almost intimidating handshake, and indicated a desk he had had set up overlooking the expansive gardens and the greenhouse fairly bursting with a profusion of flowers of every variety.

"Let us sit over here. I like to enjoy the sunshine over here by the windows, in the mornings. Will you take tea?"

"Thank you, Your Excellency," the Prime Minister replied. "It really is lovely here today. Yes, I would like tea, with lemon if you please."

"I presume you have received the Foreign Office statement," Davidson said, coming directly to the main order of business. The Governor held up a copy of the declaration of war that Morris had received earlier.

"It speaks, of course, for the Empire – all of us, in Great Britain equally with Canada, Australia, New Zealand, South Africa, and right here in Newfoundland. Now we must consider and decide what is to be done to implement it. There are two aspects as I see it – what must be done in support of His Majesty's armed forces in the actual conflict, and of course, what may be required in terms of home defence.

"I propose that steps be taken immediately to raise a force, beginning with perhaps five hundred men, to train as infantry, and as well to enlarge the Royal Naval Reserve to one thousand. That would seem to be a reasonable contribution for this colony to make, at least initially, and I shall advise London to this effect immediately. I am certain they will welcome the news. In the meantime, the Constabulary should be alerted to the need for greater security measures – checking up on aliens, such as that troublesome fool of an artist in Brigus – and it would be a salutary lesson for the press if they were to be subjected to a degree of censorship. We cannot have idle editorialists sowing the weeds of doubt and distrust among the good seeds of loyalty and patriotism, now, can we?"

"Ah . . . Yes, of course, Your Excellency," Morris replied, his breath taken away by the directness of it.

"I should think that the House of Assembly should be called to ratify the declaration, as it were, and to consider the proposals for recruitment – and in particular, the cost of Newfoundland's direct involvement in the war and how we shall pay for it.

"The most economical approach, perhaps, would be for our men to enlist directly in, or be assigned to, existing units of the Imperial forces. As well, when men give up their ordinary occupations to go to war, their families must still be supported, and we shall have to consider those costs. A special session of the House could, perhaps, be summoned to meet in a week or two."

But Davidson was having none of it, and his response was scathing.

"Good God, man, what are you saying?" he demanded, all formality abandoned.

"Do you not understand that there is a war on? Do you not comprehend what that means? Do you think for one moment that the Kaiser and his generals are going to sit back and wait for your little House of Assembly to ratify the declaration of war?

"Come to your senses. The die is cast, and we have no choice but to move ahead. I intend to call upon the public for the creation of a Newfoundland Regiment that will preserve its separate identity in the field, and I am certain the people will support it.

"I suggest you wait to open the House, say for about four weeks after the summer vacation, when people can pay proper attention to the issues. Is that agreed?"

Sensing the meeting was over, the Prime Minister had risen to his feet.

"If that is your wish, Your Excellency, then I feel I have little choice but to agree," he replied deferentially.

"Very well." Davidson spoke with finality as he, too, rose, and added a dismissive, "Thank you for coming."

He was now convinced beyond any doubt that, so far as Newfoundland's part in the war was concerned, and for the sake of his own reputation and future career (he had his eye on the Governorship of New South Wales, Australia's richest and most populous province) he must take a direct hand – even if it meant stepping outside strict constitutional bounds. The war, he told himself, could not be left to the bumbling incompetence of Morris and his crowd of colonials.

A few days later *The Daily News* reported on a large public meeting – all classes being represented, it said, and indicating that the matter at hand was attracting the keenest interest. The gathering took place in the cavernous Church Lads' Brigade Armoury "to consider the question of enlisting citizens for land service abroad in the War, and to establish a corps for home defence."

The newspaper recorded that promptly at eight o'clock the Governor arrived, and his appearance was the signal for a great outburst of cheering, while the C.L.B. Band rendered the national anthem. The Prime Minister briefly stated the subject of the meeting, and requested that His Excellency take the chair. The Governor did so, and thanked the gathering for the reception accorded him. The present question, he stated, was the most momentous in the history of the country:

"England has been forced into war by Germany; she will take up the challenge and give the Kaiser war in full and overwhelming measure and show that we are Britons of the old stamp. It behooves all Britishers to aid the Mother Country in speedily settling the trouble, so that the world may again progress peaceably, and Newfoundland should do her part. If we don't, then goodbye to our claim of being the oldest and most loyal colony."

He then got to the purpose for which he had called the public meeting.

"In my telegram to the Home Government, I stated that we were poor in money and rich in men, men who are accustomed to meet all difficulties without wavering. I pledged myself that Newfoundland would furnish five hundred men, but I hope the number will be five thousand. The struggle may be desperate, but we will win hands down, and I hope our folks will get in the front so they may have a chance to uphold our reputation."

Two resolutions were put and roundly approved: one for establishment of a committee of twenty-five citizens "to take such steps as may be deemed necessary for enlisting and equipping . . . several hundred efficiently trained men for service abroad in the present war," the appointment of the committee to be left in the hands of the Governor; the second for that committee to take steps to provide for enlisting and equipping "serviceable men between eighteen (18) and thirty-six (36) years of age, to enrol themselves in training for Home Defence wherever Corps Instructors are available."

During a subsequent meeting, Davidson declared his willingness to assist the new Newfoundland Patriotic Committee – now described as having the chief purpose of "initiating a Newfoundland Regiment" – in any way possible. As if to more adequately demonstrate support for the idea, he himself moved, seconded by former St. John's mayor W. J. Ellis, that he himself be elected a member of the Committee, which was approved. To finalize the matter, on motion of leading businessman Hon. Marmaduke G. Winter, seconded by Major C. H. Hutchings, commander of the Methodist Guards and Deputy Minister of Justice, the Governor was elected chairman of the Committee, whose membership was expanded to include fifty of St. John's most prominent citizens.

"The first duties of the Committee," His Excellency declared, "are to enlist, equip, and dispatch a regiment, five hundred strong, for service abroad, and to appoint a subcommittee to draft a proclamation to this effect."

In this way, the formation and equipping of the Regiment, by which the cream of an entire generation of Newfoundland youth would go off to war, many never to return, took place completely outside the ambit and responsibility of the government and the House of Assembly. Constitutional or not, by the time the House convened in September, the country had been fully committed to the actions of the Governor operating virtually single-handedly.

* * *

Not to be outdone by her husband, the Governor's wife also called a public meeting. She presided over formation of the Women's Patriotic Association, whose main work would be to provide "comforts" – knitted socks, shirts, surgical bandages – for men serving overseas.

"I felt sure," she explained, "that there were many women who would wish to do something for our brave soldiers, risking their very lives for us, and who yet did not know the best way of helping or what the needs of those at the Front might be."

The following day, September 15, readers of *The Daily News* were informed that, long before the appointed hour, the hall was thronged, and if the meeting was "any criterion of the willingness of Newfoundland women to assist . . . in the present crisis by providing for our soldiers at the Front, then such assistance is assured."

Resolutions were approved providing for establishment of the Patriotic Association of the Women of Newfoundland and naming a General Committee with Lady Margaret Davidson as its president.

From a rear bedroom of the Brownsdale Hotel just off New Gower Street, inexpensive and reasonably inconspicuous lodging house of outport visitors to "town," Karl Otto Stroesser kept careful track of these matters, duly reporting to his superiors.

The German national, a low-level member of the Kaiser's fledgling international military espionage organization, had arrived in Newfoundland posing as a crewman on the herring collector *Fischboot I* operating in and near Bay of Islands. He had taken the train to St. John's, a distance of 405.9 miles on the slow, narrow-gauge Newfoundland Railway, in order to get a better view of the colony's preparations for war. His cover story was that he had come to the capital to secure herring export permits.

In the privacy of his hotel room, he carefully clipped items from each day's local newspapers to supplement his own summary reports, paying particular attention to noteworthy political events. These were sent by post daily to a senior operative in Ottawa, the capital of Canada – via a rotation of fictitious names, used to confuse any suspicious local censors – and fed into intelligence reports to the High Command in Berlin.

"Ye certainly are a great one for the papers," Tryphena Batstone, also known as Triffie and a distant relative of the hotel owners, remarked one day. Miffed at having to pick up the newsprint scraps littering the floor, she added, "and for cutting them up, too!"

Stroesser declined to rise to the bait, instead returning her a haughty look that said, "And who are you, chambermaid, to be questioning me?"

He was of medium height, wiry, with a swarthy complexion and a goatee that hid almost entirely a knife scar along his left cheekbone. The eyes, dark and brooding, flashed with anger when he was annoyed . . . which he was just now.

Triffie had resolved to mention to her brother-in-law, a member of the Newfoundland Constabulary, what she regarded as unusual behaviour on the part of the man with a foreign accent – German, she was sure. It was common knowledge that the police were under orders straight from Governor Davidson to keep a sharp eye on all foreigners.

Indeed, an eccentric artist and open German sympathizer from the United States by the name of Rockwell Kent, who had been living in Brigus, was suspected of spying and ordered out of the country. No doubt there would be others.

Plump, pretty, and more than a little pregnant, Triffie was nothing if not daring. She made obvious to all her willingness to impart to male patrons of the establishment the ultimate comfort and companionship – for a price. And Stroesser seemed willing.

Still, she was unable to resist provoking the man.

"Sure, ye could be a German spy, for all I know, Mr. High-and-Mighty Stroesser," she foolishly teased him, unwittingly inviting what happened next.

The day after the spy took the train back to the West Coast, Triffie's bloated remains were discovered floating in nearby Steer's Cove. Obvious signs of violence were lacking – she had been suffocated with one of Mrs. Brown's feather pillows.

Finding no water in the woman's lungs, the physician who conducted the autopsy concluded that she was dead before landing in St. John's harbour.

THREE

Captain Cook's Brook,
Western Newfoundland, 1914

THE FIRST BRILLIANT rays of the August sun burst over the
summit of Mount Moriah, the landmark promontory that rises
sphinx-like from the picturesque South Shore of Newfoundland's
Bay of Islands. They slanted down through early-morning mists
rising from the sea pool near the place where Cook's Brook
empties into the broad expanse of the Humber Arm, invading its
murky depths to project shadows of the furtive fishes lying there.

Humber Arm is one of three offshoots, but the largest by far,
of this important waterway, a deep indentation of the Gulf of St.
Lawrence that separates the historic Island of Newfoundland from
Canada. The others are North Arm and Middle Arm, the latter
being itself divided into two lesser inlets, Goose Arm and Penguin
Arm. The mouth of the bay is guarded by no fewer than a dozen
islands, hence the name Bay of Islands.

At the head of the sea pool, an angler's catgut leader fractured
the calm waters. His perfectly tied Silver Doctor created a neat
"V" as it riffled the mirror surface.

Suddenly, there was a heart-stopping swirl as a sleek Atlantic
salmon lurking below took the artificial fly in its left jaw. In the
same lightning motion, it dove for the bottom of the pool. *A fine
fish*, the angler speculated. *At least ten or twelve pounds.*

Instantly there commenced the deadly game: the skill of the
fishermen – *keep the rod up . . . keep the tension on . . . keep his
head up . . . give him more line . . . take back the slack* – matched

against the desperate struggle on the part of the magnificent *salmo salar* to free itself from the steel hook that had embedded itself in its flesh and now threatened its very life.

The man was tall and well-proportioned, his movements exhibiting top physical condition. Under a traditional New-foundland salt-and-pepper cap, steely blue eyes squinted against the bright sun now reflecting on the water. The pure white of a short goatee indicated his age as early or mid-sixties.

He wore a light undershirt and nondescript trousers, but on a flat rock nearby was a carefully folded military-type black tunic, and on top a "cheese-cutter" forage cap fronted with a badge that signified its owner was a member of the Newfoundland Constabulary.

He kept the line taut and prepared himself for the inevitable series of wild jumps that the fish would employ in its attempts to shake free. It was all part of a well-worn ritual. The frantic manoeuvre would quickly drain the salmon's energy, enabling its tormentor to take back more and more line as the fish faced exhaustion and eventual capture.

The first jump came with startling suddenness. The salmon leaped clear out of the water to fall back with a *slaapp!* and a mighty splash that sent ever-widening circles to all sides of the formerly placid pool.

At that precise moment, a shrill sound burst upon the tiny river valley. It shattered the illusion of peace in this small corner of a world about to explode into the hell of war. The man recog-nized the sound of a police whistle and, his attention momentarily diverted, felt the line go slack; he knew at once that the fish was lost.

"Damn it to hell," he growled, beginning at once to reel in the line, then turning to break down his fine split-bamboo rod from Scotland. It was his first use of a gift that his cousin, celebrated Arctic navigator Capt. Robert Abram "Bob" Bartlett, had picked up on his latest well-publicized international speaking tour in conjunction with the National Geographic Society.

A few years earlier, in 1909, "Skipper Bob" – the respectful title accorded by the family, and indeed by all residents of the ancient town of Brigus, to honour the hero that he clearly was – had captained the USS *Roosevelt* and brought Admiral Robert E. Peary and the Stars and Stripes to within striking distance of the North Pole. He was disappointed to be sent back, at that point, by the great man who wanted all the glory of a successful expedition for himself.

Hauling off his thigh waders, the fisherman spied and raised a hand in recognition to a uniformed figure beginning to make his cautious way down the steep, rocky embankment from the public road.

Little more than a cart track, the road linked, to the east, the village of Petrie's, then Petrie's Crossing where the railway and the road intersected with the main population centre of Curling, formerly Birchy Cove, and the hamlet of Corner Brook with its Fisher's lumber mill, and Humbermouth, developing site of railway divisional operations. To the west lay a further series of small, mainly fishing communities lining the south shore of the bay.

"You certainly picked a good time to sound that bloody whistle," Head Constable Isaac William Bartlett grumpily greeted the new arrival. "I was just about ready to land my supper here!"

"I was afraid you might have a salmon on, sir," his youthful assistant, Constable Nathan Azariah Kelloway, confessed apologetically, "but I couldn't see for sure that it was you from up there on the road, and this is very important."

He held up a pink form displaying the heading "Department of Posts and Telegraphs, Newfoundland." Surrounding the official Coat of Arms of the ancient British colony were the words "Operating in Connection with Commercial Cables to All Parts of the World."

On the left side, reading bottom to top, large, bold capital letters announced that the telegram was "URGENT."

Bartlett took the paper and immediately noted the name of the sender: John Sullivan, Inspector General of Police. He had good memories of Sullivan, and a good deal of admiration for this native of the historic town of Trinity. As one "bayman" to another, he was cheered by the fact that an outport man like himself had risen through the ranks to the very top. Sullivan was the first Newfoundlander to do so.

Only the third man to enlist in the newly constituted force in May 1871, Sullivan made Acting Sergeant six months after entering, Sergeant after a year, Head Constable second class three years after that, and Head Constable first class two years later. When Inspector and General Superintendent Paul Carty was retiring in 1895, he recommended Sullivan to be Sub-Inspector of Police, and two years after that he was appointed Superintendent. Bartlett himself joined up a couple of years after Sullivan, in November 1873, and was promoted to Acting Sergeant in 1876, Sergeant in 1879, Head Constable in 1895, and aimed to retire as District Inspector in 1918.

In the wake of the Great Fire of 1892 that ravaged most of St. John's, Sub-Inspector Sullivan had been made first Chief of a newly organized fire brigade, and sent to Québec to study the establishment and practices of firefighting services in the City of Montréal, and to purchase equipment and apparatus required for Newfoundland's capital. In 1909 he became Inspector General of the Constabulary as well.

Young Nathan Kelloway was a graduate of the Church Lads' Brigade, one of the paramilitary youth organizations operating under church sponsorship. Others included the Catholic Cadet Corps, the Methodist Guards, and the Newfoundland Highlanders – plus the Legion of Frontiersmen, an independent group. It was founded in England at the turn of the century and within a decade had local units in many parts of the British Empire. This short-lived organization – short-lived in Newfoundland, at least – was imported from the Mother Country by Arthur Wakefield, a physician on the staff of Sir Wilfred Grenfell's first hospital, in

Battle Harbour, Labrador, and Edward W. Vere-Holloway, who had immigrated with his family in 1910 to become brewmaster with the Bennett Brewing Company in St. John's.

Training young men in rifle drill and marching in the interests of healthful physical activity and personal discipline – "It's not only cleanliness that's next to godliness," C.C.C. founding chaplain Rev. Patrick Crooke was given to say – these organizations were the only semblance of military preparedness in Newfoundland, with the exception of a small contingent of naval volunteers.

Kelloway had been a policeman for about a year, and like most young Newfoundland men felt a patriotic stirring at the thought the British Empire was taking up the cudgels against the forces of the Kaiser half a world away.

In fact, he had confided in Bartlett that he had pretty well decided to join up as soon as Governor Davidson in St. John's issued the expected proclamation establishing a distinct and separate Newfoundland Regiment. He clearly relished the thought of going off across the ocean to fight "for King and Empire."

"Imagine, Newfoundland having her own regiment in the field," the young constable had remarked proudly, as if it were some kind of miraculous happening to be wondered at and celebrated. And, perhaps, in a way, it was.

"I don't want to say anything yet, Head," Kelloway informed his superior, "because I want to tell Mother and Father myself. But they'll be proud as punch when they hear that I'm going over there to fight the Hun, don't you think, sir?"

Bartlett had nodded, but was noncommittal – hesitant to encourage the young man's patriotism for the mortal danger in which he would place himself, but unable to deny it. He remembered all too vividly a cousin and a fellow policeman who had both gone off to fight in the South African War a decade and a half ago. The glamour and excitement that marked their departure soon changed to grief with the news, much delayed, that Bartlett's police colleague had been killed in the British relief of Ladysmith. Perhaps he had been the lucky one.

The cousin survived, but was so horribly mutilated during a Boer guerilla attack near Mafeking that he might have been better off dead. Invalided to a hospital for the hopelessly insane in England, he likely would never again see his sorrowing family in Newfoundland. Bartlett had little difficulty persuading himself that, for all concerned, this probably was for the better.

For the moment, in any event – and Kelloway's countenance reflected it – there was a real sense of anticipation. Until something better came along, Newfoundland and Bay of Islands seemed about to become, in some small way, part of the great international events that were taking place. Kelloway carried on with a notable degree of excitement. "The orders from St. John's are to proceed to pick up some German fellows right away," he announced, "or, I suppose, as soon as we can find them. Six of them left their ship and are wandering around the country. We're to lock them up and keep them under guard until further notice. It's right there in the telegram. I don't know where we're going to find room to keep all those prisoners, though. I wonder how we're going to feed and guard them?"

"That's enough, Kelloway," his superior cut him off. "I can read it for myself," he barked in that perpetually gruff Bartlett voice. "And something else. We're not here to wonder why – we just do it, follow orders, right? As you'll find out soon enough if they take you in the army, where they leave no opportunity for discussion. Now, I wonder where those bloody Germans are supposed to be?"

A half-dozen miles further out the bay, at Benoit's Cove, the three-masted schooner *Fischboot I* let go her lines earlier than planned. Taking advantage of a southwesterly breeze, she raised sail and moved away from Basha's wharf to anchor a few hundred yards offshore.

The vessel had loaded only half the contracted cargo of herring under salt, but Captain Kurt Bruggemann had received orders from the owners to quit Newfoundland waters immediately. As the senior of the two, he had sent word overnight to his colleague, Captain Wilhelm "Willi" Meunch of the sister ship *Fischboot II* up the bay in Curling, that it was time to make waves, else the vessels and their crews might well be seized for the duration of the war. Like Bruggemann, Meunch lost no time getting under way. He hoped to rendezvous with *Fischboot I* at Benoit's Cove so they would sail from Bay of Islands together. However, Bruggemann had a serious problem on his hands, if not several.

"Six members of this crew have gone ashore, with permission, and have not yet returned," he pointed out to the first mate, Karl Lagerman. "If they do not soon return, we may have to sail without them. I am unwilling to abandon them, but we may have no choice. We have our orders."

"Perhaps we could send a party to look for them," the other man replied, and Bruggemann nodded in agreement.

"But we can only allow them so much time. Six hours at the most," the captain said, consulting his watch.

"Now," he added, "we also have Lutz missing – away *without* permission. I am guessing his intention is to carry on his feud with Herr Stroesser, if he can catch up with him. I believe I already told you confidentially that he – Herr Stroesser – in reality is an agent in the employ of the High Command," he said somewhat sourly.

Lagerman nodded, well aware that Bruggemann had little use for the arrangement that required him to carry an espionage agent in his crew, but that he had been given no choice. The owners had made that decision, no doubt under pressure from politicians. During the voyage from Cuxhavn, however, Lutz had recognized Stroesser as the man who had brought charges against his father several years earlier for theft from a military supplies warehouse in Hamburg. The old man was serving a long sentence and might well end his life in a prison cell.

"Bloody, despicable spy," Lutz had raged, and in their latest confrontation threatened to kill Stroesser if their paths crossed again – which was virtually inevitable sailing on the same ship.

To cool down the issue, Bruggemann arranged with Meunch to have Stroesser switch vessels, but before that could happen an incident occurred in which Lutz produced a gun and might have made good his threat had another crew member, Schmelling, not deflected the firearm at the last minute. As it was, Stroesser was shot in the leg and in need of medical attention that he could not obtain aboard ship.

"To forestall any further confrontation, while you were busy getting the cargo loaded, I authorized Stroesser to leave for Curling to get medical help, and then join *Fischboot II*, " the captain informed the first mate. "I sent his nephew, Schmelling, along to assist him in case he got in trouble. Whether they can reach our sister ship before she sails, that's another matter. And whether Lutz can catch up with them." His voice trailed off.

"*Mein Gott*, what a mess," Bruggemann said, realizing that, if they ever got back home to Germany, the owners would demand an accounting and he would certainly be the man on the spot. "I've never before experienced anything like this!"

Lagerman slowly shook his head, sharing his captain's expression of disbelief over what was happening. "I'll get a party ashore right away," the first mate said. "I think we'd better be ready to sail as soon as we get those fellows back on board."

FOUR

Curling Police Station,
Western Newfoundland, 1914

BARTLETT WAS A man who, above all, kept himself well informed. As a policeman, he knew that it behooved him to be aware of everything that was going on around him, maintaining a network of usually reliable sources. But there was more to it; of curious mind and a compulsive reader, he maintained a respectable library of classical and currently published books, and soaked up every scrap of information from the limited number of newspapers regularly available. The latest issues were piled up on his desk in the Curling police station – the local *Western Star*, published right in the community, was printed on a gasoline-powered cylinder press that sounded a lot like a two-stroke fisherman's engine, in a white-shingled building just east of the Newfoundland Railway station. *The Evening Telegram* and *The Daily News* arrived by train every few days, sent out by Constabulary headquarters in St. John's.

News by radio was still a thing of the future. Bartlett knew from his reading that although German physicist Heinrich Hertz had created radio waves in the laboratory as far back as 1887, nobody had yet figured out how to broadcast voice and musical sounds to a mass audience, or equally important, how they would receive them. In the meantime, reports from London had it that Signor Guglielmo Marconi, who in 1901 had chosen Newfoundland as the site to demonstrate for the first time his invention of long-range wireless telegraphy, had now revealed wireless telephony as an accomplished fact and provided his latest device to ships of the Italian navy. However, he had "refused to receive" agents of the German government seeking to have its fleet so equipped.

In any event, Bartlett was well aware of what had been reported in the newspapers – not to mention what he had heard by word of mouth from informants – that numbers of foreign nationals, many certainly German, were on the ground in Newfoundland and certainly here on the West Coast.

He was sure the majority were exactly what they purported to be – ordinary fishermen and fish buyers. But it was inevitable that a few were there for other purposes: information gathering, otherwise known as intelligence, and perhaps even sabotage. There was, however, little enough in this region, he judged, to justify or attract such activity.

Typical of the newspaper reports were the following:

> HARBOUR GRACE (*Evening Telegram*) Three Germans were arrested here and brought by train to the Penitentiary in St. John's by Sgt. Benson and Const. Fardy. They were members of the crew of a ship that loaded fish here recently.

> ST. JOHN'S (*Daily News*) Sgt. Kent of Placentia came in by last night's train bringing along a German seaman who was later taken to the Penitentiary as a prisoner of war. The man was a member of the crew of a vessel loading fish at Burin for European markets.

And there was this item, admittedly vague, but much closer to home:

> CURLING (*Western Star*) A number of Germans have been conspicuously active along the West Coast and no one seems to know what they are really doing. Some of

them have been cruising up and down the Coast the past three or four months. It is said they pass themselves off as representatives of various business houses and already one business firm has found it necessary to issue a warning to the trade.

This last report had not only excited Bartlett's curiosity, but also got his policeman's blood boiling. His training had ingrained the rule that confidentiality – not to say secrecy – was the hallmark of successful police operations, and he lived by it.

The next morning Bartlett turned up early on the doorstep of the *Western Star*'s managing editor, Andrew L. Barrett, who ran the paper in partnership with Dr. Alexander Campbell, a physician with political connections in St. John's. Campbell had acquired the financially troubled publication, in the years after founding publisher and editor Walter March left to accept a position with Robert G. Reid's Newfoundland Railway. The new, unlikely proprietor for a time had been the Roman Catholic Bishop of St. Georges, Neil McNeil. His Lordship had made a fire sale purchase in order to keep a local paper going in the place until someone came along who was interested in operating it permanently.

"Good morning, Isaac." The grey-haired, bespectacled Barrett greeted the policeman cordially. "It's a beautiful day. Come in and have a cup of tea."

But the journalist could see right away that something was amiss.

"This story here in the paper," Bartlett began without acknowledging either the greeting or the proffered beverage. With his left hand, he held out a folded copy of the *Star*; right index finger tapping the paper at approximately the location of the item in question.

"I suppose you could call it a story. As far as I'm concerned, it's nothing better than rumour mongering and certainly doesn't do anything to help police work or the security of the country in the present circumstances."

"Whoa . . . . Hold on there a minute, Head Constable. I'm the editor here," the suddenly stern-faced Barrett retorted stiffly. "I'll decide what's news and what's rumour, and I'll thank the Constabulary to keep that in mind. In the meantime, my eggs and toast are getting cold, but the offer to join me in a cup of tea stands."

He stepped back and opened the door to its full width.

Bartlett hesitated just a moment, then removed his service cap and stepped inside, following the newspaperman to his kitchen table.

"The wife is out back working in her garden," Barrett explained, pulling out a chair for his visitor, setting a cup and saucer in front of Bartlett as he sat, and removing a fancy, crocheted cozy from a huge china teapot. They were silent as he filled Bartlett's cup. Then he asked quietly, "Now, what's all this about rumour mongering?"

After twenty minutes the two men, who, despite their normal professional differences, were actually good friends, and indeed much alike in attitude and disposition, had agreed to disagree about Barrett's right to exercise his editorial judgment as to what went in the newspaper, and his readers' right to be informed. And about Bartlett's duty to express concern (as did any citizen, but especially one responsible for the security of the population) if and when it appeared that security might be jeopardized.

As well, Bartlett had to admit that the *Star*'s information, in all probability, was solidly based. Despite the virtual certainty it would alert any aliens in the area and put them on their guard, he knew such reports were routinely days ahead of official advisories from Constabulary headquarters in St. John's; for as must inevitably be the case, bureaucratic systems could never keep up with the journalistic demand for news immediacy.

There also was the point Barrett made that people not only should be told if their safety was in any way threatened, but their being informed might well help, rather than harm, police work.

There now would be thousands of citizens on their guard, many or all no doubt prepared to alert the authorities to any suspect activity.

Bartlett tied his fishing waders together and slung them over his left shoulder as he and Kelloway started the exacting climb up the steep embankment from Cook's Brook to the public road. As he climbed, the older man reluctantly admitted to himself something else: His assistant had a point, namely that there could be dozens of undesirable aliens in the area on foreign vessels engaged in catching and collecting fish, especially on this coast where herring and mackerel, particular favourites of eastern Europeans, abounded. *If we have to pick up a large number, where, indeed, will we put them?*

He continued to turn the problem over in his mind as his heavy, standard-issue leather boots scraped and skidded on rocky terrain. Clearly the cells on Courthouse Hill in Curling were unsuited for long-term incarceration of foreign internees, and in any case were required to serve the ongoing need for which they were provided, the custody of ordinary lawbreakers from the area. As well, Bartlett, Kelloway, and one other were the only law officers on the station, and their day-to-day policing duties were more than enough to keep them busy without having to guard virtual prisoners of war.

And another thing: As Constabulary members they were required to go about their daily business unarmed, in the same fashion as Robert Peel's London "bobbies" after whom their force was patterned. The local people knew this and responded accordingly – incidents involving firearms were extremely rare. The question was, would foreigners react in the same way?

Finally, he wondered, how and what *will* we feed them? It was rare to have more than one or two ordinary prisoners at a time, and there was an arrangement with a woman in the neighbourhood to provide their meals. When necessary, Bartlett's wife would help. As the mother of ten, her attitude, like that of most hospitable Newfoundland housewives, had always been, "What's one more mouth to feed?"

He was not so sure she would react the same way to having an extra dozen men around the place, and in any case, there wasn't the physical space to accommodate them.

Preoccupied as he was with such considerations, Bartlett permitted his right boot to skid on the flat surface of a large boulder of dolomite limestone, and began to slide back down the way he had come. He could easily have taken a tumble and received a serious injury, or at least a bad shaking up. Fortunately, Kelloway was directly behind and the younger man managed to impede his superior's unintended downhill progress. The latter grunted his gratitude and they completed the climb without further incident.

Their bicycles were lodged in alder bushes at the dusty road-side and as they reached the spot, the ever-inquisitive Kelloway posed a question.

"By the way, Head" – Head Constables were always addressed as "Head" – "maybe it's not very important, but why do you always call it 'Captain Cook's Brook' instead of just 'Cook's Brook' like everyone else around here?"

"Well, it's like this, sonny," Bartlett replied, his tone indicating annoyance at the question, or the ignorance of history that made it necessary, or both. "I just want to be sure everyone knows that one of England's greatest explorers and cartographers – that means map-makers – spent time in this little corner of the world in the eighteenth century, and mapped it all, and very likely did what I was doing a short while ago until interrupted by your whistle. That is, fished for a salmon for his supper. I just hope he had better luck and fewer interruptions!"

That peremptory history lesson delivered, he nimbly threw a leg over his bike and set off in the general direction of Curling, his headquarters for the Bay of Islands region, with Kelloway following close behind.

* * *

Higher up on the western slope of Mount Moriah, well-hidden in the dense profusion of alders and young spruce and fir, a man sat on a large rock studying the movements of the policemen through powerful binoculars, his left leg drawn up so the knee supported the hands holding them. The right stretched straight out, and part of a bloody bandage was visible between the trouser leg and the top of his heavy boot. After a while he returned the glasses to their battered leather carrying case whose Imperial German Navy insignia had been roughly scraped away.

Nearby a much younger man, one eye closed, squinted along the barrel of a rapid-firing Mauser rifle. He had the policemen in his sights.

"I could very easily pick them off," Werner Heinz Schmelling suggested quietly, and made a minor focusing adjustment with thumb and forefinger. "Two shots would do it," he mused, proceeding to slide a pair of long-range, brass-jacketed bullets into the chamber.

"Put that damn thing away, and come and help me up," Stroesser ordered. His companion was his nephew who, he knew, loved to play with guns. The older man worried that the obsession would sooner or later get them both in trouble and endanger his mission.

"*Jawöhl, Herr Öberleutnant*," Schmelling responded, but with little enthusiasm.

Still holding the gun in his left hand, he reached down with his right to help the other man struggle painfully to his feet. Stroesser was in his early thirties, hair thin and greying prematurely; only when he was standing did it become obvious that he had a serious injury. He supported himself by means of a crude crutch cut from the forked limb of a birch tree.

"Now, bury the guns and the rest of it. And don't forget, we are not here to engage the enemy. Our job is to learn what he is about – to gather information that will help the Fatherland in whatever way the High Command may decide, not take a chance of shooting a pair of unarmed local police officers and setting the whole country on our trail. Is that clear?"

They had been over this subject a dozen times, with Schmelling accepting their role as spies only reluctantly. His one-dimensional concept of war was limited to killing the enemy, nothing more, nothing less. But he followed orders, however reluctantly, and immediately set about preparing to stow their Morse sending-receiving set, spare batteries, and other paraphernalia, Luger pistol, and Mauser, all carefully wrapped in waterproof material, in a hole already prepared. The handgun had given Stroesser pause; he felt naked without it. Was it wiser to keep it for personal protection and take the risk of apprehension as an armed combatant, or to be rid of it and claim civilian, if alien, status? In the end, especially in consideration of his injury which left him basically immobile and in need of medical help, the latter had won out.

The hole was filled in with the use of the collapsible shovel, which also was wrapped and placed in it, just below the surface where it could easily be retrieved. Then the young man employed a heavy boot to spread the last of the gravel over the top and scattered leaves and twigs to give an appearance not unlike the surrounding terrain. The hole had been dug near a large boulder, its exposed bulk the size of a man's body. They should have no trouble locating it later.

"I doubt anyone will come by here," Stroesser said, "but if they do, it's unlikely they will notice any disturbance of the ground.

"Now, I must have medical attention for this leg before blood poisoning sets in and our mission is ruined. Let us go and meet the gentlemen of the local *gendarmerie.*"

At the base of the hill, Kelloway happened to glance upwards just as Schmelling, rifle still in hand, turned to assist his superior, and the policeman's eye caught what appeared to be the briefest reflection of sunlight on metal.

"Sir, I think there's someone up there, " he informed Bartlett, nodding towards the general area of the hillside. "Maybe the people we're looking for?"

Bartlett hauled a telescoping brass spyglass, a relic of his family's participation in the Conception Bay fishery, from a tunic pocket and extended it to its full length of about a foot. He put it to his left eye, but scanning the area indicated, detected nothing of interest. He was not greatly surprised; whoever it was would not be anxious to be discovered.

"Good eye, Kelloway. If it's those German fellows, we could encounter them anytime now. Let's just pretend to be completely surprised and see what develops. But we have to be careful — remember, they're most likely armed, and we're not."

FIVE

On the Side of Mount Moriah,
Newfoundland, 1914

"*Güten morgen, mein herr!*"

The two policemen gave every appearance of being momentarily taken aback, as if the last thing in the world they expected was to encounter a pair of German-speaking strangers on the side of Mount Moriah. They had pedalled their bicycles slowly up the long slope, and stepped off to make the remainder of their dusty way to the top of the grade on foot. A few hundred yards more and it would be mainly coasting to at least Petrie's Crossing, halfway home. Both were breathing heavily, but the younger man suffered the most. He was overweight, and in the blistering sunshine of the August forenoon, the heavy melton Constabulary tunic with its high collar might have been invented as a particular form of torture.

"You all right, Kelloway?" Bartlett called back over his shoulder.

More than twice his subordinate's age, he had learned to pace himself and, tall and spare, was in excellent physical condition.

"Yes, sir," the constable replied somewhat weakly, as he struggled to keep up, his response at variance with his obvious shortness of breath. Then he exclaimed:

"Head – look there, two men. Strangers for sure. Maybe they *are* the Germans we're supposed to be looking for!"

The pair – a young, blond fellow and an older man leaning on a makeshift crutch and nursing some kind of injury – stood at the side of the rocky cart track awaiting their approach.

* * *

Stroesser had calculated that the greeting in German would help to disarm suspicion that they were anything other than they pretended to be – merely members of a fish boat crew with nothing to hide, posing a danger to no one, caught in circumstances beyond their control. The deferential tone, therefore, was quite deliberate, a show of respect for the authority represented by the Constabulary uniforms that might just be enough to ensure their freedom. Rather than a potential threat, he reasoned, they might even be seen as representing a welcome opportunity for local fishermen to sell their catches into traditional European markets, caught up in a situation nothing worse than unfortunate.

But, make no mistake about it, Stroesser was part of a widespread mission, and an important one: to provide Germany with the reliable information required to deploy its forces so as to win the war. In the process, there was being constructed the most widespread spy network the world had ever known.

Scores of hand-picked operatives, their orders first and foremost to determine and report back to Berlin the state of military preparedness in assigned areas of the British and French possessions in North America, were infiltrating all levels of society. If, at the same time, they were in a position to undermine defences or to frustrate support for the mother countries, well and good, but on the scale of priorities intelligence was to take precedence over all else. The model was the so-far neutral United States of America, where already full advantage was being taken of a climate of isolationism and lax security to carry on an intensive campaign of espionage activity and sabotage. Agents were being placed in sensitive positions in government and industry, in the crews of passenger and cargo vessels, and among the personnel of great flying boats and dirigibles that were harbingers of the new age of international air travel – in short, wherever they could secure the most vital, useful information and cause the greatest damage to the Allies in the coming war.

If anyone doubted that this was so in Newfoundland, there was the case reported in the *The Western Star* concerning one

Gerhard von Stoekl, a recently deceased former employee of the government in St. John's and later the Newfoundland Railway, who was now reported to have been secretly "in the pay and employ of the German Emperor." Quoting the North Sydney, Nova Scotia *Herald*, the Curling newspaper described von Stoekl as a clever professional who moved in the best circles. After his death, however, personal papers were found that proved what he was really up to. The *Herald* had learned that, when the general manager of the Scotia Steel Co. visited Germany on business, he was amazed to find his contacts there had detailed maps of Bell Island, including the Wabana iron ore mines, and the wharves and ship anchorages, all supplied by von Stoekl.

"Good morning," Bartlett replied evenly, reciprocating Stroesser's greeting and reaching automatically for the notebook in the breast pocket of his tunic. "What are you men doing around here?"

Technically, since no crime had been committed, nor was there any suspicion thereof, this was not an arrest in the ordinary sense. However, the Germans were being taken into legal custody, and despite the absence of charges Bartlett quickly decided the usual police caution was in order. He began by identifying himself and his fellow officer, then went on.

"I expect you speak and understand English, else it would be extremely stupid to have sent you, whoever did send you, and whatever the reason you are here in this country." The older of the two men nodded.

"You do not have to say anything," the policeman continued, "but if you do say anything, it will be taken down and may be used as evidence in a court of law. Now, I need to know your names, where you are from, and what you are doing here. You first."

He indicated the older of the pair, a man of average height and weight, with thinning har, but seemingly in good physical condition except for his leg injury.

"Karl Otto Stroesser," he declared, in the methodical fashion of the military, "of Cuxhavn, Germany, in the estuary of the Elbe

River. I am second mate on the schooner *Fischboot I*, presently loading herring from T. Basha & Son at Benoit's Cove for carriage to Bremerhavn. My papers . . . "

Taking the proffered documents, the policeman noted the man's precise response and near-perfect English, marked by only a faint accent and entirely free of the guttural inflections apparent in the speech of most European fishermen he had come in contact with in his days enforcing fisheries law. Not exactly what you would expect from an ordinary crew member off a stinking fish-collection vessel. This, he guessed, was no rough fisherman. Rather, he likely belonged to the professional or officer class, and had possibly served in the Imperial German Navy.

He made a note to check the story with Thomas Basha, the Lebanese-born businessman who had emigrated to Newfoundland in the early years of the new century, and was well on the way to becoming a leading citizen and one of the most prominent businessmen in Bay of Islands.

"Just a minute," Bartlett interrupted sharply, as the police practice of interviewing prisoners separately took over a tad belatedly. He glanced in Kelloway's direction, and was thankful the younger man seemed not to have noticed.

"Constable Kelloway, take this man" – he indicated the tall, blond, pimply-faced youth – "down the road a bit, so this gentleman and I can have some privacy."

"At once, Head Constable," Kelloway replied, and turning to the younger prisoner, inclined his head in the direction from which the officers had come. They walked back down the road until the policeman called a halt, and the youth sat in a patch of grass at the roadside.

"All right, Mr. Stroesser. You were saying . . . ?" Bartlett held the pencil poised over his notebook.

"My young friend and I – his name is Werner Heinz Schmelling – we set out yesterday evening to walk up to Birchy Cove, or Curling as some call it, to visit friends on our sister ship, the *Fischboot II*, which is tied on at Mr. Basha's wharf up there doing the same as we, buying herring. Well, unfortunately I tripped over a rock in the dark and injured my leg. Now I am barely able to get along."

The policeman nodded and ordered, "Turn around."

Stroesser complied with some difficulty and Bartlett ran his hands over the other man's body from shoulders to shins without finding any trace of a weapon – not even a fisherman's knife. *That's strange,* the policeman thought to himself. *A fisherman without a knife? Too smart by half!*

It was a small thing, but he knew it was often the little things that made the difference in an investigation.

"I am not going to handcuff you," he informed the prisoner, "but you must understand that, as an enemy alien, a citizen of a country with which the British Empire, of which Newfoundland is part, has been at war for some days, I must take you into custody.

"Because you have broken no law that I am aware of, you will not be charged with any crime. If, however, you attempt to escape lawful custody, that will change; I shall be obliged to charge you, and you will thereupon become subject to the penalty or penalties provided. Is that clear?"

He watched Stroesser's face closely, and saw him tense momentarily and seem, for an instant, about to protest somehow against the detention. Then his control returned. He relaxed, nodding in compliance.

"I understand, Head Constable," he spoke carefully. "May I request that steps be taken to advise the German authorities of what has transpired here, so that our families will be made aware? And as well, that the master of the *Fischboot I* to be informed . . ."

His voice trailed off as he evidently realized that, in all likeli-hood, both his own vessel and its sister ship had been detained by now – unless they had managed to leave the bay before detention orders were received.

Bartlett nodded, but was noncommittal.

"Be assured that whatever is required will be done," he said.

With that, he called out, "Kelloway bring the other man here," and sent Stroesser down the road.

The interrogation of Schmelling, who gave his home address as rural Hamburg, ran along similar lines – to a point. With the same caution given, Bartlett questioned him about the circumstances under which the pair left their ship at Benoit's Cove, and the youth was surprisingly frank.

"Two days ago," he replied, obviously shaken at the prospect of dealing with the police in a strange land. His memory of the brutal treatment meted out to detainees in Germany was still fresh; there was no point, he concluded, in risking the same thing.

His use of English suffered badly by comparison with his older compatriot as he asked, "Did Herr Stroesser tell what happened there?"

"Why don't you tell me?" Bartlett suggested, glancing down the road to ensure the other man was out of earshot.

"Well . . ." he hesitated, uncertain what to disclose, then continued. "There was some bad trouble. Someone accused Herr Stroesser of being a spy – I think it was Lutz, from Lubeck – and of having his father put in prison. A shot was fired and my uncle was struck in the leg, so we were lucky to escape. We had hoped to reach the other ship."

Now, there's a discrepancy, Bartlett noted, *from the story of an injury from a fall as told by Stroesser*, and continued to write in his little notebook. *There will, I expect, be others.*

The difficulty now lay in getting the prisoners to the cells in the basement of the Courthouse in Curling, some seven miles distant, given Stroesser's injury.

"Kelloway," Bartlett called, "go down to Mr. Cooper's and tell him I need to borrow his horse and cart to bring an injured prisoner to Curling."

"Yes, sir, right away," the constable responded. He jumped on his bicycle and was gone in the direction of James Cooper's farm, well-known as the only one in the area that used oxen to haul wood in winter. The huge animals were a curiosity that brought more than a few visitors around "just to see."

Turning to the Germans, Bartlett said, "Gentlemen, we'll just have to wait here until he returns with some transportation. We can't have you trying to walk that distance using a crutch." He indicated Stroesser's injured limb. "It would take us all day."

"*Danke . . . danke schon . . . .* Thank you very much," Stroesser said. His face was wreathed in pain, and he indicated obvious relief.

A few minutes later, the clank and crunch of iron cart wheels on a rocky surface announced the arrival of an elderly farmer, his plough horse hauling an all-purpose long cart known as a dray. With help, Stroesser was able to get aboard the conveyance, head resting on his rolled-up jacket, and the injured limb cushioned by a potato sack of hay that the farmer carried for the horse.

"Mornin' Isaac," Cooper said. "Lucky to catch me. Fifteenth of August, ye know, an' I was just headin' out to the field to get the first o' the new 'taties for me supper."

"Appreciate your help, Jim," Bartlett said. "Sorry to interrupt your plans for Lady Day, but this is official business."

The whine of a rifle bullet, and then another, and a double *thwack, thwack* of gunshots, came just as Cooper picked up the reins and cluck-clucked Bill, the horse, into motion. The movement caused the first deadly projectile to miss Stroesser, who Bartlett correctly guessed was the intended target. It kicked up a little geyser of dirt at the side of the road. The second caromed off the left-hand shaft of the cart, then struck Bill a glancing blow in the left hindquarter.

The animal squealed in pain and reared up in the shafts, threatening to upset the cart and take off down the road. It was all Cooper could do to keep him under control.

They scrambled for cover at the side of the road nearest the hillside – Bartlett, Kelloway, Stroesser who rolled off the cart and painfully dragged himself as far out of harm's way as he could, all except Cooper, who took a chance moving to the front to stroke Bill's face and murmur in his ear to quiet him down, and Schmelling . . .

The youth raced down the road twenty yards to the place he had waited with Kelloway during Stroesser's questioning, plunged his hand into some leaves behind a stump, and produced the Luger he was supposed to have buried up on the mountain a few hours earlier. Wheeling, he began firing in the direction from which the rifle shots had come, and was immediately rewarded by a muffled scream of pain from the woods above them, followed by a sudden silence.

Bartlett stood and brushed dust and twigs from his uniform.

"Hand over that pistol," he ordered, fully realizing that if the youth refused there was little that he could do about it.

When Schmelling hesitated, Stroesser added his voice to the policeman's demand.

"Werner, I order you to turn over the gun to the Head Constable . . . . Do it now – *schnell!*"

To a greater degree than others, it was said, in the armed forces of Germany the voice of a superior was the voice of God. Bartlett took the pistol, offered to him butt-first, and put it in a tunic pocket. Leaving Kelloway in charge, he set off up the hillside in search of the rifleman.

He discovered him lying face down in a well-worn footpath, a youth not much older, perhaps, than Schmelling. A bullet from the Luger had torn away his throat and exited at the back of the neck. He was, of course, quite dead.

Absolutely amazing . . . . Either an unbelievably lucky shot, Bartlett thought as he picked up the dead man's rifle and searched his pockets for identification, *or we have discovered in Schmelling the world's number one marksman!*

They loaded the corpse, whose papers bore the name Wilhelm Albrecht Lutz, date of birth March 7, 1894, of Lubeck, Germany, on board Cooper's long cart. It lay stretched out alongside

Stroesser, his intended victim, for the bumpy ride to Curling. Bartlett thought it only right to cover the face, which he did with a large white handkerchief.

SIX

Constabulary Residence, Curling, Newfoundland, 1914

ELIZABETH ANN BARTLETT, née Bishop, typified that magnificent legion of Newfoundland housewives to whom has been accorded the title of "good managers." It meant that they were the de facto bosses of their households, well capable of looking after things whether their husbands were at home or away – but generally deferring to them as "head of the family." It was their choice that it was so.

They disciplined the children and fed and clothed them, saw that they regularly attended school and paid the requisite attention to their studies, that they carried out their assigned chores, that they went to church on Sunday, and that they conducted themselves in such a way as not to shame or embarrass the family. It was in keeping with the grim tradition of fishing families whose experience was that the father was away for long periods – and in all too many cases failed ever to return from the fishing grounds. The history of Newfoundland is replete with the stories of scores of fishing vessels, large and small, that disappeared in storms, capsized when the burden of fish in the hold shifted suddenly, or foundered because the catch was perhaps too great and the vessel overloaded, their crews never seen or heard from again.

Tall, grey-haired, and exhibiting a self-confidence born of a long line of "good managers," Elizabeth Ann Bartlett was born near Spaniard's Bay, a bustling harbour in Conception Bay North, on October 1, 1853. She was exactly four years younger than her husband, Isaac William, who first saw the light of day in the neighbouring fishing community of Brigus, in the same district but some dozen miles away, on October 7, 1849. Their children were Frederick William, Allan George, Walter James, Emily Lavinia, Annie Emmeline, Effie Maude, Robert Bishop, Charles Boone, Wilfred, and Ethel May. Eight survived childhood, all but Emily and Effie, and by now had gone their separate ways, establishing families of their own.

As the wife of the police officer in charge of the district, Elizabeth Ann felt she had a responsibility, which she carried out to an exacting degree, to assist her husband in the performance of his duty. Thus, when Isaac William left before dawn for what were intended to be a pleasant few hours fishing for salmon on Cook's Brook, she heard the back door close on her mate and thought, *God knows he can stand a day of relaxation.* Simply put, she was prepared to be the unofficial Head Constable for Bay of Islands until his return.

Constable B. J. Quinlan, whose ordinary station was Petrie's Crossing, rapped on the door about noon with three strangers in tow, and Elizabeth Ann gave the appearance neither of being surprised nor taken aback.

"G'mornin', ma'am," the tall beanstalk of a man greeted her, "is the Head Constable about?" He spoke with a low drawl that seemed to be impeded somehow by a huge, black moustache.

"Not at the moment, Constable, but he shouldn't be too long. What have we here, now?"

She indicated the trio in rough foreign fishermen's garb – the caps and boots, especially, definitely not of a style local men wore – who stood around uncertainly, seemingly resigned to the fact that, sooner or later, someone would decide their fate.

"Well, they do be hangin' around down to the Crossing, not knowin' what to be doin' what with the war situation and all, I imagine. When they went in Mr. Dunphy's store, scoopin' sauerkraut out of the barrel with a stick, he decided to send for me. I figured the best thing was to bring them here. There are supposed to be two or three more around, but no sign of 'em so far."

"You did the right thing to bring these men along," she said. "Constable Kelloway went to fetch my husband with a telegram from St. John's ordering the arrest of some aliens. I presume these men have documents?"

"I have 'em right here," Quinlan replied, removing a wad of paper from a tunic pocket, and reading out the unfamiliar names as best he could.

"Walther Heinrich Stoerk, thirty-eight years old, from Wilhelmshavn, Germany," he read, indicating a tall, slightly balding, bearded man with a swarthy complexion.

"Over here we have Heinz Rickard Diemke, age twenty-seven, address given as Lower Freiberg," he said, pointing to a short, burly individual with flaming red hair and beard.

"And here, Otto Josef Rasch, from Hamburg . . . ah . . . oh, yes, he is nineteen years old." Quinlan indicated a gangling youth with straight, black hair that had been allowed to grow as long as a girl's.

All acknowledged the tall, grey-haired matron with small bows in her direction, except for Rasch who also smiled and attempted a greeting in English.

"Ver-r-ry plissed . . . to meet you," the young man stammered.

"Thank you," Mrs. Bartlett replied, colouring slightly. It was the first time she had encountered foreign nationals in custody – innocent men, she reminded herself, men who had committed no crime, as far as she knew – who actually seemed relieved to be facing incarceration. She tried to imagine the confusion and uncertainty in their lives; any one of them could be one of her own sons.

"Constable Quinlan," she continued, "I think it would be a good idea if you escorted these men to the cells now."

"Yes, ma'am," he replied, "right away." Tugging open the heavy door to the jail area in the basement of the combined courthouse, police station, and Head Constable's residence, he signalled for the men to enter. He placed them in alternating cells to preserve a degree of isolation until Bartlett's arrival and their subsequent questioning.

When Quinlan emerged Mrs. Bartlett invited him in for a cup of tea, and he did not refuse. Her tea biscuits and raspberry jam were famous in the district.

"And how is Mrs. Quinlan," she inquired, cringing as he tipped strong tea into his saucer and blew on the steaming liquid to cool it, "after that terrible fright you people had last week?"

They had awakened in the small hours of the morning to the smell of smoke. The Soper house that the government rented for them at Petrie's Crossing was on fire; someone had piled brush against the back of the dwelling, poured fuel oil over it, and set it alight. Only the quick action of neighbours carrying water from their wells saved the structure from serious damage or destruction.

"You'll appreciate, ma'am, that the wife is pretty nervous. I'm suspicious that it was connected to a big bootleg operation out the Bay; I think it's the foreign fish boats probably going by St. Pierre, and their local connections, sending a warning that we'd better be careful about interfering with the biggest industry around here next to fishing and lumber – illegal alcohol. I suppose you know the government is sending out special agents to help with the investigation."

"Yes," she said, "my husband mentioned that. Give Mrs. Quinlan my best wishes. Here are a few tea biscuits she might enjoy."

"Thank you very much, ma'am," he said, and took his leave.

Within the hour the crunch of cart wheels on gravel announced Bartlett's arrival. They removed the body of the dead German from Cooper's conveyance and placed him in a shed directly behind the main building. A few large blocks of ice from Basha's fish plant, buried in sawdust, would serve well enough to keep the shed cool and preserve the body until the doctor could come for the required post-mortem examination. At the same time Stroesser's injury would receive attention.

Bartlett alerted Dr. George Pullin via the rural telephone system that had just been installed, with the police station linked to various prominent sites. For some reason, however, it had not been decided that one of the fifteen boxes should be put in the local Post and Telegraph office, so it was necessary to send Kelloway down, paper in hand, to dispatch a report to Constabulary headquarters:

```
SECRET
INSP GENERAL OF POLICE
ST JOHNS


FIVE GERMAN NATIONALS ARRESTED NAMES KARL
OTTO STROESSER WERNER HEINZ SCHMELLING
WALTER HEINRICH STOERKE HEINZ RICKARD
DIEMKE OTTO JOSEF RASCH ONE MAN WILHELM
ALBRECHT LUTZ DECEASED EXCHANGE GUNFIRE
BETWEEN ALIENS POST MORTEM ARRANGED DR
PULLIN AWAIT FURTHER ORDERS CUSTODY
ARRANGEMENTS ENDS.


BARTLETT HEAD CONST
CURLING
```

By the grapevine, Bartlett knew that temporary holding facilities for aliens were being prepared on the north side of Quidi Vidi Lake in St. John's. However, he also knew that when these would be ready to accept prisoners and where the funds would come from to pay for their construction were unanswered questions.

In the meantime, he would have to consider how to deal with the security, accommodation, feeding, and other aspects of looking after the men he already had in his basement in Curling, and the others who might follow.

And, of course, there was the day-to-day business of a busy police station to carry on. Bartlett was especially concerned over the attempt to burn Quinlan's home with the constable and his wife in it, and determined that the investigation would be pressed and those responsible apprehended. He had no doubt Quinlan was right, that it was the work, directly or indirectly, of bootleggers; he had requested revenue department assistance that should be arriving from St. John's in the next day or so.

Elizabeth Ann raised this matter as soon as they were alone in their private quarters. She referred to the constable's visit, and the worry, particularly on the part of his wife, that the arsonists might strike again. Finally, she suggested that the Quinlans might move in with the Bartletts until the perpetrators were found.

"I understand your feelings in the matter, but I'm not so sure that would be a good idea," her husband replied. "For one thing, it might look like Quinlan was running away, which would certainly not engender respect for the force or for the rule of law. For another, it would leave their home and their belongings unguarded and vulnerable for anyone who might want to destroy or steal them. No, my dear, it will be far better for all concerned if the Quinlans stand their ground."

She did not reply, so he continued.

"By the way, was that Quinlan's idea, that they move in here?"

"Oh my heavens, Isaac, no," she quickly replied. A bit too quickly, he thought.

"He just happened to mention that his wife was nervous over what happened. She is expecting, you know. I would be nervous too, for heaven's sake!"

When Kelloway returned from the Post and Telegraph office, he brought news of an early season storm to the north, in the Bonne Bay area and beyond. Overnight, houses had been unroofed and barns and sheds blown down. There was snow in the higher and medium levels of the Long Range Mountains north of Bonne Bay up to two feet deep. There was much damage to fishermen's boats, wharves, and stages from what was unusually severe weather for this time of year.

Bartlett was thankful the fury of the storm had left his Bay of Islands territory unscathed. What he did not yet know was that *Fischboot I* and *II* had both departed hurriedly – and suspiciously coincident with the order to various police stations around the coast to pick up enemy aliens – and had sailed directly into the teeth of the gale. Was there a leak somewhere, he wondered when he got the news, that permitted them, and perhaps other foreign ships and their alien crews, to flee when they did, and thus elude capture?

The herring collectors had left Curling and Benoit's Cove with the intention of making a rendezvous in the outer Bay of Islands, lying-to in the East Arm of Bonne Bay until the expected storm had blown itself out. Then they would escape together up through the Strait of Belle Isle. But an urgent warning that the authorities might be hot on their trail caused them to ignore the storm warnings, abandon their rendezvous plan, and unwisely head on up the St. Barbe Coast.

The viciousness lashing the land turned out to be even less kind to those on the water. The wooden-hulled *Fischboot II* drove ashore on Martin's Point between St. Paul's Inlet and Cow Head – the same rocky shore that one day would claim the steel-hulled Newfoundland Railway steamship SS *Ethie* – at two o'clock in the morning with the loss of all hands. The bodies of crew members, together with wreckage and cargo, including casks of French liquor with labels still affixed, bearing the name *F. Labelle, St. Pierre-et-Miquelon,* were washing ashore for days and weeks afterwards.

Unaware of what had befallen her twin, *Fischboot I* barely escaped a similar fate. After limping along the shore as far as Port aux Choix, she managed, with the assistance of local entrepreneurs happy to exchange repairs, supplies, and water for a supply of strong drink, to depart the scene before the authorities realized she had been in the vicinity.

As the storm subsided, she sailed well offshore from Reef's Harbour, Black Duck Cove, and Anchor Point, Flower's Cove and Eddie's Cove, and Boat Harbour. Once she passed L'Anse aux Meadows – the place Leifr Eiriksson and the first Europeans made land in North America nearly a thousand years before – it was clear sailing out into the broad expanse of the Labrador Sea.

Now, Bruggemann felt, there was a reasonable chance that they might make it safely home. As to what had befallen their sister ship, he had no idea – nor did he feel it wise to wait around to find out.

In the house in Petrie's Crossing, Constable Quinlan and his wife, Catherine, who was carrying their first child, had decided they would retire early.

At 2:30 a.m., Catherine awoke in a state of high alarm to the distinctive odour of woodsmoke, and in an absolute panic roused her husband.

"My God, Jim," she screamed, "it's happening again. The house is on fire!"

Their bedroom was on the second floor. They grabbed street clothes and fled downstairs to the front entrance, to find that it had been blocked by heavy logs and debris that had been doused with kerosene and set alight. The couple turned and raced to the back door only to find it similarly obstructed. Fires had been started, as well, at several other locations around the exterior of the dwelling.

Quinlan picked up a dining-room chair and used it to smash a window at the back of the house. As he and his pregnant wife stepped gingerly through shards of glass into one of her prize flower beds, flames were leaping high up the walls. This time no bucket brigade would save the structure. Had Catherine not been a light sleeper, they very well might have been trapped in the flames.

The determined bootleggers on board the *Fischboot II,* who had paid a large sum to arrange the arson, would never know of this second failure to eliminate the Quinlans. Nor would the dead men get another chance.

SEVEN

Government House, St. John's, Newfoundland, 1914

As THE REALITY of war descended upon the Newfoundland of 1914 like a dark, forbidding cloud, the practicalities of the situation also began to assert themselves. For one thing, the Old Colony – which by war's end would consider itself to have earned the title of "Dominion" and a new status to accompany it – was virtually bereft of any semblance of military preparedness. With the exception of a 600-man contingent of Royal Naval Reserve volunteers, most of whom were involved in the fishery which was at its peak at this time of year, and the mainly church-sponsored cadet corps, there were virtually no men in uniform, no weapons to speak of, and no training facilities.

There had been no British military garrison in Newfoundland for the past half-century. With international hostilities about to envelop nations bordering the broad Atlantic Ocean, the island that conventional wisdom would hold to be of enormous strategic importance to North American security found itself totally unprotected.

Should the German navy decide to invade St. John's – London had reported that the cruiser *Dresden* was operating off the South Coast of the Island, more or less in striking distance of the capital – it could expect to meet with very little armed resistance. Perhaps the most striking response to the news from the British Admiralty was the entry Governor Davidson made in his daily log before retiring:

"[I]f the . . . Dresden *enters the harbour of St. John's, we shall block the entrance to the Narrows by sinking two of our own ships in the fairway, and if the* Dresden *threatens retaliation [by] opening fire on the town and arresting or executing the Governor and leading people as prisoners or hostages, the people are armed and will exact the fullest retribution on the whole crew . . ."* [2]

As matters turned out, and no doubt very fortunately for the people of St. John's and all Newfoundland, the Admiralty's information was quite less than accurate.

Davidson's policy was knock and enter, and Captain Goodridge was always careful to respect the Governor's rules. He rapped smartly, three assaults by a middle knuckle on solid oak, and turned the knob. He stepped over the threshold into the private office.

"Your Excellency, it appears that this is the latest word the Admiralty has in the *Dresden* affair . . ." He held out a decoded dispatch, just delivered by special messenger from the Marconi receiving station at Cabot Tower.

Davidson, standing at the tall windows with hands in trousers pockets, chewing over what he would say at tonight's meeting of the Patriotic Committee, did not turn around.

"Read it to me, Goodridge," he commanded.

"Of course, sir," the aide-de-camp responded, removing a single sheet of stiff, official stationery from its OHMS envelope. He cleared his throat, and began:

```
MOST SECRET FOR H. E. EYES ONLY
FROM: DIRECTOR NAVAL INTELLIGENCE LONDON

RE:  WHEREABOUTS CRUISER DRESDEN

LATEST INTELLIGENCE CONFIRMS SUBJECT VESSEL
IN CARIBBEAN WATERS STOP BELIEVED DESTINA-
```

```
TION  IS  SOUTH  AMERICAN  ZONE  STOP  DISCON-
TINUE   ALERT   NEWFOUNDLAND   WATERS   STOP
CONFIRM STOP
```

"Well, that's it then," said Davidson, who had earlier ordered nighttime blackouts, and the harbour entrance blocked from dusk to daylight, against the possibility of attack. "Mark my words, Goodridge, faulty intelligence will double the length of this war – it could go on for six months or more, instead of the six weeks the Kaiser has estimated.

"However, having said that, the news about the *Dresden* has done more to screw up the courage and determination of the people here to win the war than even I could have done, were I to give a dozen speeches. I'd wager we are going to see recruitment oversubscribed, and the special fund go over the top – provided, perhaps, the news of the *Dresden* false alarm doesn't get out. So let's keep this absolutely between us, eh, Captain?"

Goodridge smiled thinly. "Absolutely right, sir," he said. "Not a word to anyone."

"And, Captain," Davidson added, "that especially includes the press. If those fellows come around asking questions, remind them about the censorship rules and the fact they can go to jail if they violate them. But you could also suggest that the danger of attack and invasion is ever-present in a city located right by the ocean. That might not do any harm at all. In fact, don't wait for them to come to you. You go to them."

The wherewithal to finance "the great adventure," as some foolishly referred to the war, was simply unavailable, short of massive public borrowing. Easily the most expensive undertaking involved the creation of an independent Newfoundland regiment, including support in the field and the future costs of pensions, allowances, and medical care. It had started out in the range of $10,000,000, but the cost would very likely grow to three times that, and contribute heavily to Newfoundland's eventual bankruptcy.

However, remarkably few objected as Davidson, aided and abetted by the leading citizens of St. John's, pursued an objective that, quite aside from the financial cost, could hardly be sustained without resort to conscription. If any were perturbed by his invidious suggestion that Newfoundland was in a position to send men, but not money, no one said so.

The call to arms that a young Newfoundland Constabulary member named Kelloway, and thousands like him, waited to hear came in newspapers of August 21. Scanning the latest batch of papers from St. John's, Bartlett spotted it right away.

"Kelloway," he called to his young colleague, who was busy checking the German prisoners into their cells at the end of a period of outdoor exercise, "here's what you've been waiting for, the Governor's call for recruits. I suppose this means we'll be losing you to the Regiment. Have you told your parents yet?"

"No, sir, not just yet, but I'll be talking to them when I go home on leave next week. I'm sure they'll be very proud to have a son serving over there!"

Newspapers carried the proclamation calling on men aged nineteen to thirty-five to help fulfill Davidson's earlier commitment to the "Home Government" to furnish five hundred men – he hoped it might turn out to be be five thousand – who would enlist "for the duration of the war, but not exceeding one year." Clearly, the Kaiser and his High Command were not alone in the mistaken belief that it would be over quickly!

Couched in the most patriotic language, it was addressed "To the People of Newfoundland" and signed by the Governor, Morris; James Mary Kent, Leader of the Opposition; and Eric R. Bowring, Chairman of the Finance Committee of the Patriotic Association.

Fellow Countrymen:

The Mother Country has been compelled to go to war to preserve, among other things, the rights and liberties which we all enjoy as citizens of the Empire.

Newfoundland, in common with the other Overseas Dominions, has pledged itself to assist the Mother Country with material help in the present extremity.

This is to take the form of an increase in the Naval reserve, from Six Hundred to One Thousand Men, and the raising of a Regiment of Five Hundred Men for land service abroad, and the Colony has further undertaken to assume the full cost of this contingent of Five Hundred Men during the course of the war.

It is our duty and privilege, as loyal and patriotic citizens of the Empire, to voluntarily assist in supporting this movement, and, to raise a fund for that purpose. This Patriotic Fund will be applied primarily in making provision for the dependent relatives of those who Undertake to fight the battles of the country and the Empire by land and sea and afterwards to such other objects connected therewith as may be deemed desirable.

The need is great and in the confident expectation that this appeal will evoke a prompt and generous response, we respectfully but strongly urge all who can to give as liberally as possible towards this most deserving object.

The undersigned, on behalf of the Patriotic Committee appointed to undertake the organization and despatch of this Regiment, appeal for subscriptions toward this fund. Contributions may be sent to the nearest magistrate, to the branches of any Banks doing business in the Colony, or to the Treasurer, J. S. Munn, Esq., and they will be gratefully acknowledged.

A further "Call for Recruits" would begin with the declaration, "Your King and Country need you!" and then ask, "Will you answer your country's call?"

The Empire was engaged in "the greatest war in the history of the world" and was calling upon young men to "rally around their flag and enlist in the ranks of her army." Which, of course, they did, and in unpredictably large numbers. Newfoundland had already sent to the Front her "first contingent, 540 strong" – known as the First Five Hundred, also called the Blue Puttees because of the colour of their leg wrappings (no khaki material was available). But it was made clear that "further drafts will be needed." In fact, when all the numbers were totted up, the faceless bureaucrats who keep such statistics concluded more than 12,000 men had offered themselves as volunteers. Of these, more than half were accepted.

The casualty list was devastating, in excess of 1,300 dead and 2,300 wounded. In other words, twenty per cent of Regiment personnel – or one in every five – would never see Newfoundland again. According to one analysis, this was proportionately more than double the losses suffered by their nearest neighbours, the Canadians. Of the rest, half came home with wounds that in many cases marked and impaired them, physically and psychologically, for life.

It was certainly true that over the course of the conflict the Regiment distinguished itself. The phrase on everyone's lips, attributed to Lieutenant-General Sir Aylmer Hunter-Weston, the Corps commander, in the wake of Beaumont Hamel: "Better than the best." As had no other regiment in the British forces in the history of modern warfare, it was granted the title "Royal" in the field. There were regimental battle honours for Gallipoli, Arras, Langemark, Cambrai-LeTransloy, Ypres, Poelcappelle, and Bailleul, and Beaumont Hamel, of course. Individual honours and decorations numbered 280, including one Victoria Cross.

However, people were coming to realize that Davidson's insistence on the concentration of Newfoundland soldiers in a single infantry unit, rather than distributed throughout elements of the British forces, was proving to have been an enormous blunder. In terms of lives lost, it was the worst tragedy by far in the long, tragic history of the Old Colony.

This was most dramatically seen in the debacle of July 1, 1916, when the result was not only virtual annihilation of the battalion that went "over the top" that day, but a huge and terrible toll on a tiny community of little more than 200,000 souls. Hardly a family in the length and breadth of Newfoundland was spared.

Almost nobody gave much thought to the cost of arresting, guarding, sheltering, feeding, and transporting prisoners of war – or, if non-combatants, as was more than likely the case, enemy aliens.

However, it was a difficult challenge faced by men such as the Constabulary's Bartlett in Bay of Islands: where and how physically to accommodate foreigners who might be taken into custody. A few areas had limited jail space, provided for the purpose of holding local residents and others serving light sentences or awaiting trial, but unsuited to long-term incarceration. Other places had none. Their expedient was to convey internees under police escort to His Majesty's Penitentiary in St. John's which had, perhaps, a little room to spare, but not very much.

"Isaac, we have to be sure we can take proper care of our prisoners during the winter," Elizabeth Ann Bartlett said after supper one late September night, as the sun sank behind the Blomidon Mountains, flooding the outer Bay with colours of dark red and gold. "That sky tells me summer is long gone, and we can expect just about anything from now on," she said. "If we're going to keep those men here, we have to shelter and feed them, but they also don't have much in the way of clothing and boots for the winter."

Her husband removed the pipe from between his teeth and carefully folded the latest copy of *The Evening Telegram*, laying it on a side table.

"My darling wife," he replied with a small touch of impatience, "my reports have gone in to St. John's. They know what needs to be done. I have asked for an increase in budget for foodstuffs, and an additional allocation for boots and heavy clothing. As recently as yesterday I inquired as to the status of those requests. What else would you have me do?"

"Yes, well, I hope they realize the problem we have here, or will have, if they don't hurry and approve those requests."

"I don't disagree with you, Elizabeth Ann," he replied, "but you know as well as I do that headquarters moves at its own pace."

With that Bartlett donned cap and tunic and descended the stairs to the jail section of the building. Stroesser seemed to be the acknowledged leader of the internees, and the policeman had developed a habit of dealing with the men through him.

"Mr. Stroesser," he greeted him, unlocking the cell.

"*Jawöhl*, Head Constable," the man acknowledged.

"How is your injured leg coming along?"

"Good, very good," the German replied. "I would wish that you tell the physician – *Herr Doktor* Pullin, is it? – that his good work is very much appreciated."

"I shall do so the first time I see him," Bartlett said. "However, there is something I wish to speak to you about, since it is my understanding that the men have chosen you as their spokesman. You are likely to be here for some time, and from the point of view of physical condition – that is to say, your personal health – I do not think we can keep you penned up without ever getting any exercise.

"What I would like to propose is this. I have some work to be done on property I own about an hour's walk from here. I am prepared to pay to have the work done, which would allow you and your compatriots to earn some money against the time that you are repatriated, whenever that may be. Now, what do you think of that?"

"I am sure," Stroesser replied, "the men will want to know what kind of work, and how to work outside without proper clothing."

"I have requested," Bartlett informed him, "funds to purchase winter clothing and boots for all of you, which I am certain will be approved. As for the work, it will be physical, outdoors work – for example, I want a rock wall built on the property – but it will be nothing too strenuous. Better than being cooped up here all day long."

"Very well, Head Constable," Stroesser said. "I shall let you know tomorrow if the men are interested. But only, I would say, if provided with proper clothing and boots."

"The men are all fishermen by trade," Stroesser added, "and they would also like the opportunity to go fishing occasionally – if a small boat could be found for jigging a few codfish, for example. We could even help feed ourselves. We realize we are a burden on your local operations here."

Bartlett agreed in principle, but would have to consider practical details such as security, which Stroesser understood. Soon they worked out an amicable arrangement.

It took several months, but eventually it was decided that, rather than build its own detention facilities, Newfoundland would send its internees to Canada – there were far fewer than expected – and of course, pay the cost of doing so. On July 30, 1915 Governor Davidson penned a formal memorandum to W. W. Halfyard, the Colonial Secretary:

"It is suggested that this telegram be dispatched to the Canadian Government as a convenient method of disposing of civilian prisoners of war. Will you ascertain if members (of the Cabinet) desire it to be sent?"

```
TO: H. E. GOVERNOR GENERAL OF CANADA


TWENTY CIVILIAN ENEMY ALIENS INTERNED WAR
ST. JOHN'S BUT QUESTION OF ERECTION OF A
CAMP PRESENTS DIFFICULTIES. MY MINISTERS
ENQUIRE IF SUCH ALIEN PERSONS MAY BE TRANS-
FERRED TO AHMERST FOR INTERNMENT THERE AT
THE EXPENSE OF THIS GOVERNMENT


DAVIDSON
```

On Christmas Eve, 1915, the British government advised as follows:

```
TO: H. E. GOVERNOR OF NEWFOUNDLAND

GOVERNMENT OF GERMANY HAVE AGREED WITH H. M.
GOVERNMENT TO RELEASE ON CONDITION OF RECI-
PROCITY MERCHANT SEAMEN UNDER 17 AND OVER 55
EXCLUDING ALL OFFICERS. ARRANGEMENT IS
INTENDED TO APPLY TO THE WHOLE EMPIRE. SECRE-
TARY OF STATE FOR FOREIGN AFFAIRS REGRETS THAT
OWING TO AN OVERSIGHT YOUR GOVERNMENT WAS NOT
INFORMED AT AN EARLIER STAGE BUT TRUSTS THAT
MEMBERS WILL NOT HAVE ANY OBJECTION.


BONAR LAW, SECRETARY OF STATE
```

The reply brought the matter to a close, a year and a half after it began:

```
TO: HON. SECRETARY OF STATE:

YOUR TELEGRAM 24TH DECEMBER. ALL GERMAN
MERCHANT SEAMEN INTERNED IN NEWFOUNDLAND
HAVE BEEN TRANSFERRED TO CANADA. NONE NOW
HERE UNDER 17 OR OVER 55 YEARS OF AGE.


DAVIDSON
```

Bartlett was glad to see the German prisoners leave for Canada and a proper internment arrangement. Now he could return to normal policing of the area under his responsibility. But he sometimes wondered what had become of his German "guests." Had they been returned to their native land? Were they alive and well?

The war over, a letter arrived from Hamburg, Germany from Rasch, the shy young man who had become Elizabeth Ann's favourite among the internees. He had reached his home after three years in the prisoner exchange system.

"I shall never forget the good times we had in Curling," he wrote. "I wish I could get some of your codfish and rabbit pie. I hope this letter finds you in good health. Kind regards to you and Mrs. Bartlett."[3]

At least one of Bartlett's prisoners subsequently returned to Newfoundland. At the start of the Second World War, Stroesser was back as a spymaster for the *Abwehr* military intelligence agency, with the support and confidence of its head, Admiral Canaris. In time, Canaris would be hanged for his part in an assassination attempt on Hitler.

By then Stroesser and his agents would have cost Newfoundland hundreds of lives and cruelly affected thousands of others.

EIGHT

The Battlefields of France,
First World War, 1918

DURING HIS FIRST year overseas, Fred Banting made the rounds of military hospitals in England, providing medical aid and comfort to many in the continuous stream of wounded men of the British Expeditionary Force and others shipped back from the Front. But he was increasingly impatient to get to the scene of the action. Finally he was promoted to Captain and assigned to France in June 1918, in the final, bitter months of the war, to tend to the needs of Canadian and other Empire troops on the battlefields of Amiens, the Arras sector, and Cambrai. By this time sheer exhaustion – of men, of *matériel*, of money – had sapped the collective energies and the economies of belligerent nations. There was talk of an armistice by Christmas and to the surprise of many, that hopeful but speculative deadline was, in fact, bested by several weeks.

Banting, meanwhile, came perilously close to losing his right arm from German shrapnel when a shell exploded virtually on top of a field hospital where he was working. Awarded the Military Cross for bravery, and after being hospitalized in England for several months, he was finally repatriated home to Canada in March 1919.

The man who recommended him for the coveted medal was Senior Major L. C. Palmer of the 13th Field Ambulance Brigade.

"Twice I had to order him out of the line at Cambrai," the officer reported to his somewhat incredulous British Army superiors. "It was really quite inspiring, if exceedingly foolish. There he was, despite his own wound, continuing to treat our stricken soldiers."

The first time, Palmer recalled, was one mid-morning in September.

"When I returned the next day he was still there, so I ordered him out again. I thought any man who would stand from ten-thirty one morning to four-thirty the next, dressing the wounded under fire while wounded himself, surely deserved a decoration."

However, Banting's wound became seriously infected, and he suffered a life-threatening hemorrhage while being treated at a field nursing station. The medical officer in charge of the hospital in England to which he was evacuated, a full Colonel, saw no point in trying to save the limb, just as he had seen no point in trying to save the limbs, or even the lives, of many a wounded soldier before the Canadian officer arrived at his institution.

"No question about it, Captain Banting," he declared. "The infection is too massive, far too dangerous. It will have to come off at the shoulder. Unfortunate, of course, but I would think you can always resume civilian medical practice with one arm. Won't be much good at surgery or delivering babies, perhaps, but there must be things a one-armed physician can do to earn a living."

Banting received the news, and the supercilious commentary that accompanied it, with cold fury. He refused absolutely to submit to amputation.

"Damn you," he exploded, oblivious of the other man's superior rank.

"I will live with two arms, or I will die."

He thereupon laid down a course of treatment for himself that pulled him through after a hard fight – but with the injured arm intact.

Nearly two decades passed, and with war again on the horizon, Banting re-enlisted and was promoted to the rank of Major. He began at once to look for ways to become usefully engaged in the approaching conflict.

In the meantime, his personal life had taken some unexpected, even disastrous turns. The long courtship with Edith Roach, the minister's daughter, came to an unhappy end.

Next, Banting met and married hospital X-ray technician Marion Robertson in 1924, and although the union produced a son, William, it dissolved a decade later after a messy, much-publicized divorce proceeding that for months titillated news-paper readers in puritanical Toronto and beyond. In 1939 the hard-drinking Banting took a new wife, laboratory technician Henrietta Ball, a woman more than twenty years his junior. Beyond his domestic escapades, Banting turned to painting as a hobby, showing himself to have uncommon talent, and made fast friends among the famed Group of Seven artists.

While all this was going on in his personal life, the general practitioner in London, Ontario became world-famous. Working with colleagues J. J. R. MacLeod, Charles H. Best and others, he became the first to isolate the hormone insulin from the pancreases of dogs. It would lead to one of the great medical achievements of all time: the control, if not the cure, for diabetes in humans. This brought Banting a share of the Nobel Prize for medicine in 1923, a life annuity granted by Canada's House of Commons, and honours and recognition around the world, including a belated knighthood in King George V's 1934 birthday list.

He was thus enabled to travel repeatedly to, and to be welcomed as an international celebrity and a featured lecturer in, Britain, Europe, Scandinavia, the Soviet Union, and the United States. What he saw in his travels, particularly in Europe, as Hitler rose to power, was not encouraging. He became preoccupied with the prospect of another war – a major conflagration that he was increasingly certain would soon erupt to engulf the world.

"War is not a pleasant thought," the eminent Canadian remarked at one point, "but it is a fair bet that boys now ten to fifteen years of age will be in uniform as their fathers were."[4]

His principal concern continued to be that Canada, and the British Commonwealth and Empire of which she was a part, be adequately prepared for the inevitable cataclysm, fully capable of dealing the threatening Huns a decisive defeat.

A genuine celebrity, Banting was often in the public eye and did little to avoid it.

It seemed never to occur to him that his outspoken views might place him in physical danger, a serious mistake that one day would become a fatal one.

Michael Grattan O'Leary was a descendant of the famine Irish who helped populate eastern areas of Québec in the eighteenth and nineteenth centuries. Born in the Gaspé Peninsula in 1889, he aspired to be a newspaper reporter and took out membership in the Ottawa Press Club in 1911 as a representative of *The Ottawa Journal*. He would go on to become one of Canada's most respected journalists; the newspaper was one of Canada's leading dailies under his editorship, chronicling and commenting upon key events and decisions from the vantage point of the nation's capital. Years later, on being purchased by the Thomson interests, it would be closed after a few months, by which time Prime Minister John G. Diefenbaker had put O'Leary in the Senate.

O'Leary was well-acquainted with leaders of the Conservative Party of his day, and was invited by Arthur Meighen, Canada's prime minister in 1921, to accompany him to that year's Imperial Conference of British Empire prime ministers.

"It will be a tremendous opportunity for you," Meighen assured him. "You will gain an intimate, and, for a journalist – an editorialist – a tremendously valuable insight into the moods and aspirations of Commonwealth and world leaders in the wake of the Great War."

It also helped whet the newspaperman's taste for domestic Canadian politics, to the extent that he decided to stand, albeit unsuccessfully, as the Conservative candidate for Gaspé.

But O'Leary also made no secret of his admiration for the great Liberal leader Sir Wilfrid Laurier, and penned a column-and-a-half editorial tribute on the statesman's death. He got along with Liberal Prime Minister W. L. Mackenzie King, whom he described at one point as "an extraordinary combination of sentimentality and toughness, of tenderness and cruelty, of monastic exclusiveness and political sophistication. . . . Not before or since have we had a politician like him." And he could even be supportive of King's "minister of everything," U.S.-born Clarence Decatur Howe, the powerful "Get-it-done-now!" politician who would enable Canada to significantly help England win the war – but was anathema to the Tory Party and its leader George Drew.

"I've played golf with Howe," the newspaperman told an acquaintance. "That's one of the best ways to get to know a man. He's tough, sometimes crude, absolutely honest, a great engineer and builder, laughable as a House of Commons man. But personally, I enjoy C. D."

And concerning Lieutenant General Andrew George Latta McNaughton, O'Leary rejected, as editor of the *Journal*, "the childish contention that Canada is lacking in real leaders." He pointed to the much-admired Chief of the General Staff to make his case.

Thus, when Conservative Prime Minister R. B. Bennett dumped McNaughton, who had led the mechanization of Canada's permanent army and modernization of its militia, O'Leary was appalled. It seems Bennett – himself an aspiring future member of the British peerage – was much annoyed by the general's attitude towards what McNaughton considered the snobbishness of the Mother Country's military leaders, his resentment of the way they looked down upon Canadians as inferior "colonials," and his demand for independence of action for Canada's military leadership.

Suddenly, the general was out as Canada's top soldier – and into the presidency of the moribund National Research Council, considered by many as a poor sop.

However, the outcomes of political machinations are frequently uncertain to predict, and their results often surprising. Under King, who had lost the government to Bennett in 1930, but won it back in 1935, McNaughton invigorated the NRC. He doubled the staff to 300 and set it on a new course, preparing for the war that both he and the Prime Minister could see coming, with research turning to weapons, medicines, and synthetic fuels.

Indeed, visiting Germany in 1937, a bellicose King seized the opportunity to warn Hitler personally that, if Britain came under attack, Canada would not hesitate to back her up.

"That would be the case," he advised the Nazi dictator, "even if Canadians had to swim the Atlantic to get there."[5]

In the meantime, the transformation of the NRC, sanctioned by the prime minister, was made complete when Banting, a frank admirer of McNaughton, was invited by King to join its board.

"At my personal request," the general wrote, "he gave up unselfishly [his intention to serve the Canadian Medical Corps in the field] to undertake the organization of research of far-reaching importance to us, and which he alone could do."

In particular, this meant the promotion of chemical and biological warfare research. Banting was thus presented with the opportunity he sought – to be involved in what he considered a significant way in Canada's, and by extension in Britain's, preparations for war. He became chairman of the NRC's Associate Committee on Aviation Medicine, as well as its Associate Committee on Medical Research. Soon the two old soldiers – McNaughton was then fifty, Banting forty-six – with their memories of Germany's First World War poison gas attacks, were discussing chemical and biological weapons as a threat to the peace, notwithstanding the fact that a 1925 Geneva Protocol had outlawed their use.

"Major, perhaps you should begin preparing a general memorandum on the subject," McNaughton suggested, "and the sooner the better."

Banting agreed. Indeed, in his eagerness, he could hardly wait to get at it.

"I will gather up everything we have here," the general said, "and between us we may well come up with enough evidence to get our own defence department moving, and perhaps spur the British to action as well."

"The new reality," Banting pointed out, "is that development of the airplane means that, in future, war will explode far beyond the battlefields for the first time, to involve civilians on a broader scale than ever before known – people in cities, towns, and even the countryside, to a degree never before visualized."

He speculated that water reservoirs could be contaminated with typhoid, cholera, and dysentery, ocean fishing grounds poisoned, and farm fields sprayed to destroy livestock and render crops unfit for human consumption.

"In the end, it is just as effective to kill or disable ten unarmed workers at home as to put a soldier out of action, and with less risk."[6]

It could well become acceptable to employ any mode of warfare to accomplish this, Banting reasoned, and being attacked, one must be able to effectively fight back.

"The evidence is that Hitler is getting ready to launch an unprecedented assault against England. Ordinarily, the way to offset it would be to achieve an equal level of preparedness. However, we know that England lacks the ability to retaliate in kind – either by conventional means, or with chemical and biological weapons should the Führer choose that method. Consequently, the Old Country is terribly vulnerable – unless means can be devised, and quickly, to meet the Nazi threat head-on and defeat it.

"Biological and chemical weapons are the surest way to meet a German invasion, if only we can persuade the British powers that be. And of course, our own Canadian authorities as well."

* * *

On a press junket to England in the early days of the war, O'Leary reported that what he saw first-hand "shattered the state of euphoria many of us had indulged in" about conditions there, writing about "'business as usual,' Britain 'muddling through,' and all that sort of bosh." The truth, he discovered, was that the British people, noble and gallant as they were, were suffering. Food was being rationed, children were being sent out of London, bombing raids were taking place with alarming frequency, and "not all of the ringing hyperbole of Churchill's 'Give us the tools and we will finish the job' can alter the simple fact that Britain's back is against the wall."[7]

He thus confirmed in the minds and hearts of readers of the *Journal* what men like McNaughton, Banting, King, and Howe well knew already: Britain was in dire need of more substantial Canadian backing if the war against Hitler was to be won.

In a luncheon speech that he gave to the Canadian Club in Ottawa, the newspaperman declared that Britain "cannot finish the job with tools alone. The Nazis will not be beaten until Canada and America send their young men to do the job as in 1914 and 1917 "– clear reference to the hugely divisive issue of conscription in Canada.

"After the luncheon," he recalled, "Mackenzie King, who was present, came up and congratulated me. 'As Prime Minister, I could not say what you said; but I agree completely and I think your saying it will do some good.'"[8]

In the days following the fraud of Hitler's non-aggression pact with Stalin, the genocidal obscenity of the invasion of Poland, and the initial, half-hearted response of the Anglo-French declaration of war on Germany, the British Medical Council had invited Canada to send over representatives to witness the progress they had made in the field of wartime medical research. Banting eagerly took up the invitation, along with colleague Israel Rabinovitch, a Montréaler and an expert in poison gas whom McNaughton would later install, with the rank of Major, as tactical officer to the Canadian forces in Britain.

But after two months in England, Banting threw up his hands. His efforts to persuade the British to espouse biological weapons were to little or no avail. He complained to the general that the British were refusing to take the threat of biological attack seriously and no research was being done in Britain such as he was convinced was under way in Germany. An extensive memorandum he had written on the subject was, in effect, being ignored – which was not really strange, since in it he virtually accused the British scientific-military establishment of failing in their essential duty to prepare adequately the nation for war.

"I am all the more convinced," he despairingly confessed to McNaughton, "that there will be the attempt [by Nazi Germany] of biological warfare . . . . (A) most serious situation faces our dear old England."[9]

Back in Canada, however, Banting was greeted by a far different circumstance. NRC scientists were working on more than two dozen military projects, and where private donors – the T. Eaton Company, the C.P.R., and Consolidated Mining & Smelting Company, Bronfman Brothers, International Nickel Company – had previously provided over a million dollars in support of War Technical and Scientific Development, otherwise known as the Santa Claus Fund, the King government had now stepped in. It had decided to approve and support completely and actively Banting's program of biological warfare experiments, looking towards both defensive measures and possible offensive weapons development as well.

McNaughton, meanwhile, had been summoned back to military service as Inspector General and General Officer Commanding Canadian troops in England, his place at the NRC being taken – but on an acting basis only, the general made plain – by Dean C. J. Mackenzie of the University of Saskatchewan.

Mackenzie regularly reported to the general on the status of NRC programs, including the creation of a highly secret biological warfare unit at Grosse Île in the St. Lawrence River, a co-operative project between the United States and Canada, and a chemical warfare facility at Suffield, Alberta, with a tract of land about twenty to thirty miles square for field testing. The model for Grosse Île was Porton Down, the British chemical warfare facility where Banting and Rabinovitch had spent a good deal of time. It had even sent a top official to help get Canadian operations off on the right foot. These were among the many projects that Banting had been instrumental in initiating, and Mackenzie was unstinting in giving him full credit.

"Sir Frederick Banting has just come into my office and told me that he is leaving for England tomorrow by bomber plane, and I am dashing off this note which he has agreed to take," Mackenzie wrote to McNaughton that fateful day in February.

"Banting has been feeling for some time that someone should go to England and get first-hand information concerning medical problems. Dr. Best has been wanting to go and we finally made arrangements, but he then decided he had other work to do so Banting is going. He is bucked up about the prospects of flying."[10]

Mackenzie was well aware of Banting's frustration that the British continued to rebuff his biological weapons advice, but the term "medical problems" seemed a useful way to cover off that aspect; obviously, his intention was to give it one more try. However, the NRC head did not commit to writing his worry over the extreme danger in which his colleague was placing himself as a passenger on one of the earliest airplane flights to cross the wild Atlantic in mid-winter. The thought of Banting being tossed about in an unarmed, unheated bombing plane, piloted by a virtually unknown American stunt flyer who must rely on bare minimums in the way of aerial navigation to reach a far-off wartime destination, caused Mackenzie to shudder involuntarily.

My God, he thought, *this whole episode is absolutely ridiculous. If they come down in the ocean – they could even be shot down by Nazi patrol planes – we'll likely never hear of Banting again.*

He told himself he should have done more to prevent the folly of the trip, even appealing to the top, to the Prime Minister. King, he felt, would have stepped in to stop it. But it was too late for that now.

Mackenzie also realized that if the expedition ended in disaster, as might well be the case, he would have to accept a large share of the responsibility – he would certainly blame himself. But that took second place to his overriding concern for Banting's personal safety.

NINE

Hitler's Eagle's Nest, the Austrian Alps, 1937

BEFORE ADOLF HITLER rendered its very name infamous to decent people everywhere, Berchtesgaden was a little-known village an hour's drive from Munich – Bavarians seem to prefer the medieval name Munchen – in the mountains to the southeast. In one writer's description, it was "beautifully situated at a height of 1,700 feet on the Untersberg . . . and celebrated for its mines of rock-salt and for its charm as a summer resort."

Then the Chancellor-Dictator of Germany chose it as the site for his so-called Eagle's Nest, a securely guarded mountain villa that he himself designed and named the "Berghof," accessible only by an elevator and tunnels burrowed in solid rock. To this remote retreat Hitler frequently withdrew for rest and relaxation, and to contemplate his plan for the conquest of Europe and the world – for their domination by the Third Reich, in his mind a mighty empire to last a thousand years.

Soon other members of the Nazi hierarchy joined him in what came to constitute an executive compound: Martin Bormann, destined to be Hitler's deputy after National Socialist Party Chairman Rudolf Hess fled to Scotland in a stolen *Messerschmitt 110* fighter plane; Reichsmarschall Wilhelm Hermann Goering, founder of the Gestapo and chief of the *Luftwaffe;* and Albert Speer, the Führer's architect and head of armaments production. It was said that Bormann delighted in his habit of summarily evicting local property-owners whenever this hierarchy decided that they wished to acquire additional buildings or lands.

Here, in the fall of 1937, Hitler entertained two of the world's most famous personalities of the time – the former King Edward VIII of Great Britain, and Wallis Warfield Simpson, the twice-divorced American adventuress for whom the King had renounced history's most famous and most durable throne.

The Instrument of Abdication had been signed almost a year earlier, on December 10, 1936, following which Edward ("David" to his family) broadcast a farewell message to the nation and the Empire, perhaps the most famous swan song of modern times:

> *A few hours ago I discharged my last duty as King and Emperor, and now that I have been succeeded by my brother, the Duke of York, my first words must be to declare my allegiance to him. This I do with all my heart.*
>
> *You all know the reasons which have impelled me to renounce the throne. But I want you to understand that in making up my mind I did not forget the country or the Empire, which, as Prince of Wales, and lately as King, I have for twenty-five years tried to serve. But you must believe me when I tell you that I have found it impossible to carry the heavy burden of responsibility and to discharge my duties as King as I would wish to do without the help and support of the woman I love.*

Permitted by the new monarch, George VI, to use the titles Duke and Duchess of Windsor – but denied, for Wallis at least, the coveted designation "Royal Highness" – they had left England for effective exile.

First it was France, where they married after her divorce from U.S. shipping magnate Ernest Simpson became final, and then and more permanently the British dependency of the Bahamas. They might have returned to England after the fall of France, but the Duke refused unless the Duchess was given "proper" recognition and respect. This was denied her, it was believed, at the instigation of the new Queen Elizabeth, who was widely held responsible for what would become a lifelong rift between her husband, the new King, and his brother. Eventually the Duke was appointed wartime Governor and Commander-in-Chief of the collection of Caribbean islands some 700 miles southeast of Florida, far removed from the primary zone of hostilities.

The British had been extremely nervous to have the ex-King residing and travelling on the Continent, and were understandably shocked to learn of his plan to tour Germany – culminating in a visit to Hitler in his fortress at Berchtesgaden.

As the inevitable war approached, they feared the still immensely popular former monarch might be kidnapped and held by the Nazis for ransom – or, of even greater concern, the enormous propaganda value that might be derived. Such a saga would surely occupy newspaper front pages for as long as the Germans wished to detain him, and would give rise to predictable and continuing outrage among the British people and would threaten to destabilize a government, already facing the prospect of disintegration, all-out war, and, very possibly, invasion.

Soon after being summoned by George VI to replace the bumbling Neville Chamberlain following the devastating surrender of Norway, Winston Churchill felt it prudent to order the Windsors' gubernatorial mansion in Nassau, the Bahamian capital, guarded by squads of British Army commandos and machine-gunners.

The Duke had long and openly exhibited sympathy for the Nazis and their objectives, even employing on the German visit, and on this very occasion, their *"Heil, Hitler!"* salute, borrowed from the *"Hail, Caesar!"* of imperial Rome.[11]

The British, Churchill in particular, burned to know what had passed between the ex-King and the German Chancellor that October day in Berchtesgaden, and the Prime Minister considered bringing the Duke back to Britain in custody to face a charge of high treason. Only concern over the extent of the Duke's popularity and the obvious embarrassment to the Royal Family dissuaded him. But it seemed hardly likely that, on the eve of the most destructive and bloodiest conflict in human history, the Duke and the Chancellor would not have discussed the condition of the main participants of the coming international cataclysm.

On the one hand, there was Great Britain, her people divided (not the least by the Royal abdication) and her defences neglected and, in keeping with the Versailles Treaty, significantly scaled back; on the other hand Germany, united under the Führer, had with "impunity and abandon" repudiated the onerous armistice agreement that ended the First World War. She had withdrawn from the Disarmament Conference and rejected treaty limitations on rearmament. Most spectacular had been the secret building up of the *Luftwaffe* to more than 4,000 planes and 550,000 men – over twice as many aircraft as England and five times her manpower!

The scream of Junkers 87 *Stuka* dive-bombers, terrorizing military and civilians alike in attacks on the side of General Franco's forces in the Spanish civil war, had become the terrible new trademark sound of modern warfare, and provided a glimpse of the wider conflict soon to come.

"How can the English warmongers possibly hope to meet and defeat the onslaught that we are well-prepared to launch against them?" Hitler demanded rhetorically, exhibiting supreme confidence, as the Duke and Duchess listened in shocked silence.

"This is no longer 1918, when they had their heel on the throat of the Fatherland. How can they be so stupid and short-sighted as to think they can win a war with today's Germany?

"I had believed, at one time, that an entente with England was possible, indeed greatly to be preferred," he went on, speaking in German, which the Duke understood but the Duchess did not. He strode back and forth as if on a military parade ground, in front of large windows overlooking the Bavarian Alps, gesticulating with his right hand while the left was hooked by the thumb into the belt of his military-style uniform.

"With that I would have been quite satisfied," he went on, his voice rising.

"Now I am convinced that the English do not want peace. It is the furthest thing from their minds. Therefore, invasion of the British Isles by our superior German forces will be inevitable.

"With your help, my dear Duke, we shall surely succeed. Then I shall see that you return to occupy the throne that is rightly yours as the legitimate leader of the British people . . . along with your lovely wife," he added pointedly, with a small bow to Wallis.

The Duchess, although annoyed that Hitler had kept them waiting for more than an hour while he finished his afternoon nap, nonetheless assumed that he paid her a compliment – which the Duke afterwards assured her that he had. She acknowledged it with a tentative smile, shivering inwardly under the glare of the brilliant blue eyes that appeared, she thought, somewhat wild. The eyes of a madman?

"Perhaps . . ." the Duke spoke quietly, choosing not to respond directly to the suggestion of his regaining the throne of England, which, he had already been assured by von Ribbentrop, Hitler's ambassador in London, would be accompanied with an infusion of cash, say fifty million Swiss francs. "Perhaps the English will have a nasty welcome waiting for any invader. Really, I shouldn't be surprised were they to resort to biological weapons."

"I must ask you to explain," Hitler said, the sharp edge in his voice indicating displeasure at the interruption of his soliloquy.

"Germ warfare, my dear fellow," the Duke repeated with some emphasis. "It may well be the only effective defence we – that is to say, the British – could mount at this stage," he went on. "But strangely, it is not our British scientists, not our generals, not even our politicians who are pressing the matter, but rather a prominent Canadian scientist – possibly the most prominent – and he seems to be making a number of influential converts to his way of thinking."

"Well, who is this individual? What is his name?" Hitler demanded, his level of annoyance increasing markedly.

"His name is Banting, Sir Frederick Grant Banting, an officer of the Canadian Army Medical Corps, and a co-discoverer of insulin," the Duke responded.

"However, it seems he also is one of the world's foremost proponents of the development of biological weapons, and is forever pressing the British scientists and politicians to make such obscene methods a major part of military preparedness. I have, of course, seen Cabinet papers on the subject, and although I am not prepared to discuss in detail the confidential information contained in them, I may tell you he may be planning to come from Canada again soon to pursue the matter and to reinforce his arguments, which already have been accepted by his own government.

"Personally," the former King went on, while Hitler became an unaccustomed listener, "I find it monstrously at variance with his standing and reputation as the humanitarian discoverer of insulin. His scientific invention is saving the lives of thousands of people, many of whom may now suffer horribly from microbes from his very laboratory. He received a knighthood and the Nobel Prize for *saving* lives, for God's sake."

"You are quite certain of all this?" Hitler asked, unable any longer to disguise the depth of his interest.

"Of course," the Duke replied. "My wife is terrified of the possibility of large numbers of innocent people, not to mention fighting forces, becoming victims. A dear friend of hers, a nursing sister, was gassed in the Great War, you see, and suffered indescribably. But I expect that what this Banting proposes will be very much worse.

"We discuss it often. Indeed, the Duchess has horrible nightmares about it. She refers to the whole confusing business as the Banting enigma."

The Duke and Duchess of Windsor had barely regained their limousine for the return journey to Munich, state police motorcycle outriders clearing the way, when Hitler was on the telephone to Goering.

"I have just heard a most amazing and disturbing story," he advised the *Reichsmarschall*, who was greatly annoyed at being interrupted in the midst of a sumptuous dinner party. However, he managed to avoid letting his annoyance convey itself to the caller at the other end of the line, as Hitler repeated what the Duke had told him.

"If this Banting has been in England already, apparently more than once, peddling his germ warfare proposals, why haven't we heard about it?" Hitler demanded. "What is Ribbentrop doing in London?" he raged, shaking with an anger that was palpable to Goering, who was given no opportunity to respond.

"He is supposed to be so close to the Windsors, especially the Duchess. Why in God's name has he not made us aware of this inherent threat to the success of the invasion?"

Hitler had a right, as they say, to be upset that Joachim von Ribbentrop may not have been performing as anticipated. The general belief was that the Führer had had the previous ambassador, Leopold von Hoesch, eliminated – the cause of death reported as a heart attack – to provide an official position in London for the former wine salesman, and to give von Ribbentrop the prominence he craved, including the friendship of people like Mrs. Simpson.

He would remain in Hitler's favour, and having become Foreign Minister of the Third Reich in 1938, would keep that position throughout the war. As a consequence, he would take a leading part in negotiation of the Rome–Berlin Axis with Mussolini, and the short-lived Russo–German non-aggression pact of 1939 with Molotov. He was also prominent in planning the rape of Poland that started the Second World War, and perhaps for this, more than anything, would be condemned to death by the Allied war crimes tribunal. He would become the first of ten high-level Nazi defendants condemned to the gallows under the hand of U.S. Army executioner John Wood in a Nuremberg school gymnasium on October 16, 1946.

Scheduled to share the same fate on the same day, Goering contrived to cheat the hangman. He would be found dead in his prison cell a few hours before the time set for his execution, having somehow obtained a lethal cyanide pill with which to end his own life.

"Obviously these are questions I am not in a position to answer, my Führer," Goering replied, somehow managing to pacify Hitler, "but I assure you that I stand by the advice that I have previously given.

"The *Luftwaffe* will prove to be the key to the successful invasion of Britain. We shall destroy in the air and on the ground whatever the British may have in the way of air power, and we shall pulverize their factories, their cities, their power plants, their rail lines, and their naval and merchant ships in port and on the high seas.

"That achieved, it will be well within the capability of our sea and land forces to take care of the rest. The invasion will be a success. You may count on it."

"Hermann," Hitler said, mellowing, "somehow I always feel better after discussing a problem with you, which, I suppose, is why I often think of you as my successor. Nonetheless, I shall certainly speak with von Ribbentrop about this Banting fellow. There is no excuse for not knowing what the mad Canadian scientist may be up to."

"Thank you, my Führer," the corpulent Goering gushed, and smiling a smile of smug satisfaction, returned to his dinner party. Once again, he told himself in a mood of happy self-congratulation, he had demonstrated his ability to control the greatest individual Western civilization had produced since Alexander the Great, perhaps since Julius Caesar.

It was an especially heady thought even for Hermann Goering, a man quite accustomed to entertaining heady thoughts.

TEN

Poli. Sci. Class, Memorial University, St. John's, Circa 1965

IT WAS SOMETIMES said by those who knew no better that, given the determination of Democratic President Franklin Roosevelt and the United States of America to stay formally away from the fray – a determination comparable to that exhibited by President Woodrow Wilson in the First World War until the sinking of the *Lusitania* – that Britain and her Commonwealth family alone stood in the path of Hitler's brazen scheme for world domination. But this thesis failed to account for Lend-Lease. It was the ingenious method devised by Roosevelt to put up fifty billion dollars in credits so Britain could purchase from United States industrialists the implements of modern warfare, while allowing the President to maintain, for domestic political purposes, the fiction of neutrality. In particular, the Royal Air Force acquired thousands of short-, medium-, and long-range bombers with which to pulverize Germany and its war-making assets.

"It was the perfect example of what we might describe as enlightened self-interest," Political Science professor Malcolm McCommon would explain some two decades later to his students at Memorial University in St. John's. The former junior college, erected in the 1920s in memory of Newfoundland's First World War dead, had been elevated to degree-granting status as one of the first acts of Premier Joseph R. Smallwood's government, following implementation of the postwar referendum decision to become part of the Dominion of Canada in 1949.

"So keep in mind the term Lend-Lease. Not only did it cause the American economy to accelerate into boom phase, thereby bringing the Great Depression in the United States to a final, spectacular end," he went on, "but America was buying time, building up her own armaments, developing her 'military-industrial complex' as Republican President Dwight Eisenhower later and derisively termed it, while assurance was being purchased, we might as well say, that Hitler would be kept at bay in Europe.

"Roosevelt knew that, sooner or later, they would be in the fight, boots and all, but also that, in the meantime, keeping the war in Europe meant American cities and civilians would be spared the devastation wrought, yet again, on the people of London and Paris, Berlin, and Brussels – the very thing generations of Americans in their millions had fled to the New World to avoid."

There was yet another highly advantageous side to the arrangement – advantageous for both the Americans and the British, as McCommon described it:

"Fifty over-age United States Navy warships were taken out of mothballs and handed over to Britain's Royal Navy. These would replace to some degree the millions of tons of shipping, from frigates to battleships, that had been scrapped in naïve compliance with the disarmament requirements of the 1919 Treaty of Versailles that Germany had been pleased to ignore.

"In return, without the slightest reference to the people of the places affected, ninety-nine-year leases on huge tracts of lands in Newfoundland and Labrador were given to the Americans on which to construct army, navy, and air bases by which to establish the forward defence of their homeland. In some instances, such as Placentia and Stephenville, land was taken that farming and fishing families had lived on for generations, their private property where they had raised their families, grown their own vegetables, and grazed their own cattle. They had no choice but to make way for major military installations. Homes, barns, and outbuildings were either dragged to new locations or bulldozed to smithereens, and their owners forced or induced to abandon traditional livelihoods to go to work for 'the Yankee dollar.'

"Even their dead were uprooted and re-buried to make way for it."

A young woman in the third row had her hand up.

"The way I understand it," she said, "and from what I remember, many people were only too pleased to have a steady job, at good wages, instead of the hand-to-mouth poverty they had to live with before. That's what my grandfather tells me, anyway, and he lived there, in Little Placentia. Was one of the ones who had to move, to abandon the home where his grandfather lived before him."

"Thank you for that, Miss Collins . . . and you're quite right," McCommon replied. "There was a price to be paid for the new economy. For some it was an acceptable price, but for others it was too high, perhaps much too high. One of the Americans who came to Argentia in 1941 was a friend of mine who always had mixed feelings about what happened, about the effects on the local people. But he also recognized that it was absolutely necessary for the freedom of the people of North America, as for the people of Europe, and I suppose we can say the world, that Hitler be prevented from carrying out his plan to take over the world.

"Seen in this light, the bases that the Americans established in Newfoundland and Labrador were a critical part of the Allied strategy, as important to people in Pittsburgh and Paris and Plymouth, England as to the people of Placentia and Paradise River and Port au Port."

Another student signalled that he had a question. "From what I've read," he began, "the war – or, maybe I should say the wartime economy – really saved Newfoundland from starvation?"

"Well," McCommon replied, emphasizing his main theme, "these arrangements unquestionably went a long way to seal Hitler's doom and that of the Third Reich. But they also solved –

and this goes directly to your question, Mr. White; you're a Stephenville man, right? Your family name used to be LeBlanc? – They solved almost without the need to lift a finger, the twin problems faced by the Newfoundland Commission of Government.

"The first of these was the economy; that the London-appointed body of seven men, three Englishmen, and three Newfoundlanders, plus the English Governor, had struggled without success to invigorate the economy since 1934, when they were set up to replace the elected legislature and the government of the bankrupt Dominion.

"Then there was the military defence of both Newfoundland, the Island, and its huge dependency of Labrador which, prior to the arrival of the Americans, in particular, was totally non-existent. The Canadians also put in an appearance, but they were little better than a junior partner in the enterprise.

"But to answer your specific question. The Great Depression had hit Newfoundland very hard, harder than other places in North America, because she was so small and all on her own. The wartime economy, with hundreds of millions of dollars in defence expenditures pouring in, and thousands of Newfoundlanders employed, and the big American military bases which remain in operation were, and continue to be very, very important to the economy. These produced an era of prosperity that could not have come about in any other way. Of course, it was not built to last, and something had to replace it, but something much bigger and more lasting was required.

"That's where Smallwood's campaign for Confederation with Canada came into play, and whether you like it or not, it changed Newfoundland forever."

In a real sense the floodgates on the Second World War were flung open on August 23, 1939. On that date von Ribbentrop for the Nazi Third Reich and Molotov for the Union of Soviet Socialist Republics signed the non-aggression pact that, as

Nicholson described it, "secured Soviet connivance with Germany's designs on the Poles."

Eight days later, on the thirty-first, Hitler issued his "MOST SECRET: DIRECTIVE NO.1 FOR THE CONDUCT OF WAR." It began: "Now that all the political possibilities of disposing by peaceful means of a situation on the Eastern Frontier which is intolerable for Germany are exhausted, I have determined on a solution by force."[12]

The Führer made no secret, however, of the date or even the hour of the attack – the following day, at 4:45 a.m. – though this could hardly be construed as a formal declaration of war. For days German motorized units had been massing on the Polish border. At dawn on September 1, Panzer and infantry forces began the attack. The *Luftwaffe* was already in the air, had already begun the assault, and in a few hours, more than two dozen Polish cities were bombed and burning.

Britain and France had both pledged to the defence of Poland, and though the attack was well under way, British Prime Minister Neville Chamberlain continued to strive to dissuade Hitler. But he finally had to admit to the House of Commons that all efforts had failed to obtain "satisfactory assurances" of the suspension of "all aggressive action against Poland."

His note to the German Foreign Secretary, he told them, had declared: "Although this communication was made more than twenty-four hours ago no reply has been received, and German attacks on Poland have been continued and intensified. I have accordingly the honour to inform you that unless, not later than 11 a.m. British Summer Time, today, September 3, satisfactory assurances to the above effect have been given by the German Government, and have reached His Majesty's Government in London, a state of war will exist between the two countries as from that hour."[13]

Chamberlain hesitated, and Members of Parliament shifted uneasily on their House of Commons benches. A hush descended as all strained forward to ensure they heard his next words.

"That was the final note," Chamberlain advised, his voice nearly breaking. "No such undertaking was received by the time stipulated and consequently this country is at war with Germany."

A few hours later King George VI, Queen Elizabeth by his side, broadcast to the people of the British Empire:

> In this grave hour, perhaps the most fateful in our history, we are called, with our allies, to meet the challenge of a principle which, if it were to prevail, would be fatal to any civilized order in the world. It is the principle which permits a State, in the selfish pursuit of power, to disregard its treaties and its solemn pledges; which sanctions the use of force, or threat of force, against the sovereignty and independence of other States. Such a principle, stripped of all disguises, is surely the mere primitive doctrine that might is right; and if this principle were established throughout the world, the freedom of our own country and of the whole British Commonwealth of Nations would be in danger. But far more than this – the peoples of the world would be kept in fear of bondage, and all hopes of settled peace ended. This is the ultimate issue which confronts us. For the sake of all that we ourselves hold dear, and of the world's order and peace, it is unthinkable that we should refuse to meet the challenge. The task will be hard. There may be dark days ahead, and war can no longer be confined to the battlefield. But we can only do the right as we see the right, and reverently commit our cause to God. If, one and all, we keep resolutely faithful to it, ready for whatever service or sacrifice it may demand, then, with God's help, we shall prevail. May He bless and keep us all.[14]

His Majesty had hardly finished speaking when air-raid sirens began blaring out their mournful wail over the city of London for the first time. Goering's *Luftwaffe* was about to let loose the terrible *blitzkrieg*. The Battle of Britain had begun.

* * *

In the private family quarters of Government House in St. John's, as the royal broadcast ended, Governor Sir Humphrey Thomas Walwyn sat back, looking pensive, and asked the aide-de-camp, his twenty-six-year-old son James, a Royal Navy man like his father, to switch off the radio. The overall appearance was that of an anxious family gathering, replicated in millions of homes throughout the Empire on which the sun never set. Lady Eileen was present, of course, and Captain Charles M. R. Schwerdt, the private secretary, with his wife Violet and their daughters Pamela and Rosemary.

"This is, as His Majesty has just stated, a fateful and an historic moment," Walwyn said, "and the question is, how will it all turn out? How will we all fare – those of us who live in Britain, or elsewhere in the Empire, and right here in Newfoundland where we have virtually no protection?"

"Well, Father," said James, "we'd better hope that the ships-for-bases deal with the Americans comes together, and soon. The sooner the Yanks establish a garrison in Newfoundland the better – once they do, we should be able to breathe a lot easier."

"We cannot leave it all to the United States, however," the Governor replied. "Every part of the Empire has to do its bit, and we are no different from the rest. I do not, unfortunately, have the freedom that allowed Davidson, over the heads of the elected Government of Newfoundland in 1914, to take firm steps both for the defence of the Island, and for the recruitment of men to go overseas. In our situation, I can make recommendations, and the Commission will certainly do so. But the final decision as to what will be done rests with London. It is effectively out of our hands."

"Excuse me, Sir," Schwerdt intervened. "I'm afraid it is past the girls' bedtime. May we be excused?"

"Oh, yes, yes, of course," Walwyn said, getting to his feet in order to see them out. After the private secretary and his family had said their goodbyes and departed, the Governor continued.

"On the same day Hitler invaded Poland – the same day, mind you – Emerson, on behalf of the Commission, announced the Emergency Defence Measures, the arrangements for a limited number of Newfoundlanders to enlist in the British Army and Navy, and the setting up of the Home Defence Force. A hundred and eighty men may not seem like much, but we have to be aware that it does involve a quite serious financial consideration."

Lewis Edward Emerson held the dual portfolio of Justice and Defence. His EDMs, as they were referred to in civil servant circles, included "registration of all persons not of British nationality, registration and control of aircraft [and] imposition of censorship on communications systems."

"It is a beginning," Walwyn said, almost as if seeking reassurance from his own family, "and it shows that we haven't been slow to move."

However, he had felt it necessary to make Whitehall aware of a certain level of local upset that some of the measures were both puny and bureaucratic, and "not in keeping with the loyal spirit of this community," as the editor of *The Evening Telegram* had phrased it. *The Daily News* was more accepting, even suggesting that "in the event that a local unit will not be established, [Newfoundlanders] might prefer to enlist with the Canadian forces."

In the end, however, the general patriotic feeling that, regardless of the financial situation, volunteers should feel free to come forward "to serve their King and Country" in various units that would be identified with the Old Colony, was satisfied as thousands enlisted in the 166th Newfoundland Regiment, Royal Artillery; the 59th Newfoundland Heavy Regiment, Royal Artillery; the Newfoundland 125th Squadron, Royal Air Force; the Newfoundland Overseas Forestry Corps; as well as the Royal Navy, the merchant navy, and any number of British and Canadian units including the Canadian Women's Army Corps and the Women's Royal Canadian Naval Service.

William R. Callahan

When the British War Office belatedly posed the question, "What degree of importance do you attach to having a separate Newfoundland unit?" Walwyn knew that the Whitehall bureaucracy had seen the writing on this particular wall.

ELEVEN

The Royal Scot Motel,
Near Oceanside, California, 1941

SHE HAD ARRANGED connecting rooms in the Royal Scot Motel in Oceanside, California on Interstate 5, halfway between Los Angeles and San Diego. They had dinner and drinks in a secluded restaurant in nearby Carlsbad, followed by a long night of pleasant, and at times exciting, sex. He awoke early out of habit, and following a brief, but largely disappointing, attempt to revive the night's frenzied activity, stumbled towards the bathroom, pausing momentarily to inspect the bleary-eyed, crew-cut image in an oversized mirror of a rather handsome male well on the way to middle age. Before stepping into the shower enclosure, he answered nature's call and pressed the flush button. Then he flipped on the water and was blasted instantly by hot spray, sharp needles searing his muscular frame.

Naked on the bed, she picked up the phone and asked for room service.

"Always hungry when it's over," she called out. "How about you?"

There was no reply, so assuming she hadn't been audible over the noise of the shower, she got up and went to the bathroom door, which he had left open about a foot, and pretty much shouted.

"Jimmy, did you hear . . . ? I'm going to order some food. Interested?"

This time he heard. "Yeah, thanks. Get me steak and eggs and lots of coffee. And orange juice, good and pulpy . . . and extra toast."

"You've got it."

Clad only in spike heels she strutted back to the bed, pausing to glance appreciatively at her own mirror image. She reached for the Hawaiian-design silk dressing gown that came with the room, and turned once again to the phone. Shrugging into the garment, and sweeping back her long blond hair, she placed the order: two sirloins, medium rare; eggs over easy; extra toast; coffee and pulpy juice; and, she added, a newspaper. By the time he had showered and shaved, the order had arrived.

"Last thing I ever expected, to hear from you like this." Master Sergeant Alvin James Altehouse, United States Army Air Corps, shook his head in frank admiration as they consumed the food before the picture window with its spectacular view of the Pacific Ocean. A brassy sun edged into a corner of the room, giving promise of yet another delightful mid-winter day ahead, its reflection playing on her finely chiselled features. He made no effort to keep his eyes off the voluptuous woman opposite, loosely tied gown failing utterly to hide a magnificent cleavage and the tops of long, sun-browned legs crossed beneath it. Eva Johanna Haussling smiled knowingly, and daintily licked strawberry jam from well-manicured fingers.

They had not seen each other since the early days of the California *Bund*, otherwise known as the German-American Friendship Society, Pacific command. Avid participants in the meetings and marches, they had become personally and frequently intimate. For them sex and politics had seemed to go very well together.

But then she had been summoned to far-off New York, noticed by someone high up in the headquarters of the Nazi spy-and-sabotage operation in and for the entire United States and Mexico. He had been devastated, and on the rebound married Miranda – a disappointing substitute, he had to admit – and before long, for no good reason, he enlisted in the U.S.A.A.C. He had neither seen nor heard of Eva for more than three years, until her telephone call a few hours ago suggesting that they meet.

During dinner she explained that she was back in California on a matter of utmost importance – a matter with respect to which, she assured him, as a loyal son of the Fatherland, he would have ample opportunity to render service beyond anything he had done up to this time.

"Germany needs you, and needs you now, Jimmy," Eva assured him, adding that she was speaking with the full authority of the *Bund* leadership.

"I cannot tell you more at this moment; wait until we are in the security of the motel. But I can say that the very life and death of the Third Reich, nothing less, may be in the balance."

The *bund* had been formed during the First World War, with the specific intention of persuading both state and federal politicians that the United States should stay out of the bloodletting that the nations of Europe seemed bent on bringing upon themselves – which the country indeed did, for the first three years of the conflict. However, it was increasingly obvious to all that the weapon that Germany might employ to greatest advantage in an attempt to starve its main opponent, Great Britain, into submission, was also the one that held the greatest threat to neutral nations, especially the United States. Indeed, there arrived a point at which the indiscriminate use of U-boats against any ships routed to or from England, among which U.S. merchantmen and passenger vessels certainly predominated, offered Germany its only possibility of winning the war.

The issue crystallized suddenly in May 1915 when a German submarine torpedoed and sank the pride of the British merchant fleet, off the Irish coast. The RMS *Lusitania*, together with her famous sister, *Mauretania*, had earned a reputation as one of the fastest and most luxurious ocean liners ever built. When attacked, the *Lusitania* carried 1,200 passengers, together with her crew, a total human complement in excess of 2,000 souls – of whom barely 700 survived. Although it was not much spoken of, her cargo consisted largely of armaments destined for the support of British armed forces.

In terms of lives lost, it was a disaster to rival that of the RMS *Titanic*, but the latter was considered a "natural"occurrence – a collision with an iceberg on the Newfoundland Grand Banks. To many, the sinking of the *Lusitania* represented the deliberate murder of hundreds of defenceless non-combatants, including a large number of women and children.

Among those on board were some 150 U.S. citizens, of whom only two dozen lived to tell the tale. President Woodrow Wilson reacted with an angry protest against the wanton destruction of innocent American lives on the high seas, and for many months, diplomatic notes were exchanged between Washington and Berlin. It took a full year, which brought further U-boat attacks, before Germany finally bowed to U.S. demands. A promise was given that in future no merchant vessel would be attacked without warning, or without adequate provision for the safety of passengers.

There could be no doubt about the self-limiting effect of this decision on the Kaiser's most effective means of indirectly inflicting serious damage on Great Britain in the conduct of the war. Too late to recover fully, on the last day of January 1917, Germany gave notice to the United States and other neutral powers that earlier promises were withdrawn and that ocean traffic in the vicinity of the British Isles, France, and Italy would be subject to being "prevented by all weapons" and without notice. In future U-boats would sink on sight any merchant vessel they encountered, no matter which flag flown or if passengers carried. Wilson, the peacemaker, to this point said to be "too proud to fight," had had more than enough. He immediately ordered diplomatic relations with Germany severed, and on April 6, after prolonged debate, the U.S. declared war.

Now, two decades later, like a recurring nightmare, dark clouds were gathering once again on the European horizon, and many – those who genuinely opposed sending American boys overseas for the second time in the still-young century, as well as the German-American Friendship lobby – were determined the United States would not be drawn into the fray. Typical of those considered to be in a position to influence matters was Joseph Patrick Kennedy, the multi-millionaire whisky baron who had married Rose, daughter of Boston's famous Mayor John F. "Honey Fitz" FitzGerald, and like his father-in-law was regarded as a power to be reckoned with in U.S. Democratic politics.

President Franklin D. Roosevelt appointed Kennedy, father of a future President of the United States, as Ambassador to Great Britain – or, as it is formally stated, to the Court of St. James – in 1937. However, this did not deter the outspoken ex–saloon keeper from East Boston, with his deep Irish or anti-British roots, from telling the world how he felt about the possibility of American involvement in the Second World War, and about the British as well.

"This is not our war," Kennedy declared, and informed the President that he hated all Englishmen "from Churchill on down." Many believed this just may have had something to do with his replacement as ambassador in 1940 by John G. Winant.

Kennedy was hardly alone in his controversial views. Another prominent anti-war spokesman with a growing following was the popular hero Charles Augustus "Lucky" Lindbergh, the American aviator credited with the first solo non-stop flight across the Atlantic in 1927. His pro-German, isolationist views were denounced in New York, media which labelled him as "the spokesman for the Fascist Fifth Column in America" and "if not pro-Nazi, definitely not pro-British." He testified before the U.S. House Foreign Affairs Committee and expressed views that the newspapers condemned as being "utterly at variance with the studied opinion of the large majority of his countrymen." Critics said he did not "make sense . . . [as]

he refuses to see any danger to the U.S. . . . should Germany win the war."

But not everyone believed the newspapers, and not everyone in America was prepared to send their offspring to fight in another European conflict.

In the face of significant opposition to involvement, Roosevelt struggled to avoid direct American participation in the conflict, while striving to find creative ways of helping Britain and the Allies. Out of a secretly arranged meeting between the President and Prime Minister Winston Churchill at Ship Harbour, near Argentia, Newfoundland on August 14, 1941 came the Atlantic Charter, affirmation of the right of all peoples to national independence and self-determination.

In more concrete and pragmatic terms, Churchill agreed to the lease of lands for development of American military bases in Newfoundland and its northern territory of Labrador. In return, the Americans would deliver fifty over-age, mothballed destroyers to strengthen the Royal Navy's hand in the battle for supremacy of the Atlantic. And there was invention of the policy of Lend-Lease, designed to assist the Allies to resist aggression by enabling them to buy airplanes and other engines of war from manufacturers. The total bill would come to exceed fifty billion dollars, serving to strengthen the Allies' ability to defend themselves, enabling the development of U.S. war industries, and thereby – also critically important – helping to mould U.S. public opinion in favour of involvement in defence of the free world.

These moves came none too soon. A diplomatic agreement between Hitler and Italian Dictator Benito Mussolini, known as the Rome–Berlin Axis, was reinforced in 1939 by a joint military accord, and in 1940 it was joined by Japan. Then, without warning, on December 7th, 1941, the Japanese attacked and devastated Pearl Harbor, headquarters of the U.S. Pacific Fleet, on the island of Oahu, Hawaii. There were disastrous losses in ships and planes, and some 2,000 Americans were killed. Four days later, Roosevelt declared war on the Axis powers.

The U.S. war industry of greatest importance, fostered and financed by Lend-Lease, was aircraft production; mainly centred in Southern California, it was the focus of much of the *Bund*'s effort to create disruption. It was hardly unexpected that the anti-war lobby would demand that the burgeoning aircraft industry be directed towards peaceful rather than military purposes, and churchmen and politicians alike mounted attacks on what would come to be referred to by many as the "military-industrial machine."

"Jimmy, honey," Eva gushed, "I always knew that we'd be together again someday . . . and here we are! When I phoned you yesterday, I didn't realize you were married," she lied. "I wasn't even sure it was your name in the Burbank telephone directory. I hope I don't cause you any trouble with that wife of yours. What's her name . . . Miranda?"

The truth was, she knew all about Altehouse – probably more than he knew about himself. It was all there in the extensive files the *Bund* maintained on immigrants from Germany and other expatriates and their families. In Altehouse's case, his parents had made their way to the United States after the First World War, settling first in New Jersey, and when things were really bad in the Great Depression, making their way to California. As a check supervisor representing the military, he was in a position to approve or not individual aircraft coming off the line, while being privy to secret information. The *Bund* knew that Altehouse was, in fact, selling secret information to agents, its own and the Japanese.

He put down his coffee cup and took her hand in his own.

"Eva, from what you've told me, I realize we have an important mission to perform for Germany," he declared with passion, "and nothing must be permitted to interfere. It goes far beyond considerations of personal feelings or comfort. I am certain

Miranda will understand – and if she doesn't, well, I'll just have to deal with that."

"But I *am* serious," Eva pursued the point. "We don't need anything to happen that will draw attention to our project, okay?"

He got the distinct impression that a hidden message was being conveyed, and rather than merely stating a preference, she was giving an order that she fully expected to be obeyed. It was an impression that was about to be confirmed.

"Excuse me a moment," Eva said abruptly, and disappeared into the adjoining room, which she had made clear was her private quarters. Returning she had undergone a startling transformation in both appearance and attitude. She had donned a dark blouse and skirt outfit to help turn his mind to business. Besides rearranging her hair in a tight bun and adding heavy glasses, she wore a uniform identical to that of *Bund* members whose photographs had appeared with growing frequency in newspapers and in magazines, such as *Time* and *Life*, accompanying reports of anti-war and pro-German demonstrations.

Attached to her left sleeve was the black, white, and red swastika armband of the National Socialists. Her entire demeanour had undergone a startling alteration; clearly it was her intention to move their meeting into a new phase, and she could see that the effect on Altehouse was as she desired, immediate and dramatic.

"Now . . . we have important work to do," she declared, opening a large dispatch case and producing a pair of scrapbooks containing newspaper clippings from across the United States, Canada, and Newfoundland. "Take a look at this," she commanded.

The very first thing he noted on opening the cover was a story from a publication he had never before seen, in a place he had never heard of, the Corner Brook, Newfoundland, *Western Star.* The headline on the story read, "PLANES BOUGHT IN U.S. MAY BE FLOWN VIA NEWFOUNDLAND."

"What very few people in the United States may realize, or even care about," Eva informed him, spitting out the words as her face flushed and her voice suddenly hardened with anger, "including the stupid Californians who are building those planes just up the road in that plant in Burbank, is that within a matter of days many of them will be in England loading up with bombs to blast the people and the cities of Germany. Yet, this U.S.A. is supposed to be a neutral country!

"This is why I have brought you here. It is critical to act on this matter right away. Given your experience, we require your assistance," she said with the air of a superior making a demand of an underling.

"Of course," he said, without pausing even to think about it.

"Now," Eva said, "look at this."

This time she held up a clipping from a California newspaper, the San Francisco *Chronicle*. Under the headline "ARMY MAN ACCUSED," a dispatch from a British United Press correspondent told of a United States Army Air Corps mechanic accused, at a general court martial, of conspiring to pass vital information to enemy agents for money.

"Well," she asked, "what do you think of that?"

Altehouse blanched, his face turning ashen beneath the California suntan.

My god, he thought, *she knows . . . they know . . . that I've been selling information to the Japs that should have been made available to the* Bund. *But they can't turn me in, that would only blow the roast on the whole organization . . . . Or would they?*

He was totally confused, so much so that he was unable to answer.

"Well, I'll tell you," she said. "The FBI are onto it, and they could catch up to you in a few days – maybe even by this time tomorrow, who knows – unless we get you out of town fast. So that's what we're going to do."

* * *

Military personnel like Altehouse, who was responsible for inspecting the final product, were well aware of the expanding volume of production at the Lockheed Aircraft Corporation. As to where precisely the orders were coming from and to whom and for what purpose the planes were to be delivered, that was another matter. Leaders of the *Bund* had become convinced, however, despite frequent assurances of continued neutrality emanating from the White House, that the aircraft, foremost strategic implements of modern warfare, were being built for delivery to belligerent powers: the Allies. Recently, with the Burbank production lines crammed with fuselages in various stages of completion, Lockheed President Robert Gross had ordered that long lines of twin-engine Hudson bombers be moved outdoors for final assembly. No problem in the California climate. It was impossible for thousands of workers and passersby to miss the identification painted on them – said to be Canadian, but with striking resemblance to the multicolour roundel of the Royal Air Force.

In fact, the aircraft orders were originating in Canada, but with a private company: Canadian Pacific Railways. It was itself entering the world's newest mode of public transport to carry thousands of passengers annually on aircraft as it had for decades on its trains. But Canadian-born British newspaper baron Max Aitken, otherwise known as Lord Beaverbrook, had been appointed by Churchill as his minister of aircraft production, and it was he who came up with the idea of having the Montréal-based C.P.R. purchase warplanes in California and organize civilian pilots, navigators, and mechanics to ferry them safely across to Britain.

At first, concerns over the neutrality issue were so intense as to cause American bureaucrats to decide that aircraft bound ultimately for Britain could not be flown out of the U.S. into Canada. They dreamed up the awkward, time-consuming method of transporting them across the Canada-U.S. border *on the ground* – towed across the line by draft horses.

Mercifully, this not very useful attempt at subterfuge was short-lived.

"Exactly what do you want me to do?" Altehouse asked.

"These are your orders," she stated, holding up the documents, "and I mean military orders. The *Bund* has arranged to have them cut, and they are perfectly legal. You will leave by train tomorrow morning for New York, to join a troopship for Newfoundland. Ironically, it is our former SS *Amerika,* which the United States took as a war prize twenty years ago, but which hopefully will be regained by Germany in the near future.

"It will be taking on board a thousand American troops to begin preparing military defence bases in Newfoundland, and you will be among them. When you get to St. John's, Newfoundland, you will report to the *Abwehr* agent in charge, Herr Stroesser. He will give you further orders. The instructions tell you how to contact him. One thing you must not do is tell Miranda, or anyone else, that you're going away, let alone where you're going. Is that clear?"

He nodded absently as he accepted the portfolio, shocked at the way his life was being taken over, but unable to think what to do about it. Eva stood to signal he was dismissed, and raised her arm in the Nazi salute.

"*Heil Hitler,*" she declared.

"*Heil Hitler,*" he echoed obediently, if regretfully.

Early the next morning, as Eva prepared to check out of the motel, her telephone rang. It was a California *Bund* official calling urgently to advise of the arrest by Military Police and the Federal Bureau of Investigation of Staff Sergeant Frederick Hurst, a senior U.S.A.A.C. mechanic and close associate of Altehouse. He would face court martial, accused of conspiring to pass vital information to foreign agents, for which the penalty was the firing squad. The investigation was in its early stages, but appeared certain to spread, with more arrests promised. Altehouse could very well be next.

Eva said not a word, but hung up quickly, avoiding discussion in case the telephone was tapped. She glanced at her watch, and breathed a sigh of relief – by her calculation Altehouse had left Los Angeles on a train for New York forty-five minutes ago; with any luck, he would be on board ship on the high seas before the MPs and the FBI figured out where to find him.

TWELVE

On Board USAT Edmund B. Alexander, New York, 1941

AN ENDURING IRONY lives on concerning United States participation in the Second World War, namely that the first American troops to arrive on foreign soil – the island of Newfoundland – long before a state of hostilities had been declared against the Third Reich by President Franklin D. Roosevelt, reached their assignment on board a captured German passenger vessel, the former Hamburg–America ocean liner SS *Amerika.*

Her skipper, U.S. Navy Capt. William Joensen, was not a man to be much bothered by quirks of fate. Of much more practical bent, he was annoyed as winter daylight was breaking over New York City on the morning of January 21, 1941, that although United States Army Transport *Edmund B. Alexander* was finally ready to cast off at 6:47 a.m. Eastern Time, they were nearly an hour behind scheduled departure.

"Not a good way to begin a long voyage – or any for that matter . . . . I like to be on time," he pointed out to the executive officer, Lt.-Cmdr. Raymond DiMaggio, whose private opinion was that his superior was overdoing it, being just a tad too picky.

Joensen's main concern, however, and DiMaggio's too, was the fact that in the coming days they would be steaming, counting zigzag avoidance procedures, through over a thousand miles of submarine-infested waters. It was beyond imagining that any Nazi U-boat commander alive would not give his eye teeth for the opportunity to sink a torpedo or two into a shipful of U.S. troops and supplies – especially when that same ship had been seized from Germany as a war prize in the first place!

Joensen realized all too well that the only real protection the big ship and her 1,200-plus passengers and crew could rely on was the U.S. Coast Guard cutter *Duane*, due to rendezvous with them in a couple of hours in Lower New York Bay, and assigned to escort them to their ultimate destination. He had all kinds of confidence in the Coast Guard to do its job to the utmost. But whether anyone could reasonably be expected to keep them safe in the face of the hidden menace lurking beneath the roiling surface of the unforgiving Atlantic Ocean was another, very serious and worrying question.

There was developing, however, one other factor that might work in his favour, thanks to the unseen hand of Mother Nature. The gangplanks were withdrawn, and deep in the bowels of the ship, stokers stripped to the waist shovelled coal by the ton to build up steam in her boilers, when the early-morning weather forecasts were coming in.

The news might not be welcomed by the ship's mainly land-lubber passenger complement, for many of whom it would mean a miserable few days of extreme discomfort, but her skipper was suddenly buoyed and grateful: the mid-winter storm that had appeared to be losing strength as it left the Florida Panhandle behind was actually picking up speed and force. The outlook now was that it would probably accompany them all the way to the eastern Grand Banks, after which they could expect to be enveloped in the thick, clinging fog for which the western Atlantic shoals were famous. Perhaps it would not totally prevent U-boats from operating effectively, he reasoned, but it would certainly cramp their style. What you couldn't see would be damned hard to torpedo.

"That's what we needed to hear," the captain remarked, as Lt. (J. G.) Michael Noonan, the man responsible for keeping tabs on the weather, arrived on the bridge to deliver the latest verdict.

"It may not make for a pleasant time below decks, but it could be a lifesaver, literally speaking. Okay, Mr. DiMaggio, let's get this ship under way."

Standing by the voice pipe, experienced New York harbour pilot James McGuinty at his elbow, the executive officer spoke to the engine room and ordered slow astern – just enough power to begin moving the big ship away from her berth. On command, the helmsman put the wheel hard to starboard, and her stern began slowly to swing out from the dock. As the vessel achieved turning room, the engines were reversed and she began to move forward, almost imperceptibly at first, out from the East River into Upper New York Bay, past Liberty Island with Freder Bartholdi's famous 300-foot bronze figure of *Liberty Enlightening the World*, gift of the people of France in 1876 on the hundredth anniversary of the Declaration of Independence. A powerful, snub-nosed service tug, engines rumbling like a caged tiger, stood by in case it was needed to help the troopship counter the force of the rising gale as she eased into the ship channel.

DiMaggio reached for a lanyard above his head, and the whistle attached to the forward stack gave a couple of deep-throated burps to signal all was well. The man on the bridge wing of the tugboat raised his hand in a farewell gesture, and towering six storeys above him Joensen waved back.

Minutes later McGuinty shook hands with DiMaggio.

"I can't leave, Commander," he said, "without asking if you're related to the Yankee Clipper. That's my team, and he's the guy in baseball that I admire the most."

The executive officer smiled a knowing smile, having been faced with the same question, or variations of it, many times before.

"I'm asked that a lot, sir, but I think I may only be a very distant cousin of Joseph Paul DiMaggio. Our grandfathers probably came from the same village in Italy – but I've got to confess my team is the Red Sox!"

McGuinty shook his head as if finding that unbelievable, and turned to Joensen to wish him a safe trip.

"Hope I'll see you again, sir, the next time you come to New York," the pilot said, with a firm handshake. He did not envy him the North Atlantic in mid-winter, with the added risk of submarine attack.

"Thank you, Captain. I'll be looking forward to it."

McGuinty was led by a quartermaster's assistant to a hatch well down on the port side. There a Jacob's ladder dropped him to the deck of a New York Harbor Authority launch waiting below which, as soon as it recovered the pilot, turned off and headed without delay for the shelter of the Brooklyn docks.

On the bridge with Joensen, but displaying the good sense to stay out of the captain's hair as he oversaw the ship's departure into the teeth of a biting northeast gale, whose snow squalls at times obscured other ships and installations only a few hundred yards away, Col. Maurice D. Welty warmed his hands by cradling a steaming cup of coffee. Welty was the man responsible for the nearly 1,000 troops on board – men from the 2nd, 3rd, and 7th Army Corps from New York, New Jersey, Delaware, West Virginia, Pennsylvania, and Maryland. In future they would be assigned to the U.S. 3rd Infantry, 24th Coast Artillery, and the 62nd Anti-Aircraft Artillery – a reflection of the job they would be expected to do in their first overseas posting.

And where exactly might that be?

They were supposed to sail under secret orders – so secret that before boarding the ship most knew neither where they were headed, nor how they were getting there. Troops arriving by train at New York's Grand Central Station were rounded up and transported by bus and lorry to the Brooklyn Navy Yard, where mystery seemed to prevail as to the name of their ship and where she was docked.

"I soon found out our ultimate destination after speaking to several workers (Italian) who were helping to renovate the ship." [Many years later Dominic "Tony" DeAntonio from Altoone, Pennsylvania, member of an advance Quartermaster Detachment, would relate to historian John Cardoulis how he cracked the mystery:] "When I inquired if they knew where the ship was headed for, they said 'Don't ja know – this ship she go to Newfoundland.'"

DeAntonio admitted he and his buddy, Joseph F. "Midge" Mellon, had never heard of the place, let alone known where it was.

As for the name of the ship, it had been changed long ago from SS *Amerika* when the 21,085-ton liner was caught in Boston harbour at the outbreak of the First World War, to USS *Amerika* when seized and turned over to the Navy for use as a troopship after the U.S. entered the fray in 1917. The name was soon anglicized to USS *America* when she returned to her original purpose.

Launched in 1905 at the Harland & Wolff shipyards in Belfast, Ireland, she spent her first ten years plying the Atlantic Ocean between Germany and the United States. Following seizure she was turned over to the U.S. Navy for conversion into a troop transport at the Boston Navy Yard, and began carrying servicemen to France. She made nine round trips, and after the war, eight additional return voyages bringing some 47,000 Americans home from the European war zone. In 1919 she was decommissioned and then transferred to the U.S. Army Transportation Service. She completed two additional trips to and from Europe as an army transport, and then between January and August 1920 undertook a long voyage, via the Panama Canal and the Pacific Ocean, transporting members of the Czech Legion from Vladivostok, Russia to Trieste, Italy.

The ship was then converted to her original use, and made her first Atlantic crossing as SS *America*, a civilian passenger liner, in 1921. She continued in this role – except for time out for repairs following a serious fire, a collision that sank the merchantman *Instructor,* and her own sudden and mysterious sinking at her dock in Hoboken, New Jersey, and her subsequent refloating and refit – until the early 1930s, when she was laid up at Patuxent River, Maryland.

The Second World War caught up to the old steamer and brought her back to active duty in 1940. Taken from the laid-up fleet and towed to Baltimore, she was rehabilitated by the Bethelehem Steel Co. and renamed the USAT *Edmund B. Alexander.* The voyage to St. John's, where she would serve as a floating barracks while accommodation was being built on land at the newly established Fort Pepperrell, headquarters for Welty's Newfoundland Base Command, was her first under this persona.

Preparations for the voyage had begun three weeks before Christmas, and continued through mid-January. By that time, all pretense of secrecy had been abandoned. Armed Forces Public Relations was putting out photographs showing officers inspecting the rifles of troops clad in fur helmets and other winter garb, boarding the *Alexander* in New York, and newspapers reported them "outbound for Newfoundland, the first hemisphere defence base acquired from Great Britain in the destroyer deal."

The news reports not only named Welty as the first Newfoundland base commander, but also identified in some detail the stateside units from which the troops were drawn. Little wonder Joensen was concerned about German U-boat activity off the Eastern Seaboard; official United States neutrality notwithstanding, Admiral Karl Donitz and his Nazi commanders had been provided with a virtual road map with which to track and destroy his ship. The media reports might be just what it would take to provoke them.

A change of name had done little to alter the reputation of the *Alexander* as the "swankiest" troopship afloat. In length 668 feet, and at the beam 72.2 feet, her five upper decks and three lowers were marked by spacious corridors and luxurious staterooms and cabins. Many of these had been subdivided to accommodate up to four enlisted men each, with others retained in nearly original form for officers, and all comfortably furnished. Large recreation rooms were provided on each deck, and there were well-stocked libraries, pianos, radios, Ping-Pong tables, and log-burning fire-places. Motion-picture equipment was installed in the largest of the recreation rooms so full-length features, newsreels, and training films could be shown. It was expected the troops would inhabit the luxurious "barracks" in St. John's for at least six months.

In a cabin on "C" deck that he shared with three others, Altehouse considered his situation. Unlike other enlisted men on board, he belonged to the United States Army Air Corps, and had a very different agenda – officially and otherwise. As a secret member of the German–American Friendship Society, he would ultimately be taking his direction from the *Abwehr* agent for Newfoundland. The orders he carried, and presented on boarding, had the appearance of being both official and authentic, but that did not prevent the ship's security from taking a hard look – he was an anomaly, the uniform he wore saw to that. Accordingly, Altehouse made up his mind to stay out of sight as much as possible.

Two decks up, the Military Police Commander on board the *Alexander*, Maj. James Adams Goodfellow from Woonsocket, Rhode Island, was proving to himself that he certainly was no sailor. In fact, he had never before been to sea, and almost from the moment of setting foot on board ship his stomach reminded him of that fact. It was so bad that, to avoid a major embarrassment right in the Military Police On-board Office, Goodfellow had turned his private cabin into his personal work area. It put him a lot closer to the "heads" – the navy term for the toilets, he had learned – in case of emergencies, which were proving frequent, and afforded him a certain level of privacy in his distress.

Despite the worst bout of illness he had ever experienced, Goodfellow struggled manfully through the mass of reports compiled by men of his detachment who interviewed troops boarding the ship in New York, checking their orders and inspecting their equipment. Among them he found a handwritten notation, made by a sharp-eyed, quick-witted MP corporal, appropriately named Thomas Avery Bright, who spotted the apparent anomaly of an Army Air Corps type in among the foot soldiers. Altehouse's papers were in order, but since he did not seem to fit the general profile of the ship's military complement, his file was flagged. Understandable, since the voyage was a U.S. Army undertaking, Goodfellow reasoned. No doubt there was a reasonable explanation as to why a fly boy was there in the midst of all those soldiers, but it was worth looking into.

Running once again for the heads, one hand over his mouth and the other clutching a stomach about to erupt for the umpteenth time, he resolved that at the first opportunity, if he ever became well again, he would check it further.

It was a few minutes past midnight, and therefore very early on the twenty-fourth of January, 1941. His mother's birthday, James Winright Stubbs reflected, as well as his own. How many blokes, he wondered, had been born on the same date as their dear old mums? It was the first time he had not been at home in Bournemouth, for the double family celebration; instead, at nineteen years and a few minutes of age, here he was keeping graveyard watch on the port wing of the flying bridge of the SS *Sheaf Crown*, a merchantman with holds full of grain from the Canadian Prairies, already a precious commodity in early wartime Britain. Her destination was Land's End.

The ship was making eight knots, all the speed her master dared in worsening weather with zero visibility due to dense Grand Banks fog; this was risky business in a time when all you had were rumours that an Englishman named R. A. Watson-Watt – only an inventor could get away with a name like that – was close to perfecting a device that would "see through" fog, snow, or darkness. The idea was that it would send out radio waves to bounce off an obstacle in a ship's path, giving adequate warning to stop or change course, and it was clearly revolutionary.

Suddenly a break opened up in the solid wall of fog. One instant Jimmy Stubbs was fighting to keep his tired eyes open, tired from peering into grey nothingness, the next he had a startlingly clear view of – *Oh blimey!* – a German submarine. It sat there on the surface, an evil, black whale of a craft, clearly outlined against the ghostly opaque of the fog bank. In a matter of seconds, almost before the *Sheaf Crown*'s lookout could react, she was gone as the fog closed in again. By then he had whistled twice into the voice pipe to the officer of the watch, and the officer had quickly appeared to hear the report which he immediately communicated to the master.

Capt. Robert M. Buckwhiler surmised the U-boat had surfaced in the relative protection of the fog to recharge batteries, air out the boat, or for some other purpose, and would be slow getting under way – even assuming her lookouts had, in turn, spotted the grain carrier. Despite the risk he decided to increase speed to twelve knots, the best the freighter's engines could do, to put the maximum distance between them. After an hour of faster steaming, he decided it was safe to break radio silence to report the sighting to the authorities in St. John's, Newfoundland, the nearest friendly port:

```
URGENT
FROM: SS SHEAF CROWN
TO:   ST JOHNS ADMIRALTY RADIO
01:22 GMT 24 /01 /41

U-BOAT SIGHTED ON SURFACE LAT 47.52 N LONG
50.34 W TIME 00:10 GMT NO CONTACT

R. M. BUCKWHILER, MASTER
```

In St. John's – or in sailors' wartime parlance, Newfyjohn – they immediately plotted the position provided in the freighter's message, and concluded the U-boat was only sixty miles from the port when spotted. Immediately warships of the Royal Canadian Navy, a destroyer and two corvettes, were ordered to begin a systematic sweep of the area.

At that same moment, the *Alexander* was making her way north along the eastern seaboard in desperate ocean conditions – giant seas, northeast winds approaching hurricane force, and worsening fog. Captain Joensen got the news from the SS *Sheaf Crown* in his bunk just before two o'clock in the morning. He had it flashed at once to *Duane*, the Coast Guard escort, somewhere off his ship's starboard beam. Then he informed Col. Welty.

"I never thought I'd hear myself say it, Captain," the army commander breathed fervently, "but thank the Good Lord for this absolutely lousy weather."

On the second-last day of January, Frederick C. Oechsvey, British United Press correspondent in Berlin, filed a story that received top placement in newspapers on both sides of the Atlantic:

HITLER BRAGGING THREAT TO THE U.S.
Says Every Ship Going to Britain To Be Torpedoed

BERLIN (BUP) – Adolf Hitler said today that American aid for Great Britain "will be torpedoed" and "Europe will defend itself" should the people of the American continent enter the war.

Hitler told a cheering crowd of 30,000 at the Berlin Sports Palace on the eighth anniversary of his assumption of power that "If the United States wants to send help we say this: Every ship with or without convoy that approaches Britain will be torpedoed."

At about the same time Associated Press correspondent Howard W. Blakeslee turned in the following item at the news agency's headquarters in New York's Rockefeller Center:

SHIP CARRYING NEW FLU VACCINE TO BRITAIN SUNK

NEW YORK (AP) – A German submarine has sunk a ship carrying 500,000 doses of the new American 'flu vaccine en route to Britain, says the American Medical Association News.

The date and name of the ship were not given.

Shipments of the new hope for stopping influenza have been kept secret.

THIRTEEN

Southside Hills, St. John's, Newfoundland, 1941

IF EVER THERE existed the title Inveterate Trout Fisherman, Edward John Rogers would surely deserve it. When not glued to his powerful Emerson "Electric Eye" radio, the one with an undulating green spot indicating when it was finely tuned to Station WOR (New York), KDKA (Pittsburgh), or WBZ (Boston) for major league baseball broadcasts, he was almost certain to be out tramping the countryside around St. John's in season, angling gear at the ready. He had never been to the United States, so he had never actually attended a professional baseball game, but he knew by heart the records of every team and player, and was as familiar with the top performers as if they were personal acquaintances. However, even baseball took second place to trouting.

His favourite ponds lay in over the Southside Hills, the high, brooding promontory guarding the harbour of St. John's with its growing population of Allied warships attesting to the reality of a war threatening to expand to engulf the whole world.

The one-time copper miner in Betts and Tilt Coves on the northeast coast of Newfoundland, was paid off as a moulder and pattern-maker three years ago, about the time his wife Bridget passed away suddenly after a stroke. He had worked more than fifty years for the United Nail & Foundry Company, manufacturer of kitchen ranges and parlour stoves, cast-iron pots and frying pans, manhole covers, and, of course, nails. He had been trekking up over these hills for as many years as he could remember.

Armed with an expensive English green-heart rod fitted with an exquisite Shakespeare reel, which he considered the great extravagance of his life, he regularly took into his creel the legal limit of native muds, the occasional rainbow, and even an elusive eel. He fished flies or bait depending on the time of year, and was very successful at it.

This May morning his first destination, as usual, was Beaver Pond, followed by Duck Pond, and to cap off the day, the incomparable Muddy Hole. Whatever an angler's luck at the first two, he could always be sure of a couple of pan fries, as mud trout of a quarter to a half-pound were called, at Muddy Hole.

A creature of habit who never smoked, swore, or drank – a supply of bay rum was kept on hand to soak his feet after a long day standing in the hot clay of the moulding floor, then poured back into the bottle – "Ned" Rogers was always up with the sun. Most Sundays, after early Mass at St. Patrick's Church in the West End, he breakfasted on roasted salt codfish – just wrap in newspaper and lay it right in the kitchen range, on top of the splits – accompanied by two thick slices of homemade bread and strong tea. Then he set out from his home on Deanery Avenue, walked down Plank Road to Job Street, crossed Water Street, and traversed the Long Bridge over the Waterford River past the Newfoundland Dockyard to the Southside Road. Now began the long, rocky climb to the summit.

Often along the way he met up with one or another of his former work buddies, Jim Cantwell or Bill Caul, and sometimes both. He was a bit surprised and certainly disappointed that today neither was in evidence up to the point that he passed through the squatters' village of Blackhead Road, also known as The Brow, whose residents enjoyed a superlative view of the city below. The trio had an informal competition going – who, at the end of the season, would have had the best day's catch by numbers and weight?

Under their honour system, each was required to deposit in a pickle jar, through a slot cut in the sealed lid, a twenty-cent piece for each fish caught, the spoils to go to the most prolific angler at the end of the season. A minor controversy had blown up at one point when Rogers was found to have entered three eels into the contest.

"Go 'way, b'y," Cantwell objected. "Sure, you know as well as I do that an eel's not a fish – not what we Newfoundlanders call a fish, anyway!"

"Ned, the only people that likes to eat them eels is Germans." Caul was more emphatic, if tongue-in-cheek. "I might have to report you to Mr. Outerbridge down to Civil Defence Headquarters as a dangerous person, if you're not careful," he warned with considerable hilarity. "You just can't be counting eels in our contest, my son!"

The lighthearted outcome, by a vote of two to one, was that the rules were clarified to recognize only native mud trout and rainbows as "fish." Eels were thus relegated to the status of aquatic nonentities – good eating, perhaps, for the likes of Rogers who savoured them as a delicacy, cut into inch-thick rounds and fried with fat-back pork, but possibly to be considered unpatriotic.

By this time a brilliant sun was transforming the clear May morning into the equivalent of a midsummer's day. When Rogers came to Beaver Pond Brook, mopping his sweating brow, he decided it would be a good spot to stop for a rest and a drink of cool, clear water. He had just settled on a large rock when two boys – he guessed they were twelve or fourteen years of age – appeared from around a bend in the narrow, dusty road, talking and gesticulating in obvious excitement.

"You should've seen it, mister," one of them blurted as soon as they spotted Rogers. "He had to be a German spy, with a secret suitcase radio and everything. Just like in the movies down to the Crescent!"

"Yah," his companion added, "he must've been sending messages to German submarines or something. First it looked like a fishing pole he had, but then we saw it must be the aerial for his radio, and we could hear the sounds – short dots and long dashes. It was some scary. We were afraid he'd come after us, so we got out of there!"

The man had surprised them as they were lying around, passing back and forth their single Gem cigarette, and enjoying the lovely spring day. There seemed no doubt the individual was what the youths thought him to be, a spy, and had they surprised him, the consequences for the pair might have been serious.

Like most everyone else in St. John's, Rogers was well aware of the rumours and speculation about agents and saboteurs in their midst, and he had decided there was possibly something to it. He was certainly not so naïve as to think that Newfoundland might be spared the presence of enemy agents, or even attack by enemy forces; very early after the commencement of hostilities, reports had circulated of the presence of German surface raiders and submarines in the waters around the Island.

He was mindful, too, that his son James, who had served with the Newfoundland Regiment in the Great War only two decades ago – and returned from the fighting in Europe, and its aftermath, thankfully unscathed – had reported that many a German in defeat was outspokenly adamant: "The next time, it will be *your* cities, *your* wives and children and old people, who will suffer because we will carry the fight to where *you* live!"

To be sure, there was plenty of evidence accumulating that Newfoundland would play a major part in the latest international cataclysm, thanks to its strategic location as the virtual gateway to the heart of North America. Avid newspaper reader that he was, Rogers took special note of headlines such as that in the Corner Brook *Western Star* reporting "PLANES BOUGHT IN U.S. MAY BE FLOWN VIA NEWFOUNDLAND" – the same headline that had attracted the attention of the California *Bund*. Translation: bombers built in American factories and destined to devastate Germany, its cities, its factories, its war machine, would be ferried across the Atlantic Ocean to Britain via the newly constructed

Newfoundland Airport near Gander Lake, a couple of hundred miles west of St. John's.

Another prominent headline, this time in the St. John's *Evening Telegram*, announced "U.S. SEEKING NAVAL AND AIR BASES IN NEWFOUNDLAND." Soon thousands of American troops would take up station in the British colony in some four dozen separate locations. As well, there was a clear reflection of growing concerns that the place could come under direct attack or invasion in headlines such as this one in the St. John's *Daily News*: "NEWFOUNDLAND TO HAVE HOME DEFENCE FORCE."

Nor was that all, by any means. The newspapers reported that Dr. R. J. Manion, director of Air Raid Protection for Canada, had told a civil defence conference in Toronto that he would be "very much surprised" if Toronto, Montréal, and Ottawa, and Canadian coastal cities did not come under attack in the form of bombs, poison gas, and enemy landings. And perhaps inspired by Manion, Leonard E. Drummond of the Alberta and Northwest Chamber of Mines was quoted in Montréal and Toronto newspapers as suggesting in a speech that invasion of northern areas of Canada was only "logical." Speaking in Edmonton, he referred to reports that German submarine bases had already been established in Greenland and on the Labrador coast and said these reports "lend colour to the theory that a northern invasion is not beyond the limit of possibility."

All this had brought a predictable response in Newfoundland, especially when viewed against the background of: the surrender of Norway; the German invasion of Belgium, Holland, and Luxembourg; the Dunkirk disaster with 140,000 Allied troops literally pushed into the sea, narrowly escaping a Nazi death trap; and the fall of France.

In 1939 Newfoundland was even less prepared, if that was possible, than it had been at the start of the First World War. The legislature having been abolished, the bankrupt colony was under control of a British-appointed commission chaired by Governor Walwyn. He soon announced emergency measures that, besides recruiting for service overseas, allowed for establishment of the

Home Defence Force referenced in the newspapers – in time named the Newfoundland Militia – which would grow to some 500 men, under command of Lieut.-Col. Walter F. Rendell. Meanwhile, under pressure from Canadian, American, and British authorities, the commission launched an enhanced Air Raid Precautions Organization headed by Col. Leonard Outerbridge, honorary private secretary to the Governor and, like Rendell, a First World War veteran.

The principal concern was that St. John's, a wooden city with approaches "wide open to the Atlantic," would be especially vulnerable to attack – from even a single airplane dropping incendiary devices on a windy day, from shelling from hostile shipping, or from commandos put ashore by submarines or surface raiders.

Then came what some on the Allied side saw as a desperate move – the replacement of British Prime Minister Neville Chamberlain by political gadfly Winston Spencer Churchill who offered "blood, toil, tears, and sweat" as the price of eventual victory.

To many it seemed more than mere coincidence that the summons from King George VI put "the most hated man in Germany" in charge at 10 Downing Street at the very moment Hitler was preparing to launch the aerial *blitzkrieg* that Goering had persuaded him would soften up the British, paving the way for an intended invasion. Instead, in the Battle of Britain, 144 days between May and September when world freedom hung in the balance, the vaunted *Luftwaffe* daily rained down death and destruction on cities, towns, and villages, but failed to pound a nation into submission. It was massive, naked aggression foiled by British and Commonwealth airmen, despite their lesser numbers, by the uncommon determination of a people not to be cowed, and by the leadership provided by the King and Queen and a bulldog of a Prime Minister, who insisted on remaining in besieged London and sharing the danger with its residents.

Rogers's patriotic heart soared on hearing, on the shortwave, the reports of Churchill's tremendous, encouraging speeches and his tributes to England's fighting forces:

"This is London calling, in the Overseas Service of the BBC The next voice you will hear is that of the Prime Minister, the Right Honourable Winston S. Churchill:"

"I expect that the Battle of Britain is about to begin. Upon this battle depends the survival of Christian civilization. Upon it depends our own British life, and the long continuity of our institutions and our Empire.

"The whole fury and might of the Enemy must very soon be turned upon us. Hitler knows that he will have to break us in this island or lose the war. If we can stand up to him, all Europe may be free and the life of the world may move forward into broad, sunlit uplands. But if we fail, then the whole world, including the United States, including all that we have known and cared for, will sink into the abyss of a new Dark Age made more sinister, and perhaps more protracted, by the lights of perverted science.

"Let us therefore brace ourselves to our duties, and so bear ourselves that, if the British Empire and its Commonwealth last for a thousand years, men will still say 'This was their finest hour.'"[15]

And when that battle had been won against seemingly impossible odds, and Hitler's thoughts of invasion had, consequently, all but vanished, the Prime Minister offered this tribute:

"The gratitude of every home in our island, in our Empire, and indeed throughout the

world, except in the abodes of the guilty,
goes out to the British airmen who,
undaunted by odds, unwearied in their
constant challenge and mortal danger, are
turning the tide of the world war by their
prowess and by their devotion. Never in the
field of human conflict was so much owed by
so many to so few."[16]

At about the same time the Battle of Britain was being won in the air, word was reaching Newfoundland of the sinking by Nazi U-boats of the SS *Humber Arm*, pride of the newsprint carrier fleet of Bowater's Pulp and Paper Mills in Corner Brook, off the Irish coast, and soon after that, in mid-Atlantic, the SS *Waterton*, also out of Corner Brook, and then the SS *Geraldine Mary*, carrying a cargo of paper for Britain from the Anglo-Newfoundland Development Co. in Grand Falls. Had the schedule of their sailings from Newfoundland been flashed to enemy submarines by secret agents, equipped with clandestine radios, such as the one detected by pure accident this very morning on the Southside Hills?

Amidst periodic reports of German and other foreign nationals, usually described as seamen, being rounded up or escaping custody, and criticisms that "unrealistic" blackout rehearsals were being held in daylight hours, *The Western Star* in Corner Brook carried a report that "wives and sisters of the capital's leading citizens" were demanding, by means of a petition, that the authorities put a stop to Nazi fifth-column activities in Newfoundland. Their fear was that "Newfoundland might be as lax in protecting itself against the enemy boring from within as were Holland, Norway, and Belgium."

Having just witnessed two badly frightened youths describe what they had seen, Rogers thought there could no longer be any doubt that Newfoundland was indeed being infiltrated by enemy agents, and that the war was being carried to North America's very doorstep. Suddenly he found himself chilled by their excited apprehensions.

"Jingoes!" he exclaimed. "Where did this fellow go, the man you say you saw? Was he on foot or did he have a car? You boys had better go down right away and report this to the police," he told them.

They took to their heels, and despite his misgivings – not much he could do about it anyhow, and a day's fishing was not to be wasted – Rogers returned the fishing basket to his shoulder, picked up the green-heart, and resumed his trek up the brook. Although not by nature a nervous man, he was unable to shake the uncomfortable, oppressive feeling of being watched. There was the unaccustomed sense that danger might well lurk around the next turn as he followed the well-worn footpath. Reaching the shores of Beaver Pond, he was relieved he would not be alone; a couple of fishermen he recognized were there ahead of him. He smiled to realize how little annoyed he was that they occupied the best fishing spots!

Stroesser had become accustomed to going to the Southside Hills to transmit and receive radio messages; to do it down in the city was both risky, because of the chance of detection by local police and military, and uncertain, due to the interference of the surrounding hilly terrain. He cursed his own carelessness. He realized that, having been seen, he could now be described to the police and thereby be recognized by them – a virtual death sentence for anyone in the spy game. He had watched from dense bushes as the two youths excitedly described to a fisherman on the trail how they had observed a man sending a radio message in Morse code, and knew he could not permit them to reach the police security office.

He found the stolen car where he had hidden it in a grove of trees, and caught up to the pair just a hundred yards ahead. Closing the distance slowly so as not to alarm them, he suddenly put the accelerator pedal to the floor. They tried to run, to get out of the way, but it was no use. The car hit them with a sickening thud, sending one up over the windshield and the other into bushes at the side of the road. Both lay still, either unconscious or dead.

Stroesser jumped out, and taking no chances they might still be alive, picked up a large rock and bashed each youth several times in the head and face. He then dragged the bodies to the car and placed them inside.

It was not difficult to find a spot where the vehicle could be run over a steep drop. He manoeuvred it to the edge, got out, retrieved his suitcase radio, and with a firm push sent the auto with its macabre cargo hurtling over and over to crash on rocks a hundred feet below. When the police found it, there was a very good chance they would conclude the youths were common car thieves who had caused their own sorry end.

FOURTEEN

Railway Station, St. John's, Newfoundland, 1941

CONFORMING TO THE principle of safety in numbers – the bigger the crowd, the greater the degree of anonymity – Stroesser hung back in the shadows of the Newfoundland Railway round-house opposite the foot of steep Patrick Street, waiting for larger numbers to gather on the passenger platform. The roundhouse was the place where locomotives and train cars underwent major servicing and repair. The sprawling, grey-black structure in the West End of St. John's, and the mechanical miracles performed within its walls, had fascinated generations of boys attending nearby Holy Cross School for whom it was a favourite, if forbidden, hangout. There was always the chance of some youthful excitement – like the day the Pullman car *Ferryland* missed the connecting rails to the giant outdoor turntable and plunged into the pit. It could happen again, couldn't it – and maybe an engine this time?

More seriously, the railway yard represented for many the security of a lifetime job with a free travel pass and maybe a government pension on retirement, hardly an unworthy ambition in 1940s Newfoundland.

Stroesser waited and watched from a distance, unobserved as far as he could tell, as one of the fire-eating, steam-and-smoke-breathing monsters emerged into the cold, soft drizzle of the late February afternoon. The locomotive eased slowly onto the turntable which, in revolving, would enable it to reverse direction and back onto the main line at the Riverhead station and couple onto the waiting train.

"Paper, mister?"

The Nazi agent started involuntarily as a sharp-eyed newspaper boy spotted him standing there in the shadows. There had not been time to fabricate an identity, to obtain false papers, and he was feeling vulnerable, unusually jumpy. His orders required him to get on the road at once. He was left no choice. The assassination must take place within three or four days, and the uncertain timetable had unnerved him as well.

The youngster, a typical street urchin, poorly dressed with a trademark salt-and-pepper cap canted over one eye, dragged a sleeve across his runny nose and reached into the sheaf of papers under his left arm. With a grimy right hand, he held out the day's issue of *The Evening Telegram*, Newfoundland's oldest daily journal.

Stroesser took it and quickly scanned the headlines, heavy and black in contrast to the pink newsprint. They trumpeted British Royal Air Force raids on Germany and German-occupied seaports in northeastern Europe – news that was hardly unexpected, but nonetheless caused a sharp constriction of breath, a pain around his heart. He had a sudden image of Ilse in the little house in a Hamburg suburb, with British bombs raining down.

His wife of three decades had declared she did not want ever to see him again after their son and only child, Bernhardt, was blown to bits when his patrol group was ambushed by partisan bombers in occupied Norway. She blamed his father for encouraging the twenty-three-year-old into the *Wehrmacht*. But what choice had there been, Stroesser asked himself for the millionth time. It was either the regular army, where there seemed to be some chance of surviving the war; the *kriegsmarine*, which was losing far too many ships and suffering huge casualties; or the *Luftwaffe*, whose losses of planes and personnel over Britain were beginning to cast shadows of doubt on Goering as successor to the Führer. He continued to hope that the rift in this marriage, caused by indescribable shock and sorrow, could be bridged sometime.

The newspaper speculated over the sensational defection to Britain of Rudolf Hess, Hitler's deputy, in a stolen *Luftwaffe* fighter plane. And it reported on the revelation that a Nazi-dominated movement, bent on creating disorder in the United States and Mexico, had been revealed to have its headquarters in New York City. At this latter disclosure he cursed under his breath – from now on, he realized, the *Abwehr* would operate with increasing difficulty – and he shivered to read the forecast of the Newfoundland weather: plenty of snow and falling temperatures. Abruptly he thrust the paper back into the boy's grubby hand.

"What's the matter, mister," he sneered, "ain't ya got a coupla coppers . . . only two cents?" He turned away in disgust at losing a sale.

Despite the gathering darkness, Stroesser could see in the distance increasing numbers of men, women, and – surprisingly, he thought – children, moving in the direction of the imposing railway headquarters and sheltering as best they might under the sloping roof of its open passenger platform. With the numbers growing, it would soon be safer to approach the train. He especially noted that a considerable number of those in the crowd wore military uniforms – the khaki of the army, sailors in the navy blue of the "senior service," as the British regarded it, and the lighter blue of the air force. On the platform an atmosphere of anticipation grew, rising to near-excitement, as the train, consisting of mail, express, baggage, dining and passenger cars, completed its assembly.

A hush fell over the crowd as a pair of railway employees and a man attired in the unmistakable garb of an undertaker trundled a cart along the platform to the baggage car. It carried a rough wooden box, stencilled with the stark legend "OF NO VALUE," which was manhandled aboard the train. The mournful faces of a few people who accompanied it, an elderly woman and, apparently, her sons and daughters, left scant mystery as to what it might contain.

Now the engine and its coal tender arrived, bell clanging, amid clouds of steam and smoke pressed close to the ground by atmospheric low pressure.

Conductor Michael Walsh, in a carefully pressed dark-blue serge uniform with brass buttons and a round, pillbox-shaped cap with shiny peak and gold piping, oversaw the process as workmen in contrasting grimy, greasy coveralls, striped caps, and big, stubby workboots walked the train's length. They inspected couplings and steam lines and flicked up the covers of hot boxes to ensure adequate lubrication, where steel wheels and axles joined, to minimize friction and provide against fire or derailment or both.

The train was ready at last, huffing and puffing in the station, waiting impatiently for the conductor's call of *"All aboard!"* – universally heard as *"'Board!"* – the signal that it was finally ready to set out on its twenty-three-hour run across the ancient Island of Newfoundland, first settlement of Europeans in the New World, to Port aux Basques where fishermen from overlapping regions of France and Spain were said to have harboured as early as the fifteenth century. The southwest coast town, with the neighbouring village of Channel, served as home port to the passenger ferry SS *Caribou*, nearest thing to a luxury vessel in Newfoundland waters, that had been bridging the ninety-six-mile ocean gap between Newfoundland and the Canadian port of North Sydney, Nova Scotia, for nearly two decades. A steel ship with powerful engines, capable of operating in the heavy ice of the Gulf of St. Lawrence, the railway had had her built in Rotterdam where she was launched on June 9, 1925.

Stroesser had good reason to know all about the *Caribou*, having submitted not one, but two reports to Berlin, in meticulous detail, on the operation of the ferry. A man with a naval background who had come up through the ranks of the *kriegsmarine*, he had switched to naval intelligence just before the beginning of the First World War and, following a brief training period, was assigned to Newfoundland. In light of his familiarity with the place, he had been selected from private industry, the manufacture of marine engines, by old friend and navy colleague Wilhelm Canaris, to set up and run a cell of the newly established *Abwehr* military intelligence in the British colony. Both had been closet Nazis during their early service together. Then Canaris was chosen personally by Hitler – and promoted to the rank of admiral – to run the spy agency that was claiming marked success both infiltrating German diplomatic ranks abroad, and planting agents in key displomatic, economic, and industrial sectors of foreign governments.

In Stroesser's estimation, the *Caribou* was as much a troop-ship as any military transport vessel he had ever heard of, and should be subject to the same rules of war. Officially regarded as a civilian service and ostensibly operated as such, the ferry was the principal passenger vessel operating between Newfoundland and Canada, and consequently handled most of the traffic, including the burgeoning military sector.

It was no secret, therefore, that her passenger manifest regularly included scores of travellers with direct and indirect British, Canadian, American, and other Allied military connections and responsibilities. It was clear what should and could be done, bearing in mind that besides virtually non-existent security at dockside, only a pesky but relatively harmless Canadian minesweeper was assigned to protect the vessel at sea. What a priceless opportunity was afforded to deal a solid blow to the Allies – for the price of a single torpedo, the chance to snuff out as many, perhaps, as 250 enemy lives.

But there were important echelons of the Third Reich, up to and including the Führer himself, who worried – as had the Kaiser in the First World War – that an attack on a ship classified officially as a civilian passenger vessel would be viewed by the civilized world as an act of barbarism. Hitler's hesitation, however, had a strategic basis. To the increasing consternation of his generals, and particularly his admirals, Canaris included, Hitler had decreed that everything must be avoided that might cause the Americans to enter the war before he was ready – which meant, before an anticipated Nazi victory on the Russian front.

As the *Abwehr* spymaster in Newfoundland, Stroesser had been assured that adequate help would be provided in carrying out his task, and the first agents were quickly in place. But he himself had been kept extremely busy. Not only had he investigated and submitted reports on shipping movements – for example, the ridiculously vulnerable situation at nearby Bell Island, which did not even provide the shelter of a harbour, and the various sabotage opportunities. He poured out a succession of reports, paying particular attention to the big military bases and scores of smaller detachments being created by the "neutral" United States and the Canadian government in St. John's, Argentia, Gander, Stephenville, Goose Bay, and a couple of dozen lesser locations in Newfoundland and Labrador.

As well, in response to an order from Canaris, a First World War U-boat commander with a distinguished record and an abiding conviction in the efficacy of the submarine service, he had undertaken a preliminary assessment of potential sites in Newfoundland for a U-boat base. Repair, refuelling, and resupply would be provided to the expanding German submarine fleet whose vessels currently must make their way to the other side of the Atlantic, to the northern European ports of Lorient, Brest, Cuxhavn, and Kiel, to be refitted and re-equipped to fight another day.

The lack of such a base was "a very serious problem" and "seriously depleting the effectiveness of our U-boat resources," Canaris had pointed out.

"Your assignment," he informed Stroesser with grave formality when they met for a long lunch in a private restaurant alcove in the elegant Europaischer Hotel in Hamburg's

Kirchenallee, "is very much in line with the General Staff Memorandum, classified top secret, that underscores the Führer's interest in occupying certain Atlantic islands. This is of great importance now, but will be even more critical for the purpose of prosecuting the war against America which, realistically, cannot be far off.

"Newfoundland, with which you, of course, are so familiar, is at the strategic centre of interest, commanding not only the North Atlantic sea lanes, but also the gateway to the North American continent at the mouth of the St. Lawrence River."

"I remember the place well," Stroesser nodded, "especially the primitive state of public transportation. Almost no roads anywhere. I wonder if it has improved?"

"Unfortunately," the admiral went on, "the treachery of Roosevelt and his gang, who have seen fit to make a complete mockery of the principle of neutrality, has pre-empted the occupation of most of Newfoundland and Labrador by our forces, by undertaking to establish huge military bases there.

"Our sources tell me that at any one time, in addition to whatever the British and Canadians do, the Americans will have in excess of fifty thousand troops, hundreds of planes, and scores of ships there. We know full well that the naval station at Argentia will become home to a fleet of destroyers and antisubmarine aircraft that could cause us a lot of difficulty.

"However, it is a very large island with many large, isolated bays and only a small, scattered population. As well, there is its extremely large dependency of Labrador, with only a relative handful of aborigines and white settlers. Keeping in mind the serious limitation imposed for several months of the year by sea ice . . ."

He paused to refill their glasses with a fine Moselle wine, pressed from superior Reisling grapes and unique for both its body and lightness, as well as a slightly effervescent quality.

The admiral stood, arm extended, glass in hand, and Stroesser followed suit.

"A toast . . . to the Führer, and to the ultimate victory of the Third Reich," Canaris intoned, standing ramrod straight, imperious even in severely cut civilian clothes.

"*Seig Heil!*" Stroesser responded, heels clicking.

They resumed their seats and Canaris picked up where he had left off.

"We badly need, nonetheless, land-based communications and weather forecasting in Labrador, and I look to you and your people to see to the establishment of these important, and I would say vital, services. The success of our submarine operations and, in time, all ship operations, will increasingly depend on them."

"*Jawöhl, Herr Admiral*," Stroesser had replied without hesitation, maintaining the official nature of the occasion. "You may absolutely rely upon us. I understand completely what is required. It shall be pursued immediately I arrive in St. John's."

The formality of the luncheon over, the old friends strolled for half an hour towards the area of Hamburg's old free port warehouses, engaging in a friendly conversation about families, careers, and colleagues, some of whom had already given their all in the expanding war. They parted with a warm handshake, in contrast to the chill fog rolling in from the Elbe Estuary to remind them that out there on the North Sea, as in the English Channel, and on the broad Atlantic Ocean, the fate of nations, and the lives of countless thousands of comrades hung very much in the balance.

"I wish you Godspeed," Canaris said as they parted, fully aware that in a few hours Stroesser would be hostage to the vast, grey expanse, a spy masquerading as a crewman on an Estonian fishing trawler. What was not obvious was the fact that the trawler itself was now a spy ship, captured in the Gulf of Finland and its crew replaced by Nazi collaborators. The tipoff was that it sailed from the German port of Cuxhavn rather than the Estonian port of Tallin where it was registered.

"And I wish you every success, Herr Admiral, in your endeavours," the other man replied, conscious of the critical importance of his friend's work.

However, he harboured an unspoken concern. He had heard it said that the outspoken Canaris did not always see eye to eye with the Führer, which could be the equivalent of a fatal disease.

Soon reports began to flow over Canaris's desk. One possibility raised by Stroesser was the seizure of the tiny island of Ramea off Newfoundland's southwest coast, in much the same way as the Channel Islands, the British-ruled archipelago in the English Channel, were occupied by German invaders at the end of June 1940. Situated in waters ice-free year-round, Ramea was virtually at the centre of the North Atlantic sea lanes.

Another possibility was the broad inlet that Newfoundlanders unaccountably called Bay Despair, rendered on maps and marine charts as Bay (or Baie) d'Espoir – the exactly opposite meaning. However, it was located well to the east and somewhat off the shipping lanes. A third prospect was the anomalous French possession of St. Pierre-et-Miquelon, still further eastward and just south of Newfoundland's Burin Peninsula. But whether the Vichy regime that had taken control could be trusted was another matter. Ramea was a very different, and, Stroesser felt, a very attractive, proposition.

"With a population of only a few hundred fishermen and families," Stroesser wrote, "the island could easily be captured and sufficient numbers of residents held hostage so as to dissuade the British authorities from any attempts to retake it."

But as in the case of the SS *Caribou* and various other recommended projects, his masters could not seem to make up their minds. This he found incomprehensible, since success would be so relatively easy to achieve. The damnable thing, however, was the silence. It was impossible to get an answer out of Berlin, hence there existed a climate of continual uncertainty. *If someone does not decide something soon, I may have to take matters into my own hands*, he permitted himself to think out of pure frustration. *Hah*, he finally decided. *How ridiculous of me to even think such treasonous thoughts.*

But they would not go away and, if anything, grew more frequent and more intense. And now, to compound his disquiet, there had come out of the blue special orders direct from Berlin – delivered by U-boat, no less – to mount an assassination plot against a prominent Canadian scientist, to attend to it personally, and to carry it out in a matter of a few days. It was a mission for which he felt completely unsuited; he had not the slightest idea of how he would carry it out. All due respect to the High Command, he could not accept that it was the best use of his time and talents.

FIFTEEN

Security Conference,
Hotel Newfoundland, St. John's, 1941

THAT AGENTS OF the Third Reich were active in wartime Newfoundland came as no surprise to the Allies. It was of particular concern to the Americans, maintaining the fiction of neutrality while busy constructing, equipping, and staffing in this outpost of the British Empire their biggest military bases outside the continental United States. They thus had a huge and growing establishment to protect. The Canadians, too, were extremely conscious of the real possibility of subversion and sabotage, but had a double-barrelled motivation in being here: the protection of their own exposed eastern approaches; but also the need to establish a presence that would be adequate to ensure a future stake in the neighbouring Dominion, comprising the Island of Newfoundland and its much larger dependency of Labrador. Above all, they were determined that it not fall into the hands of the Americans. The third member of the "big three" occupation force, the British, kept an anxious watching brief on the conduct of the Battle of the Atlantic, fought primarily to protect and preserve their North American lifeline of troops, supplies, and engines of war against the growing destructiveness of Nazi U-boats. "About all we can do, really," a senior officer remarked with a mixture of regret and surprising frankness; in the circumstances, they were powerless to do more.

A joint mission of British admiralty and secret service had examined the state of security in Newfoundland. Given its strategic importance, no one seemed shocked by the conclusion that the landing of enemy agents in the colony was "a real possibility."

"Like flies to honey," was the way Emerson, the dapper lawyer who served as Commissioner for Justice and Defence, and was considered a safe bet to be knighted and become a future Chief Justice, characterized it. As he prepared to preside over a top-secret session of Allied commanders and their security chiefs in the cavernous ballroom of the posh, government-owned Newfoundland Hotel, the fact that bees might make for a more appropriate analogy appeared to bother him not at all.

"Show me the honey pot, Carew, and very soon I'll show you the flies."

Unknown to Emerson, to government chief civil servant William J. Carew, or anybody else, was precisely how many flies – or bees – there were, and where and when they might swarm. Discovering the answer and swatting them successfully was precisely what this conference was about.

Governor Walwyn, the British-appointed chairman of the Commission of Government that had replaced the elected legislature, after a century of first representative and then responsible govern-ment, had intended to preside over this conference himself. But at the last minute His Excellency had been forced to send his regrets.

"A case of double pneumonia," warned his personal physician, First World War medical officer Cluny MacPherson, MD.

In the master bedroom of cold, draughty Government House, he warned, "The risk of leaving your bed is just too great, Your Excellency. I realize this conference is extremely important, but so is your health, and then some. As your physician, I must insist that you not get out of bed until further notice."

Unused to taking orders from anyone, the career navy man snorted impatiently and seemed about to argue the point. But he was restrained by his wife, Lady Eileen, who placed a hand on his arm even as she smiled dismissively in MacPherson's direction.

When the doctor had gone out, she pulled the blankets up under her husband's chin and finally settled the matter.

"I shall be taking command here for the next few days, my dear, until I get you well again," she declared firmly. "Now, I want you to take your medicine and stop worrying about all the things you could be up and doing. As for the conference, you know Emerson will have it well in hand."

In the absence of the Governor, Emerson, who in the ordinary course would have attended in support of Walwyn, received last-minute instructions to take over.

On hand, in response to the Governor's urgent, personal invitation – none would dare decline – would be Brigadier Philip W. Earnshaw, chief of the combined Canadian–Newfoundland military command, which included the Newfoundland Escort (Convoy Protection) Force; Col. Maurice D. Welty, the officer in charge of the U.S. Newfoundland Base Command that shortly would be headquartered at the Pepperrell army (later air force) installation in East End St. John's; Maj.-Gen. G. C. Brant, Welty's designated successor; and Admiral Arthur L. Bristol of the big U.S. Navy installation at Argentia, ninety miles away, and destined to become the principal anti-submarine and convoy security base in the North Atlantic. Along with them, in addition to the heads of military security, would come senior officers of the Royal Canadian Mounted Police, the U.S. Federal Bureau of Investigation and the U.S. Secret Service, and the British secret service, MI5.

Emerson would be accompanied to the conference by Newfoundland's most senior security and intelligence officials.

"Carew, I wish to go over the ground, in advance, with the heads of the Constabulary and the Ranger Force – let's say tomorrow morning at ten o'clock," he had indicated a couple of days earlier to the man who was Executive Secretary to the government.

"And perhaps O'Neill should bring along Mahoney, Whelan, and Cahill for good measure. They should have a good appreciation of who we're dealing with here, and we want to be sure the

Americans, the Canadians, and the British know we are well-prepared with experienced people ready to handle any problems that arise, and have the confidence that we shall do so."

The Commissioner's wish being tantamount to a command, all were present for a preliminary meeting in the Executive Council chamber of the Colonial Building.

"Gentlemen, I do not believe I have to emphasize the threat that may be facing us," Emerson told them. "It is a matter of being well-prepared for whatever may come. But let us not be lulled into thinking that the only danger is from Nazi spies and saboteurs.

"If independence and sovereignty mean anything, and they do, then regardless of the temporary suspension of the House of Assembly, we must be careful to exercise our proper functions and responsibilities in terms of the maintenance of law and order, otherwise others will contrive to step in and do it for us. Do I need to say more?"

As the conference got under way, Emerson formally introduced his people: Patrick J. O'Neill, chief of the Newfoundland Constabulary, doubly qualified by his First World War experience as commander of an anti-submarine vessel patrolling Newfoundland waters; District Inspector Michael P. Mahoney, officer in charge of the Constabulary's wartime Security Division; Inspector Edward Whelan, head of the Constabulary's Criminal Investigation Division; his deputy, Inspector Michael J. Cahill; and Eric W. Greenley, chief of the Newfoundland Rangers, the colony's rural police force. All had had Scotland Yard, Federal Bureau of Investigation, or Royal Canadian Mounted Police training.

Carew had fetched along a battered, well-used gavel in a velvet-lined case. He passed it to Emerson, who rapped a few times for order, and after a few preliminary remarks got quickly down to business.

"Gentlemen," he said, "it is obvious that the enemy cannot afford *not* to be right here among us. I do not mean in the room, of course." He paused to acknowledge a somewhat tentative response to his attempt at gallows humour. "And to do all in his power to frustrate our intentions."

The Commissioner for Justice and Defence was especially concerned to offset the growth of inter-service rivalries – in particular, the American tendency to attempt to "take over the whole show," as he had expressed it privately, and thus turn everybody else off. The attitude would be voiced openly by Brant, who would soon succeed Welty, making no bones about the fact he believed the U.S. forces, with by far the biggest investment in men and resources, should be totally in charge.

Divisions thus spawned, Emerson knew, could jeopardize the Island's protection against German attack, and even invite invasion.

"The enemy well knows what is transpiring here, in the middle of the Atlantic Ocean," he suggested with deliberate ambiguity. "However, if we do our job right, we shall pose the greatest threat to his bellicose ambitions in Europe and elsewhere.

"Therefore, he must do everything in his power to attempt to cripple our efforts to keep Great Britain, as well as our Russian allies, supplied with tanks, guns, and ammunition, with bombers and fighter planes, with soldiers and sailors and airman. And we, for our part, must see that the Atlantic convoys get through, and that the ferrying of bombers from Newfoundland is successful, so that together with our allies we may defeat the Nazi aggressor where he is – else the day will come when he will be launching attacks on the North American continent.

"This is the great task before us, gentlemen, our primary responsibility, and we must, above all, work together." He paused for emphasis. "We must not be found wanting, due to any feelings of rivalry or for any other reason, in carrying it out."

Reports were then received regarding the level of infiltration suspected in both the military and civilian sectors, by agents of the Third Reich. The speakers were generally unprepared to acknowledge that their services might be at fault. Mahoney, as the officer in charge of the Constabulary's security division, gave it as his opinion that, just as the war was in its early stages, so German espionage efforts in Newfoundland had only begun.

"I am afraid we must be prepared to see them grow, and perhaps quickly, with the passage of time. Whatever we may have seen so far, and I think it is fair to say it has been very little, it can be expected to escalate – to double, triple, or perhaps quadruple, in the months ahead. Quite obviously, there must be a comparable increase in anti-espionage activity.

"If I may say so, Mr. Commissioner," he said with a slight incline of his head in Emerson's direction, "with the resources available to it, the Constabulary cannot even begin to cope, on its own. We expect arson and other forms of sabotage. We will need equipment and men for aircraft and submarine spotting. We will need to board and arrest enemy vessels and crews. There are frequently occurring immigration and detention problems, the guarding of strategic sites and infrastructures such as electricity plants, and the inspection of trains and passenger vessels. All in addition to the regular work of civilian policing. I should point out also that the Newfoundland Rangers have been asked to add to their regular duties the security of the Newfoundland Airport at Hattie's Camp, and coastal surveillance of shipping and aircraft spotting.

"I could go on, but we all know what is involved here. But I will venture to state that, lacking a tremendous improvement in operating systems, the support of additional trained personnel, and mutual co-operation, we can expect major problems to affect us all."

Emerson was grateful for Mahoney's frankness, and would make a point of telling him so privately. For now, he signalled that the conference was over.

"That's it, then, gentlemen. I believe we have covered the agenda, and that we have ended up on a good note, thanks to Inspector Mahoney. Over the next few days, His Excellency the Governor and the Commission will finalize a draft functional plan and suggest protocols that will guide our joint actions. We have some extremely serious challenges ahead, and . . . . General Brant . . . is there something that I missed?"

"Well, not exactly, Mr. Commissioner," the cigar-chomping American replied, half-smiling, "but there is a matter that I'd like to mention before we leave. I'm very pleased to advise you that the United States Army has just completed a new shooting range up on Signal Hill, and we're planning our first annual turkey shoot. I'd like to invite everyone here to participate, and I certainly hope you all will."

"Excuse me, General," Emerson replied, displaying genuine puzzlement, "a turkey shoot? I'm afraid you will have to explain. We do not have wild turkeys here in Newfoundland."

"Oh, I know that, Mr. Commissioner," Brant said, "and it's too bad, too. But I explain with pleasure. You see, we don't plan to shoot real, live turkeys, but rather clay pigeons – one good bird deserves another, you might say."

He laughed heartily at his own joke, and continued.

"Those with the best scores will win frozen turkeys, big ones too, flown in from stateside especially for the competition. So the shooting is really about turkeys – or at least *for* turkeys!"

Emerson struggled to keep a straight face.

"Thank you, General. Clay pigeons are not exactly the shooting priority I have in mind these days, but having said that, there may be some value to be derived from the target practice."

"Well, I do hope you'll all come," Brant concluded, a trifle lamely.

As intelligence officer at Fort McAndrew, Lt. Jethro S. Cook, Jr. was responsible, among other things, for investigating possible breaches of security in the general area of the base. The "general area" included the many villages of sprawling Placentia Bay, Newfoundland's largest with an area of 3,600 square kilometres, as well as the southern part of neighbouring Trinity Bay, separated from the larger water body by the three-mile-wide Isthmus of Avalon. There were persistent, if unconfirmed, reports of suspicious persons and incidents, speculation that included the possibility of enemy U-boat incursions, with agents put ashore for espionage or sabotage. Or both.

Maj. Robert L. Mushen, officer in charge of security for the Newfoundland Base Command, called in Cook to help him decide what steps they should take to determine, once and for all, what if anything was going on. The conclusion: it was a huge area, to which the United States forces were complete strangers; so they would seek the assistance of the Newfoundland Constabulary's Security Division.

Shortly O'Neill informed Mahoney, who in turn advised Sgt. E. J. Carroll at Placentia, that Staff Sgt. Edward E. Knauss and Sgt. Edward J. Flynn, special agents of the United States Army Counter-Intelligence Corps, were being dispatched to Fort McAndrew to undertake a security reconnaissance of the Placentia Bay area.

"Confirming our telephone conversation, and in compliance with the Chief's instructions, you are directed to send Constable James J. Lynch on this tour. On his return he will furnish Headquarters with a detailed report."

A member of Carroll's detachment, Lynch reported in detail on visits to the rural communities of LaManche, Little Southern Harbour, Arnold's Cove, Arnold's Cove Station, Come By Chance, and Sunnyside. Residents were interviewed – fishermen, housewives, a postmaster, a railway agent, a co-op store manager, a cottage hospital doctor, a merchant who was also a volunteer aircraft spotter. The reconnaissance "observed the coastline with the aid of binoculars, watching for anything of a suspicious nature," but turned up no firm evidence of anything awry, no tampering with rail lines or equipment, and no strange boats seen, although a number of steel buoys had washed ashore "of the type used on the submarine gate at Argentia harbour." Had they been cut adrift by enemy agents tampering with the gate?

A highly laudatory letter for O'Neill from Major C. H. Coyles, the U.S. Marine Corps commandant, commended the "splendid co-operation and assistance" rendered by the local police.

"In all my dealings with them I have found them friendly, courteous, fair and just, tactful, painstakingly helpful, and ever mindful of the cause they serve. The services rendered by these men are in keeping with the finest traditions of the Newfoundland Constabulary."

"We wouldn't want this to go to our heads." Showing the letter to the head of his Security Division, the Chief of Police expressed satisfaction at the state of relations – but with reservations. He cautioned, "Especially since we know with complete certainty – whatever may or may not be going on in the wilds of Placentia Bay – that the German spy and sabotage network is alive and well, and the U-boats as well. To think that this is not the case right here in Newfoundland would be a fatal delusion."

Tragic events would soon bear out O'Neill's grim caution.

The turkey shoot took place right on schedule, and somewhat surprisingly won space in the local newspapers – perhaps because of the unusual nature of the event.

The first prize, a twenty-two-pound bird, was won by none other than Maj.-Gen. Brant with a score of 45 (out of 50 clay pigeons shot at). Last prize, a twelve-pound turkey, was won by Lieut. Wilson, of the Army Air Force and aide to Brant, with a score of 33.

"Skeet shooting at clay birds with shotguns is practically unknown here in Newfoundland," *The Evening Telegram* informed its readers, "but recently ranges have been installed at Fort Pepperrell, Fort McAndrew, and the Gander Lake airdrome."

SIXTEEN

Troopship Edmund B. Alexander,
Off St. John's, 1941

As FAR AS anyone was able to make out visually – for those on board were hardly able to see land, and the former ocean liner was very nearly invisible to persons onshore – the big vessel was hove to a mile off Cape Spear, the most easterly point in North America. It was early on the morning of Saturday, January 25, 1941. A gale was blowing hard out of the northeast, raising the danger she could drag her anchors. Twenty-foot waves crashed on the rugged shore, uncomfortably close in a mixture of snow squalls and dense fog.

In the radio room, the Morse key kept up its incessant chatter as the St. John's pilot station poured out coded instructions via the radio station high up over the harbour entrance in Cabot Tower, where Marconi had received the first international wireless transmission four decades earlier. Principally, the advice was that given the combination of extreme weather and her deep draft and wide beam, the *Edmund B. Alexander* should not attempt to squeeze through the Narrows, as the harbour mouth was appropriately named, until the storm abated. That meant, to judge from information provided by weather forecasters, that the former ocean liner, carrying some 1,400 souls, might be required to lay-to in the open sea off the Newfoundland capital for three, possibly four days – a dangerous, worrying possibility.

The same was true, of course, of her Coast Guard escort. The *Duane* carried a crew of nearly 150, and, although most, if not all, were experienced sailors, they were taking a severe battering. She could have made port without difficulty, but her duty was to shield the *Alexander* no matter what – as she had done faithfully since leaving New York five days earlier. No doubt the weather offered a certain level of protection from U-boat attack, but it also was the cause of the very danger in which the troopship found herself, a sitting duck in the open water of Freshwater Bay, where it would have been well worth a U-boat captain's attempt, even taking the chance of getting into dangerously close quarters, to put a torpedo or two into her vitals. And, if there was ever any doubt about the U-boat danger, the urgent message from the SS *Sheaf Crown* had served to erase it.

On the *Alexander*'s bridge, Captain Joensen received the latest weather report with a large measure of frustration. Having delivered the bad news, DiMaggio, the executive officer, suggested what might have to be their next move.

"The local pilotage people will attempt to come aboard in the next hour or so, Captain, but they're suggesting we move into Conception Bay." He indicated the large, sheltered inlet on a marine chart. "At least until the wind abates, which may not be before tomorrow morning. We will have zigzag room there, without having to remain on the open sea."

Despite her size, even with her bows held to the wind, the ship heeled to starboard under force of the waves, with their energy gathered over hundreds of miles of ocean, and rolled heavily back to port.

Below decks, hundreds of seasick soldiers who had hoped for early relief from their misery received the news of delay with groans of despair.

Their commander decided to break with custom and go personally on the ship's intercom to explain the delay in making port. "This is Colonel Welty speaking." He cleared his throat with a great, startling "harrumph!" that boomed throughout the ship and wittingly or otherwise served to get him attention.

"I realize that many of you men . . . landlubbers like me . . . are having a miserable time," he began, giving rise to a broad chorus of agreement, outspoken and otherwise.

"I had hoped, believe me, that we would make port today, but it looks now like that will not be possible due to the very severe weather. On the other hand, the weather has also been the factor protecting us against the action of Nazi U-boats, so we have that to be thankful for.

"Captain Joensen informs me that we're going to move to a more sheltered location until the storm blows itself out. It may take a couple of hours to get there, but after that you should have a far less unpleasant time while we wait to make port.

"I realize the last thing many of you want to think about right now is food, but the truth is that the worst thing possible in trying to deal with seasickness is an empty stomach. I have instructed that we put on a special menu tonight to celebrate the fact that we're at the end of the voyage, or at least very close to it.

"Now, I trust you will enjoy your dinner as I intend to try to enjoy mine!"

Within the hour, DiMaggio reported back to Joensen that the senior St. John's harbour pilot, Captain George Anstey, had advised he found it impossible in the heavy seas to approach the *Alexander* in order to come aboard and assist with navigation in local waters.

"They just can't take the risk, Captain, and I can't say I blame them. I watched their launch circling the ship two or three times – once they came right in under our bows. It was a near thing whether they'd be capsized or smashed to matchsticks."

"So what are they suggesting . . . to go around into, what is it, Conception Bay? Just how do we get there?"

As a first-class exec should be, DiMaggio was ready for the question.

"They're offering to send out a steamer of some kind to lead us around . . . let's see." He consulted the chart. "Cape St. Francis. We steam due north about twenty miles, then make a left turn around into this big bay, coming back to the south'ard about fifteen miles to what they call 'The Grounds' – which I think means the fishing grounds, pretty well sheltered – between two islands, Bell Island which is a large, inhabited place, and Kelly's Island which is neither."

"Very well. I suppose that's the best we can do," Joensen replied wearily. "Signal that we're ready to move anytime they are. And alert Lt.-Cmdr. Jones on the *Duane* as to what we're up to."

"Aye, aye, sir," DiMaggio replied, heading for the radio room.

Soon, lookouts on the *Alexander* reported a sturdy-looking steamship emerging from the Narrows, plunging into huge waves that all but buried it, and heading towards the troopship. In a few minutes the Newfoundland Railway coastal steamer SS *Kyle*, Capt. Thomas Connors master, was standing by the much larger vessel, waiting like a friendly sheepdog for the signal to lead the way to the entrance to Conception Bay. In short order, they set out together for the anchorage off Bell Island.

The delay in making port in St. John's had a serious consequence that was not immediately apparent: the *Alexander*'s water supply had run critically low, adding seriously to the already urgent need to complete the voyage.

This had been made known to the authorities in the capital and Capt. Connors returned the following day, Sunday the twenty-sixth, to transfer a hundred tons of water, or about half her requirement, to the troopship. He came back with the remainder on Monday, the twenty-seventh, but by this time the weather in the bay had deteriorated to the point that a further transfer of water could not be made.

Early Tuesday morning, Joensen decided to make another attempt to enter port. The *Alexander* weighed anchor at 8:00 a.m., and with the *Duane* off her port bow, started out on the forty-mile run to the shelter of one of the world's best-protected harbours. But it was not to be. *The Daily News* described the drama as the troopship tried again – and failed – to make it into the harbour, and United States government officials attempted – and failed – to make it on board the ship:

Sometime before noon [*Alexander*] was signalled from Cabot Tower and the enthusiasm of Saturday was reawakened as it was made known that the transport was outside.

The *Shulamite* in charge of Captain Sinclair and the *Marvita* in charge of Captain Hounsell were both on the alert, and two local steamers, one in charge of Captain T. Connors and the other in charge of Captain W. B. Kean, were also active and in close proximity to the incoming steamer.

The weather . . . was fairly clear, with a little snow, but from the wharves of the harbour visibility failed at the entrance. A wireless was received from the transport about 1 p.m. that the ship would enter at 2 p.m. and dock a half-hour afterwards. With this information it was arranged that the *Marvita*, in charge of Captain Hounsell, would leave Campbell's wharf at 2:45, and when she left there were on board United States Consul General H. B. Quarton, Vice Consul F. Walter and Lt.-Col. Philip Bruton, who expected to contact the transport and pay an official call on Col. Welty, the officer commanding the troops.

Arriving some miles outside . . . the transport could be seen looming up in the distance and about four miles off with the two local steamers some distance away, one north and one south of the transport, which appeared to be heading southerly. After a very short time, Captain J. J. Whelan, who was on board the Customs cutter, was satisfied that both the transport and the accompanying ships were headed for Bay Bulls, and the cutter was put about and headed for port, arriving at her berth about 3:30 p.m. The cutter will leave port at 7:30 p.m. today on another venture, which is expected to be the last, to place on board the transport United States officials.

* * *

Captain Joensen was just beginning to feel the strain of the protracted delay, but Col. Welty had become decidedly edgy.

"I realize you can't do much about the weather, Captain," the army commander began, "but somebody should have foreseen the possibility of this ship, because of its size, being unable to get into port here."

"Yes, no doubt they should," Joensen replied. "But let's look at that. It was a decision growing out of the Board of Experts visit here to St. John's last summer, in September, actually. Admiral Greenslade's and General Devers's report" – he was careful to make clear the army, as well as the navy, was involved in the decision – "recognized there might be risks in mid-winter, but it was crucial to get troops on site here without delay. To put it bluntly, Colonel, if we hadn't acted right away, the Germans possibly might have got here first."

The crew of the *Alexander* was used to coping with extremes of weather at sea, but not so their guests. The mood among many of the troops on board, many of whom had never been on a ship before, was turning decidedly ugly. The decision to begin rationing water, necessary because of a depleted supply and the difficulty of bringing more on board, had precipitated a state of near-mutiny and Welty had ordered that armed Military Police patrols be stepped up throughout the ship.

"Be prepared to confiscate all firearms," he ordered Goodfellow, "and don't hesitate to throw any troublemakers into the brig. The only way to control situations like this is to act quickly and decisively. Any delay in putting a stopper in the bottle will produce a situation you'll not be able to control.

"Gentlemen, I recognize fully that we have an extremely difficult situation here," Welty said, delivering a similar message to a conference of platoon commanders in the ship's main ballroom, "but, as with any military problem, the first resort must always be to the maintenance of discipline. I am depending on you officers to see to it that difficulty does not turn into disaster."

It was late afternoon, just after five o'clock, which in mid-winter meant nearly dusk, when the *Alexander* hove to off Bay Bulls, a couple of hours' steaming south of St. John's. Sea conditions had moderated, and this meant much less discomfort on board. Welty took advantage of it to again go on the ship's intercom with encouraging words, and an optimistic report on the weather.

"It looks very good now for getting into port in the morning, on the high tide, at about 9:00 a.m.," he told the troops. "Then we can all begin to look forward to our first liberty ashore!"

An hour after sunrise the weather was perfect for bringing through the Narrows on high tide the biggest ship ever to enter the harbour in the more than 500 years since international fleets first began sheltering there. The sky was clear, there was scarcely any wind, and wave action outside the entrance was minimal. Inside, the harbour was smooth with an oily sheen. As she slipped through the entrance, with St. John's Master Pilot Captain George Anstey on the bridge, the *Alexander* had less than fifteen feet of leeway on her bows and perhaps less than ten feet of clearance under her keel. Nobody could tell for sure.

Mercantile premises ringing the harbour, and not a few homes, displayed the Stars and Stripes and red, white, and blue bunting, and shipping in the port blared out a welcome as the big vessel, nearly 700 feet long, was nudged into her berth on the Southside. There for the next six months, she would serve as a floating barracks while permanent accommodation was being constructed ashore. On board, a military band played, appropriately, "Hail, Hail, the Gang's All Here!" and hundreds of soldiers lined the rails trying to get a glimpse, through the fog and snow squalls, of the place that would be their home for months, if not years, to come.

Soon the flag-bedecked Customs cutter *Marvita* headed across the harbour to ferry Col. Welty to courtesy calls on Governor Walwyn, Mayor Andrew Carnell, Chief Justice Horwood, and other government officials, as well as Brig.-Gen. Earnshaw, commander of Canadian forces in Newfoundland. Later the cutter brought Col. Leonard C. Outerbridge, representing the Governor, and the other officials to the *Alexander* as Welty's luncheon guests. A guard of honour was drawn up and the ship's band played "The Star Spangled Banner" and "God Save the King."

"You know, there's only one thing wrong here," Joensen remarked thoughtfully, pouring Seagram's V.O. into large tumblers and adding ice and 7-Up brought from New York for the occasion. The formalities over, he had invited DiMaggio and Lt.-Cmdr. Jones from the *Duane* to his cabin for a quiet, relaxing drink. They clinked glasses and wished each other "Cheers!" and "Good luck!" and "Bottoms up!" before going to work on the contents. After all, they had survived a trip through the most dangerous waters in the world, possibly the most dangerous a troopship and its escort had ever sailed.

"Okay, Captain, I'll bite," the executive officer replied. "What is it, sir?"

"Well, I was just wondering. Why is it that the Canadians have a Brigadier General in charge here, and we've only got a Colonel?"

"Hmmm, good question, Skipper. Maybe someone will do something about that before long!"

As things turned out, it was a very good guess. Welty's successor turned out to be a Major General.

When Colonel Welty's adjutant posted Orders of the Day for January 30, 1941, the troops learned shore leaves would be permitted on their first full day in port.

However, the so-called "friendly invasion" of the Newfoundland capital would take place in stages. Following consultations with Governor Walwyn, Chief of Police O'Neill, and Brigadier Earnshaw, it was decided that instead of letting loose on the unsuspecting city a thousand troops – not counting the *Alexander*'s crew of 200 – the number of passes issued each day would be limited, at least for now, to 250, given out on a rotation.

Among the first to be granted liberty, thanks to both his rank and special, if counterfeit, orders, was Master Sergeant Alvin

James Altehouse, United States Army Air Corps. By pre-arrangement, as soon as he had been delivered to the north side of the harbour in a fisherman's open punt that had been converted to water taxi, he made immediate contact with Stroesser and received his assignment.

"You know why you are here, Sergeant," Stroesser said, "at least as much for the purpose of slowing down or halting the delivery of bombing planes to England, as for your own safety from the United States authorities.

"Here are your further orders and your train ticket to the seaport of Botwood, which is also the base for the transatlantic flying boat service. I will require you to maintain daily communication with me, as things change very fast in this business; we cannot afford to miss any opportunity, however unexpected, to advance the war effort of the Third Reich."

"I understand, Herr Stroesser," the American replied, adopting the form of address that he assumed was preferred. "I shall establish contact with you as soon as I arrive there."

By late afternoon Altehouse was on a train to Central Newfoundland, little realizing, any more than Stroesser himself, how prophetic those parting words would turn out to be.

SEVENTEEN

Quidi Vidi Gut, Near St. John's, Newfoundland, 1941

THE MISSION UPON which Stroesser embarked this dreary February day was intended, after all was said and done, to target a single individual, and was therefore a very different proposition from both his experience and his inclination. Moreover, Berlin had demanded that it be carried out *immediately and without fail.* It was even hinted that the idea originated with the Führer himself, its success so highly desired as to cause the High Command, in the interests of heightened security, to forgo the usual coded radio communication, which could be intercepted. Instead, the senior patrol submarine then in Newfoundland waters, *U-69* with Kapitanleutnant Ulrich Gräf in command, was instructed to make a risky rendezvous with a tiny fishing skiff, hired by Stroesser from a fisherman in the village of Quidi Vidi. Ostensibly, the purpose was to procure "a meal of codfish" – the spymaster had employed the local idiom – but in fact it was to ensure personal delivery of the sealed orders to Stroesser.

This had taken place before dawn in dense fog off Quidi Vidi Gut, a narrow hole-in-the-wall passage to the sea barely a mile north from the barricaded entrance to St. John's harbour.

Fifty-year-old Roderick Chartwell, although bursting with curiosity, knew enough to keep his mouth shut as he got some fishing gear together and they slithered down the slime-covered ladder from his stage, as fishermen called their combination wharf, workplace, and storage shed, into the boat. They put to sea without delay, heading straight out from shore for a thousand yards, when there suddenly appeared before them the black outline of a Nazi U-boat.

"My God, what is this?" the fisherman gasped, fear in his voice.

"Be quiet," Stroesser snarled. "You have seen nothing!"

These were the only words spoken as, cutting the engine, Chartwell threw the tiller hard over to prevent a head-on collision with the bulk of *U-69*, its powerful diesels pulsating as it sat there on the still, oily sea. As the wooden boat eased up to the great steel hull a seaman in oilskins – the only person in sight – wordlessly swung out a long pole with a package suspended. Stroesser grasped the package with both hands, and the pole was immediately withdrawn.

The seaman turned to climb the conning tower ladder and disappear inside the vessel as Stroesser signalled to Chartwell to get out of there, fast; if the U-boat were to submerge suddenly, their small craft would surely be sucked under with it. The skiff's engine coughed backed to life, and they turned away as quickly as they had come. The submarine disappeared from view. The entire episode had taken perhaps thirty seconds.

Back in the Gut, Chartwell was in the midst of tying on to the stage when the butt end of a stout sculling oar struck him in the side of the head, once, and then as he began to topple over, a second time. Stroesser quickly eased the motionless body over the side, climbed out of the boat, and in seconds had vanished into the fog.

In rooms over a Water Street tobacconist's, which he had rented for privacy in addition to his "official" bed at the nearby Seamen's Institute, Stroesser opened the package. To his great surprise, he was ordered to proceed urgently to the newly established Newfoundland Airport at Mile 213, a remote logging site on the trans-island railway line near the shore of Gander Lake. There his assignment was to arrange the elimination of one of the world's most prominent scientists: a leading proponent of germ warfare, Frederick Grant Banting, whose work with the British threatened to frustrate the Führer's plan to invade England.

His first reaction on learning the nature of the assigned task was a less than happy one. He even thought of directly questioning the wisdom of it – foolhardy and dangerous, he knew that it certainly would be. Though a loyal and committed member of the National Socialist Party and an enthusiastic supporter of everything that Hitler stood for, Stroesser worried nonetheless, that the Führer and his close advisors frequently acted on impulse, without proper consideration or an adequate assessment of the odds for success of an undertaking. Or perhaps simply on bad or questionable advice. In the present instance, there was little or no time to plan, to consider how the mission might best be carried out, or to develop an alternative course should the original plan go off the rails.

Moreover, the fine art of political assassination was far out of his line. He had killed before – as recently as this very morning – and likely would again, but that with one exception was a matter of self-protection, of kill-or-be-killed whether on the battlefield or elsewhere. He still experienced a cold sense of shame remembering his participation, as a youthful member of a Munich street gang, in the beating deaths of an elderly Jewish couple who failed to yield the sidewalk. But to set about to carry out the planned, deliberate murder of a stranger . . . that, he thought, should be the business of an experienced professional.

Yet, as he thought about it, Stroesser began to appreciate that there very likely was here the element of unforeseen opportunity which could change everything. Who could have predicted the chance to eliminate a prominent figure in the war plans of the British would so easily present itself? Who knew how many German lives might be saved? Finally, and beyond everything else, there was the matter of duty. He had been ordered to carry out this mission, and it was the wish of his leader, the Führer, that it be done. The habit of strict obedience was strongly ingrained.

In the end, he became reconciled to the fact that, whether or not he was happy about it, the moment must be grasped. His principal concern now must be that he had perhaps three days, barely seventy-two hours, to develop a plan and carry it through. Too little time, surely, but it would have to be enough. He was determined not to fail.

But what precisely would be the plan? he asked himself yet again. Here he was, barely half a day after the order had been delivered, setting out for the Newfoundland Airport, where he had never been before – or as close as he could get to it. As far as he could find out from discreet inquiries, it consisted of a high-security collection of hastily erected temporary buildings – a single airplane hangar, an administration building, living quarters still under construction for communications and technical personnel, and while they waited, a few Pullman railway cars on a siding to accommodate pilots and aircrew flying bombers across the ocean to the British. These were bombers that, delivered to the Royal Air Force, before long would be raining destruction and death on German cities and German people. He felt anger rising in his throat like bile at the very thought of it.

Stroesser had not had time to consider an identity change or a disguise, any more than he knew how he would carry out the assignment. He only knew that the airplane, on which his quarry planned to travel to England on official business for Canada's National Research Council, was a newly minted Lockheed Hudson bomber, twin-engined, serial number T-9449, manufactured in Burbank, California. So much for American neutrality!

He must contrive either to eliminate the man directly – or much better, to somehow cause that aircraft to crash into the sea, carrying all on board to their deaths.

Burbank, California . . . *Burbank, California!*

Suddenly, the name of that far-off American city rang a bell in Stroesser's memory. Only a couple of weeks ago, thanks to the intervention of someone high up in the California *Bund*, a United States Army Air Corps sergeant from Burbank, a check supervisor at the Lockheed aircraft factory, had fled to Newfoundland with papers and forged special orders on board the USAT *Edmund B. Alexander*, one step ahead of a federal espionage investigation. The suggestion had been that this man, himself a secret *Bund* member, could be used to sabotage the operation ferrying bombers to England. For this purpose, he could be located either at the Newfoundland Airport, the takeoff point for the flight over the Atlantic Ocean, or in St. Hubert, Québec, near Montréal, staging area for the planes before they moved on to Newfoundland. Because the troopship was headed for St. John's, the Newfoundland Airport had, literally, won the toss.

Until it was decided how best to employ him – his name, Stroesser remembered from their brief meeting in St. John's, was Altehouse – the airman had been assigned to a small Allied detachment in Botwood, sixty miles west of the Newfoundland Airport. His cover, the ostensible reason for his assignment to Newfoundland, would be to complete a status report on the international flying boat service, about which the *Abwehr*, to its chagrin, knew very little.

Although Altehouse's report would, in itself, be genuine and done by and for the U.S.A.A.C., the German authorities would secretly receive a copy. It would detail the operations of the big Pan-American *Clippers* and British Imperial *Caledonias* regularly landing to refuel on the harbour waters of the Newfoundland village. They were providing the world's first reliable intercontinental airline service, passengers crossing the Atlantic in relative comfort in a matter of hours, rather than days on an often raging ocean, and had taken over where Germany's unreliable Zeppelin dirigibles had left off after a series of disasters.

It was at least useful, if not vitally important, for the Third Reich to learn more, much more, about the service, including who was using it, and why. For example, according to the newspapers – there was no serious attempt to hide it – some of the highest officials of the British, American, and Canadian governments used this method to cross the Atlantic. The potential for espionage, and ultimately for sabotage, was considerable, as it was with regard to the program to ferry bombers to Britain that Eva Haussling had described.

However, that would all have to wait, Stroesser decided. There was a much more urgent task now for Altehouse to concern himself with, an assignment the air corps sergeant would learn about tonight when the two met in the paper mill town of Grand Falls. Stroesser immediately busied himself framing the innocuous wording of a telegram to arrange that meeting, and shortly made his way along Water Street to the public telegraph office.

Stroesser could see from a distance that the numbers of people heading towards the railway station platform had grown considerably, so it now seemed safe to move closer. He joined the flow hurrying singly or in twos and threes along a narrow, tree-lined boulevard that ran parallel to Water Street, the main thoroughfare that extended the length of the harbour. Then he abruptly crossed to the other side, for he had suddenly realized he was out of cigarettes. He headed for a corner store bearing the sign, "T. Ricketts, Druggist."

The man behind the counter was approaching middle age, stout with receding, sandy hair and horn-rimmed glasses. Stroesser indicated a stack of locally manufactured Royal Blends in a red package, the nearest thing, he had found, to the strong European brands he was used to. The druggist plucked a package from the shelf and placed it on the counter, in the same motion scooping up the coins the customer proffered. These days, many people favoured Canadian-made Players Navy Cut, with a bearded seaman on the box, perhaps a tiny nod to wartime patriotism – unless you had a friend or relative among or employed with the newly arrived American troops, in which case you could get a cheap supply of Camels, Lucky Strikes, or Chesterfields.

"Going out on the train?" Ricketts asked conversationally, with a friendly smile.

Mixed smells of pharmaceuticals, perfumes, and tobaccos filled the air. A large, brown-metal, oil-fed space heater struggled to offset the draughts of an old, creaky-floored wooden building. Its inadequacy for the task was made obvious every time the door opened and the damp, cold air blew in.

"Ja. Ah, yes," Stroesser caught himself. "Danish merchant marine." Not an unreasonable persona to adopt, since his mother had been born in Denmark. "Going to meet a ship in Grand Falls. A newsprint carrier," he added by way of explanation, and immediately regretted it. Signs everywhere displayed one or another version of "Loose Lips Sink Ships." The slogan could as well apply to spies; he would have to be more careful.

"You mean Botwood," the shirt-sleeved proprietor corrected him in a quiet voice, and noting the questioning look on the man's face, went on to explain.

"Botwood. It's the seaport for Grand Falls, where the ships come in to load newsprint paper. About twenty miles down the line, the company's private railway line."

"Yes, yes . . ." the other man repeated weakly, feeling the blood drain from his brain. He felt he might collapse in a faint.

Gott in Himmel, it is him . . . die Englander, from the trenches!

Stroesser was close to panic.

That voice!

Recognition took him back in a flash to 1918 and the blood-soaked fields of Flanders. The war had been going badly when the High Command ordered into the trenches those not already engaged in combat roles. Like many of his desk-bound colleagues, Stroesser the intelligence officer was forced overnight to trade his impeccable officer's uniform for the drab, untidy, mud-soaked garb of a front-line fighter.

One October morning, in the final days of the conflict, he found himself a member of a battery trading fire with British forces. Suddenly, the British stopped firing. There could be only one explanation, their young officer told them – the enemy was out of ammunition – and his guess was quite correct. He ordered an advance, but it led them into a trap. He could not know that a seventeen-year-old youngster from a village in White Bay, Newfoundland had doubled back to replenish the supply of Lewis gun and rifle ammunition.

Stroesser had never been able to erase the memory, the shock, of the young soldier – no "Britisher" he now belatedly realized – coming up behind the German battery and single-handedly taking them prisoner.

"Raise your hands – high – and keep them there," he ordered, a mere boy brandishing a .303 Lee Enfield rifle, salvaged off the corpse of a British soldier. Ricketts had then thrown away his own regular-issue Canadian Ross firearm, slow-firing and susceptible to jamming, of which Governor Davidson had ordered 500 at twenty-eight dollars each for the Regiment because Lee Enfields were in short supply.

The youth was joined immediately by several of his fellows and, in brief moments, for Stroesser and his compatriots the war was over.

They all stood around or lounged against the sides of a rat-infested dugout, waiting for the provost unit to come and take charge of the prisoners. The youthful soldier who had led the capture offered them tea, and bread laced with a sharp-tasting compote – "Homemade bread and partridgeberry jam. A mug-up from home, thanks to my mother and the Red Cross," he explained.

He next decided to bandage the head wound of one of the prisoners, replacing the muddy rag the man held to it.

"Now, my son, you sit down here. I'm going to clean that up a bit, and put a new bandage on it. And the rest of you, have a hot cup of tea, now!"

The German soldier looked dubious about submitting to the ministrations of his captor, but his officer, who understood some English, assured him it would be all right and the fellow allowed Ricketts to treat him. A small thing, perhaps, but Stroesser never forgot it, or the voice of the man who was prepared to help those who a few minutes earlier were doing their best to kill him, and he them!

He had no way of knowing that the other man had later been declared a hero out of the action, and received the Victoria Cross, the British Empire's highest honour for valour, at the hands of King George V at York Cottage, Sandringham, on January 21, 1919.

"The youngest V.C. in my army," His Majesty announced proudly. (Another member of Newfoundland's tiny wartime contingent to win the Victoria Cross was Private John B. Croke of Little Bay, less than three dozen miles from Ricketts's birthplace of Middle Arm, White Bay. Croke, who served with the Canadian Expeditionary Force, was cited for valour in an action during the Battle of Amiens in August 1918.)

And now, Stroesser thought, hardly able to believe it, here was that same fellow, more than two decades later – no *Englander*, in fact, but what the British derisively looked down upon as a damned colonial, and the Americans these days called a Newfie – standing not more than three or four feet away.

Ricketts interpreted his customer's struggle with his emotions as an attack of some sort, which in a way it was. He rushed out from behind the counter to offer a chair and a glass of water.

"Are you all right? Would you like me to call you a doctor?"

Stroesser shook his head, gulped down the water, and stumbled out the door, leaving Ricketts staring after him in mild wonder. However, the druggist reflected, the war did strange things to people, so he really was not greatly surprised by the man's behaviour. Little did he realize that they had met on the killing fields of an earlier war, and under very different circumstances!

Re-crossing Water Street, Stroesser paused, leaning momentarily to get his breath and recover his mental equilibrium against the base of the statue of Industry as she guarded the imposing railway headquarters. He cautiously skirted the structure and came to the passenger platform at the station's rear. There he could spot only one uniformed policeman, a seeming giant in heavy black melton greatcoat from neck to ankles, under a tall hat of black seal fur. It added at least another foot to the five feet, ten inches required of Newfoundland Constabulary recruits.

He moved quickly along to the edge of the crowd, carefully avoiding treacherous patches of ice, out of concern for his old leg injury – sustained here in Newfoundland, he remembered with a grimace – that had resulted in a noticeable limp. Ducking inside the grey stone station building, he purchased a ticket to Grand Falls Station, some sixty miles beyond Hattie's Camp, a lumbering whistle stop that was the site of the Newfoundland Airport, sometimes referred to as Gander after the huge lake nearby. He knew it had been included under a recently published government designation of "Prohibited Places." The regulation declared, in the best bureaucratic parlance, "If a railway passes through such a Prohibited Place, no person shall enter or leave the Prohibited Place except as a passenger on such railway." Just getting access to the airport would have been an insurmountable problem until Altehouse fortuitously came along. Now, perhaps, the problem could be solved.

He emerged just as a five-minute warning bell sounded to indicate the train's departure was imminent, and was startled to see off to his right a man he had encountered before – except that the bearded former deckhand on the Estonian trawler on which both had secured working passage to Newfoundland, Stroesser as an engine room assistant, had now assumed the appearance of a peddler, a not unfamiliar figure in Europe. Moving quickly towards the train, the man wore a rough woollen suit and had a packsack on his back.

Any number of Yiddish-speaking Jews had been turning up in Newfoundland, fleeing the *shtetls* of Eastern Europe in the face of Stalinist purges, and these days what he believed to be the justifiable efforts of the National Socialist government to end Jewish influence over German society. He had never questioned the murderous avalanche of the Nazi purification under which as many as six million would eventually be exterminated – a fate richly deserved, so far as Stroesser was concerned.

In Newfoundland not a few found a living, and a stake in future small businesses, as travelling salesmen once they received a letter of clearance from the Constabulary; most eventually set up clothing and variety stores in St. John's, Grand Falls, Corner Brook, and other centres. It was not difficult for those who secured a place with well-connected firms such as the big dry goods dealer I. F. Perlin & Co.; its founder, Israel, and his brother, Pyoter, had similarly emigrated from Eastern Russia via New York many years before. Their descendants had successfully integrated into the upper crust of St. John's society.

Stroesser knew he had no time to lose. He could not take the chance this man, who had given his name on the trawler's manifest as Chaim Isdor Friedmann, was not also a secret agent of some sort, representing some interest other than his own. The Newfoundland capital was full of them these days. The two had had heated arguments, on one occasion coming to fisticuffs, over the merits of Hitler's policies, especially the treatment of Jews in Germany. Friedmann – if that, indeed, was his name – could cause trouble, perhaps even denounce him to officials of the government railway, who would turn him over to the secret police that surely must be on board. As Friedmann mounted the steps to the railway coach, Stroesser, close behind, drove a snub-nosed pistol into the small of his back.

"Don't look around, *schweinhund*," he hissed. "Just keep moving!"

A few yards along the narrow corridor leading to the passenger seating area was a compartment prominently labelled "Toilet."

"Wha . . . what is this about?" the peddler stammered in heavily accented tones, thoroughly alarmed.

Stroesser growled, "In here," giving his prisoner a warning jab of the gun. "Be quiet or I'll kill you!"

Friedmann did as ordered. He turned a knob, the slatted door opened inwards, and together they pushed into the small space. Stroesser slammed the door shut with his left foot and reaching behind, locked it. As he did so, the train's whistle gave two quick, shrill blasts, its bell clanged, and clouds of steam and smoke issued from the engine as the drive wheels skidded into life.

With all that noise, Stroesser was certain nobody heard the report as the pistol slammed a bullet into the back of the peddler's neck just above the collar, ending his life instantly.

EIGHTEEN

On Board the "Newfie Bullet,"
February 1941

THE NEWFOUNDLAND RAILWAY had grandly named its trans-island passenger service The Overland Limited. American troops had another term for it – they derisively tagged the narrow-gauge line, with a top speed of forty-five miles per hour but in practice most often much less, the "Newfie Bullet." Filled to capacity with some 200 passengers and a dozen crew, the train lurched forward and began to pick up speed as it left the St. John's rail yards and entered the Waterford Valley. In the last couple of hours, the outline of a plan to assassinate Major Sir Frederick Grant Banting of the Royal Canadian Army Medical Corps had begun to fall into place in the mind of Karl Otto Stroesser.

But right now he had to deal with a body.

There was remarkably little blood from the neat hole beneath Friedmann's hairline, just at the point where the neck joins the torso. The body had convulsed a few times. Then, weighed down by the peddler's heavy packsack, it collapsed upon the brown-stained porcelain sink, slid down, and became wedged between it and the toilet bowl.

Stroesser freed it of its burden which he found, on quickly slipping the straps, to be neatly packed with jewellery and trinkets, women's lingerie, and other small items of apparel, plus pencils and India rubber erasers, various colours of chalk, and magnifying spectacles. There were packages of needles of all sizes, and spools of thread of many colours. He lost no time in going through the dead

man's pockets, and right away found what he was looking for –
identification papers. An official document, neatly typewritten and
contained in a manila envelope stamped OHMS, was in an inside
breast pocket. Under the Newfoundland Coat of Arms it read:

```
NEWFOUNDLAND CONSTABULARY
The Chief of Police


TO WHOM IT MAY CONCERN:


The bearer of this paper, which is issued in
duplicate, is Chaim Isdor Friedmann, a Subject of
the Union of Soviet Socialist Republics, latterly a
resident of the Weimar Republic (Germany) whose
request for Refugee Status is currently under
consideration by the Colonial Secretary in behalf
of the Commission of Government. Mr. Friedmann's
Guarantor pending a decision on his status is his
employer, I. F. Perlin & Co. For purposes of iden-
tification Mr. Friedmann's signature appears at
the foot hereof.


GIVEN UNDER MY HAND & SEAL OF
THE DEPARTMENT OF JUSTICE, THIS
10TH DAY OF JANUARY, A. D. 1941


PATRICK J. O'NEILL, J. P.
Chief of Police


MR. FRIEDMANN'S SIGNATURE
```

Stroesser inspected the heavy scrawl and decided it would not
be difficult to approximate if he had to satisfy some representative
of authority that he was the person named in the document. Mein
Gott, *what good fortune!*

In those few moments he decided that he would become Chaim Isdor Friedmann.

In other pockets he found a leather coin purse that contained a couple of small bills, a few coins, a small pocket knife, a pair of reading glasses in a case, and of course a train ticket, to some place named Badger, which he guessed was somewhat beyond his actual destination, that the peddler had purchased minutes before departure. Stroesser pocketed the purse with its contents, the knife, and the ticket. The glasses he also kept; they might help him change identity at some point. Then he switched off the lights and forced open the window of the little room. He grabbed Friedmann's overcoat by the lapels and, thankful for the gathering darkness outside that made it highly unlikely anyone along the train's route would notice, began to stuff the body through the opening.

Fortunately the peddler was not a big man and, after a brief struggle, the cadaver toppled into the darkness. As an afterthought, Stroesser tossed out his own "quiff" hat, as Newfoundlanders called it, a soft felt chapeau with a brim, exchanging it for the peddler's fur helmet, complete with earflaps, that would help his disguise.

At that moment the train was rattling across the South River trestle in publicly operated Bowring Park on the western outskirts of the city. The park was frequented by few people at this time of year. It should be months before the river, freed of its cover of ice and snow, would give up its macabre burden, which then would be swept down to the harbour. When discovered, it would be entered into police files as badly decomposed, unidentified remains, most likely of a foreign seaman.

No sooner had Stroesser slammed down the window, shutting off the blast of cold, damp air laced with coal smoke, and inspected his clothing for telltale spatters of blood – he found none – than a fist hammered on the door of the cubicle.

"Tickets! Have your tickets ready!"

He turned the lights back on, hoisted the packsack onto his right shoulder, picked up his suitcase, and turned the knob to yank open the door.

Conductor Walsh and his assistant, Anthony Spurvey, were standing by the water cooler where the younger man had just withdrawn a folded-up paper cup from a dispenser. He squeezed it at the sides to open it, held it under the tap, and depressed a handle to obtain a drink of ice water.

"Well, Spurvey," the older man asked, "did your sister get married on the weekend as planned?"

"Yes, sir," the assistant replied, "and quite the party it was. Up to St. Patrick's with Monsignor Kitchin doing the honours. The good Monsignor had a few words to say about wartime romances and the courage it takes for couples to stay together in good faith when they're split apart by the war. My mother says it was really a warning that true love is hard to find, or to keep, when you're far from home and dodging bombs, bullets, and torpedoes. I'm sure she's afraid my sister's husband is already married, with a wife somewhere in the States."

He rolled with the movement of the train, holding the cup away from his body to avoid spilling the contents on his uniform, a poor replica of that of his boss.

"You know, my new brother-in-law is a top sergeant in the U.S. Corps of Engineers. They're building the base down to Quidi Vidi Lake. He told me there's lots of jobs down there, and going to be more. The pay is good, too, but the government won't let Newfoundlanders make the same money as the Yanks."

"That's right," Walsh confirmed. "They don't want Newfoundlanders working on the base earning more than the rest of us. Could cause a lot of trouble – with perhaps a lot of the best people leaving their ordinary jobs, like here at the railway, for instance, for to go to work for the Americans. Could cause quite a bit of social disruption, I should say. We can do without that!"

Spurvey thought for a moment, not anxious to differ with his superior. "Well, I don't know . . . . I like the idea of equal pay for equal work – I think I'd be really upset to have the guy next to me getting more for the same job."

"Speaking of work," Walsh cut the conversation short, "let's get on with the tickets. Is there someone in that toilet?"

"Yeh, here he comes now," Spurvey said as Stroesser emerged, free hand fumbling with a button at the front of his trousers to suggest the visit to the facilities was completely normal.

"Ticket, please." Walsh appraised the man who emerged with knapsack and suitcase.

"Didn't you see the sign, 'Do Not Use Toilet When Train Is Standing in Station'?" he demanded. "Where are you bound?"

Stroesser fumbled in the leather purse and produced the ticket he had purchased minutes before, trying not to look nervous, or guilty, or too nonchalant.

"Grand Falls Station," he answered. "Travelling for Mr. Perlin." He had read the identification letter carefully, and now was glad he had done so.

The conductor applied his punch, cancelling the ticket by leaving a small cutout in it, and he and his assistant moved on.

"Tickets, please. Have your tickets ready!"

In the dim light of the coach, Stroesser had to search for a seat that was not already occupied, and finally found it near the middle of the car. There a pleasingly plump young blond woman was hanging on to three young children and had stowed some of their luggage in the unoccupied space. As she moved their things onto the floor, under their own seats, he caught a flash of slim legs, a well-turned ankle.

"Here, you could sit here," she offered with a welcoming smile, gathering a thin cloth coat closer around her and indicating the empty seat. Wary of the unsolicited offer, his first instinct was to decline. But the prospect of possibly standing the entire distance made him think better of it. Besides, as a travelling companion, she presented a tempting prospect.

"Thank you, thank you," he said in deliberately heavily accented English, determined nonetheless to keep to himself if that was possible. He had too much on his mind, far too much, to engage in frivolity, far too much of importance to allow his attention to be diverted.

However, the children, two boys about five or six or seven, and a girl somewhat older, occupied the seats opposite. He was no sooner settled, suitcase under his seat and knapsack between his feet, than they introduced themselves.

"I'm Ingrid; how do you do?" the girl announced. Her blond hair like her mother's, he guessed she was perhaps ten or twelve, no more. She offered her hand and Stroesser had little choice but to take it.

"And I am, ah, Chaim . . ." A split second's hesitation, but he'd had to search his memory for the first name on the identification paper. *Mein Gott*, he thought to himself, *what is the matter with me? Good thing it was just a youngster I was dealing with, not the conductor or a policeman!*

". . . Friedmann, how do you do?"

He was more than ever aware that his accent, while foreign-sounding to most people, might not convince certain others that he was neither Dutch, nor the Soviet Jew that he now pretended to be, but exactly what he was trying to hide – both German and a spy!

"I am Torstein," the older of the boys informed him. The younger added gravely, "And I am Knut."

All Norwegian names, he told himself, as each in turn held his hand out and Stroesser took them in his own. *Bloody Norwegians!*

His mind went back to the bitter resistance mounted against occupying German forces in Oslo, Bergen, and Trondheim. His own son had died of injuries after an insurgent's bomb destroyed a popular café in the capital.

What are they doing here?

Now it was their mother's turn.

"And I, sir, am Gudrid . . . . Our family name is Nilssen."

As if reading his mind, she related how, with her husband and the children, she had come to St. John's some weeks earlier to be with her father, resident buying agent for Norwegian fish merchants. He had suffered a stroke and died soon after their arrival. The husband, Knut, Sr., a naval officer, had been summoned to join his ship in the Norwegian coastal patrol, but with the occupation of their homeland, it would not be possible for the family to return to their home in Bergen. Instead, they were bound for the Canadian capital of Ottawa to stay with her married sister for the duration.

"Do you know anything about the ferry ship to Canada?" she asked, explaining that they came from Norway via England, crossing the Atlantic on one of the Furness Line ships direct from Liverpool, the RMS *Newfoundland*.

"Not much," he lied. "But I have heard that the SS *Caribou* is a very nice boat . . . . Very nice, very safe . . ."

As the train progressed, its whistle sounding at level crossings and the passage of steel wheels over track joints producing a rhythmic *clackity-clack*, he turned away and pretended to yawn broadly, feigning sleepiness to escape further conversation.

On fine mornings, even in winter if there was not too much snow on the ground, Jack Ryan and his wife Amy liked to exercise their hunting dog, a Blue Belton setter named Grouse, on walks in Bowring Park.

"The jewel in the crown" of the ancient city, people called the beautifully landscaped area in the West End of St. John's. It had been donated to the citizens by the merchant family whose name it bore, Bowring Brothers Ltd., prominent in many areas of the economy for well over a hundred years. With motorable roads and walking trails, facilities for tennis, swimming, and boating, developed picnic areas, together with a wide variety of planted trees and extensive flower beds, it was a popular destination most of the time for residents and visitors alike.

In mid-winter, however, it was little frequented except by a few hardy souls like Ryan, a First World War veteran of the Royal

Newfoundland Regiment who had left an arm in France, and his Trinity-born wife, hunting buddies in season on the Southern Shore barrens.

Near the spot where a railway bridge spanned the South River, Grouse began acting strangely. He raced out on the river ice and began running in circles around what appeared to be a bundle of some sort lying in the snow.

"Here, Grouse . . . . Grouse, get back here!" Ryan demanded in his normal gravelly voice, but to no avail. Instead, the well-trained, ordinarily obedient canine stood there, legs planted wide apart, barking at his master and seeming to say, "No . . . . You come here and see what I've got."

In the end that's what the Ryans did, moving carefully so as to avoid breaking through the ice. Brushing away the snow that partially buried the object, they saw at once the reason for the hunting dog's excitement. The bundle was the body of a man, slightly built, bearded, with what immediately drew a hunter's eye – a telltale purplish entry-wound at the back of the neck and powder burns. He had been shot at close range with a small-calibre pistol.

The headquarters of the Newfoundland Rangers, the country's rural police force, was in the process of being relocated from Whitbourne, some sixty miles away, to a location only a few hundred yards away near the Kilbride Bridge over the main Waterford River, of which the South River was a tributary. In a few minutes the Ryans had reported the grisly find to this nearest police station.

The Rangers soon cordoned off the area, but because it was within the jurisdiction of the Newfoundland Constabulary, and they themselves were not yet officially established at Kilbride, they turned the matter over to the Constabulary's Criminal Investigation Division. Three men from the C.I.D.'s plainclothes force, led by Inspector Cahill, searched but found nothing – either on the body or around it – to identify it or to tell what had happened.

A sketch was prepared for the newspapers. Perhaps a reader would recognize the face and help solve the mystery of the body in the park.

In the offices of the St. John's *Daily News* on Duckworth Street, Albert Benjamin Perlin was working on his "Wayfarer" column of personal observations on the news for the next day's Editorial Page, having already "put to bed" the editorials that represented the paper's institutional position. He was sure there were readers who, knowing editor and columnist were one and the same person, must have wondered that the two did not always or necessarily agree. As he pecked away with nicotine-stained fingers on an ancient typewriter, the street door opened, and on a gust of cold wind a familiar figure entered – Inspector Cahill of the Newfoundland Constabulary's Criminal Investigation Division.

"Good afternoon, Inspector," Perlin greeted him, stubbing out his cigarette. "Can I help you?"

"Mr. Perlin," Cahill said, taking the proffered hand. "I was hoping to catch one of your news reporters – Jack A. White, perhaps, or Art Pratt, or Eric Seymour."

However, Perlin explained that most of the morning newspaper's staff, of necessity, worked an evening shift, so there were few people about in the mid-afternoon, especially reporters. "But, maybe I can do something for you?"

"Well, it's like this," the policeman said. "We've had a body discovered in Bowring Park, a man who could be thirty-five or so, but with not a stick of identification on him. I have a facial photograph, but if you prefer not to publish such unpleasantness, we've also provided an artist's sketch, in the hope your readers can help us figure out who he is."

Cahill slid the photograph, taken at the General Hospital morgue, and the sketch, from a large official envelope. He handed them to the newspaper editor, who studied them intently.

"In Bowring Park, you say." He was pensive, lit another cigarette, and inhaled deeply. "How did he die, and do you know when?"

Cahill told him it appeared the man had been shot to death, possibly within the past couple of days. There was even a chance he might have fallen or been dumped from a passing train.

"Inspector," Perlin said quietly, "I may be wrong, but I believe I know this fellow, or at least that I have seen him before, alive and well. He was hired a few weeks ago to work for our family firm, I. F. Perlin & Company, name of Chaim Friedmann.

"But he's supposed to be on a selling trip out west of Grand Falls, in the Badger area. My God – shot, and in Bowring Park. I wonder what could have happened?"

On emerging from *The Daily News*, Inspector Cahill instructed his driver to take him to Bowring Park. In conformity with blackout regulations, the sedan's headlights were hooded to permit only narrow slits of light aiming downward, invisible from the air. In the gathering gloom of a winter's afternoon, it would soon be time to switch them on.

"Any particular place in the park, sir?" Constable Selby Hounsell asked, thinking in terms of snow conditions and his ability to navigate unplowed park roads, even with tire chains.

"I'd like to take a look around the railway trestle over the South River," Cahill replied, "so get as close as you can short of becoming stuck."

The weather had been unseasonably mild, with little new snow. There was nothing notable to be seen. Other than a better sense of exactly where the grim discovery had occurred, a chilly walk-around added little to Cahill's knowledge of the man in the photograph, or what had happened to him.

"All right, Constable, let's go down to the railway station," he said, climbing back into the vehicle.

Approaching the imposing granite building on Water Street, Cahill remembered he had to pick up a prescription, and instructed Hounsell to stop at T. Ricketts, Druggist.

"Tommy, how are you?" he greeted the proprietor.

Ricketts smiled a slow smile and said, "Well, Inspector" – he paused as Cahill grimaced slightly –"all right then, Mike . . . . We don't often see you up this way. What can I do for you?"

"Oh, don't worry – you're not in any trouble with the law," Cahill laughed. "I came in to get some medicine for the wife."

The druggist had the preparation ready in a few minutes, and as Cahill fished some money from his pocket, said half apologetically. "Mike, this may sound a bit crazy, but . . . . There was a man in here the other day. I'm sure he was a German soldier in Flanders in the Great War. I couldn't help wondering what he was doing in Newfoundland, going out on the train to Grand Falls, or Botwood, I think it was.

"The thing is, he seemed so nervous. I was concerned that he was going to collapse, and then I thought, 'Is he up to something?' Maybe there's nothing at all to it, but . . . . You know, I think I may have his name somewhere. If I can find it, I'll call you. Good to see you again!"

Back in the car, Cahill checked his notebook. Was there a chance the same conductor would be heading out again on today's train, leaving in a matter of minutes?

He was in luck. Walsh was standing on the platform, smiling and greeting passengers as they arrived, preparing to call his "All aboard!" that the policeman thought must be the highlight of his day.

Cahill lost no time describing his interest, and displaying the photograph earlier shown to Perlin.

"Sorry, Inspector," Walsh told him, "but I can't say I've ever seen this fellow. Can you tell me his name?"

"Friedmann. Chaim Isdor Friedmann," Cahill told him. "Not what you'd call a common name around Newfoundland, I wouldn't say."

172

"Hmmm . . . Now *that* rings a bell," the train conductor said, "but this" – he tapped the photograph with a fingernail – "isn't his face."

The American officer assigned to the tiny Allied detachment in Botwood was Lt. William Parmiter Graves, United States Army Air Corps, from Little Rock, Arkansas. He couldn't help himself. He glared at the man standing to attention in front of him, and would have refused him leave only a couple of weeks into his assignment there – if he could have.

But he dared not. Altehouse's orders gave him specific authority to be away on temporary duty, in air corps short-hand TDY, at his own discretion. It was an unusual arrangement.

"I have to tell you I ain't never before heard of such a thing," Graves sputtered. "Just imagine, a man being free to take off whenever he feels like it. I intend to take an official exception to it, I can tell you that."

"Yes, sir," Altehouse said, in an obvious attempt to humour him. "That is perfectly understandable in your position, but . . ."

Adopting a conspiratorial tone, he went on.

"The truth is, sir, that General Martin in Burbank had to get someone on the scene up here in Newfinland to check out what's happening with his airplanes. Three crashes last week alone, in Texas, in New Jersey, and one in Canada.

"Reporting on the flying boats, as I'm sure you know better than I, is a cover. The real reason for my being here is to find out why some of those bombers that are supposed to be going over to the Brits never reach there. It's a critical matter, sir."

"All right, Altehouse, I'll sign your TDY. Guess I don't have much choice, since you're here on the General's personal order," Graves said, sounding somewhat mollified at the explanation. "Do I dare ask why you're going up to Grand Falls. Do you figure there are some spies and saboteurs up there?"

"Thank you, sir," Altehouse replied with some relief. "I wish I could tell you more, but I'm sure you appreciate it's all top secret. Ah, I wonder . . . "

"Is there something else . . . ?"

"Yes, sir, I need you to arrange for me to get on the train up to Grand Falls this afternoon."

"Damn . . . this afternoon! That's a tall order."

He got up and went to the door connecting to the Orderly Room.

"Sergeant," he instructed Newfoundland Militia member Robert Innes, a soldier in full battledress who presided over detachment administration, "we need to arrange for our friend here to get up to Grand Falls this afternoon. Maybe a bottle of good Scotch for the man in charge will help, but" – he turned to Altehouse – "you'll have to take it out of your liquor allowance. We're on rations here, you know."

"Yes, sir . . . . It'll be my pleasure. I'm a beer drinker, anyway, so it won't bother me too much."

NINETEEN

Canada's National Capital,
Ottawa, Ontario, 1941

A STRANGER TO Canada's capital, not knowing any better, might be forgiven for mistaking the Chateau Laurier for an integral part of the sprawling government complex generally referred to as "Parliament Hill," rather than a commercial, railway-built hotel just down the street from the seats of power.

Not only did it closely resemble the architecture of nearby stone-and-brick government structures, which had come to be characterized by some as "high Victorian gothic" or "chateau style," but it was the favourite haunt of most prominent politicians and government officials, as accommodation, as a meeting place, or both. So it was that, at virtually any time of the day or night, it might appear from the proliferation of ministers, deputy ministers, Members of Parliament, Senators, senior staff, lobbyists, and just plain folk looking for just plain favours, in the lobbies, the bars, the conference rooms, and, in particular, the famous Canadian Grill, that this was where the nation's business was mainly transacted. And in so concluding, the stranger might as often be right as wrong.

The Chateau Laurier had taken four years to build, from 1908 to 1912, as the Grand Trunk Railway sought to compete with other lines, especially the Canadian Pacific, in the provision of "dining stations . . . with sleeping rooms" for travellers. When the bankrupt G.T.R. was taken over by the federal government and reorganized into Canadian National Railways between 1919 and 1923, the 485-room hotel was along for the ride.

The best part of visiting the national capital was the night train over from Toronto. Leaving downtown Union Station in the late afternoon, there was time for a civilized drink or two in the club car with the attendant, pleasant camaraderie one could expect there, prior to partaking in the perennially excellent fare in the dining car. Otherwise, Banting did not much like Ottawa, or the powerful bureaucracy that populated it. But the truth was that, at least in a peripheral way, he was part of the whole thing. And, he did enjoy the power; it really got things done.

Unbeknownst to him, there was planned to take place tonight a farewell reception for a man who was leaving the senior bureaucracy, after a period of distinguished public service, to return to the world of private business. And it was here that fate, in the guise of a series of unanticipated events, and with the assistance of Nazi agents, would begin to arrange the death of Sir Frederick Banting.

As a member of Canada's National Research Council, chairman of its Associate Committee on Medical Research, and chairman of its Associate Committee on Aviation Medicine, Banting could always be certain of a full agenda on his visits to Ottawa. Today was no exception. He had completed his business and was rushing out the door to catch an evening train back to Toronto, when the telephone rang in his room at the Chateau.

The caller was Chalmers Jack Mackenzie, former dean of engineering at the University of Saskatchewan, who had recently been appointed to head the Council. Its president, Lieutenant General A. G. L McNaughton, on being given command of Canadian troops in England, had personally selected Mackenzie to replace himself – in an acting capacity, however, as he hoped in time to return to the NRC – and the King government had concurred. The New Brunswick–born engineer had thus become Canada's chief scientist at least for the duration of the Second World War.

"Banting? It's Jack Mackenzie here . . . . Look, there's a small reception this evening in the Canadian Grill – cocktails, hors d'oeuvres, the usual thing – for Jim Duncan.

"You know he's headed back to the private sector, but he did put his business interests on the shelf to get the Air Ministry on a solid footing as deputy minister, and he deserves all our thanks for that. Thought you might like to come along."

"Well, I'd have to cancel my train reservation," Banting replied, "and arrange a later one. And let my wife, Henrietta, know I'll not get home until tomorrow. But I believe you're right, Jack. It's important that we show appreciation for someone who has made a tremendously significant contribution to the war effort."

Duncan, formerly a powerful Toronto businessman, would have even more influence now, Banting thought shrewdly. His support could mean much to the future of the Banting Institute and the work carried on there.

As for the war, it was perpetually on Banting's mind. Fifteen months had passed since the invasion of Poland blasted open the floodgates of death and destruction. Even though British and Commonwealth airmen had beaten Goering's *Luftwaffe* at its own terrible game in the Battle of Britain, and, subsequently, there was no suggestion Hitler had abandoned or would abandon his plan to invade and subjugate England, as he had done most of Europe.

Therefore Germany must be defeated utterly – and Banting burned to be part of it, to be on the scene in Britain, playing a more significant role in the fight for freedom and against tyranny than he felt was possible in Canada.

He had made several overtures in this regard to McNaughton, and more recently, since the general's return to uniform and his own departure for England to become Canadian commander overseas, to Mackenzie. Each had been reluctant to let him go, even temporarily. He was needed in Canada, they said. Besides, the long ocean passage on a corvette or destroyer, and more especially a merchant vessel, would be dangerous as well as time-wasting. In any event, what could he achieve of value? He had already and repeatedly assailed the British for their failure to mount a substantial biological warfare program – both defensive and offensive – and there seemed little more that could now be done to persuade them.

"I suggest that we consider the matter closed," Mackenzie said when they last discussed it. "I just don't feel we should take the risk of having you go over there. Indeed, I'd appreciate it were you to turn your mind to other things, priorities that we have to deal with here in Canada."

It was a reproof that Mackenzie would have preferred not to deliver. The very idea of having to accuse a Nobel laureate, a decorated war hero, and a serving officer with the King's commission, of the next thing to insubordination troubled him tremendously. But he did not feel he had a choice. Banting, meanwhile, had been determined to keep trying, and although he had no way of knowing it, the reception to which he had just been invited – ironically by Mackenzie himself – would turn out to offer his best opportunity so far.

Rather than have an extra charge for keeping a room in which he did not intend to sleep, Banting went down to the lobby and checked out as planned. He lodged his suitcase and briefcase with the bell captain, to be picked up later. Then he headed for the Canadian Grill.

As the tall, striking figure in the uniform of a decorated Canadian Army officer entered, heads turned and there was a scattering of applause among the gathering crowd as word quickly spread as to his identity – a genuinely famous Canadian of the age.

One of the first to approach Banting, hand outstretched, was Air Marshal Albert Abraham Lawson Cuffe. An Irishman who emigrated to Canada in 1914 from County Mayo, Cuffe had enlisted in the Canadian Expeditionary Force in the First World War, and become one of the first instructors in the Royal Flying Corps. As the Second World War began, he had risen to the top ranks of the Royal Canadian Air Force, and now was the man in charge of its Eastern Command.

"It's good to see you again, Major Banting," Cuffe greeted him warmly.

"I can't tell you how much we appreciate the work you chaps in aviation medicine have been doing to develop pressurized flying suits. They have been making a huge difference in the ability of our pilots, and the British and other Commonwealth fellows, of course, to stand up to the G-forces in high-speed manoeuvres. A huge difference. No more blackouts, or fear of blackouts, means a higher degree of confidence – which, of course, equals a higher degree of success. It really is helping us to win the war!"

Banting was obviously flattered.

"Thank you, Air Marshal –" he began to reply, pausing to obtain a Scotch and water, no ice, from a passing waiter.

"– but you know, it's a tricky business. We can try to gauge the effects, or more importantly, the overcoming of the effects, by simulating steep dives and pullouts, that sort of thing, but the actual experience of your pilots cannot really be duplicated. We should be grateful to have any documented reports of how well the suits work – or don't work, as the case may be. Sort of like testimonials from the men who wear them.

"While we have a minute, Air Marshal, I want to explore the possibility of hitching a ride to Britain on one of your airplanes," he said. Their glasses recharged, Banting used the opportunity to further his chances of getting to England.

"It's quite important, actually, that it be soon. I can go by ship, the Navy are agreed to take me, but the delay and, quite frankly, the seasickness factor, make it a rather daunting proposition. Besides, Jack Mackenzie is extremely concerned over the increase in Nazi U-boat activity. He's convinced that for me to go by ship would be a highly dangerous journey, and is not anxious to lose a double associate committee chairman of the NRC. What can you do for me there?" He did not reveal that Mackenzie was totally against his going at all.

"Well, Sir Frederick, I don't see why not, really," Cuffe replied without hesitation. "Now that Atfero – that's the Atlantic Ferry Command, which is really the C.P.R., not quite 'ours' yet – has begun flying Hudsons via St. Hubert and the Newfoundland Airport to the other side, there should be empty planes going over every other week. It shouldn't be a big problem to arrange it for you.

"I'd have to go through channels, of course, but I'm sure I could have a positive answer in a week or so."

Banting had hardly finished expressing his appreciation to Cuffe when the guest of honour, Duncan, arrived and was escorted around the room by Mackenzie. Coming to Banting, the retiring Deputy Minister was obviously pleased and flattered to find the famous, and, he assumed, extremely busy scientist honouring the occasion.

"Sir Frederick!" he exclaimed. "So good of you to come. I know how much you must have on your plate. I was hoping to see you again before I left Ottawa, but of course, we'll run into each other in Toronto."

"To tell you the truth," Banting responded with a firm hand-shake, "I'm looking forward to it. I'd like you to visit the Banting Institute – might even try to entice you to become involved in the good work we're doing there."

"You've got me interested already," Duncan replied with a broad smile.

To say Mackenzie was upset on learning that Banting had taken matters into his own hands in making the request to Cuffe, and had done so in defiance of what was virtually a direct order to abandon the idea of going to England, would be an understatement.

The question, of course, was what to do about it. The National Research Council president was loath to allow the issue to become a public controversy, which he was sure would happen if he involved the government. In truth, he harboured an inherent distrust of politicians, and his experience as a bureaucrat had served to reinforce it. He also had little desire to become embroiled in an open disagreement with the armed forces concerning one of their own, and a very prominent one at that. The outcome, were he to pursue that route, could be disastrous.

Mackenzie's alternative was to refer the matter to McNaughton, in Britain. The general, he was certain, would know what to do.

As it turned out, the general chose to allow matters to take their course.

"A decision to do nothing," he told himself, "is a decision nonetheless."

In the Ottawa railway station, not far from the entrance to the marble-lined tunnel that permitted travellers bound for the Chateau Laurier to cross the confluence of Wellington and Rideau Streets without ever going outdoors, Eddie Henninger was engaged in a heated argument on the telephone.

"I'm telling you he didn't show – didn't come to the station, and damn well didn't board that train," Henninger repeated, voice rising. He jammed a foot against the folding door of the telephone booth, keeping it tightly shut so as not to be overheard outside. He held the phone away from his ear while the person on the other end fulminated.

"Look," he finally shouted, "you told me to wait for him on the platform, which I did. When he didn't turn up there, I let you know and you said to check the train, which I did. Then you told me to make sure he checked out, which I did – and he had. Now you say you've lost him, and it's all my fault?

"What I want to know is, where do I collect my thousand bucks? And make it snappy – I haven't got all night, or you'll be sorry you messed around with Eddie Henninger!"

"Please don't threaten me," the voice on the other end of the line snapped, coldly clipping off the words. "I don't like it one bit."

A sharp *click* on the line indicated that he then hung up.

A petty criminal with a long record, Henninger needed the money to pay the rent and keep the flat or his girlfriend would walk. He hadn't done anything like this before, and was close to making up his mind that he wouldn't again. He didn't like the smell of it. But for now, he had to have the cash, so he headed for the Bank Street tavern where a mousy little man with a German accent had hired him to stick a knife in Sir Frederick Banting – an ill-conceived, carelessly arranged, clumsy effort totally lacking in the sophistication and finesse that the importance of the target demanded.

Banting never knew that the price on his head that evening was a paltry one thousand dollars, but someone in the Nazi hierarchy had decided it would be simpler and easier to get rid of the scientist here in sleepy Ottawa than, say, on University Avenue in Toronto. They would have to try again.

"Okay, where's my money?" Henninger demanded.

"Come in the toilet," the mousy little man said. "I'll get it for you."

A couple of hours later, the manager forced open the door of one of the cubicles. Eddie Henninger was sitting there, staring silently into space, his throat slit from ear to ear.

Jack MacKenzie's worrying over stepped-up German submarine activity was underscored one placid Saturday morning when his home telephone rang at an ungodly hour.

"Jack! Have you heard about Howe?"

"What? Who?" he replied, hardly awake.

"Your friend C. D. Howe – the Minister of Everything . . . . He's been torpedoed on the way to Britain. Nobody knows yet whether he's dead or alive!"

The caller, a former colleague at the University of Saskatchewan, recently recruited to Ottawa to work in the Privy Council Office, had heard the rumours almost as quickly as the news reached the Prime Minister: Howe had been en route to England with several aides for an important defence conference when their ship, the SS *Western Prince*, was sunk by a Nazi U-boat on approaching the English Channel. One of his colleagues, Gordon Scott of Montréal, was lost, and Howe with other survivors spent several days drifting in a lifeboat before being rescued.

Eventually the ebullient minister found his way back to Canada, hitching a ride on board HMS *King Gerorge V*, a newly minted, 35,000-ton Royal Navy battleship assigned to deliver Lord Halifax, the new British Ambassador to the United States, to Annapolis, Maryland. Howe arrived at the Ottawa railway station to be greeted by Prime Minister King and other colleagues.

"Well, Howe, I'm glad to see you back," said King. "How are you?"

"Oh, I'm fine," the minister replied. "It wasn't really so bad."

He declined reporters' requests for details of his narrow escape, saying they had already been reported in the newspapers. However, he spoke sorrowfully of the death of Scott.

Meanwhile, in Conception Bay, Newfoundland, practically on the doorstep of St. John's and under the noses of Royal Canadian Navy patrols, as crew members of the SS *Saganaga* slept late, a torpedo buried itself in the port side of the freighter at 11:37 a.m. Newfoundland Daylight Time. Seconds later, a second "tin fish" struck the ship, loaded with iron ore from the nearby Bell Island mines and bound for the Dominion Steel and Coal furnaces in Sydney, Nova Scotia.

A cloud of wreckage, human body parts, and a geyser of red haematite ore rose hundreds of feet in the air. When it dissipated the ship had vanished, taking with her thirty members of her forty-eight-man crew.

A half-hour passed while the search continued for missing members of the *Saganaga*'s complement. Suddenly, an explosion tore open the hull of the freighter SS *Lord Strathcona*, also loaded and prepared to sail for Sydney and waiting off nearby Little Bell Island for convoy protection. After a second torpedo struck, she sank in less than two minutes. Fortunately the crew of forty-two plus three naval gunners had been ordered to take to the lifeboats right after the *Saganaga* was attacked, so all survived.

Two other vessels, the SS *PLM 27*, similarly loaded for Sydney, and the SS *Evelyn "B,"* waiting to discharge a cargo of coal, remained on the anchorage between Little Bell Island and Lance Cove. And as well, to the east, the SS *Rose Castle* was loading iron ore at the Scotia Pier and the SS *Drakepool* was offloading freight at the nearby Dominion Pier preliminary to also taking on iron ore. The crew of the collier, who fired their deck gun in the submarine's presumed direction, as did a Newfoundland Militia shore battery, were credited with driving the marauder off, but more likely it was the belated arrival on the scene of Canadian corvettes and Fairmile patrol boats that did it.

A few weeks later, it happened that Governor Walwyn, who had been pursuing a customary vice-regal duty, was returning to Government House from an official visit "around the Bay" to the nearby heavily populated communities along the Conception Bay shore. As the chauffeured limousine swept through Long Pond, Manuels his practised sailor's eye caught sight of vessels lying-to in the same unsheltered Bell Island anchorage where two ore carriers had so recently been torpedoed and sunk. His binoculars picked up a patrolling corvette, barely visible and so far out to sea as to be useless to protect the ships against attack.

"Bloody hell," he railed at the Commissioner for Defence the next morning, "the navy should know better than to permit it, and I should hope you would tell them so. It is nothing short of ridiculous for those ships to be out there, unprotected, waiting for some damned U-boat to pick them off, instead of inside the protection of St. John's harbour . . . and the corvette, of course, too far off to do any good.

"I tell you now, Emerson, we are going to have another disaster at Bell Island" – another embarrassing incident, he might have said – "if they don't wake up."

TWENTY

Grand Falls Station, Central Newfoundland, 1941

THE TRAIN RATTLED along with Stroesser, in common with most of his fellow travellers, dozing uncomfortably in his seat. A few took turns curling up so as to temporarily occupy an entire two-person space, while their mates moved aimlessly around, stood half-asleep where they could find some wall space to lean against, or sat on the floor. Some of the men lounged in the smoker, while occasionally a passenger would seek fresh air on the break between cars, only to flee back inside moments later to escape the extreme cold, the swirling engine smoke that attacked the lungs, and the cinder ash that inevitably assaulted the eyes.

In view of the fact that he had been pressing the High Command to take action against the SS *Caribou*, Stroesser told himself that he probably should not have assured the woman Nilssen that the ferry was "very safe." At any time, in fact, it could come under U-boat attack, perhaps during the very crossing when this mother and her three children were on board.

Considering the fact crossings between North Sydney, Nova Scotia, and Port aux Basques, Newfoundland were made at night, if the ferry should be attacked, the chances were that the loss of life in the darkness of the often stormy Gulf of St. Lawrence would be enormous. He had considered offering the woman a revised opinion, as it were – perhaps suggesting that the ship was not so safe after all. But to what end? Would she then cancel the trip to Ottawa? He seriously doubted it. Besides, this might have required him to provide an explanation that he obviously was not prepared to give.

In the end, he shook himself mentally and abandoned the idea and any further consideration of it. *Damn it . . . what is going on with me?* he wondered. *Am I having a belated attack of guilty conscience? These may be the relatives, or at least fellow citizens, of those who murdered my own son. Why am I suddenly concerned for their welfare?*

It was just after half past five in the morning when Conductor James Templeton, displaying remarkable consideration, passed through the car to announce quietly, so as not to awaken the whole train, "Grand Falls Station, next stop." Within a very few minutes there was a perceptible slowing down. Then the train came smoothly to a halt with a long sigh as excess steam escaped from the drive cylinders.

Railway Agent Edward Callahan emerged from the station building into the bitterly cold early morning with train orders in his hand. He shivered, pulled the collar of his overcoat tighter around the neck, and hauled his salt-and-pepper cap down over his ears. Approaching the engine he handed the documents up to his old friend, Engineer Joseph Byrne, a bear of a man known to everyone who worked for the railway.

"Just talking to Millertown Junction on the key, Joe," said Callahan, who had learned his trade as a railway telegrapher after he and his wife Anastasia decided to give up the risky Labrador stationer fishery for the security of a railway job. They moved their family from Harbour Grace to the growing community literally across the tracks from Grand Falls, booming economically, thanks to its pulp and paper mill. Grand Falls Station would shortly be incorporated as the Town of Windsor.

"There's starting to be a buildup of snow on the Topsails. I'm sure you and Tom'll be glad to hear that!" Callahan said with a grim laugh. Byrne reacted with an oath and Tom Robertson, the fireman riding beside him in the cab of the engine, made a face and swore as Templeton came up in time to get the bad news first-hand.

All had had their experiences with trains being stuck for days, even weeks, on the inland plain that was home to the Main, Gaff, Mizzen, and Fore Topsails – a succession of rocky promontories named for the masts of a sailing ship and rising hundreds of feet. The fierce winds, extreme cold, and snow buildup in the area were legendary. One story, likely apocryphal, had it that with food running low after two weeks snowbound on the Gaff, Byrne found a bare flat rock where he lodged a signalman's lantern fuelled with the last cupful of kerosene oil on the train. Returning the next morning, he harvested a dozen rabbits frozen to death staring at the light.

On board, the Nilssens did not stir, neither the mother, whom he regarded with some small regret for not having time or opportunity to get to know her, nor the children. Stroesser heaved himself out of his seat, picked up his suitcase and the peddler's packsack, and in seconds was out into the night, clear, moonlit, and bitterly cold. Minutes after his feet touched the ground, the locomotive's whistle gave two short, almost plaintive blasts, and the train was smoothly under way again.

Altehouse was waiting. In response to the urgent telegraph message sent the previous morning, right after Stroesser returned from the U-boat rendezvous off Quidi Vidi Gut, Altehouse had come up from Botwood on the Anglo-Newfoundland Development Company's railway, which was how it got its newsprint product to the docks for shipment to market. Then, using his master sergeant's rank and authority, he managed to scrounge a three-quarter-ton lorry on loan from the local United States Army communications detachment known locally as the Repeater Station.

"I am very pleased to see you again," Stroesser told him civilly as he climbed into the warm comfort of the vehicle. "Right on time, too."

They had considered Altehouse's situation following his arrival on board the *Edmund B. Alexander*, and agreed that a brief sojourn in Botwood, while his role was being sorted out, was advisable. There was no need for more discussion of that matter at this stage.

"You know, there is one thing above all others that is to be admired in military personnel," Stroesser remarked pointedly, as they got under way, "and that is punctuality. The absolute foundation of discipline. I don't see how we could ever function without it. I should also say that I do not like being kept waiting.

"I also admire a man who appreciates that there are times when action, fast and decisive, is necessary," he went on, "and that there is no room for questioning or quibbling. I myself am here under rather precipitate orders, and the selfsame situation exists, of course, for you. Thank you, Master Sergeant, for your ready co-operation."

He could see that Altehouse was pleased to be so complimented. Stroesser had learned a long time ago that, to inspire confidence in subordinates, it was necessary to display confidence in them in the first instance.

"I greatly appreciate your saying so. Thank you, sir," the younger man replied respectfully, disregarding the fact that he was unaware of Stroesser's military rank – if, indeed, he had any. On the other hand, the older man's *Abwehr* credentials were signed personally by Admiral Canaris, a right-hand man of the Führer, and that was certainly impressive.

"I appreciate the opportunity to work with an experienced agent such as yourself. I hope to learn quite a lot from you about the espionage business."

The lorry wheeled up to the front door of the Cabot House hotel on the main street in Grand Falls, where Altehouse had rented a double room. On the way upstairs, they stopped at the kitchen. It was still too early for staff to be up and about, but he had ordered sandwiches to be left, and coffee waiting to be perked, only to be switched on.

"The first and most important thing to remember is that we have a very limited time in which to get the job done." Once in the privacy of the room, Stroesser began to outline for Altehouse the nature of their assignment. "The job being, of course, to eliminate Sir Frederick Banting, the 'humanitarian' who has been showing his true nature as an ardent proponent of biological weapons. He presents a major threat to the Third Reich and its objectives in the present war.

"Secondly, security has been growing tighter almost daily at the Newfoundland Airport, and presents currently an extremely serious challenge.

"Let us look at the security problem first.

"The Black Watch Regiment of Canada, perhaps the finest, best-trained troops available for the purpose, is doing primary guard duty, with rifles at the ready and fixed bayonets, at the railway station and around all buildings on the installation – the administration building, the airplane hangar, the temporary accommodation in the Pullman cars, and the Eastbound Inn, which should be just finishing construction.

"It is only possible to reach the airport by train, and nobody is permitted off the train unless they can meet the security requirements, which include first-class identification and specific letters of authorization or military orders. I have little doubt that you should be able to satisfy the security concerns of the Black Watch and any others they may have guarding the place.

"Thirdly, Banting will be flying out of Gander within forty-eight to seventy-two hours, as soon as the weather improves, on one of the Lockheed Hudson bombers manufactured in the very plant in Burbank, California in which you have been working. We have an extremely fortuitous situation here, in terms of your expertise, plus the fact that your papers will give you access to these planes for the purpose of ensuring that they are airworthy – except, of course, that in the case of the Banting plane your real task is to ensure that the opposite is the case."

Stroesser smiled at the cleverness of it.

"The important question to be asked and answered in that regard is: What precisely can be done to ensure that the Banting plane never reaches the other side of the Atlantic Ocean?"

This was the signal for Altehouse to have his turn, having first returned to the kitchen and got the pot of coffee and a pair of cups.

"Well, Herr Stroesser," he began, "you seem to be of the opinion that I should have no problem meeting the security requirements, whether of the Black Watch or any other force, and I am certain you are correct. I anticipate no difficulty whatsoever in this regard, as the documentation provided by the *Bund* is perfect in every detail.

"Where I do see the possibility of trouble is in getting access to the particular ship and doing what needs to be done to cause a failure during flight. Pilots as a group are very jealous of their planes. They usually do not want anyone laying a finger on them, certainly not without their express consent. Some have been known to sleep in or near their craft to ensure that this is so."

"That would certainly limit the opportunity to do anything effective, wouldn't it?" Stroesser asked.

"Fortunately," Altehouse replied, "it seems the latest flight of Hudson bombers to arrive at the Newfoundland Airport are parked outside the only hangar, and are mostly buried in the snow – that's the word in Botwood, anyhow. So there is little chance of anyone sleeping in them. On the other hand, it makes it some-what difficult, out in the open, to carry on a sustained 'inspection' during which to tamper with the engines or the controls. But, I believe it can probably be done."

"All right, then," Stroesser said as he considered the problem. "Where does that leave us?"

Altehouse poured himself a second cup of coffee, and went on.

"The clear alternatives are either the introduction of sugar or water into the fuel supply, or an abrasive directly into the oil reservoirs.

"On the face of it, presuming security doesn't get in the way, either of these could be easily and even quickly accomplished. In the Hudsons, the fuel tanks are in the wings – or to put it another way, the wings *are* the fuel tanks. It might not be difficult to get enough sugar into the tanks to cause congealment and reduce the fuel to jelly. The difficulty is that it could be too fast-acting – the plane might not even get off the ground, if in fact you got the engines started, so I would rule it out.

"Water, on the other hand, can starve the engines of fuel – perhaps only intermittently, but sufficiently to cause a crisis, or a crash – or freeze to cause carburettor icing, with a similar result. However, it would require a lot of water, and the plan could fail because of premature freezing. It might be difficult to accomplish without the hazard of detection.

"That leaves an abrasive," Altehouse went on, "which for best results almost certainly means sand with iron filings mixed in. It will impede the flow of lubricating oil to the engines, and will begin to be carried into the engine mechanism to cause damage and possibly jamming. It will obstruct the screens, and without the normal flow level the engines will begin to run hot. The important thing is that sand is inert and will not affect start-up in any way, so the takeoff should be normal. I estimate a maximum of one hour's flying time before serious trouble develops."

Stroesser thought for a few moments.

"Sand mixed with iron filings," he said finally. "It seems so simple, but from what you have said, this clearly is the answer. You could probably carry enough in your pockets. Do you know if it has worked before? And just where are those oil wells located, anyway?"

"Reservoirs," Altehouse corrected him. "They're inboard in the wings, over the engines, right behind the fuel fillers.

"As for whether it has worked before, perhaps you've heard of the American aviator Wiley Post? His ship, the *Winnie Mae,* force-landed in a dry lake – Lake Muroc in California – while he was trying to set an altitude record. He thought at first that his trouble was an oil leak. Then he received a laboratory report and realized someone, maybe a rival aviator, had put sand and iron filings in his engine oil. Well, I have good reason to know, though I won't say just how I know, that he was right the second time!"

He laughed conspiratorially, to underline the fact that he was sharing a secret.

"Of course, Post was lucky. It was daytime, so he was able to see where to put the ship down. And something else. On takeoff from the Union Air Terminal in Burbank, he jettisoned the landing gear, leaving just wooden skids built onto the fuselage. They were just right for coming down for a smooth landing in the desert. But your question had to do with the cause of the force-down, and you have your answer."

"And I believe I can say that I am convinced, Herr Altehouse," Stroesser said, his tone reflecting satisfaction, if not outright admiration, of the other man's thoroughness.

"However, I must stress the importance that this plane crashes into the ocean, and that there are no survivors. As they say, dead men tell no tales. It will be very good if there is no physical evidence lying around to indicate that anything untoward happened."

"There is no need to worry," Altehouse said, very sure of himself. "No need at all."

That night when the eastbound version of the Overland Limited came to a stop in what seemed like the middle of nowhere, Stroesser, alias Friedmann, ran a hand over a steamed-up window and peered out into the darkness. A dozen yards away, across the westbound tracks, he saw a tarpaper shack, perhaps thirty feet long, with a single window and a rough signboard that read NFLD. AIRPORT. A naked overhead bulb in a white enamel fixture provided a modicum of illumination, but only a red-and-white striped signal arm lent any suggestion that this was, indeed, a railway station.

Two dozen military personnel, in a variety of uniforms, were already on their feet and spilling out of the train, overwhelming the trio of Black Watch security assigned to check their credentials.

In the middle of the queue – neither too close to the front nor too far to the rear – was Altehouse, passing though the checkpoint without apparent difficulty. Riding the train back to St. John's, Stroesser, alias Friedmann, observed this with satisfaction. He held his breath as a young soldier glanced at Altehouse's papers, looked him in the face for a few seconds, then waved him on. The American joined the crowd moving towards a pair of khaki-coloured military buses waiting to take them to their quarters.

Stroesser made the most of his peddler's disguise by offering his wares to a pair of elderly Roman Catholic nuns who seemed flattered by the attention.

Altehouse's big test came the next morning when he appeared before H. A. L. Pattison, the retired Royal Air Force Squadron Leader who was the Newfoundland government's Aerodrome Control Officer and advisor on air policy.

"We had word from General Martin's office to expect you, Master Sergeant," Pattison said, without offering to shake hands. He was attired in civilian clothes, so Altehouse did not feel obliged to salute. At the mention of notification from General Martin, he could only admire the thoroughness of Eva Haussling and the California *Bund*.

"Please sit down, and let me see if I precisely understand why you are here," Pattison continued. "Now, according to the general – or, I should say, according to the word we've had from his office, the Pacific Command of the United States Army Air Corps – you are to carry out final pre-flight inspections of Hudson aircraft coming out of the Lockheed plant in Burbank, pre-flight meaning, of course, before they depart for the U.K."

"That's correct, sir," Altehouse replied smoothly. "We have experienced two unfortunate crashes in the past number of days – one at St. Hubert Airport where three men were killed, and a few days before that at El Paso, Texas where two men unfortunately lost their lives. Not only were these incidents tragic, but they could have a serious effect on the program to supply planes to the

Royal Air Force if prospective civilian pilots got the idea that our ships are not safe to fly.

"So General Martin has decided that we should have an experienced check supervisor take a look at the Hudsons before they start on the last, long leg to England."

"Yes, well that certainly sounds logical, Master Sergeant. Do you know the general circumstances of these crashes?"

"Yes, sir. In the St. Hubert crash, it apparently was engine failure – the ship only got fifty feet off the ground. Two men died instantly, and the third later in the hospital. We don't know what caused the crash.

"In El Paso, the story was that they veered into a radio mast. There was a suggestion of pilot error, but something put the plane off course. Once again, we don't know what. Neither of the two crew members survived that crash.

"The thing is, the ships you have on the ground here came off the line about the same time as those crashed Hudsons, and we are concerned that there be no repeats."

"That's a very persuasive argument," Pattison admitted. "We're talking about the lives of flyers, the bravest men in the world, and I personally support anything that will increase the margin of safety for them. However, we have a peculiar situation here. We – meaning the Government of Newfoundland – neither own the aircraft in question, nor have any right to provide you with access to them. Or deny it either, I suppose. They simply are not our ships, as you call them, and therefore permission is not ours to give."

An oil burner in a corner of the spartan office sputtered noisily as it poured out an uneven heat. Pattison got up from his desk and went to the window, which was partly frosted over. Outside, the wind howled and snow swirled around isolated buildings and half-buried planes on the tarmac. For the thousandth time he asked himself, *What am I doing in this godforsaken place?*

Altehouse kept silent, almost afraid to breathe while waiting for the answer that could mean the success of the Banting assignment, or throw it into a tailspin of failure.

"Having said that, who does own them?" Pattison asked rhetorically. "It's just possible that, until they are physically in the hands of the Royal Air Force, those bombers continue legally to belong to the people who manufactured them, namely Lockheed – and you, Master Sergeant, represent those people, more or less, more than anyone else around here. Atfero and the C.P.R. are simply the transit agents, as I see it. So, on the basis that a final inspection will likely help to safeguard everyone's interest, I am prepared to say that you should be permitted to undertake it."

"Thank you, sir," Altehouse said, barely able to contain himself.

"One last thing, however, Master Sergeant," Pattison added. "It is because of the urgency – these planes need to clear this aerodrome as soon as the weather is right – that I intend to allow you to proceed with your inspection.

"But I must tell you that I shall also begin immediately to verify the information that you have given me, right up to General Martin. I am sure you have no objection?"

"No, sir, of course not," the Nazi agent replied smoothly. "I understand perfectly."

TWENTY-ONE

Argentia U.S. Naval Base,
A Few Months Earlier

CANARIS HAD BEEN as good as his word. When they met in Hamburg, as Stroesser was preparing to leave for his assignment in Newfoundland, the head of the *Abwehr* had assured him that he would have assistance in carrying out his work on behalf of the Third Reich in the British colony, and help was, indeed, beginning to appear.

The Banting affair, and the arrival of Altehouse which would ensure its success, was wholly unanticipated. It had resulted from unforeseen circumstances, not in any way related to Stroesser's original agenda. But the pieces were coming together unbelievably well, thanks to the willingness of the spy agency and the California *Bund* to work together on a project whose implications as a major coup might not have been immediately obvious to everyone.

The more he thought about it, however, the more Stroesser realized that it bore out Canaris's thinking, and the admiral's ability to see matters in the round.

"This war involves a complicated global strategy," the *Abwehr* chief had pointed out, "and we have to think about it that way. What occurs in America, or in Newfoundland, or in London, England, may have profound effects thousands of miles away. We must remember that it is the Führer, the master strategist, with the advice of his High Command, who must decide what, in the end, is to be done."

In keeping with Canaris's earlier commitment, Stroesser would be provided with two female agents.

The first to arrive was Eloise "Ellie" Miller. American by birth, she was the thirty-five-year-old daughter of New Jersey construction contractor and self-taught explosives expert Ronald "Ronnie" Miller, his name long ago anglicized from Reinhart Mueller. With his wife, Hilda, he had left Germany thoroughly disgusted with the ignominy of the First World War reparations settlement. They had no compunction, however, about making their way to the comparative luxury of life in the United States.

"After the way they destroyed my country, these Americans, it is no more than they should do to look after me and mine," Miller would quite openly declare. And he meant it. Therefore, although prospering in New Jersey, he continued to resent the fact of having to leave his native Germany, and never ceased to blame America for it.

Then Ellie's husband, U.S. Navy Lieutenant Edward O'Banion, was posted to Newfoundland as a member of an advance party preparing the ground for a huge military establishment. Local civilians, both living and dead, were to be transplanted to free up land for runways, hangars, docks, military barracks, gasoline and ammunition storage, family housing – for what would become Fort McAndrew and Argentia Naval Station. Miller set about planning for his daughter to follow O'Banion, ostensibly so she could be near her mate, but in reality to do everything possible to erase the sting of what had been her father's obsession for two decades, in his words "the shame of Versailles."

Miller had taught his daughter everything he knew, and in fact they worked together in a successful partnership. Now, under the direction and influence of the local Newark *Bund,* a secretarial position was arranged for her with a civilian contractor engaged on construction of the biggest United States military base in the North Atlantic, and perhaps anywhere overseas. Subsequently, the *Bund* got word to Stroesser concerning the date of her arrival in Newfoundland. He was waiting when she stepped down from the train from Port aux Basques, and very quickly they agreed on a communications plan to ensure regular and reliable future contacts.

Then she set out for Placentia to locate her sailor husband, who was both surprised and delighted to see her – and kept ignorant of her real purpose for being there.

"I just couldn't stay away, darlin'. When the chance came to be up here and to be near you, I just had to grab it," she said as they made love that night in her assigned room in the contractor's newly constructed staff house. However, they saw each other only occasionally after that, each being too involved in their day-to-day work. Besides, the Navy and its contractors had strict rules about fraternization between members of the military and civilians – even married ones.

Stroesser was plainly chagrined that the German intelligence apparatus had failed to discover, until it was virtually all over, the Atlantic Charter meeting between Roosevelt and Churchill in Ship Harbour, Placentia Bay, a stone's throw from Argentia. The secret conference not only settled Allied plans for the future conduct of the war, but laid down the principles of national independence and self-determination that became the basis for the postwar founding of the United Nations Organization and spelled the end for Hitler's grand design for world domination.

"Not very much we here could have done," he remarked, when discussing it with Ellie later. "The single, greatest opportunity to win the war, and our espionage people missed it completely. I presume they just took for granted what the American and British media were reporting – that Roosevelt was on a fishing trip on his yacht, and Churchill supposedly laid up with gout or pneumonia or something. And all the while they were holding hands here in Newfoundland, right under our noses. Unbelievable!"

"Well, we'll show them yet," she remarked. "The day will come when they'll be sorry!"

Stroesser was taken aback by the vehemence with which she spoke, but he would later have reason to recall it – and to appreciate Ellie's work. Her father's long-held grievance would at last be redressed.

Stroesser's chagrin would later be assuaged late one night by the news of two United States Navy ships – USS *Truxtun,* a destroyer, and USS *Pollux,* a supply ship – lost when they ran ashore in brutal weather at Chambers Cove at the entrance to Placentia Bay, en route to Argentia. The fact 239 of the 425 personnel on board the two vessels perished was sufficient to cheer him up – even if it was an accident, an act of God without any assistance from the *Abwehr.*

Argentia had been made responsible for supervising and controlling all convoy operations in the Northwest Atlantic, and became the western headquarters for dozens of Allied warships providing protection for merchant vessels ferrying munitions, supplies, and machines of war to Britain and the European and Russian fronts. The harbour was thronged with destroyers and other escorts at anchor, and lined up three and four abreast at the docks, when suddenly one night the air was rent by an explosion and fire that occurred mysteriously on board HMS *Spry*. The Royal Navy gunboat was secured astern of USS *Prairie*, command flagship of Rear Admiral Bristol, the man delegated by Washington to run North Atlantic convoy escort operations.

As planned by the saboteur, Ellie, and carried out with the help of a man she engaged for the purpose and handsomely rewarded for his efforts, the fire quickly became a major conflagration, spreading to the *Prairie*, mother ship to a fleet of destroyers, and a floating magazine. Because of the danger of a devastating explosion, the flagship had to be towed out of the harbour, jettisoning ammunition all the way, until the fire was extinguished. Then, with extensive damage, she was moved to the Boston Navy Yard under tow for repairs that consumed many months.

Other vessels were also damaged in the incident, together with a large section of the marginal wharf. The Navy admitted to two deaths, several injuries, and losses in the many millions of dollars. The customary censorship provided a complete media blackout on the disaster, but could not prevent word-of-mouth transmission of the spectacular event by the thousands of military and Newfoundland civilians who witnessed it. It was impossible to measure the effect on the health of the admiral who died soon afterwards.

No one would admit to sabotage, but it was obvious that warships do not usually explode all by themselves in the middle of the night. An inquiry concluded precisely what Ellie had come to in planning the project – the Admiral's flagship was well-protected by security forces, but the much smaller and less-important British vessel lashed to her stern had been given virtually no protection. Consequently both were vulnerable.

Ellie considered that up to this point her work in behalf of the Third Reich at Argentia had only just begun. However, security was tightened substantially following the *Prairie* incident with a detachment of tough U.S. Marines being shipped in from stateside.

"Movement around here has become damn difficult," she complained to Stroesser. "The Marine commandant is Major Harold H. Eagelburger from Poughkeepsie, New York. As they say, a nice guy, but he is ever determined to make a name for himself. You can't move around here anymore, but there's a Marine right on your tail!"

Nonetheless, without rhyme or reason, a new storage tank that was to be the basis of the station water supply, and the steel tower supporting it, suddenly collapsed. In so doing, it crashed down on top of the harbour control post, destroying it utterly. Fortunately the two enlisted men inside heard a grinding noise and got out in time, but the work of controlling the movement of scores of ships in and out of the crowded harbour became nearly impossible until the post was rebuilt.

In the investigation that followed, the best anyone could come up with was a suggestion that a blueprint section somehow slid down behind a desk in the contractor's engineering office, leaving the load factor design specifications incomplete.

"You know, we'd never be any the wiser except that Mrs. Ellie O'Banion accidentally dropped her wedding ring, and they had to move the desk to find it." Major Eagelburger, conducting the investigation, was left shaking his head in disbelief. "And right there, of course, was the blueprint. What a piece of luck!"

Ellie's next – and as it turned out, her last – target was the newly constructed Bachelor Officers Quarters. She had discovered that her husband was playing around with a Navy nurse, which explained why she was having trouble contacting him.

So she staked out the B.O.Q., and sure enough, they strolled in, large as life, laughing and kissing. They waved to the security Marine, who waved back – obviously they were no strangers to him – and pressed for the elevator.

It was the same the next night, and the next. Ellie had had enough. The fourth night she waited a couple of minutes, and, when the Marine's attention was diverted by a pair of transients whose orders he insisted on inspecting on checking in, followed her husband and his lady friend by the stairs to the fifth floor.

During the day she had already planted incendiary bombs in his room. She had only to block the single exit – easily done with the metal bar which she brought with her, placed across the frame, and connected to the doorknob by a few links of chain – then activate a remote control device invented by her father. In a matter of seconds O'Banion and his nurse would be history. She sprinted for the fire escape at the end of the corridor, but as she passed the elevator it opened suddenly and a security Marine stepped out.

"Ma'am, I need to see your ID and your authority to be in this building."

He carried an automatic rifle at the ready, and gave every indication of being prepared to use it. He never got the chance.

Ellie's explosive devices went off with a tremendous roar, demolishing the concrete block wall where she and the Marine stood glaring at each other, and burying them in the debris. Instantly a sheet of flame turned the corridor into a raging inferno that ultimately destroyed the structure and cost a dozen lives, Ellie, the Marine, O'Banion, and the Navy nurse among them.

Stroesser received privately the news of the B.O.Q. destruction – as per usual, the wartime censor had purged it from the Newfoundland news media – with a good deal of satisfaction, dampened, however, by the knowledge that a valuable agent had perished in the event. He dispassionately reported the success to Canaris, pointing out that a replacement for Ellie would be required, and as expeditiously as possible.

TWENTY-TWO

Airborne, East of Gander, Newfoundland, February 1941

THE MARK IIIA version of the twin-engine Lockheed Hudson light bomber, judged suitable, as well, for maritime reconnaissance and troop transport, was designed to be flown by one man. Thus no provision was made for a second person in the cockpit – no dual control system, no allocated position for a co-pilot.

Certain rudimentary instructions might usually be given to the navigator crew member, accommodated in the glassed-in nose of the aircraft three steps below and forward of the pilot's position. He would be informed on the maintenance of instrument records, and generally required to assist in any way required. For example, at the command of the captain, his job was to raise and lower the undercarriage and the flaps.

Otherwise, he was unable to do very much to help in the actual flying of the airplane.

Therefore, when thirty-three-year-old Joseph C. Mackey, a former stunt-flying, air-racing veteran pilot from Columbus, Ohio, realized his craft was in trouble over a dark and brooding Atlantic Ocean on a winter's night in 1941, he knew at once that he was effectively on his own. He, and he alone, could do anything necessary to wrestle his ship, as he called it, back to land, and perhaps return its four occupants safely to the Newfoundland Airport from which they had taken off less than an hour earlier.

Was he surprised that the aircraft suddenly developed trouble, and so early into this final segment of its journey from California to the British Isles, a 2,000-mile "hop" over the North Atlantic?

Hardly. As a member of a long line of superstitious, barnstorming aviators, Mackey had undertaken this leg of the trip with a sense of foreboding. He just knew that things were going to go wrong – if for no other reason than the fact there were too many people messing around with the ship. Besides, it was no longer merely an aircraft delivery project. In Montréal it had unexpectedly become a VIP flight. The addition of a Very Important Person as an unscheduled passenger had changed everything, and so far as Mackey was concerned, in no sense for the better. A last-minute, fundamental alteration of this magnitude was definitely a bad omen . . . like leaving a strange house by a different door from the one by which one entered, or carelessly walking under a ladder when there was a clear and obvious path around it.

A tangible hint of trouble ahead had come while he was having lunch in the dining room of the just-completed Eastbound Inn at the Newfoundland Airport. A man he didn't know and had never encountered before, Jerome Coulombe from Drake, Saskatchewan, the engineer in charge of maintenance on all Canadian Pacific Railway Company planes at the airport, stopped at his table.

"You're Captain Mackey, flying Hudson T-9449, aren't you?" Coulombe asked, and when Mackey acknowledged that he was, went on to explain that he, Coulombe, had been flying the previous day, when Mackey arrived from St. Hubert, and was sorry he could not make his acquaintance sooner.

"We'll get to inspect your machine first thing this afternoon," promised the twenty-eight-year-old engineer, who had his licence from the Canadian Department of Defence and had worked for Trans-Canada Airlines. But Mackey stopped him cold.

"My engines are working good. One of them may be idling a bit fast, but as far as I'm concerned, I've flown the ship this far, and I intend to fly it the rest of the way over as it is. So I don't want anyone laying a finger on that bloody ship!"

"I'm sorry, Captain Mackey," was the calm response from Coulombe, who had frequently dealt with prickly pilots, "but I and my assistants have a job to do for the owners, and we're obligated to do it."

"Well, my left tachometer does seem a bit sticky . . . . It was like that when I got to Montréal. I asked the engineers there to look at it, but it wasn't fixed. Perhaps you fellows could check that out," Mackey conceded, his tone softening. At a thousand dollars a week, he had no desire to unnecessarily endanger his employment with the C.P.R.'s Air Services Department. They could well have concerns about keeping on the payroll someone who might appear to be some kind of maverick.

"If you're satisfied with your ship, I'm satisfied, Captain," Coulombe said. "I would like my people, Norman Brown and Angus Steel, two very fine mechanics, to carry out the usual routine check and fill out the check sheet. However, I won't go through the complete drill for an airworthiness certificate without your concurrence."

The afternoon of the takeoff, Coulombe visited T-9449 on the snow-covered runway to ensure that the "little things" were looked after – for example, that there were emergency flares on board – or other details that his mechanics might possibly have missed. He was surprised to find in the cockpit a man in the uniform of the United States Army Air Corps. Altehouse informed him that he was there, in effect, as a manufacturer's and owner's representative to carry out a special inspection against possible sabotage – essentially the same explanation the Nazi agent had given to Pattison.

"That would have been between three and four o'clock," the engineer told Mackey when he ran into him later.

"I was satisfied that everything was in order. But to my knowledge, there was no special guard near the machine. I know it was in the hangar for servicing and for the check sheet, and there would have been guards there, but when it was moved outside again – I don't know. I didn't see any security around at the time."

Mackey swore. Once again he told himself that he didn't like what was going on, didn't like it one bit. *Too damn many people messing around with the ship!*

An American citizen, Mackey had a pilot's licence from the United States government, number 12800, and had been flying for fifteen years – with the C.P.R. for the past six months. He had experienced everything from engine failure, to severe icing that very nearly brought down the ship he was flying, to undercarriage collapse resulting in a fiery crash-landing. However, nothing in his experience had prepared him for the series of events that occurred over a few days in February 1941.

He was first surprised, then appalled, at being summoned to a sumptuous lunch in the elegant main dining room of Montréal's Queen's Hotel, and then to a high-level meeting at the Air Services Division offices, located in the granite edifice that housed the Canadian Pacific Railways Windsor Station. There he was informed by Captains A. S. Wilcockson and D. C. T. Bennett that they had chosen him to take along a famous passenger on his first ferry flight to England. They had been Mackey's recruiters for the aircraft ferry operation and perhaps were in the best position to make the selection.

"Gentlemen," he protested, "you can't mean this. That ship isn't fitted out for passengers, even one passenger. And certainly not one of the stature of Sir Frederick Banting." They had explained to Mackey just who Banting was, and he was both suitably impressed and very, very reluctant to accept the responsibility being thrust upon him.

But they were adamant, with Bennett, a future Air Vice Marshal who would become leader of the Royal Air Force's famous Pathfinder Force of Bomber Command, going so far as to invoke higher authority.

"I believe you should know, Mackey," he intoned, "that this is not just our idea." He swept a hand around in semicircular motion to include himself and Wilcockson, a former Imperial Airways flying boat pilot. "It comes down from on high, from Air Marshal Cuffe," he said, explaining just who this personage was.

"We two have simply made the recommendation as to who is the best pilot to whom to entrust Sir Frederick for what could, admittedly, be a hazardous journey. The Air Marshal, having reviewed your record of experience, has agreed.

Wilcockson had the last word of consequence.

"In my opinion, Captain Mackey," he said, "this pays a great compliment to you and to your experience, and, may I add without being invidious, with you not even a British or a Canadian citizen. There are some who might consider that, in itself, to be . . . well, unusual. But we believe that the safety and the well-being of Sir Frederick will best be safeguarded if he flies with you."

In the end, Mackey decided that he had little choice. And so it transpired that on a snowy field at St. Hubert, Québec, the municipal airport for Montréal, he met and for the first time spoke with the eminent scientist whose life would quite literally be in his hands. He had been advised that Banting was en route to the airport after being entertained at luncheon by top officials of the C.P.R., and when the company limousine swept up to the aircraft, Mackey was waiting.

"Sir Frederick," Mackey addressed the figure in military uniform. Banting insisted on removing his own bags from the vehicle and carrying them to the plane.

Banting put them down and took Mackey's hand.

"Captain, it's a privilege and a pleasure to meet you. I am very much looking forward to our journey together. I've done it several times by sea, you know, but this will be a new and certainly a different experience. Confidentially, and I wouldn't want the navy types to hear me say so, I don't much care if I ever go by ship again, the last time was that unpleasant."

"Well, sir," said Mackey, "flying can have its unpleasant moments, too, but at least it's over in a hurry. Now, if you'll permit me to stow your gear, I'll show you where you'll be accommodated – all very spartan and not very comfortable, I'm afraid, but we've put in a large cushion and some blankets that will help make it somewhat more endurable."

He introduced his crew: Navigator William Bird of Kidderminster, England, a former Royal Air Force flyer, and Radio Officer William Snailham, of Bedford, Nova Scotia. Then they assumed their positions for the takeoff for Newfoundland, Banting in the ample space in the rear of the craft, Snailham in the radio operator's cubicle behind the pilot, and Bird, the navigator, in the nose of the plane.

Mackey touched the starter buttons and the twin 1,200-horse-power Wright R-1820-87 engines with which Hudson Mark IIIs were fitted, for additional power for transatlantic flying, came instantly and smoothly to life. He performed the usual run-ups to test oil pressure and engine response to the controls, and then the Hudson trundled out to the takeoff position. Three or four minutes later, on receiving a green light from the control tower, it headed at full power down the runway into the teeth of a moderate gale laced with snow flurries, the windsock indicating it was out of the northwest.

As the bomber gained altitude, Mackey signalled to Bird to wind up the undercarriage, then to raise the flaps. In short moments they had circled the city of Montréal and settled onto a northeasterly track towards the Maritimes. Three hours later they landed at the snow-covered Newfoundland Airport without incident.

Although scarcely encountering Banting during the layover, Mackey gained the impression the famous scientist – while ostensibly looking forward to the Atlantic flight – harboured, as did he himself, a certain sense of foreboding.

"Well, Captain," Banting remarked during a brief conversation soon after landing, "we have a disagreeable job ahead of us, but it must be done. Whatever comes in the next few hours or days, I'm certain we are able for it. It is our duty, the purpose for which we are involved in the present struggle.

"There is a high degree of risk, of course, as we face the ocean and the elements, but this is our fate. Whatever may come, may we accept and endure it like men, unflinching and selflessly."

Mackey found this kind of talk fatalistic and unsettling, as he did Banting's ruminations about the possibility of the plane becoming the target of sabotage, as if he had suddenly become conscious of his own importance in the Allied scheme of things relative to the war.

"I'm sorry, Sir Frederick, but I have no reason to believe there's any threat to the airplane from enemy agents," Mackey said.

"Here at this airport, in the midst of the wilderness, would be an ideal place for a saboteur to be at work," Banting said, refusing to abandon his suspicions, "especially with planes sitting on an isolated field with a complete absence of guards. If Nazi agents really wanted to interfere with the flight, preventing such activity would be a very difficult proposition."

Mackey tried hard not to admit it, but he knew the soldier-scientist was absolutely right, at least to this extent. If anyone really wanted to do them in, they would be hard-pressed to prevent it.

They made their way to the newly constructed Eastbound Inn where Banting checked in with the duty clerk, a young Newfoundlander from St. John's named John Edward Murphy. An amateur hockey player with professional-level abilities, he was destined to rise to the top echelons of the international airline business.

"Welcome, Sir Frederick, we're very honoured to have you here with us." Murphy made no secret of his pleasure in meeting the famous guest, as he turned the register around and offered a pen so Banting could sign in.

* * *

Despite his misgivings, which had no real evidence to support them, Mackey persuaded himself that his machine was in tip-top mechanical condition, that he shouldn't doubt that it was equal to the demands of the flight across the Atlantic Ocean – otherwise he shouldn't be here. He was reassured in this as everything worked perfectly on takeoff. His was the last of five Hudsons to take advantage of the clearing weather, leaving Gander behind at four minutes to nine local time on the evening of February 20, 1941. Everything continued to work perfectly for half an hour or more.

Then, less than fifty miles out over the ocean, the port engine began to run hot, and while he was contemplating what to do about it, the engine suddenly quit. Mackey did not hesitate. He immediately put about and ordered the radio officer, Snailham, to request bearings to guide their return to the Newfoundland Airport.

"Bill, there's no need to go into detail about our situation," he shouted over the engine noise.

"I don't want to give the impression we're in distress – which we're not, or not yet, anyhow. And what could they do about it in any event? Just ask for QDMs" – in the phonetic alphabet, the acronym Québec-Delta-Mike signified a pilot's request for a reciprocal heading – "so we can get back to the aerodrome as quickly as possible." That, he thought, is the beauty of having more than one engine.

Snailham did as ordered. Between 00:58 and 01:03 G. M. T., a period of five minutes, bearings were requested, and provided, three times. The Hudson acknowledged the last at 01:03, and after that there was no further communication.

Receiving the course information, Snailham quickly passed it to Bird, the navigator, who, in turn, confirmed it to Mackey. The bomber made its way in what they believed to be the general direction of Hattie's Camp, reversing the track on which it had come, while maintaining an altitude of about 5,000 feet over the brooding Atlantic Ocean and the dark and frozen wilderness of

Newfoundland's Northeast Coast. They were unaware that strengthening northeasterly winds were causing them to drift off course.

Unable to leave his position at the controls, Mackey asked Bird to request Banting to come forward to the cockpit. The tall figure in Canadian Army uniform, military cap, and greatcoat appeared almost immediately at his side.

"I'm afraid we're having a serious problem, Sir Frederick," the pilot shouted. "We've lost our port engine, and we've had to turn back. We should be on the ground at the Newfoundland Airport in about half an hour. However, I'd advise you to make yourself as comfortable as possible and to sit tight against the bulkhead, just in case we have a rough landing. And put on a parachute. You just may have to bail out before this is over."

"Thank you, Captain," Banting replied, bracing against the starboard ribs of the fuselage with one hand, and with the other grasping the back of the pilot's seat to steady himself against the severe buffeting. Despite the outwardly calm demeanour of a soldier, inwardly the surging doubts and misgivings of recent days had crystallized into a clammy sense of impending doom.

"Parachute . . . . Yes, Captain. As you suggest, right away," Banting assured Mackey, heading for the rear of the cabin. But the truth was, he had no intention of leaping blindly out into the night sky, in the middle of nowhere, perhaps never to be found or heard of again.

TWENTY-THREE

Control Tower, Newfoundland Airport, February 1941

THOMAS M. McGRATH was the Newfoundland Airport's acting Aerodrome Control Officer – airport manager – in the absence of Pattison, who was currently up in Canada's capital of Ottawa, negotiating Canadian takeover of the airport for the duration of the war, in his other role as air advisor to the Newfoundland government.

From the vantage point of the control tower, McGrath had just witnessed the takeoff of a flight of five Hudson bombers bound for Britain, the largest flight to date under the aegis of the Atlantic Ferry Command or Atfero It was the device concocted by Canadian-born Lord Beaverbrook, as Winston Churchill's Minister of Aircraft Production, with the help of Canadian Pacific Railways Chairman Sir Edward Beatty and his Air Services Department, to speed the delivery of warplanes built in North America to Britain's Royal Air Force. Previously, they were crated up and carried by ship, subject to the ravages of Hitler's U-boats, which sank well over a thousand Allied merchant vessels during the Battle of the Atlantic, and to inevitable time delays.

McGrath would never admit, but could not deny to himself, at least, that the aircraft he was most interested in this frigid February night was the last in the lineup – Hudson No. T-9449. He was, frankly, astonished to think that that one had on board, as a passenger, one of the world's most important scientists.

Although there was really little enough that McGrath could have done to make Banting's visit more pleasant, he was nonetheless under instructions from Sir Wilfred W. Woods, the member of the Newfoundland Commission of Government with direct responsibility for the airport, to ensure that the great man was aware that Governor Sir Humphrey Walwyn and the Commission were well aware of the presence of the international celebrity on Newfoundland soil. Furthermore, they were most anxious to do anything and everything in their power to make him both welcome and comfortable.

In practice, this included such special touches as a hastily assembled basket of fruit placed in Banting's room in the Eastbound Inn, a selection of liquor – a bottle of Johnny Walker Black Label, a bottle of Beefeater gin, a sample of Newfoundland rum known as Screech, plenty of ice, mix, and glasses, and a dozen bottles of strong local beer, Dominion Pale Ale and Jockey Club. As well, a steward had been assigned from the rudimentary Officers' Mess, ordered to be available at Banting's beck and call.

However, he had made plain to his hosts, and to the steward as well, Canadian Black Watch Corporal Donald Jamie MacDonald from Halifax, Nova Scotia, that although this special attention was much appreciated, it would not be availed upon much. In his own mind, nor was it in any sense a reflection of false modesty, Banting fancied himself an ordinary soldier, entitled, so far as possible, to ordinary treatment.

It had snowed and blustered most of the day, a continuation of conditions that had delayed flights to England all week. Nonetheless, the newly re-established weather service – first set up in Botwood under the direction of Patrick McTaggert-Cowan, a Canadian world-class meteorologist, to support the international flying boat service, and later relocated to what was destined to be permanently named Gander International Airport – was calling for reasonably good conditions across the Atlantic. Accordingly, McGrath had ordered runways cleared and planes freed from their blanket of snow for takeoff at 00:30 Greenwich Mean Time, 9:00 p.m. Newfoundland Standard Time, aiming for touchdown at Prestwick, Scotland late in the morning of February 21.

He was well aware of Banting's anxiety about flying conditions over the vast expanse of water between North America and Britain, where there could be as many weather patterns as there were differentiated areas of ocean. The scientist's informal inquiries and discussions with all and sundry about ocean-flying, plus a nocturnal office visit to pursue the subject, were certainly no secret.

Young Roderick Goff was a native of Carbonear, Conception Bay whose appetite for the aviation business as a life's career had been whetted by the epoch-making flights of Earhart, Post and Gatty, Kingsforth-Smith and others through North America's first civilian airport in the adjacent eastern Newfoundland community of Harbour Grace.

Late on the night before the fateful Hudson flight, a knock came on the door of the weather office in the Newfoundland Airport administration building, where Goff had secured employment and was on duty along with his supervisor, Hugh Bindon. Goff went to the door and discovered there a tall, bespectacled man in military uniform who announced, "Good evening. My name is Fred Banting."

"Well, ah . . . good evening, sir," Goff replied, giving a good imitation of a double take. He flung the door open wide in a gesture of welcome, managing quickly to get over his surprise at being confronted unexpectedly by the international celebrity, and said, "Well, come right in, Major."

Everyone knew Banting was on the station, and speculation was rife as to what he might be doing there – or, more correctly, as to why such a famous personality was enduring the hazards and uncertainty of a journey across the ocean by military aircraft in mid-winter. After introducing himself, Goff turned the visitor over to Bindon, a Master of Arts in meteorology from the

University of Toronto. Coincidentally, the latter had worked part-time at Toronto's Banting Institute during his student days, but was reluctant to mention this to its namesake and director when he had the chance.

"In fine professional style," as Goff described it to his friend Joe Smallwood, a former journalist who had written about – and participated in – some of the early flying experiments in Newfoundland, and now was engaged in organizing a piggery to supply fresh pork to an expanding Royal Air Force contingent, "Bindon delivered a thorough, one-on-one briefing which obviously pleased, and perhaps reassured, Dr. Banting, who was unstinting in his appreciation.

"You know, Joe, this is a great story. In fact, there are a lot of great stories around here. Too bad you're not still in newspapers. You'd have a field day!"

"Well, who knows," Smallwood replied. "If this pig business doesn't work out, I just might go back to the newspaper game. I started up the *Humber Herald* in Corner Brook, you know, with the backing of my friend Jonathon Noel, a good Carbonear man like yourself. The present editor, Vincent Parsons, just might be delighted to have me back."

As McGrath watched, Hudsons piloted by Captains Adams, Rodgers, Harmes, Butler, and of course Mackey, lined up for departure. As each took off he made notes, recording that Adams "bumped at ridge" where two runways intersected, "but up OK"; that Rodgers "hit ridge at speed and bumped 10 feet into air & mysteriously stayed up"; that Harmes "bumped and swerved off strip into 'Circus' & ran towards south ditch of No. 3, but stopped in time," then went around for another, successful try; that Butler made "good takeoff." And then there was T-9449, Mackey's Hudson with Banting on board. It made "a wavery takeoff & did turn left very low but went up out of sight . . . used all runway & pulled up sharply." All in all, he wrote, "an exciting series of departures."[17]

Heading for his quarters, McGrath speculated as to why Mackey had "used all runway" in his takeoff run. Was he simply being more careful than ordinarily in deference to his passenger? Was he compensating for the additional weight of a fourth person in the plane? Or, was there some problem with the aircraft that those on the ground were unaware of, a problem that affected the ability of the engines to generate the required thrust? He discarded this immediately. Surely the pilot would turn back at once, abandoning the long flight across the ocean, if there was any sign of trouble right at its start.

In fact, McGrath concluded, aside from the snowy conditions that were the cause of the "bumps" during the takeoff runs, all five planes had gotten away quite successfully.

As the man temporarily in charge of the airport, he knew he should be feeling good about the whole exercise. The fact that he was not in the least elated, that he harboured some undefined, nagging doubts, did not lend itself to immediate explanation. He supposed that, after waiting all week for a window in the weather, the successful departure of the five aircraft was somehow anticlimactic, accompanied by a kind of psychological letdown. But there seemed more to it than that. He was not a superstitious person, but he had an acute sense that all was not right. Although having no desire to be overly dramatic, he was forced to admit to a premonition of disaster.

As the saying goes, Altehouse could take a Hudson apart and put it back together with his eyes closed. Well, not quite – but it was accurate to say that he was an expert on this particular model of airplane. If anyone understood what was the most effective means by which to cause it to fall from the sky, he was that person.

Having made perfunctory walk-arounds of the other four in the flight, stopping here and there to make it look as if it was a serious inspection tour, he clambered over T-9449, which was half-buried in a snowdrift, standard issue coveralls protecting his neatly pressed air corps uniform. He could see in the distance, around the perimeter of the airport's single hangar, members of the security guard of armed Black Watch troops, and suspected there might be inside security as well – Newfoundland Rangers, a recently formed force of rural police, he'd been told. But out on the snowy runways, no one seemed to pay any attention. Mounting first the starboard and then the port wing, he removed reservoir covers to feign checking oil levels, poured a mixture of sand and iron filings into each from carry bags in the big pockets of his coveralls. His actions went totally undetected.

He entered the cockpit with the vague intention of inflicting subtle damage on the control box, but changed his mind. Should it be discovered before takeoff, certainly if it was to any degree obvious, wouldn't the flight be immediately abandoned? While he was mulling this over, sitting in the pilot's seat, the cabin door opened and a man entered.

"Hullo, there," the newcomer said and shivered. "Boy, that's a cold wind whipping across that runway," he went on, hauling off heavy sheepskin mitts and unzipping his military-style parka. Altehouse noted he did not appear surprised that someone was already in the plane, and remembered the man couldn't have missed footprints in the snow around the craft. The man identified himself as Jerome Coulombe, chief engineer for the Canadian Pacific Railways Air Services Department.

"Army Air Corps, eh?" Coulombe said, more a statement than a question. "Heard from the Aerodrome Control Officer's people that there was an inspector here from Burbank," he explained. "Find anything especially interesting?"

Altehouse had produced perfectly forged and interrelated credentials to establish that he was representing both the Lockheed Aircraft Corporation and the United States Army Air Corps. The latter might be completely redundant in the scheme of things, but explained, and very usefully, the fact that he was in a military uniform and on military orders.

"Nope, not a thing that I've been able to discover. But then, we can't be too careful, I suppose," he replied.

After a few minutes' small talk, they parted, with Coulombe neither completely convinced of the other man's bona fides, nor in any position to challenge them. *All I know for sure*, he told himself, *is that I can smell something damn strange going on here, and I wish to hell I knew what it was.*

Having seen the Hudsons safely off, McGrath bade a good evening to the few people still on the job in the radio and weather offices and headed for his quarters, intending to make an early night of it. But he was hardly in the door when the telephone rang. It was the duty radio supervisor, William Lahey.

"Mr. McGrath, sorry to bother you, but I thought you should know Hudson T-9449, that's Captain Mackey, is asking for QDMs. No reason given, but it seems obvious he must be having some kind of trouble. Why else ask for course directions to get back here?"

McGrath shrugged back into his outer clothing and in minutes was at Lahey's side in the radio room. It was snowing again, and he noted a strong northeast wind was kicking up swirls of solid precipitation.

Operator James Dempsey, in the radio direction shack half a mile away, had provided the reciprocal heading, 238 degrees, that Mackey required to make it back to station. Radio Operator Patrick Fleming had passed it to the troubled aircraft to bring it back in a west-south-west direction to the airport it had left less than an hour before.

This was the relatively foolproof system by which aircraft crossing the Atlantic Ocean were enabled to keep on course and in contact with those who might be able to help them if trouble developed. However, the age of flight – particularly flight across the broad expanse of open water between North America and Europe – was still in its infancy, and if there was a time of year when it was a more hazardous undertaking than any other, it was right now in the middle of winter.

"Anything more from Mackey?" McGrath asked.

"No, sir . . . not a sound, but he was only . . . " Lahey consulted the big sweep-hand clock on the wall. "I make it twenty-eight minutes out. He should be overhead any minute now."

"Have you tried to reach him?" McGrath wanted to know.

"Yes, sir. Every two or three minutes since we got his last QDM request, but there's been no response at all."

The flight, all five bombers, had taken off on a heading of fifty-eight degrees. That should have taken them in an east-northeast direction over the Bonavista Bay village of Wesleyville and thence out to sea. Reversing it should bring T-9449 back the same way it had gone.

But by 11:30 p.m. McGrath had to conclude that his earlier, troubling premonition was being borne out. He began to compose a mental report to his superiors in St. John's, which a few minutes before midnight would take the form of an urgent or "pink" telegram:

```
85   DX   92    PINK   GANDER   1155 P    FEB 20
URGENT
SECTY PUBLIC WORKS
ST JOHNS


ONE  OF  FIVE  AIRCRAFT  WHICH  DEPARTED  FROM
HERE   830   PM   TONIGHT   UNREPORTED   SINCE
SHORTLY  AFTER  TAKE  OFF  STOP  COULD  YOU
COLLECT  REPORTS  BETWEEN  CAPE  FREELS  AND
MUSGRAVE  HR  TO  ASCERTAIN  IF  ALL  5  AIRCRAFT
PASSED  OUT  TO  SEA  AND  IF  ANY  SEEMED  IN
DIFFICULTIES  OR  WAS  OBSERVED  FLYING  TOWARDS
AIRPORT  STOP  PLEASE  ADVISE  IF  ANY  SHIPPING
IN  VICINITY  OF  FUNKS  OR  THAT  SECTION  COAST
STOP  DO  NOT  REQUIRE  ANY  RESCUE  OR  SEARCH
ACTION  AT  THIS  STAGE  BUT  WILL  ADVISE
FURTHER  LATER  STOP  IF  NO  NEWS  RECEIVED  BY
DAYLIGHT  WILL  ASK  R.C.A.F.  TO  MAKE  SEARCH


                              MCGRATH
                              1205A 21
```

Subsequently, in a lengthy report to the Secretary, McGrath would record that when the request for QDMs was received "it appeared that the aircraft was returning to the airport, though no signal was made to that effect. At first the aircraft's silence caused no concern, but after a period of one hour it appeared that the aircraft might have been in some difficulty possibly due to wireless failure.

"The airport rotating beacon was turned on to assist the pilot in his approach. A homing signal was sent out from the wireless station to regular intervals and watch maintained on all likely frequencies which the aircraft might use to call this station . . . . When the aircraft failed to put in an appearance at the airport at 03:30 G. M. T. a telegram was despatched to you informing you of the situation."

At 10:30 a.m. the next morning Manning, the Secretary, had received by telephone a report originating in Newtown, Bonavista Bay, just east of Cape Freels, which he recorded on the back of his telegram from McGrath. It read: "One plane sighted here last night 9 p.m. flying in a southeasterly direction and at 9:25 p.m. seen flying in a northeasterly direction." The report was never explained.

At about the same time he received a report from Musgrave Harbour. It read simply, "Saw no planes."

Later in the morning there was a further urgent telegram from McGrath, in code to signify the sensitivity of the information it contained:

```
16A C 17      GANDER 1145A      21
SECRETARY FOR PUBLIC WORKS
ST JOHNS


SPNGO APRUN GUSZN FCNOY ABABY KBSAN OTZND
GCORR UPICG MLFPP NGXXX RZSYF CORUM OFARK
RXOCE LNRRZ KLATO


                                   MCGRATH
                                   1150A 21
```

Someone in the establishment – probably Emerson's daughter Edwina, whom Manning knew to be a crackerjack at it – had translated the coded message which read:

```
DECODE

FOUR AIRCRAFT HAVE ARRIVED ENGLAND STOP
MAJOR SIR FREDERICK BANTING WELL-KNOWN
CANADIAN SCIENTIST WAS PASSENGER ON BOARD
MISSING AIRCRAFT
```

Manning wrote at the bottom, "Commissioner to see" and Sir Wilfred Woods, when he had seen it, acknowledged that fact by attaching his initials and noting the date, "W.W. 21/2/41."

Before heading off to Ottawa and a round of airport negotiations, courtesy of the Royal Canadian Air Force which had sent a Douglas Digby search and rescue aircraft to pick him up, Pattison lodged a special request with Raymond Manning, the Secretary of the Department of Public Utilities, and thus, penultimate authority over the aerodrome. It asked for an urgent security check to be made on Master Sergeant Alvin James Altehouse, United States Army Air Corps, of Burbank, California.

Over the next couple of days Manning, in his turn – and as established protocols demanded – handed the request over to Carew, Executive Secretary of the Commission of Government. Carew quite properly directed it, for vetting, to the office of Emerson, Commissioner for Justice and Defence.

Approved there, it was returned to the Executive Secretary's office, to be transmitted by Carew to headquarters of the United States Newfoundland Base Command. Welty's people, if he approved, would pursue the matter with the appropriate authorities in the United States. The bureaucratic process was guaranteed to take time, but nobody had been able to find a way around it.

As Billy Budgell, veteran OHMS messenger, was leaving Carew's Duckworth Street office for Welty's Command Post on board the *Edmund B. Alexander* bearing the formal request, a newspaper boy plied his trade nearby.

"*Even' Telegram* . . . . Get yer *Telegram* here," he called. "Famous scientis' killed in plane crash!"

It was Tuesday, February 25, 1941. Banting had been dead four days, but the news was just getting out.

TWENTY-FOUR

The Bonavista Bay Wilderness, February 1941

THE IDLE PORT engine was presenting a serious drag problem. Mackey had been unable to feather the propeller – to change the angle of the blades to parallel the line of flight, and so reduce air resistance. It took all his physical strength on the controls to keep the Hudson on a reasonably straight heading.

"The feathering lever" – he indicated one of a series of handles protruding from the top of the control box, located to the right of the pilot's seat – "seems to be jammed or obstructed," he shouted in explanation to Bird, who hovered close by, wanting to help but unable to find a way to do so.

"It means I can't reduce the drag from the prop, and that makes it damn difficult to keep the ship on course."

The explanation was interrupted as black smoke suddenly began pouring out of the control box. Without hesitation, Mackey ordered the crew to the rear to throw out everything moveable to lighten the craft, and to don parachutes.

As he did so, the right-hand engine began to lose power. Glancing at the altimeter he saw that they were dropping like a stone – it would soon be showing them down to 2,500 feet. He knew from the maps that he was not flying over particularly hilly country, and his hope was they could make it to some large, frozen lake where it might be possible to make a forced landing with minimum damage and injuries. However, another problem had been developing: oily residue spraying from the damaged port engine, accumulating on the windscreen, had further reduced visibility already bad enough due to snow and darkness.

It was practically impossible for Mackey to divert his attention from the instruments, or to do much more than keep the aircraft steady. He yelled to Bird, the navigator, to lower the flaps, and seconds later to the radio officer, straining to be heard over the racket from the malfunctioning engines:

"Bill! Snailham! I figure we're now at least five miles in from the ocean, okay? Over the land. I'm ordering everybody to bail out, now. Right away!"

The plane continued to lose power and altitude.

Fighting the controls, Mackey himself was unable to get out of the seat or put on a parachute. He was reconciled to riding the bomber in for the crash.

He depressed the levers that would cause the fuel load to jettison, and switched off the starboard engine, which was still running, so as to lessen the chances of explosion and fire.

Visibility now was virtually nil. He could see nothing but pitch black outside, and the accumulation of oil on the windscreen from the malfunctioning engines had, by now, almost completely obscured it.

He concentrated on keeping the nose up and the craft on a straight track.

Suddenly, he was conscious of crashing into the tops of trees.

Then there was nothing, only blackness.

Justice of the Peace Frank Whiteway in Musgrave Harbour had received in the day's mail an accumulation of newspapers from St. John's – *The Evening Telegram, The Daily News*, and most importantly for one in his position, from the Queen's Printer's the *Newfoundland Gazette* with its weekly quota of official government notices. He sat at his dining room table, where he could comfortably spread the papers while getting extra light from the chandelier, and methodically clipped with scissors the items he felt were important or might become so.

"Frank, there's an airplane up there somewhere," his brother's wife said, coming into the room just before half past nine. "We can hear it. Unusual in this neck of the woods. I wonder what it could be?"

Whiteway got up and followed her to the kitchen, put on a heavy sweater, and together they went out to stand on the bridge to scan the night sky.

"I hear it, Leah," he remarked. "Seems to be over there, heading in an easterly direction," he pointed. "But I can't see anything with this overcast and the snow."

"Stars over here," Leah reported, pointing in the other direction but she, too, had to admit she was unable to spot anything unusual. Abruptly, the engine noise stopped.

Over the next couple of days, several airships were seen flying in different directions, as if on a search. Then, four days after the first one, an airplane came in low over the town and began dropping leaflets. Whiteway picked one up, and in light of the aircraft activity noted over a period of several days, was not greatly surprised by the message it conveyed:

"Aircraft crash SSW of you. One alive needs urgent help. Exact position 190 degrees T from you ten miles."

Immediately some men got together, gathered food and equipment, and set out for the crash scene. Five or six miles further inland they encountered some woodcutters who joined the group. They had gone at least a dozen miles before they reached the crash area.

"About a mile from the crashed plane," Randolph Abbott said later in a statement to the police, "we saw a small slide track. In the track we discovered the butt of a Lucky Strike cigarette and [wrappers] that apparently came from a package of food." The food was presumably consumed by Mackey, who was found by rabbit hunters Walter Hicks, Dalton Abbott, Tobias Mouland, and Harold Hicks who conveyed him to Musgrave Harbour."

It appeared that when the plane came down, flying blind, its impact was cushioned by the tops of young second-growth trees and then, by the sheerest chance – some people would claim it was a miracle – it skidded onto the ice of a large pond.

"It went about a hundred yards [and] then the port wheel struck a rock in the pond," Abbott concluded, "as the wheel was left at this point. The plane swerved and headed in about a northeast direction until it struck the woods, and I noticed a few trees had fallen."

It was in this area that the searchers found the body of Banting, about twenty feet from the plane. Bird's remains were found inside the craft, one leg partly out through the door, and Snailham's near the entrance to the cockpit.

Getting the bodies to Musgrave Harbour required strenuous efforts on the part of the searchers. They were placed on slides which the men had to pull through the snowbound woods, in darkness and light snow, for nearly eight hours.

Schoolteacher Roland W. Abbott, cousin of Randolph, was conducting a meeting in the Orange Lodge. He wrote in his diary that around 9:00 p.m. Thursday evening, February 20, a plane was heard "coming in . . . making a strange loud noise." The following day, Friday, there were "planes out around; nice day," and on Saturday, in mild weather, there were more planes, and they were still around on Sunday. Then on Monday, there were "planes out dropping leaflets saying 'Plane crash ten miles SW of you, three men dead, one man alive. Need help.'"

This was the signal for "scores of men . . . to leave at once to go [and] render all assistance possible . . . Our town folk did everything possible to help the unfortunate airmen in the tragic disaster."

A series of urgent, official telegrams now conveyed the news of the crash, and the deaths of Banting and the others – as well as the survival of Mackey, the pilot – to the outside world:

```
URGENT      CARMANVILLE
TO: CHIEF OF POLICE
ST JOHNS
```

PLANE FOUND BY TRAPPERS TWELVE MILES SSW MUSGRAVE HARBOUR PILOT ALIVE HEAD INJURED NURSE PARSONS IN ATTENDANCE OTHER THREE DEAD TWO KILLED INSTANTLY DOCTOR DIED SOME HOURS AFTERWARDS BOTH PILOT AND BODIES HERE PLANE TOTAL WRECK MEN ON WATCH WAITING FOR ORDERS

CONST HISCOCK 928A 25TH

* * * * *

```
URGENT      GANDER

SECRETARY
DEPT PUBLIC WORKS
ST JOHNS
```

BODIES NOW AT MUSGRAVE HARBOUR WHERE THEY WERE BROUGHT ON MACKEYS INSTRUCTIONS BEFORE WE COULD INTERFERE STOP WILL FLY THEM HERE AS SOON AS WEATHER SUITABLE STOP UNDERSTAND FROM R.C.A.F. THAT PARTY OF NEWSPAPER MEN PROCEEDING HERE BY AIR WITH APPROVAL OTTAWA THIS NOT YET VERIFIED OR LIMITS OF PERMIT KNOWN STOP HAVE YOU ANY KNOWLEDGE THIS AND WHAT ARE MY INSTRUCTIONS THIS REGARD STOP HOPE VISIT SCENE THIS AFTERNOON AND WILL ADVISE LATER MAGISTRATE DUE THIS AFTERNOON MCGRATH 1156A 25

* * *

William R. Callahan

```
URGENT     GANDER
SECRETARY
DEPT PUBLIC WORKS
ST JOHNS

NO  PROGRESS  DUE  WEATHER  STOP  UNDERSTAND
BAGGAGE  AND  OTHER  FREIGHT  JETTISONED  FROM
AIRCRAFT PRIOR TO CRASH STOP POSSIBILITY THE
PACKAGES  MAY  BE  FOUND  BY  TRAPPERS  FROM  TIME
TO  TIME  SHOULD  SOME  ACTION  BE  TAKEN  WITH
POLICE  TO  COLLECT  ANY  SUCH  DISCOVERIES  STOP
CANADIAN  PRESS  DESPATCHES  FROM  HERE  ARE  SEEN
BY  R.C.A.F.  AND  ME  AND  JUDGED  SATISFACTORY
BUT  SUGGEST  YOU  MAY  WISH  KEEP  IN  TOUCH  WITH
CENSOR   STOP   UNDERSTAND   SOME   ST   JOHNS
RELEASES BE MADE ALSO OTHERS IN CANADA FROM
OFFICIAL  REPORTS  SENT  OTTAWA  BY  LOCAL  CANA-
DIAN  REPRESENTATIVES  STOP  RE  BODIES  BANTING
AND  SNAILHAM  TO  BE  RETURNED  CANADA  AND  BIRD
BURIED    NEWFOUNDLAND    STOP    UNDERTAKER
REQUIRED  PROCEED  HERE  TO  EMBALM  ALL  THREE
BODIES  BUT  NO  CASKETS  OR  COFFINS  REQUIRED
STOP  IN  VIEW  DELAYS  AND  DISTANCE  PROPOSE
SEND  FOXMOTH  ST  JOHNS  EARLY  THURSDAY  TO  FLY
EMBALMER  HERE  STOP  WILL  YOU  CONTACT  CARNELL
FOR  C.P.R.  ASKING  HIM  BE  READY  PROCEED  BY
AIR  TO  AIRPORT  TOMORROW  SHOULD  FLIGHT  BE
IMPOSSIBLE  HE  SHOULD  PROCEED  HERE  THURSDAYS
EXPRESS  STOP  WILL  ADVISE  YOU  RE  TRANSPORT
TOMORROW STOP HOPE WRITE YOU REPORT FOR NEXT
MAIL  BUT  OWING  PRESSURE  PRESENT  AFFAIRS  MAY
NOT  BE  ABLE  DO  SO

MCGRATH 1228P 26
```
                          * * *

```
URGENT


MANNING GANDER
SECTY PUBLIC WORKS
ST JOHNS


MACKEY AND BANTINGS BODY EN ROUTE MONTREAL
BY SEPARATE AIRCRAFT STOP OTHER BODIES EN
ROUTE TO HALIFAX


MCGRATH 1257P 2ND
```

The Newfoundland government ordered an inquiry, which was chaired by retired Royal Canadian Air Force Air Commodore G. V. Walsh. Governor Walwyn, on receiving the findings of the Walsh inquiry, would waste no time in communicating a brief summary to both the Canadian and British governments, with the implied advice appended that suggested the least said, the better:

```
TO:  Secretary  of  State  for  External
Affairs, Ottawa, No. 19,
repeated to SSDA No. 179


FROM: Governor of Newfoundland


DATE: April 2, 1941
Secret  No  19.  Repeated  to  Secretary  of
State for Dominion Affairs No. 179 Secret.


Findings of Court of Inquiry into aircraft
crash on 20th February
near Musgrave Harbour are as follows:-
```

Begins:-

Immediate cause of the accident forced landing due to engine failure. Underlying cause of the accident

(a) failure of the port engine oil cooling (broken tension adjuster ring in thermostatic unit) followed by failure of feathering motor on port airscrew and subsequent seizing of the engine (b) inability of the pilot to maintain height on the Starboard engine. In the absence of direct evidence but after obtaining expert opinion in evidence the Court is of the opinion that the partial failure of the Starboard engine was due to ice accretion in the carburettor system.

Ends.

We are issuing here brief communiqué to the effect that findings of Court deal exclusively with technical matters and that publication of report not in public interest. Copy of report will be sent to Ottawa and London with despatch by mail and to Chairman of Canadian Air Service.

Malcolm Mercer Hollett, born on Great Burin Island on the South Coast in 1891, was a Rhodes Scholar who put off his studies to enlist in the Newfoundland Regiment in World War I. Seriously wounded overseas in France in 1916, he was invalided home the following year, finally arriving at Oxford in

1918. Back in Burin as a magistrate, one of Hollett's chief tasks was to supervise relief and rehabilitation following the 1929 earthquake and tsunami that devastated South Coast communities.

Now the man whose future would include election to the National Convention on Newfoundland's future, leadership of the Progressive Conservative Party in the House of Assembly, and membership in Canada's Senate, found himself drawn into the Banting tragedy. As magistrate in the town of Grand Falls, the closest judicial officer to the Newfoundland Airport, he received instructions to go there immediately and take sworn statements from any witnesses with knowledge of the circumstances surrounding the crash of Hudson T-9449 bearing the doctor and his companions.

The instructions originated with G. B. Summers, Q.C., Secretary for Justice, to whom Hollett reported on his return to Grand Falls that, on arriving along with a court stenographer, Miss Carter, and Head Constable Humber, "I found that the bodies were still at Musgrave Harbour where they had been taken by some trappers. It was impossible to have them brought in before Friday morning, the twenty-eighth, all planes being grounded on account of weather conditions."

Hollett stressed the fact, pointed out in the statement he took from Engineer Jerome Coulombe, that "no special guard was kept on these planes whilst they were grounded at the Airport. You will note also what he says regarding the certificate as to airworthiness.

"'It had not been signed by anybody.'"

The magistrate made one further observation of importance to Summers.

"I would say too that a closer scrutiny of passes into the Airport should be made by the guard before allowing people to obtain admittance. These are, of course, matters for consideration of the military Court of Inquiry, but I pass them to you for your information."

Malcolm Hollett's observations could only add fuel to the rising flames of suspicion that all had not been right with the Banting flight.

TWENTY-FIVE

Aftermath of the Crash,
Seven Mile Pond, February 1941

MACKEY FIGURED HE had been unconscious for about an hour. He recalled that Hudson T-9449 had cleared the Newfoundland Airport after a long takeoff run at twenty-six minutes after midnight Greenwich Mean Time. Trouble with the port engine developed about a half-hour later, well out over the Atlantic Ocean, and assuming it had taken at least another half-hour to get back over land on one engine, the crash must have occurred at approximately 01:30 G. M. T.

His wristwatch, still set to Newfoundland local time, fortunately had survived the impact, and was showing 11:03 p.m. So, allowing for the fact that he had been tossed about the cockpit and sustained a blow to the head that bled profusely and had required bandaging, and that the injury might well have impaired his ability to do a precise calculation, his conclusion was that he had been "out of it" for a good sixty minutes or so.

The Hudson was deathly quiet, the only sound the moaning of the winter wind as it swirled snow around the aircraft which, by the sheerest luck, had come down on a frozen body of water known locally as Seven Mile Pond, and was relatively intact. Mackey's head felt as if it had been assaulted by sledgehammer blows, and his throat, dry and scratchy, hurt as he called out – "Hello . . . Bill Snailham! Bill Bird! Major Banting! Can anyone hear me?"

He was rewarded with eerie silence. Then he remembered ordering all hands to bail out, and his mind leaped eagerly to that as the answer. The others had done as he, the captain of the ship, had ordered. There was a sense of something distinctly odd about this conclusion, but he was unable to put his finger on it. Perhaps it would come to him later.

Lying in a crumpled heap on the floor of the cockpit, he mentally, and as far as possible physically, examined his limbs, his body mass, his vital organs, for signs of serious injury other than the smash to the right temple, which throbbed incessantly and continued to seep blood through the bandage. He discovered a painful leg bruise, and his back was wrenched, but there seemed to be nothing more serious. Fingering gingerly the bandage on the head wound, he was bothered by the feeling that there was something that he could not quite recall, something that was not quite right.

Mackey had not been strapped in the pilot's seat at the time of the crash – that much he remembered clearly – as he had been afraid to loosen his grasp on the stick to strap himself in or don a parachute, lest he lose control of the ship. The fact that he had regained consciousness on the floor of the cockpit confirmed this. He guessed that, on being thrown from the seat by the force of the collision with trees, or the ground, or whatever else they might have hit, his head had struck, and smashed, the wheel of the control column or struck a sharp corner of the metal control box to the right of the pilot's seat.

As he heaved himself to his feet, swaying slightly and feeling disconcertingly lightheaded, he had a sudden, terrible vision of what probably would have occurred had he not had the presence of mind to jettison the plane's near-capacity fuel load, and switch off the remaining, starboard engine just before the crash. He dropped into the pilot's seat and waited a few moments for his head to clear. He could see that it was pitch-black outside, but then realized the interior lights of the plane were on – strange, as he had been careful to observe strict orders to maintain a blackout while flying as a precaution against possible attack by German patrol planes.

After a while, he got out of the seat and started back towards the rear of the aircraft. He was surprised and shocked to discover Snailham, trapped by the restraints of his broken seat, head and shoulders in the radio compartment and the rest of him protruding into the after cabin. He was wearing a parachute.

"My God, Bill," Mackey said aloud, "you didn't get out after all."

He got down on his knees and felt for a pulse, but found none. He lifted Snailham's head to try to discover if he was breathing, but again there was no sign of life. He gently drew a hand over the battered face to close the eyes, and moved on into the cabin.

There were more shocks to come.

First there was Bird, also wearing a parachute, but also quite dead. Mackey looked for life signs, but as in the case of Snailham, he could find none. He could only perform the final service of closing the staring eyes. He looked around for something to cover their faces, but could find nothing suitable.

Why didn't they jump? he asked himself. *They got their 'chutes on, so why in hell didn't they jump?*

But as he thought about it, he asked himself if it was really so strange that men would be reluctant to fling themselves out of an aircraft, even a crippled one, several thousand feet in the air, in total darkness, over a bleak and frozen wilderness where they might never again be found. Far better, they may well have felt, to take their chances and remain with the ship, which as it turned out, was amazingly intact.

"In my opinion," Mackey would relate in a sworn statement given to Magistrate Hollett, "William Bird and William Snailham met instantaneous death by being thrown against hard objects in the ship."

And then there was Banting.

"I found Sir Frederick still breathing, and with some help from himself got him up on the bunk by the side of the cabin where a quick inspection found him to have a broken arm and to be bleeding about the head. I cut up a parachute to make a sling for his arm and opened another to cover him up to keep him warm.

"By this time he was talking completely incoherently," the pilot recalled, "and I spent the night trying to keep him on the makeshift bunk and covered up.

"At no time was he conscious of having been in an airplane crash. He was constantly dictating letters of a medical nature."

The scene was, in fact, surreal, exhibiting the intense irrationality of a dream – or a horrendous nightmare. There was Snailham horribly dead, slumped over and still strapped in his broken seat, at the entrance to the radio room. Bird's battered corpse had fallen across the threshold of the open cabin door – an indication, perhaps, that he had been about to bail out after all in the final moments before the crash. Yet as Mackey struggled to take command of the appalling situation, Banting was oblivious of the scene around him. He alternatively tried to stand, or slumped on the improvised bunk, and carried on a confused conversation as if he were back in his laboratory in the Banting Institute in Toronto.

"Now, then, doctor," he said, addressing Mackey. "Doctor? I don't seem to know you. Have you just been sent over by Dr. Mackenzie to help here in the lab?"

"I'm sorry, Dr. Banting," Mackey began, "but you don't understand. We've had a terrible aircraft crash and . . . "

Banting plainly did not realize he was in an airplane, let alone a crash, and would have gone outside if Mackey had not, with great difficulty, prevented it.

"Yes, yes, these things happen . . . . Now, you are Dr. . . . ?"

"No, sir, I'm not a doctor at all," Mackey explained. "I'm the pilot of this aircraft and we've just had a terrible crash and my two crewmen are dead."

"Yes, I'm sure that will all be taken care of, all in good time," Banting said, his response indicating he had no understanding of their predicament, "but I must get this letter off today to the

Prime Minister, or else there's a good chance we're going to lose the war. Do you know what that means?"

As he spoke, Banting got up, swaying as if he would topple over, and actually got one foot out the door of the plane. Mackey moved quickly to his side to support him, seating him in the doorway. He struggled, fighting his own injuries, to get Sir Frederick back into the aircraft, and eventually back into the bunk.

"I have to get to work here," Banting kept saying. "Can't be wasting time . . . have to get out of my greatcoat . . . . Oh, my, it's almost bedtime . . . but I have to get these letters done. Take a letter to Dr. Collip . . . "

"Very good, Dr. Banting," Mackey said, reversing his approach in the hope that appearing to go along with Banting, to humour him, would help to calm him down.

"Whenever you're ready, I'll begin taking it down."

"Dear Dr. Collip . . ."

Banting again insisted he must remove his outer clothing, and Mackey again insisted he must keep them on.

"I'm afraid it's getting very late," Banting said. "Henrietta – my wife, you know – would be very unhappy if I didn't get a good night's sleep."

With that, he began once more to undress, and once again Mackey intervened to prevent it.

About noon, several hours after the crash, Banting finally succumbed to exhaustion and went to sleep. Mackey now felt it safe to leave him to seek help. He covered the scientist with a parachute and two overcoats. By this time Banting's face was terribly swollen, his eyes swollen shut.

"If you are to survive, Dr. Banting," the pilot told the motionless figure, "you need immediate medical assistance, and I have the hope that I may find it nearby."

It was a vain hope. Weakened by his own injuries, which included a badly bruised leg, a wrenched back, and the loss of blood from his head wound, plus lack of sleep, Mackey struggled through dense bush and deep snow on improvised snowshoes fashioned from pieces of aircraft wreckage. Having walked about two miles and found no help, the nearly exhausted pilot struggled back to the plane about six o'clock, barely able to crawl the last few yards.

When he checked inside the craft, Mackey was appalled to find that Banting was no longer there. After resting for about an hour, he began to search the area around the crash site. The scientist was located in the brush only twenty-five feet from the door of the plane in a half-reclining position. One of his shoes was off, and he was otherwise dressed but without his greatcoat. He had obviously been dead for some time.

Mackey went to the plane, got the greatcoat, and put it over him. The body would remain where it lay until searchers arrived on the scene three days later.

As he covered the remains, what Mackey had been trying so hard to put his finger on suddenly bobbed to the surface of his consciousness. Having been knocked out by the force of the blow that left him still dazed, face and head caked with blood, he now realized it was hardly possible that he had bandaged his own head. Snailham and Bird had both perished in the impact of the crash, so it was obvious that they could not have assisted him. Clearly, then, despite his own injuries, it was Banting who, true to the last to his calling as a physician, had ministered to Mackey.

It might even be that by stanching the considerable bleeding from the head wound, Banting was directly responsible for saving the pilot's life.

There had been no distress call as such from Mackey. However, when the request for radio bearings to steer for Gander was first received, it was clear to McGrath and the others, anxiously waiting and wondering at the Newfoundland Airport, that Hudson T-9449 must be in trouble, even though it had made no clear signal to that effect. All attempts to contact the Hudson further to determine the condition and the position of the aircraft were met by silence, and so the assumption was made that there had been a wireless failure. At first this provoked no great worry, but after an hour had passed the level of concern rose perceptibly.

McGrath had ordered the airport's rotating beacon turned on in the hope it would assist Mackey in his approach, but to no avail. He had a homing signal broadcast at regular intervals, and ordered a watch maintained on all likely radio frequencies which the aircraft might use to call the station, but without result. The group leader of the five-aircraft formation of which T-9449 was a member, aircraft No. T-9445, was asked if he was in wireless communication with Mackey's craft, but he advised that he had not heard T-9449 after 01:02 G. M. T.

Not until Mackey had failed to make an appearance by 03:30 G. M. T., midnight local time, did McGrath send his original telegram to Manning, Secretary of Public Utilities.

The report from the village of Newtown, that an aircraft had been heard at 9:25 p.m., was considered highly significant. Given all the known factors, there was a strong possibility the Hudson might have come down between the area of the Bonavista North coast known as the Straight Shore and the airport, possibly due to engine trouble.

The day after the disappearance was marked by light snow and low ceiling, but by early afternoon three Digby aircraft of the Royal Canadian Air Force took off to search along the line of the radio bearings given to Mackey the night before. They patrolled the coast-line from Gander Bay to Poole's Island and seaward as far as the Funks. The area between the airport and the coast was thoroughly covered. But after three hours, with visibility totally obscured due to weather and approaching darkness, no evidence of the missing aircraft had been seen and they had to give up the search.

The searchers had no way of knowing that, in the attempt to return to Gander, T-9449 had strayed some forty miles off course, and had come to earth inland from Musgrave Harbour, rather than reversing its outward track through Wesleyville.

* * *

William R. Callahan

Mackey could hear and occasionally got a glimpse of search planes, but was unable to attract their attention. He tried to light a fire, in the hope searchers would spot it, but without success – the snow- and ice-covered wood he was able to gather without an axe simply would not burn. He managed to drain off any remaining fuel, ready to throw on some tree branches and set them on fire if a plane happened directly overhead.

However, snow falling overnight obscured the wreckage, its camouflage colours helping to hide it against the brush and trees. As a pilot himself, he realized that this, with poor visibility, made discovery of the wreckage from the air difficult or unlikely.

"It seemed a completely hopeless situation and I was tempted to surrender all hope and simply join my comrades by lying down and sleeping then and there," the sole survivor of the crash would tell *The Toronto Star* in a subsequent interview. "But there was food in the ship, sandwiches, oranges which I had brought from a recent trip to Florida, and which I had presented to Bird, my navigator, to take home to his family in England. And numerous tins of emergency rations, a sort of chocolate compound."

After battling snow and bitter winds to get back to the crash site, and finding that Banting had perished, Mackey ate a little and then dug a pit in the snow alongside the wreckage. He wrapped himself in overcoats with an aircraft engine cover beneath him.

"That was my second night. I was extremely uncomfortable and thought dawn would never come. But when it came, I had sufficiently rested and got control of my ideas to the extent that I realized I must formulate some basic plan."

It took him nearly an hour just to get to his feet the next morning, but he managed to reach a large exposed rock, fifty yards from the wreckage, that he had decided would be his headquarters. There he made a list of everything he had that could be of use, and began studying a map of the area. He figured he could intercept the railway line some twenty-five miles due west of his position.

"I decided that I would get out, even if it took me a month. Should the weather remain flyable I would remain still another day. If the weather was not flyable and no plane was likely to come near, I would set out in a westerly direction."

With makeshift snowshoes made from a plyboard map locker, and a toboggan fashioned from the metal of an engine cowling, he estimated he could travel five miles a day, or, if only one mile a day, he would reach the railway in twenty-five days. He was ready to set out the following morning. But it was not to be. The day dawned fine and sunny. A search plane flew directly overhead, then returned. It had spotted first the wreckage, and then, nearby, a madly waving Mackey with his signal fire blazing.

The searchers, Mackey's friend Captain James Allison and co-pilot William Dunnicliffe, dropped a sheet of logbook paper weighted down with a wrench from their plane's toolbox. Its simple message conveyed everything the downed flyer needed to know: "Bringing help. Jim and Dunny."

TWENTY-SIX

Dockside, Corner Brook, Newfoundland, February 1941

IT WAS INEVITABLE that they would be nicknamed the "lake-head twins."

Royal Canadian Navy Corvette *K-233* was the first of her kind built and launched at the Port Arthur Shipbuilding Co., so at the insistence of the town council she was christened – no surprise – HMCS *Port Arthur*. She was followed by the Bangor class minesweeper *J-311* which, to be fair – again, no surprise – was named HMCS *Fort William* after the adjacent Ontario lakehead community that supplied roughly half the shipyard's workers. One day the two towns would be amalgamated to form the City of Thunder Bay.

They rode restlessly side by side on the rising tide sweeping up Humber Arm from the North Atlantic, *Fort William* against the dock and *Port Arthur* in the outside position. It was pure coincidence that two of His Majesty's Canadian Ships out of the same yard happened to be in the Newfoundland port at the same time. Their berth at the Bowater's paper mill jetty in the harbour of Corner Brook was encrusted with a layer of dirty, late February snow and overnight had acquired an icy crust that made for treacherous footing.

As the worst of bloody bad luck would have it, a tipsy young rating from Nova Scotia named McLeod, returning in the small hours from the fleshpots of Corner Brook, reached for the gangplank railing and, before he could grasp it, slipped on the ice. He hurtled headlong into the narrow space between ship and wharf just as *Fort William* ("Wee Willie," the men called her when in a kindly mood; other, far less flattering names when not) lurched against the structure, driven by a particularly heavy swell. The sailor was crushed between steel vessel and wooden pilings and died instantly.

"Squashed like a bug, he was. Never stood a chance," observed Chief Petty Officer James Rivers McKay, the ship's quartermaster, though he himself was on shore leave when it happened.

Retrieving the body presented a difficult challenge. Rather than risk other lives, the captain ordered the engines started up and the ship backed away from the berth – which, of course, meant that *Port Arthur* was required to back off as well. When they were made fast again a safety net was slung below *Fort William*'s gangplank to lessen chances of it happening again.

"Shutting the goddamn barn door too late," McKay growled.

He had little liking for the captain, Lieut.-Cmdr. James Guildford Slate, R.N. Slate was among a flood of British career officers imported by the Royal Canadian Navy to make up for a perceived shortage of experienced Canadian skippers for a rapidly expanding naval fleet at the outbreak of the Second World War. Far better, McKay maintained with considerable justification, to commission experienced Canadian seamen like himself to assume command of the new ships.

Only lately had Bowater's (Nfld.) Pulp & Paper Mills Ltd. landed a profitable contract for the repair and refit of naval and other vessels banged up in convoy mishaps, damaged by enemy action, or simply in need of mostly overdue but nonetheless necessary maintenance and refit. Rumour had it that Sir Eric Vansittart Bowater, the newsprint mill's owner, was well-connected in British political circles, and the contract was the result. That might well be, but it was also true that repair yards in Canada's Maritime Provinces were unable to handle the volume of work brought about by the war.

The overflow was welcomed by the workers of Corner Brook. A production slowdown had occurred because of the recruitment of hundreds of loggers for an Overseas Forestry Unit for wartime work in England, leaving Bowater's in short supply of people to harvest raw material locally. Besides, several newsprint-carrying ships had been lost to German submarines, and the scarcity of replacement vessels meant Corner Brook's paper storage sheds, like those of Anglo-Newfoundland Development Co. in Grand Falls, were rapidly filling up and soon would reach capacity. Production output might have to be cut drastically until and unless normal flows to the market were restored. In the meantime, from the point of view of the workers, war work at home in Corner Brook was much to be preferred to having to leave, perhaps, for the L. H. Cahn Ltd. shipyard in Louisburg, Nova Scotia, or for Halifax, Sydney, or Pictou, in search of a paycheque.

Fort William had come off patrol in the stormy, ice- and U-boat-laden Gulf of St. Lawrence a full six weeks ago, and would soon be back at sea, while *Port Arthur* was a more recent arrival. A force of Newfoundland jack-of-all-trades millwrights and machinists, whose regular job was to keep the paper mill operating at a high level of production and profitability, had swarmed over the vessels to correct a myriad of problems and complaints. They might not be serious in themselves, but combined to impair performance and, although this seemed to excite little official concern, could easily put the lives of crew in jeopardy.

Members of the ships' companies who had not been sent back to Canada on leave during refit made friends with Corner Brook families who opened their homes and welcomed the Canadians to their tables. In return the sailors lavished on their hosts a variety from a seemingly endless supply of ship's stores: all manner of tinned foods, cigarettes and pipe tobacco, Canadian whisky and beer, impossible-to-buy "real" butter, and sugar and tea rationed locally. Carted ashore illegally these were clearly contraband – if not actually stolen goods – and naval and local authorities wished to crack down.

McKay prepared to head for dry land, anticipating an enjoyable weekend with the family of Bowater's machinist William

Bernard "Billy" Callahan with whom he had struck up a friendship. He filled huge pockets sewn inside his petty officer's greatcoat with such forbidden goods as a bottle of Canadian Club whisky, a six-pound tin of boiled ham, a carton of Player's Navy Cut cigarettes, a couple of tins of British Columbia salmon, and a bottle containing collected daily "tots" of black, extra-proof Lamb's Navy rum that various members of the crew were prepared to trade for something far more desirable and a lot harder to come by than the booze the Royal Canadian Navy ladled out in its daily quarterdeck ceremony – in this case, a few buns of fresh, home-baked bread.

The lady of the house, Alice Marie, had the knack of turning out the crustiest, most delicious, mouth-watering loaves any of them had eaten since leaving the Prairies, the cities of Ontario, the backwoods of Québec, or the fishing villages of the Maritimes. There was nothing more precious or inviting to young sailors away from home than a taste of Mom's cooking – either the real thing or a realistic facsimile.

Navigating from steel deck to icy gangplank McKay, a big man, stepped gingerly, remembering what had befallen young McLeod, and careful that his concealed burden not become overly obvious to the armed Officer of the Deck and a rating wearing a Shore Patrol armband and white spats. In fact, they hardly noticed as he disembarked. His destination was the West Side of Corner Brook, a considerable walk for a man carrying his burden if you couldn't find a cab, so he was relieved to see a vehicle with the label Star Taxi painted on its side, its motor idling, waiting just outside the paper mill gate. He yanked open a door only to find the back seat already occupied by a fellow pointing an automatic pistol.

"Shut up and get in, quick," the gunman commanded with an unmistakable American accent, before the sailor had a chance to utter a word. "We haven't got all night."

Soon after learning of the overwhelming success of Altehouse's assignment at the Newfoundland Airport, Stroesser received a warning that the United States authorities were on to the California airman. They had finally traced him to the *Edmund B. Alexander*, and if they had any doubt about being on the right track, it was erased by Pattison's inquiry from the Newfoundland Airport.

For Stroesser's purposes, the Civil Defence offices where a low-level operative had been installed as a secretary-clerk, proved to be just the important information source that he knew it would. The place had been abuzz with the news of the Banting plane crash and then, a couple of days later, there were rumours that the bomber had been sabotaged. The talk among Col. Outerbridge's staff was that a member of the United States Army Air Corps – or someone posing as a member of that organization – was believed to be responsible. According to the rumours the Federal Bureau of Investigation and the Military Police were now on the lookout for that person.

Altehouse had returned to Botwood, where it had been agreed he would have the least visibility until his next assignment was determined. But based on the intelligence he received, Stroesser contacted him at once, instructing that he leave immediately for Canada, preferably Montréal or Toronto. There he would be able to lose himself in the big city population.

"You will require a new identity, of course," Stroesser reminded him, pointing out that the best disguise was a military one – but preferably not American.

"Usually nobody questions anyone in an Allied military uniform around here," he added. "However, after your little escapade, United States servicemen are sure to get a second look. I suggest you start in Corner Brook to look for a Canadian uniform. There are bound to be some Canadian military personnel there, or local militia. They look the same."

When Altehouse stepped down from a Newfoundland Railway coach at the Corner Brook train station, the first thing he encountered was a cloud of choking vapour, with the distinctive odour and searing effect of sulphuric acid, carried by a stiff wind blowing in the Bay of Islands from the Gulf of St. Lawrence.

Spotting a taxi nearby, he got in and, between spasms of coughing, questioned the driver. "What in hell is that?" he asked, handkerchief daubing his watering eyes.

"You mean that lovely stuff we got to breathe around here? That's where they blow the digesters in the mill – every few hours they exhaust the steam from cooking the wood in acid to make the paper," the taxi driver explained. "It also kills the trees around town, and some of us think it's killing the people. Where do you want to go, brother?"

"Looking for my cousin," Altehouse gasped. "Supposed to be coming in on a warship of some kind today, or maybe he's already here. Do you know where they come ashore?"

"I'll take you over to the mill gate," the driver said.

A few minutes later Altehouse spied a man in Royal Canadian Navy uniform exiting the mill yard.

"There's my cousin now," he lied to the driver, as McKay approached the cab. In no time flat he had them both covered with his pistol.

"I knew damn well you were up to no good," the taxi driver swore.

"That's enough," Altehouse said. "Let's go to the quietest, loneliest place you can think of, and make it snappy! And as for you," he continued, turning to McKay, "Start getting undressed. I need that uniform!"

Nelligan, the driver, took them to an area of the West Side officially known as Crow Gulch, otherwise the Western Front. It had been declared off limits to service personnel due to the bootlegging and other nefarious practices carried on there. Military police avoided it if they could.

It ran parallel to a section of the inner harbour where Bowater's anchored its pulpwood booms, and the railway went through it. Nearly twenty years after completion of what would be the world's largest integrated pulp and paper mill, the "temporary" tarpaper bunkhouses known as Fisher's Shacks, constructed for the hundreds of workmen who had come flooding in during mill construction, were still in use as cheap rental accommodation. It was here that Nelligan lived, and here that he brought his passengers with a gun held to the back of his skull.

"What are you gonna do with us?" He was almost afraid to ask, but felt he had to say something.

"Out, both of you," Altehouse ordered. "Is this your shack?" he demanded of Nelligan.

"Yeah," Nelligan answered. "But what are you gonna do with us?"

Altehouse ordered them inside and quickly exchanged the sailor's clothing for his own. The shack was only a couple of dozen feet from the water's edge, and despite the late afternoon darkness closing in, it was possible to make out the end of the wooden boom, made up of twelve-foot-long, two-foot-wide Douglas fir sections from British Columbia. Chained together, they enclosed the mill's feedstock of four-foot spruce and fir pulpwood logs.

"Out on the boom," Altehouse ordered. They had no choice but to comply, stepping gingerly, Nelligan first, and then McKay shivering in his underwear. Altehouse, only a couple of feet behind, raised his pistol and without hesitation shot both in the back of the head. Their bodies tumbled into the water, almost indistinguishable from the pulp logs among which they fell.

Born in London, England in 1900, Henry Montague Spencer Lewin, who liked to be known as "Monty," was the boss of the Corner Brook newsprint mill and its ancillary operations. He also ran Corner Brook itself – the beautifully planned and built company Townsite, as distinct from the higgledy-piggledy, mainly squatters' areas of the West Side and the railway village of Humbermouth. Fading economically, the original main Bay of Islands settlement of Curling, to the west, was nonetheless openly jealous of its seniority and considered itself more "respectable" than the upstart industrial area.

Lewin had an insistent finger in most things connected with the broad community that surrounded the huge mill on three sides.

Some people thought his initials "H. M. S." indicated some sort of royal prerogative, and it sometimes appeared that perhaps he did too. He grandly supported the war effort, guaranteeing the jobs of men who enlisted for overseas service who would return after the conflict, and creating a water-borne Bay of Islands Defence Force in which his own cabin cruiser played a prominent part, complementing the government's local Home Defence organization. After Goering's *Luftwaffe* began pounding British cities, and British families came to the painful decision to send their children to the questionable safety of the countryside and then out of England altogether, youngsters with unfamiliar names such as Ditchburn, Packer, and Holloway began arriving in Corner Brook. They crossed the ocean on Bowater ships to become wartime members of families with names like Rendell and Hann, Sexton, Smith, and Nichols. Needless to say, Lewin had his finger in this too.

Few would disagree that the British-born accountant whom Sir Eric Bowater had put in charge of his Newfoundland empire had made a first-class job of it, redefining the term benevolent dictatorship with emphasis clearly on the benevolent.

When Britain's J. Arthur Rank organization decided to make one of the first feature-length propaganda films of the Second World War, *The 49ᵗʰ Parallel*, with such top-notch actors as Laurence Olivier, Leslie Howard, Eric Portman, Glynis Johns, and Raymond Massey, it was to Lewin that they came for assistance – no doubt with Sir Eric's approval. A replica of a Nazi U-boat was constructed and towed to the outer reaches of Bay of Islands. Some two dozen men from the community, including such prominent names as mill foremen Charles Ballam and Jack Fisher, and optometrist Karl Trapnell, director of the Corner Brook Military Band, were recruited as actors and extras for the film, whose storyline included the sinking of an oil tanker with the improbable name SS *Anticostilite* by a submarine whose principal objective was to establish a clandestine weather station on the Labrador coast – a case of fiction presaging, if not actually imitating, real life.

Lewin arranged for members of Bowater's electrical department to assist by wiring the fake sub to explode at the moment a Royal Canadian Air Force Catalina flying boat appeared to bomb the craft.

As the tugboat *Balsam Lake*, carrying the wiring crew, returned to its berth not far from the place where hot, sulphurous liquors were discharged into the harbour from the mill, those on board noticed something unusual in the water just off the port bow. When the tug diverted to the spot, they realized that it was the body of a man, clad only in underwear, floating face up. Nobody recognized him. Using boathooks, they began to tow the cadaver towards the dock. Then they spotted a second one, this one fully-clothed, and there was instant recognition – one of the men knew the face right away.

"I know who that is," he said, in a state of shock. "Henry Nelligan. A cousin of the wife's mother. Since the cutbacks in the mill he's been driving for Star Taxi. My God, I wonder what could have happened?"

They would find out soon enough.

The Newfoundland Constabulary's head of the Corner Brook detachment, Sergeant Michael Keough, came accompanied by Constables Walter Mugford and Stanley Martin. After examining the shoreline adjacent to the area of the harbour where the bodies were found, they had them conveyed to the Corner Brook Hospital. There the superintendent, William J. Cochrane, M.D., conducted a preliminary examination.

"They've both been shot to death at close range," he informed Keough, "in the back of the head, execution-style. Very unusual in this part of the world.

"Normally, I'd say they must be dead several days to come to the surface like that, especially at this time of year, but the mill outfall temperature may have helped to raise them up sooner.

"It's a nice problem you've got on your hands, Sergeant. I should have the complete autopsy reports within forty-eight hours, but I don't expect the result will be very different from the preliminary finding."

The following day Keough heard from Slate, who was concerned that his quartermaster, McKay, seemed to have gone missing.

"What does he look like, Captain?" the policeman asked.

"It's Lieutenant Commander, if you please, Sergeant. Big man, close to six feet, one hundred and eighty or one hundred and ninety pounds. Black hair cropped short. Should be easy to spot in his Chief Petty Officer's uniform."

"No uniform. What about distinguishing marks – tattoos, for example?"

"Yes, now that you mention it, he does have a striking tattoo on his right forearm – "Mother," entwined with roses and religious symbols."

"Lieutenant Commander, I'm afraid we have bad news for you," Keough said. "There's a man in the hospital morgue with just such a tattoo. He's been shot to death."

At this time the SS *Caribou* was approaching her berth in North Sydney, Nova Scotia, the end of her run from Port aux Basques, Newfoundland. Altehouse, having assumed the persona of McKay, was among the passengers. Within a couple of hours the Royal Canadian Navy man in ill-fitting Chief Petty Officer's uniform would be enjoying a large breakfast on board the Canadian National Railway's *Ocean Limited*. The following day he would fade into the burgeoning crowds on Rue Ste-Catherine in Montréal, Québec. He would never be seen in Newfoundland again.

TWENTY-SEVEN

Emergency Government Meeting,
St. John's, Newfoundland, 1941

THE GOVERNOR OF Newfoundland was damned angry – as well as extremely concerned. Not only had unwelcome world attention been sharply focused upon his jurisdiction, the inevitable consequence of the death of such an important person, under what would certainly be seen by many as suspicious circumstances, he was certain questions were being asked in high places about the quality and effectiveness of wartime security in the colony generally, as well as specific locations such as the extremely sensitive Newfoundland Airport. Regardless of who was responsible, it reflected badly upon himself as Governor, and upon the Commission of Government of which he was the chairman.

"To speak plainly, it's bloody embarrassing," Walwyn told an emergency meeting of the Commission, "and make no mistake, it casts each one of us in an unfavourable light, even though we had absolutely nothing to do with it, no responsibility for it, nothing. I can just hear the talk today around Whitehall. The professional naysayers in the Home Office and the Colonial Secretary's must be having a field day, and don't think it's the kind of thing that won't somehow affect each of our futures!"

Sir Wilfred Woods, the Commissioner for Public Utilities, which also included Public Works, under whose authority the Newfoundland Airport operated, pointed out that the security responsibility actually belonged to the Canadians. They would shortly be taking over complete control of the world-class facility for the duration of the war.

"Your Excellency, we still have every reason to believe that the security provided by the Canadian Black Watch troops was and is adequate. Brigadier Earnshaw has assured us over and over that it is in good hands, and we still have no evidence that anything untoward occurred. I really don't see how we could."

The Governor intervened.

"Sir Wilfred, if I may . . . . I'm afraid there really is no point trying to justify our position, certainly not within these walls.

"The fact is we have a first-class tragedy as well as a major embarrassment on our hands, and the question is what can we do to help ensure, so far as we are able, that nothing like it ever happens again?"

The door opened to admit Commissioner Emerson, responsible for Justice and Defence. His arm full of papers, he hurriedly took his seat.

"Good morning, Your Excellency . . . gentlemen . . . . Sorry to have been delayed," he said, looking somewhat ruffled and slightly out of breath.

"We are, of course, receiving reports continuously with regard to the terrible business at Musgrave Harbour, and as I am sure you know now that the pilot, a man named Mackey – an American citizen, as it happens – has been spotted on the ground, alive and apparently relatively uninjured, so at least we shall have some first-hand information forthcoming as to what actually occurred on the unfortunate flight.

"However, I put this to you. Five Hudson bombers are manufactured at about the same time in the same plant of the Lockheed Aircraft Corporation in Burbank, California. These aircraft, which for all intents and purposes are identical, are ferried into Canada at approximately the same time in similar circumstances, and then from St. Hubert, Québec to Newfoundland.

"At the Newfoundland Airport one, and possibly two, receive a fairly thorough inspection before all five take off in the space of a few minutes for England – we know now that the Banting airplane, if I may call it that, was *not* given a major inspection by the authorized Canadian Pacific Air Service engineers, because the pilot did not wish it. It was in fine shape, or so he told the mechanics. But it was inspected, apparently, without his knowledge, by a man purporting to represent the United States Army Air Corps and the Lockheed Aircraft Corporation. That man, it seems, has disappeared.

"So, gentlemen, we have all five of these aircraft, identical in virtually every respect, leaving for England together, and four of them cross the Atlantic Ocean as nice as you please – not a stain of trouble on the part of any of them. But the fifth and last gets twenty-five or thirty miles out and suddenly loses an engine, turns back, then loses its second engine, and crashes well off course trying to return to the airport.

"Does this suggest anything to you? To me it defies logic and common sense. To me it means that something particular occurred to cause this fifth airplane to develop insurmountable trouble. And that something, in my opinion, was sabotage."

Having delivered himself of this missive, Emerson sat back, permitting his fellow Commissioners to consider it. The Governor was the first to respond.

"Thank you, Emerson," he said. "I grant your logic, but of course, there is not a scintilla of evidence to back it up, and in the end it will be objective evidence that will be relied upon to determine the cause of the crash. Does anyone else wish to address this matter?"

In the shocked silence only Woods indicated he did, and the Governor nodded consent.

"I really do believe, Your Excellency," he persisted, "that we must ensure that the responsibility for security, and the blame if anything went wrong, is put where it belongs – which is squarely upon the Canadians."

"Thank you once again, Sir Wilfred. I believe we have captured that thought," Walwyn commented drily. "Anyone else?

Then let us move on to consideration of the next step. I believe that Emerson has a formal motion."

"Yes, Your Excellency. In my capacity as the Commissioner for Justice, I wish to advise that a formal Court of Inquiry should be constituted without delay to investigate the incident at Musgrave Harbour.

"Already, the pro forma magisterial inquiry under the Inquiries Act has been ordered, and will be conducted by Magistrate Hollett, J.P., from Grand Falls. This will consist of taking depositions of witnesses and generally describing the circumstances of the matter.

"The more extensive Court of Inquiry examining the particular, technical aspects and reporting on the crash of Hudson bomber T-9449, together with such recommendations as the Court may see fit to make, and with an apportionment of blame if such is considered desirable, should be carried out by persons with the appropriate expertise. I defer to Sir Wilfred in this regard."

"Yes, thank you, Emerson," Woods said.

"I propose to invite Air Commodore G. V. Walsh of the Royal Canadian Air Force to be president of this Court of Inquiry, with Wing Commander Adams of the R.C.A.F. and Stewart Graham, Esq. of the Canadian Department of Transport as the other members. I request the authorization of my Colleagues for the establishment of the Court of Inquiry as proposed."

"Thank you, Sir Wilfred," the Governor said. "Does the Commissioner have authority to proceed as just outlined?"

John C. Puddester, Commissioner for Public Health and Welfare and the most senior of three local Commissioners – the others plus the Governor, all from England, gave the Crown a perpetual majority – questioned why it had to be an all-Canadian court.

"Couldn't there be at least one Newfoundland member? This has the ring of the Amulree Commission, which bothered many people because no Newfoundlander was involved in deciding the future of the country. I foresee a similar public reaction in this case, and I suggest we have to be more careful. We could at least appoint our own Air Advisor, Squadron Leader Pattison, if not Captain Fraser or Captain Sullivan who are both experienced local aviators. I believe we should make use of their expertise."

"It would seem to me," said Emerson, also a Newfoundland member of the Commission but more restrained in his views than Puddester, "that the way to ensure impartiality – and the appearance of impartiality, which may be even more important – is, indeed, to have a completely outside Court. Therefore, I support Sir Wilfred's proposal."

James A. Winter, Commissioner for Home Affairs and Education, had been Speaker of the House of Assembly before it was abolished and replaced by the Commission, and was soon coming to the end of his term. He offered no objection, and the English members similarly remained silent.

The Commission operated essentially on the British Cabinet system – decisions arrived at by consensus, with votes ordinarily not taken, and none recorded. In this matter there could be no doubt that the consensus favoured Woods's recommendation.

"Very well, then, gentlemen," Governor Walwyn pronounced with an air of finality, "there being no further discussion, I declare that the proposal is approved."

As he did so, however, Sir Humphrey was overcome by the strongest conviction that the sabotage of the Banting aircraft – for, privately, he was certain it had been no accident – was only the beginning. Before this war is over, he told himself, little Newfoundland could very well undergo her own particular reign of terror, and he was the man who would have to preside over it and persuade the people to carry on, no matter what.

* * *

Constable Gilbert Hiscock of the Newfoundland Constabulary, stationed at Carmanville, had been ordered by telegram from the Chief of Police in St. John's to proceed at once to Musgrave Harbour, a distance south of nearly twenty miles over rough logging trails, to take charge of the situation there.

However, when he looked around for a conveyance, there were no horses available in Carmanville, all being in the woods, engaged in the logging operations that would supply the community with fuel and building materials for the ensuing year. The United Church minister, Reverend Francis W. Mitchinson, came to the rescue with the offer of his dog team, which was promptly accepted, although another three dogs were needed, and hired, considering the length of the journey, the difficult terrain, and the weather.

"I would like to get started right away, Reverend," Hiscock said, "even though it means we're going to be travelling mostly in the dark. I do appreciate your willingness to take me. There's no reason your expenses will not be paid, just as if I were hiring a horse and sleigh."

The clergyman, not long arrived in Newfoundland from England, was pensive. He had limited experience travelling in Newfoundland in winter, and actually was little daunted by the difficulties and dangers he was sure could be involved. Yet, he was a methodical man and exactingly careful to make preparations that, to the maximum degree, would offset the foreseeable hazards of the journey.

"It's not the expenses I worry about, Constable," he replied. "It's keeping on the trail in the dark, and besides it's getting stormy. There's always the chance we could get lost, so we need to take supplies for three or four days, dry kindling for starting a fire, and a good axe is as important as a good tent. And extra clothes. I can't imagine there's much worse than trying to keep warm in the open in wet or damp clothes."

The route from Carmanville to Musgrave Harbour, on the Straight Shore, was virtually obliterated by winter snows.

Nonetheless, they would have to leave the seacoast to head inland, skirting the inlets of Hamilton Sound – Carmanville Arm, Middle Arm and Eastern Arm – and then bear northeast roughly paralleling the course of the Ragged Harbour River.

"I estimate we're soon going to be near Alder Harbour," Mitchinson shouted to Hiscock above the howling of the wind. "Perhaps we should stop for a while and reconsider our situation?"

The policeman, who was younger and inclined to be respectful of the cloth, had insisted that the minister ride the komatik while he stood, feet wide apart, on the ends of the runners or, to save the dogs, donned snowshoes and ran along behind. Occasionally he had to use the drug chain under the runners to slow them so he could keep up. It was dark and snowing a blizzard now, and they were crossing a number of frozen marshes where the tracks were drifted in. But Hiscock was determined to press on.

"I feel we should continue," he replied. "That's our best course. Besides, my orders are to get to Musgrave Harbour as quickly as possible."

Mitchinson nodded assent, but later would record his misgivings:

"So we proceeded. It was impossible for us both to ride, so the Constable insisted that I be the fortunate one most of the time. Only those who have made a similar journey will know what this one was like. Most of the dogs we had had worked in the woods all day. Despite our handicaps we arrived at 1 a.m."

The officials were accommodated at the home of Frank Whiteway. Wisely, the Justice of the Peace had instructed the search party to bring Mackey there to await Hiscock's arrival. The pilot was being cared for by the Public Health nurse, Eleanor "Nellie" Parsons. When the policeman arrived, she reluctantly permitted him to see her patient, who had been made as comfortable as possible on a lounge in a front room, with his head wound heavily bandaged.

"It is extremely difficult to know the extent of his injuries," she said, "except that he has a serious blow to the head which looks to have been bandaged by someone who knew what they were doing. It's hard to believe he treated the injury himself, in the situation he was in," she suggested somewhat mysteriously.

"I don't plan to remove the bandage until later, because it is better that he rest. The journey from the crash site was not very comfortable for him, and rest can do more for him now than anything else."

"I understand your position, Nurse," Hiscock said, "but I have a job to do too, and part of it is finding out, as far as possible, exactly what happened to cause the deaths of three men, including one of the most famous men in the world."

Finally she agreed that Hiscock might question the injured pilot, who was conscious and alert, but "only for a few minutes."

Mackey related the sequence of events that had overtaken him and his plane. He had gotten less than fifty miles out over the ocean, he estimated, when one of the engines gave out. He tried to get back to the airport on the one remaining, but it also failed.

"He believes it exploded," Hiscock noted in a report to his superiors, "as his windshield was covered with oil. He was still flying by instruments and knew nothing until he felt the plane strike and crash. He does not remember bandaging his head."

Considering the ordeal the pilot had been through, Hiscock harboured doubts about interrogating Mackey further – Nurse Parsons thoroughly disagreed with him doing it in the first place. But the questioning was important. For example, the Constable had established in the course of the interview that, unlike Snailham and Bird, Banting had survived the crash of Hudson T-9449.

"Captain Mackey stated that the doctor lived all that morning, and until some time in the afternoon, February 21st," Hiscock wrote in his report.

"He was not there when death ensued – he had gone to look for help, and when he got back a few hours later the doctor had died. He further stated that he knew the doctor to be badly injured, in addition to a broken arm, and doubted, even if medical aid had been immediately given, of his ever recovering."

It was hardly a valid medical opinion; but then, who was in a position to dispute it?

TWENTY-EIGHT

Retrieving the Dead, Musgrave Harbour, Newfoundland, 1941

F OLLOWING HIS INTERVIEW with Mackey, difficult as it was, Hiscock faced a far less pleasant task: the need to attend to the bodies of those who, unlike the pilot, had not survived the crash. The arrival in Musgrave Harbour of searchers with the remains of Banting, Bird, and Snailham had occurred about 3:00 a.m., a couple of hours after the policeman and his clerical companion reached the Bonavista Bay village.

Once they had located the wreckage of the plane around 5:00 p.m. the previous day, and recovered the bodies which were loaded on hand-drawn sleighs, the searchers had to struggle through the night for more than seven hours, impeded by darkness, heavy snowdrifts, and dense woods, to drag them to the community. There they were laid out on large banquet tables in the Orange Hall, where Hiscock immediately assumed custody.

"I've never really got used to examining dead bodies, for all my time on the force," the Constable remarked to Mitchinson. The latter had offered to assist and surprised Hiscock by admitting that he, too, had a strong aversion to dealing with cadavers, even though, as a clergyman, he had to do it often enough.

"No matter how you look at it, Constable, it is far from an agreeable duty," he concurred, as they approached the first of the three remains in the dim light of kerosene oil lamps in the chilly cavern of a hall that had not been heated since the last Lodge meeting several days earlier. Whiteway had seen to the lighting of the big, brown space heater, but before its effects could be felt Hiscock shut it off again, realizing that the cold was required for the preservation of the corpses.

For Hiscock, it was mainly a matter of going through pockets to establish identities beyond question, if he could, and to take account of valuables that they might be carrying such as amounts of money and personal items. A general description of the condition of the dead persons, and such details as how they were attired, would prove useful, perhaps vitally important, later on. The general medical condition, such as obvious injuries that might contribute to a person's death, would be noted. The actual detailed examination, of course, would be carried out later by a qualified physician.

They turned to the corpse of Banting, still covered with his military greatcoat, where it lay stretched out on a banquet table.

"Sir Frederick Banting was wearing a khaki uniform," the policeman wrote in his report, the same officer's uniform in which he had cut such a fine figure at the Ottawa reception for Duncan, and that commanded the respect of young fellows like Goff and Murphy during his visit to the Newfoundland Airport.

Banting was a complete stranger to Hiscock, who correctly surmised, however, that cuts around the eyes probably meant he had worn glasses that were smashed into his face on impact with some part of the plane. When he mentioned this to Mitchinson, the minister agreed, saying he remembered a photograph in one of the British papers in which the dead man had been wearing steel-rimmed spectacles.

"He looked badly smashed and a considerable amount of blood was around his face and hands; his arm was broken and he was badly swollen," the Constable recorded.

"I do not know the extent of his injuries as this was very difficult to determine. He had no boots on his feet and no cap, but his greatcoat was brought out with him."

Having finished examining Banting's remains, they re-lit the space heater temporarily to hold their chilled hands over the firebox and generally warm themselves. Then they shut it off again.

"You're absolutely right, you know, Reverend," said Hiscock, in the interests of making conversation. "This is anything but an agreeable duty. But it has to be done, and we are the ones who have to do it."

Accordingly, after a few minutes they resumed their grim work.

On going through the pockets of the second victim, they established that the body was that of Flying Officer Bird, a member of the Royal Air Force, and the navigator.

"He was lying straight, with boots off," Hiscock wrote. "He had on an aviator's cap, black leather coat, and blue pants."

They saw that Bird's face also was badly smashed.

"His arms and legs appeared as if they were all broken," the Constable recorded, "and he had attached to him a parachute, which I sent along with the body. This body, I was informed, was found by the port door of the plane, which looks as if he was about to bail out when the plane crashed."

Even before they located his identification, they knew the third and final victim had to be William Snailham, the wireless operator.

The body was "bent somewhat forward," Hiscock wrote. "He was the most severely injured of the three men; his forehead was smashed in, his nose smashed and split, and his chin was broken and crushed. I could not tell if any of his limbs were broken."

The policeman also noted that Snailham was wearing civilian clothes with low shoes on his feet. He ascertained that, when found, the man "was strapped in his seat, occupying the doorway of the Control Room" – the aperture between the radio room and the plane's cockpit.

"Well, that's it then," the policeman said, closing the school exercise book in which he had been making his notes. He would transcribe them into a formal report for Constabulary Headquarters in St. John's as soon as he had access to a typewriter.

"I really do appreciate your assistance – and especially your company," he told the minister. "This is a hard place to spend the night alone, at this kind of work. I appreciate your being here . . . and also the use of your dog team."

"Very pleased to be able to help, Constable," Mitchison said. "Perhaps we'll find reason to work with each other again some-time."

With that they shook hands, and as dawn was breaking the minister left to get his dogs ready for the run back to his home in Carmanville. The weather was fine, and barring any trouble, he figured on making it by mid-afternoon at the latest. Although he did not know it at the moment, he would be asked to change his plans.

Hiscock decided a couple of hours' sleep would be a good idea, and stretched out on a couch by the big stove in the Whiteway kitchen. He awoke about 9:00 a.m. and obtained the assistance of a half-dozen men to return to the Orange Hall and sheet the bodies in heavy sailcloth and sew them up.

Two Royal Canadian Air Force planes arrived at nearby Doting Cove, named for its population of bay seals or "doters," landing on the sea ice for the evacuation of Mackey and the bodies of the dead. Hiscock had the church bell rung at Musgrave Harbour to assemble the men of the community for the purpose of conveying them to the aircraft.

In his report to Chief of Police P. J. O'Neill, he advised:

"A short funeral service was held at the Orange Hall by Rev. Mitchinson, at the request of Capt. Mackey. A procession was formed, with a brass band in attendance, and the bodies conveyed to the plane where they were passed over to the pilots.

"Shortly afterwards a storm warning was received and the planes did not get away until the next morning. The plane with the bodies on board took off some hours before the plane conveying Captain Mackey back to the Airport."

* * *

On March 2, the Toronto *Globe and Mail* carried the latest reports on the death of Banting in the crash of Hudson T-9449, consisting of its own story of the arrival of the famed physician's remains in Toronto, together with a report by Canadian Press writer Bob Daldorph:

BRING BODY OF BANTING TO TORONTO

The body of Sir Frederick Banting, who died ten days ago in the Empire's service, was returned home late yesterday by members of the civilian flying service with whom he had been associated in his mission as a soldier-scientist.

The war-painted bomber, mate to the one which crashed in Newfoundland's wastes and carried Sir Frederick and two others to their deaths, sifted slowly into Malton Airport shortly after 7:00 p.m. and in the deep dusk his body was brought into the city.

Military authorities announced last night that the funeral would be held at Convocation Hall at 2:30 p.m. Tuesday, with interment following in Mount Pleasant Cemetery. The body, said the brief announcement, would lie in state in the hall until 12:30 p.m.

Under orders of the military, enforced by a closely spaced guard of airmen in training, the entire airport, from the front gates of the civilian and air observation fields to the distant boundary fences, was cleared of visitors before the bomber's arrival. Air crews, one after the other, as they came in from afternoon flights, were hustled out of their kit and placed on guard.

Friends and relatives meeting the Ottawa plane, and passengers for the Windsor flight were halted at the entrance to the T.C.A. field and finally were permitted to enter with an escort.

Then, after the sun had set and airport lights were beginning to reflect from the ice-covered fields, the bomber stole in from the east and with little preliminary settled down before the R.C.A.F. training post and taxied up to the apron. Even from a short distance its camouflaged flanks merged into background of mud and stubble.

In the presence only of the flying men, Britain's bomber ferry crew and civilian officials, the body of Sir Frederick was carried from the plane to a hearse. As it was driven up the lane through the air-training establishment, aircraftmen on guard at the gate and drawn up on each side of the road came to rigid attention and saluted.

The bomber which bore Sir Frederick home from the Newfoundland Airport yesterday morning halted at Montréal for fuel and to exchange crews, and continued on in charge of Capt. R. Humphrey Page, First Officer Thomas I. Davis, and Radio Operator H. S. Green.

The three had supper at the airport, and within an hour were winging back to Montréal.

At the University of Toronto the flower-bedecked lying-in-state came to an end. No hymns were sung. The organ played quietly. In the distance the Hart House carillon could be heard. Lady Banting and Sir Frederick's eleven-year-old son Bill sat quietly – stoically, news reports said – as President H. J. Cody offered a brief tribute:

"Soon or late we all must die," he intoned. "It is not given to everyone to die for his country, for freedom and for justice, to die in the path of duty, to die on a mission fraught with great significance to science and to the success of the great cause for which we fight. Such was the earthly end of Frederick Grant Banting. Tragic? Yes, but also triumphant."

He had served as a soldier, so Banting was given a soldier's burial – the coffin borne on a gun carriage drawn by an armoured car and escorted by 200 members of the Governor General's Horse Guards and the Royal Canadian Army Medical Corps. Major John McGarry walked behind the bier carrying his medals and decorations.

In Mount Pleasant Cemetery riflemen fired three volleys and a trumpeter played the Last Post.

Across the ocean in far-off, war-ravaged London, where only a few days earlier Banting had planned to be, General McNaughton joined the mourners in the famed, bomb-scarred church of St. Martin-in-the-Fields in busy, historic Trafalgar Square, facing across from Nelson's Column. They heard Canon G. C. Hepburn of Ottawa, Chief Protestant Chaplain of Canada's overseas army, describe the man who lost his life coming to the aid of Britain as "a great citizen of the world."

A bright sun streamed down on bustling London traffic outside, but none penetrated the church windows – they were boarded up as a result of an earlier bomb blast.

In his brief address, muffled by the roar of traffic in the square and briefly by an air-raid siren, Canon Hepburn recalled Churchill's tribute to the Royal Air Force – paraphrased to declare that never had so many been so consciously aware of the debt they owed to Banting and his colleages in the discovery of insulin.

Hymns were sung: "From Thee All Skill and Science Flow" and "Jesus Lives." Then the congregation, which included Canadian High Commissioner Vincent Massey, representatives of the Canadian medical corps, a group of Canadian nurses, and representatives of Allied forces, bowed their heads in prayer, asking that those keeping Sir Frederick "in glad remembrance" might "live the more bravely" on that account.

Other burials were taking place – those of the men who died with Banting in the Newfoundland wilderness. The Canadian Press wires carried the report to newspapers across Canada and the world:

By BOB DALDORPH

HALIFAX, March 2 (CP) – Ten days after they had plunged to death in the Newfoundland bush, the bodies of two men who died in a plane crash with Sir Frederick Banting were flown here today from Newfoundland Airport in a Royal Canadian Air Force plane.

I travelled in the plane with the bodies of Flying Officer William Bird of the Royal Air Force, navigator of the death plane, and William Snailham of Bedford, N.S., wireless operator. Shortly before we headed for Canada, another machine left Newfoundland Airport with Capt. Joseph Mackey, the pilot and only survivor of the crackup.

(Mackey was brought to Montréal by plane Sunday. Mackey, whose head was bandaged, was taken to hospital for examination after his arrival at St. Hubert airport. He was able to leave the plane without assistance.)

On the sombre 500-mile journey the bodies of the two victims lay on cots running along each side of the heavy machine. They had been sewn into shrouds of white canvas.

Sir Frederick's body, flown to the Newfoundland Airport from isolated Musgrave Harbour Friday after being moved ten miles by land from the scene of the crash, was still at Newfoundland Airport when our plane left. It was taken by plane to the Dominion later in the day.

No Ceremony Occurs

There was no ceremony as the bodies left Newfoundland. Ambulances brought the three bodies to the airfield and they were quickly placed aboard the two waiting military planes.

Officials in charge of the Newfoundland Airport, one of the world's largest, were in attendance as they started their final journey to Canada. I was the only civilian making the trip.

A hush settled and then powerful motors of the military plane sprang into life. A few sharp orders, and with throttles wide open it roared down the runway and into the air a few minutes after we had watched the ship bringing out Pilot Mackey take off. It was the first time in the airport's history that a funeral flight was witnessed.

Climbing immediately after the takeoff over the clouds and into brilliant sunshine, the pilot brought the plane to a gentle landing on the Nova Scotia airdrome – four hours after we left Newfoundland behind.

R.C.A.F. officers and men, a private hearse, and newspapermen surrounded the plane as it braked to a stop. Immediately after, the bodies were placed in flag-draped caskets and, as airmen stood at attention, were moved once more. Tonight arrangements were being completed for burial of the two victims in this city. Flying Officer Bird will be given an Air Force funeral at St. Paul's Anglican Church tomorrow afternoon. The funeral will be conducted by Flight-Lieut. W. S. Dunlop, Chaplain.

* * *

In Ottawa, O'Leary, as editor of *The Journal,* gave Banting an effusive farewell. He expressed sorrow over the death of a friend and a great man in what many felt was a surprisingly emotional tribute:

It may seem odd that Sir Frederick Banting, going to England on a great scientific mission, should have chosen to travel in a bomber. But Banting was like that. He would have argued that the doctor must take the risks of a soldier, and it would never have occurred to him that his life was so precious.

He did not think he was a great man. Shy, modest, he had that complete simplicity which so often in history has been the mark of true greatness. He must have known that he was a benefactor of mankind, that he was in the mighty tradition of Lister and Pasteur, but he would have been hurt if one said so in his presence.

Of his discovery of insulin he talked little. When compelled to, as he sometimes was among friends, he invariably argued that he had merely carried on from where others had left off, that he had been the beneficiary of their pioneering, and that ultimately somebody else must have come upon what he found. He could never be the conventional lien.

Personally, among his circle of friends, Banting had a sweet modesty and a courtesy that were captivating. He was proud of his modest achievements as an amateur painter, he enjoyed judicious convivialty, and he loved good talk and good companionship.

There is tragedy, and terrible loss, in his death. Yet, there is gain too; the gain of the self-sacrificing gallantry for a cause dearer than life. Of such stuff, woven into tradition, comes the tale of a people in their voyage through history.

TWENTY-NINE

Sinking of SS Caribou
1942

THE SECOND AGENT DIRECTLY assigned to Newfoundland to assist Stroesser, recruited with the help of an informal German–Canadian friendship group based in Toronto, was finding her bearings. In fact, she was quickly thrust into the middle of a sensitive sector of the Newfoundland defence organization.

Johanne Rhoda Horstnagel, twenty-five, was a product of German immigrant stock who settled in what came to be known as Berlin, Ontario. But at the height of the First World War, in the face of reports of Canadian troops being subjected to German gas attacks, the city was renamed for the famous British soldier Lord Kitchener. The neighbouring community had, from the beginning, honoured the 1815 victory over Napoleon. In time the two would be amalgamated to form the city of Kitchener-Waterloo.

However, more than a few inhabitants of the former Berlin were angered by the change in name of their community, including Johanne's family. Even after more than two decades, they continued to feel that it reflected unfairly on them as good Germans and good Canadians.

When the Canadian Women's Army Corps was formed in August 1941, permitting thousands of clerks and secretaries to share the glamour of a military uniform while performing useful war work, an unexpected opportunity was created for Nazi spies to infiltrate Canada's armed forces.

"We were made to look like fools, or worse, when we were forced to change the name of our home. It was wrong, unfair, a shame on us all," Johanne's father, Seigfried, had complained over and over as long as she could remember.

On learning she was considering joining the new women's division of the Canadian Army, the old man became so angry she feared he might have a stroke.

"How can you do this, a daughter of mine?" he demanded, voice rising and hands trembling violently in his favourite easy chair before the living-room fireplace. "It is the very opposite of what I should expect."

With that he stood, tottered, and fell striking his head on one of the heavy fireplace andirons. At the hospital it was touch and go for a while, but after forty-eight hours he began to improve, and doctors decided he might go home in a few days.

Johanne's mind was made up, but overwhelmed by guilt and responsibility for what had happened, she applied and was accepted at the Kitchener-Waterloo C.W.A.C. Basic Training Centre – but had decided she wanted to work secretly to assist the German cause, an unbelievable irony when she found her new group of recruits was to be inspected by none other than Subaltern Mary Churchill of the counterpart Auxiliary Territorial Service, daughter of the British Prime Minister.

She found many Newfoundland women among the recruits, and out of those contacts was born the idea of suggesting to the Canadian version of the *Bund* that she be assigned for duty in the remote, but strategically important, port of St. John's.

She knew her plan to be a secret agent couldn't fail to please her father, and ensure his recovery. On being told, he smiled, tears coursing down his cheeks, and embraced her with a warmth she had not experienced since girlhood.

Thanks to initial low-level security, and the high demand for recruits, it was easy for women with less-than-worthy motives to gain entry to the corps. All she had to do was change her name to something that would attract less attention. A simple, if careful, alteration to her mother's Canadian birth certificate did the trick. In little more than the blink of an eye, the Johanne Schmidt of the document had become a younger Joanne Smith. A documents clerk at the training centre, concerned only that quitting time was minutes away, suspected nothing, and she was sworn in without difficulty.

Following a training period, it was arranged for Private Smith to be assigned to her preference, St. John's. She took the train east to North Sydney, Nova Scotia and crossed the Cabot Strait on board the SS *Caribou*. Arriving in St. John's, she immediately contacted Stroesser, who had been alerted by the espionage network concerning her travel plans, and was briefed on her duties as a member of the *Abwehr* cell.

"You will be attached to a significant office," Stroesser informed her, "the Civil Defense Organization, headed by one of the most prominent military and business people in the place, Colonel Leonard Outerbridge. It's mostly a volunteer organization, and I understand they are ecstatic that they are about to be given a regular army person to help with the work – can you imagine! They've even found you a nice, quiet boarding house nearby so you won't have to live in a barracks."

He smiled a thin smile, once again congratulating himself on his cleverness.

"They are responsible for Air Raid Protection, enforcing the rules concerning blackouts, lights on ships and vehicles, that kind of thing. But much more importantly, it should be an excellent listening post, and I expect you to report to me regularly, at least weekly. More often if necessary."

"That does not sound like a great challenge. I was of the impression, from the agent in Toronto, that there was more to it – sabotage, to be specific," Joanne said, after a few moments. "That's really my interest, dropping a monkey wrench into the works, as we say. Do you suppose . . . ?"

"Perhaps I shouldn't say this," Stroesser replied. "I don't know you, and there is always the possibility you could get me in trouble. But there is a certain amount of frustration to be put up with. Our masters in Berlin can't seem to make up their minds about what should be done.

"From my perspective, I believe we have to do everything in our power to cause disarray in the Allied war machine, perhaps with an occasional monkey wrench, as you put it. Otherwise, we lose valuable time and opportunity."

"Well," she said, "that's pretty plainly stated. I would like to discuss further with you what we could be doing, but as you indicated, I am expected at the Civil Defence office in twenty minutes for a general staff meeting, and from what I've heard, Colonel Outerbridge doesn't much appreciate a lack of punctuality."

"I would agree with him there, Private Smith," Stroesser said. "Completely agree."

After she left, he got out reports he had submitted to the High Command on the K. of C. Hostel, the U.S.O., the Old Colony Club, and some of the lightly guarded military barracks in the city.

Stroesser had spent considerable time scouting the men's hostel operated by the Knights of Columbus in uptown St. John's, as well as the nearby United Services canteen, and the Caribou Hut located in the government-operated Seamen's Institute down near the harbour. Along with such popular nightspots as the Old Colony Club, they offered aid, comfort, and accommodation to Allied forces who, rested and refreshed, would soon be back shooting at, dropping bombs on, and firing torpedoes at the forces of the Third Reich.

In his mind, these places furthered military objectives and should be viewed from a military perspective – especially the largest and most popular, the K. of C. Leave Centre, which presented both a legitimate target, and crowded any Saturday night with hundreds of soldiers, sailors, and airmen of a dozen Allied nations, a tremendously tempting one for a skilled and determined saboteur. Moreover, there was no security to speak of, and from his visits there – passing himself off as a Danish naval officer awaiting reassignment after having been torpedoed, and therefore some kind of Allied hero in this town – Stroesser knew the hostel on Harvey Road was an unguarded tinderbox waiting to explode.

"Time to dust these off," he said aloud, although there was no one around to hear, "now that we have a person – and in an Allied uniform – ready, willing, and able to do what needs to be done."

Stroesser first received the news the same way as most everyone else – from rumours, which might be wildly removed from reality – although there were times when output from the so-called "jungle telegraph" was a lot closer to the facts because its contents originated with people who really did know something. Thanks to wartime censorship, it took several days for a modern Newfoundland tragedy, the sinking of the SS *Caribou*, only twenty or thirty miles from the assumed safety of her home port, to be confirmed officially through the news media. However, word of the tragedy had been spreading for a full forty-eight hours or more before a headline in the St. John's *Daily News* tentatively announced, "RAILWAY FERRY ATTACKED IN CABOT STRAIT."

By this time, the Newfoundland Railway was already dropping off at stations across the island the few bodies of the dead that had been recovered from the waters off the Southwest Coast, and whose identities and next of kin and hometowns had been able to be established.

Stroesser, who did not yet know for certain but suspected it was a kill for Graf in *U-69*, could hardly contain himself. It seemed his reports to Canaris had begun to be taken seriously. The reluctance to attack what might officially be classified as civilian passenger vessels, because of what the world might think or because it might bring the United States into the war, had finally been abandoned.

"At last," he breathed fervently, mindful of his advice to Berlin, "someone in the High Command has come to their senses . . . and it's about time!"

Stroesser's self-congratulatory mood may have been a case of taking somewhat more credit than was due. Whether he realized it or not, the *Caribou* had been classified in the authoritative international directory *Janes Fighting Ships*, a British publication, as a reserve troop transport – close to the truth, unfortunately, and an open invitation to submarine attack. The mystery, people in the know had come to believe, was that the vessel survived unscathed for so long in what was arguably the war's most dangerous area for Nazi U-boat activity.

The News had a secondary headline that stated, "More Definite News Will Be Released As It Is Available," under which appeared a bare-bones statement that added little new information: "A Newfoundland Railway Ferry Boat was attacked in the Cabot Strait yesterday, Wednesday, morning and as definite information is available it will be released." Nowhere did the name of the vessel appear.

Immediately below, however, the newspaper provided passenger and crew lists under the headings Civilians Landed, Members of Crew Landed, Civilians Listed, and Members of Crew. Perceptive readers noted that the latter two lists combined were more than twice as long as the first two. It took no great feat of mathematics or logic to conclude that a blow of major proportions had been struck against Newfoundland and the Western Allies, far beyond anything it had been imagined the war might bring.

Two more days would pass before the full impact would be realized. Then, in its Saturday issue, the same newspaper carried a lengthy report from the Canadian Press in Nova Scotia. It provided detailed lists of survivors and persons missing and believed dead – segregated as between Canadian and British navy, army, air force, and United States military personnel, and civilians and ship's crew.

Stroesser read, and then re-read it, with obvious relish. He took considerable satisfaction, and derived not a little justification, from the fact that the passenger list was overwhelmingly a military one – 118 members of various Allied forces, compared to only seventy-three civilians, men, women, and children, and if truth be known, many of these were wives and children of, or otherwise related to, service personnel. According to official sources, fifty-seven of the military and forty-eight civilians, along with thirty-one members of the vessel's crew, were Missing and Presumed Dead, one less than the total number of 137 originally reported.

"There is the answer to those who argued that we were some kind of monsters, out to victimize innocent citizens," Stroesser pointed out to Johanne when she appeared to report on preparations for her plan to torch the Knights of Columbus hostel. "I believe civilians are being used deliberately as a shield for the military, otherwise they would be using military troopships rather than civilian passenger vessels to transport members of the armed services."

"It will be the same outcome when we burn down the K. of C. hostel," she said. "There will be numbers of civilians involved in it too, but the great majority will be military. I assure you that I will feel no regrets," she declared.

The morning newspaper, as the first to make public the horrific details, devoted virtually an entire page to coverage of the sinking of the Newfoundland Railway ferry, with the main report from the Canadian Press news agency headlined:

TRAGIC STORY OF SINKING OF SS CARIBOU

SYDNEY, NS, Oct. 18 – (CP) – Torpedoed in darkness, the Newfoundland-Nova Scotia ferry steamship "Caribou" was sunk in the Cabot Strait October 14th with the loss of 137 lives in the greatest announced marine disaster in the coastal waters fringing Canada.

A Canadian naval craft saved 101 passengers and crewmen after the vessel was sunk by a submarine that came to the surface after the kill and watched the finish of the "Caribou" and the struggling survivors. The "Caribou" was struck nearing the overnight run from North Sydney, NS, to Port aux Basques and sank within a few minutes. Civilians from Canada, Newfoundland and the United States perished as scores were carried down with the ship while they lay asleep in their staterooms. Out of a crew of 46, mostly Newfoundlanders, 31 went down including Captain Benjamin Taverner of Channel, master of the vessel, and his two sons both of whom were officers.

Survivors told how Captain Taverner steered the settling craft at the surfaced submarine in an effort to ram the attacker but the "Caribou" slid under the waves. Some survivors said the submarine caused a further loss of life when it came to the surface amidst a group of the ship's complement. They said the rising hull of the enemy craft smashed a lifeboat and upset one or two rafts to which swimmers were clinging. Between three and five hours elapsed before all the survivors were picked up because of darkness and the fact that the naval craft was tracking down the submarine.

The family suffering the most was that of Mrs. Hazel Tapper of Burin, Newfoundland. The 35-year-old mother and her three children, John age 9, Lillian 7, and Donald 2 are all missing. Another multiple family tragedy was that of Mrs. William Strickland of Rose Blanche, Newfoundland, and her two children, Abigail 4, and Vera 8 months.

The most prominent Maritimer lost was Hugh B. Gillis, age 61, of Sydney. Mr. Gillis was a well-known engineer with the Dominion Steel and Coal Corporation. One woman member of the crew, Stewardess Bride Fitzpatrick of Rose Blanche, was also drowned.

Most of the survivors were in good shape when they landed here, only ten being hospital cases. The survivors are unanimous the officers of the ship did everything to avert panic when the torpedo struck shortly after 4 a.m. amidships on the starboard side, the explosion ripping pieces off the lifeboats.

The 15-month-old son of Mrs. Gladys Shiers, of Halifax, was lost three times after the sinking and was found by a different rescuer each time to end in a safe arrival here. Little Leonard and his mother were en route to St. John's to visit his father, Elmer Shiers, a Canadian Navy shipwright.

Leonard is the only survivor of the 15 children aboard. He and his mother were thrown to the cabin floor by the force of the explosion. Mrs. Shiers was again swept off her feet by the force of the in-running water and lost the baby, but he was picked up by a Navy man. Again lost whilst en route to the lifeboat, he was found by Vivian Swinamer of Woodside, NS. For a third time the baby was lost. This time his mother found him, when she reached a raft, in the hands of Elizabeth Northcott of Burgeo.

Revised figures issued by Newfoundland authorities late last night put the number of missing persons at 137, following the loss, through enemy action, of SS "Caribou," Newfoundland Railway Ferry. The ill-fated vessel, which carried a total of 236 passengers and crew, was attacked by an enemy submarine in Cabot Strait Wednesday morning while en route to Port aux Basques.

Of the total listed as missing and now believed dead, 57 were service personnel, 48 civilian personnel, and 31 members of the crew. Of the 101 rescued, 61 are service personnel, 25 civilians and 15 members of the crew.

The survivors were landed at an eastern Canadian port by a Canadian escort vessel.

* * *

"The wartime censor's feeble attempts to enforce secrecy in the news media are laughable," Stroesser decided, miffed that the full details of the sinking were not coming out. "As you can see from the article, reading it carefully," he pointed out to Johanne, "it is sometimes applied and sometimes not, even in the same report. Of course, most people will not read it that carefully.

"If they did, it would be completely obvious that the 'Canadian escort vessel' that isn't named – the one that rescued the *Caribou*'s survivors – was the *Grand'mere*. That's the same warship our man in North Sydney observed leaving port right after the ferry sailed, to be its escort for the crossing to Port aux Basques," he said. "Can people be so stupid that they do not realize this?"

"Yes," she readily agreed, "and Sydney is just as obviously the 'unnamed Canadian port' where survivors were brought, with medical personnel and ambulances waiting to take them to the hospital, right on the wharf for everyone to see.

"But, if the authorities insist on playing silly games, and treating the people here like idiots, why should we worry? Aren't they really playing into our hands when they try to hide the reality and bury the truth?"

In the coming days Naval Intelligence pieced together, mainly from interviews with *Caribou* survivors and HMCS *Grand'mere* crew members in Sydney, a succinct present-time document summarizing the events of the night of Tuesday and Wednesday morning, October 13–14, which became the official version of the sinking:

```
At 3:40 a.m. Newfoundland Daylight Time,
between 25 and 40 miles south of Channel
Head, near the entrance to her home port,
the ferry is impaled by a single torpedo.
It slams into her starboard side dead amid-
ships, tears through her vitals, and roars
out through the port side, leaving utter
devastation in its wake.
```

Detonation on impact of its explosive
warhead causes a huge explosion that rips a
large hole in her structure. The result is
instantaneous death for starboard-side
passengers and members of the engine-room
crew. Amidships lifeboats on the starboard
side, swung out on leaving port for immediate launch if required, are reduced to
smithereens. The radio room is demolished.
The boilers explode.

Lights fail throughout the ship, leaving
those who have so far survived to struggle
in pitch dark and swirling waters to find
their way around scattered wreckage and
submerged luggage and the bodies of already
dead passengers in the attempt to reach the
main deck and hoped-for safety.

They have less than five minutes from
the time the torpedo strikes without
warning, until the *Caribou* vanishes beneath
the waves.

It is officially confirmed that of 236
passengers and crew, 137 are missing and
presumed dead.

The family of Captain Taverner, the sixty-two-year-old giant of a
man whose forebears were among the original settlers of the
historic town of Trinity, like the Tappers and the Stricklands
suffered multiple losses. Not only was the *Caribou*'s skipper
among the missing, but his sons Stanley, the ferry's First Officer,
and Harold, the Third Officer, as well.

Taverner himself was last seen shrugging into his greatcoat
and making his way to his command post on the bridge, apparently to give the order to ram the U-boat, still on the surface 300
yards away. However, time ran out for both the captain and his

ship. The *Caribou* sank well short of her intended target, and in the best British naval tradition he went down with her.

Loss of the *Caribou* raised a storm of critical questions, and officials of the Royal Canadian Navy and the Newfoundland Railway provided answers that were far less than satisfactory to many people. They included:

> Where precisely was the escort vessel, HMCS *Grand'mere*, at the moment of the sinking? *On station 500-700 yds. astern of the ferry.*
>
> Why was she following the ferry, rather than clearing the route using her ASDIC submarine detection equipment? *Following standing naval orders.*
>
> Why did the ferry regularly sail at night in view of increased hazards to ship and passengers that night sailings implied? *Complying with railway schedules.*
>
> Why did *Grand'mere* choose to pursue the submerged submarine rather than pick up freezing and drowning survivors? *Following standing naval orders.*
>
> Was it true that the escort dropped anti-submarine depth charges amidst the lifeboats and rafts? *No evidence of this.*
>
> Was it true that the submarine surfaced among the *Caribou's* lifeboats and rafts to deliberately upset them? *No evidence of this.*
>
> Was it true that the submarine machine-gunned or shelled survivors struggling in the water? *No evidence of this.*

The most prominent Newfoundlander to survive the sinking was a Blaketown, Trinity Bay native, forty-one-year-old William James Lundrigan, who had been in Montréal for a medical check-up. In Sydney, the businessman got around a general order given survivors on the *Grand'mere* to say nothing about the disaster by paying a newspaper boy to send a cryptic, but reassuring, telegram to his wife Naomi and family in Corner

Brook. Then he busied himself arranging to get home via Trans-Canada Airlines.

At the Newfoundland Airport in Gander he encountered Herbert J. Russell, general manager of the Newfoundland Railway, the *Caribou*'s owner and operator. In his customarily quiet but uncompromising way, Lundrigan demanded answers to the questions that were on everybody's lips, two in particular.

Significantly, within days of that brief conversation, the Royal Canadian Navy's Western Approaches Convoy Instructions were altered to require single-ship escorts to proceed *ahead* of the vessel being escorted. And, nighttime sailings on the Newfoundland–Nova Scotia ferry service were discontinued forthwith.

THIRTY

Body Blows of the War

JOANNE SMITH REPORTED THAT SHE had paid visits to the Knights of Columbus Hostel and other likely sabotage targets in the St. John's area referenced in his reports to Berlin – visits that were conducted without the slightest difficulty, thanks to her Canadian Women's Army Corps uniform. Instead of paying very much attention to IDs, she found guards at the entrances were inclined to just wave uniforms through, especially if occupied by females.

"There is some security on the main floor of the K. of C. hostel," she reported, "but you wouldn't want to try anything there anyway – too many people around, and not many hidden closets or corners.

"But upstairs – that's another matter. It wouldn't be hard to start a fire in the second storey, and unless someone spotted it right away they'd have a difficult time putting it out."

"How would you propose to go about it?" Stroesser asked cautiously.

"Well, it seems to me the simplest way is just to set a match to material in one or two of the upstairs storage rooms. You could hardly bring anything inflammable into the building without getting caught, but why do that when there's so much in there already?"

"That makes sense to me," Stroesser said. "So when do you plan to do it?"

"As soon as the opportunity presents itself," Joanne replied. "It will be one of the biggest victories of the war for the Third Reich in North America! We could also think of setting a couple of smaller places on fire earlier, to divert attention from the big one. What do you think?"

"Let's be careful not to get too ambitious," Stroesser cautioned. "This is a big and important project. But you know what you're about, so go ahead with your plans for the K. of C., as they call it, and we'll see how you get on."

Thanks mainly to the uniform she wore, Private Joanne Smith, Canadian Women's Army Corps, alias Johanne Horstnagel, *Abwehr* agent XAM 29305, had no difficulty at all obtaining a ticket for Uncle Tim's Barn Dance, the coming feature attraction at the Knights of Columbus Leave Centre for Saturday night, December 12.

As a matter of fact, based on the welcome extended by Robert Ryan, head of the K. of C.'s Canadian Huts organization, who was visiting from Montréal for the first anniversary of the St. John's centre, and centre manager Michael Quinn, it almost seemed a person might have had a dozen tickets to hand out to friends had they asked for them. But, considering what she had in mind, who would want friends to be anywhere in the vicinity?

In a show of what might have been considered elementary security, tickets were personalized – the holder's name written in – and non-transferrable, and had to be signed for. A minimum of 350 service people and their guests were expected to fill the moveable chairs arranged in the auditorium for the show. They were required to be in their places by 10:30 p.m. when a broadcast of the program would begin on radio station VOCM.

"We're only too happy to see members of the women's military services using our facilities," Ryan said, "but I have to say you're one of the very few. For some reason – I suppose it's because the Knights are a fraternal organization – the idea has gotten around that the hostel's for men only. But I assure you that's just not so."

Quinn wrote her name on the ticket, and she signed for it. When he offered to show her around the facility, she could only consider it an unbelievable stroke of luck.

"Oh, that would be wonderful," she gushed. "Are you sure you have the time?"

The U-shaped building faced on Harvey Road, what might be considered part of the fourth level of the tiered old city. Water Street, completely skirting the north side of the harbour, comprised the first tier. Then the cityscape stepped up to Duckworth and New Gower streets for the second level, followed by Bond and Gower streets and Queen's Road–Theatre Hill in the third level. Finally came Military and Harvey Roads leading into LeMarchant Road.

Two wings of the building led northward from the base of the "U." The east wing, like the front section a two-storey structure, had sleeping accommodation and storage rooms on the second floor, while the west wing was a single-storey area housing mainly the auditorium.

After half an hour the saboteur was satisfied she had all the information she required, compliments of the people who ran the place. She decided that complete destruction by fire of the Knights of Columbus Leave Centre, causing the deaths of scores of military personnel and civilians, would not be nearly as difficult as she had imagined.

Newfoundland's governor during the years of the Second World War was a career sailor and looked and acted the part, often appearing in public in Royal Navy uniform. Born in Dorset, England, in 1879, he took up a career in the navy as a youth of sixteen and, forty years later, in 1934, retired with the rank of vice-admiral. Two years after that, he accepted the chairmanship of the Commission of Government that was established to replace the elected House of Assembly. Governor Walwyn's position was one that conveyed far less in the way of executive authority than most people might reasonably have imagined. The truth was, the real power resided in London, rather than St. John's. Accordingly, for a man who had spent most of his lifetime either executing or giving orders at a high level, the appointment turned out to be a considerable frustration.

However, it was blunted by the knowledge that, even if they had little time for the Commission, which met in secret and governed by edict, most Newfoundlanders genuinely liked Walwyn as a seafaring man who did his best to run a tight ship. Consequently, a brief announcement emanating from Government House was well-received:

> *The King has been pleased to approve the extension for a further year of the term of office of Vice Admiral Sir Humphrey Walwyn, KCSI, KCMG, CB, DSO, as Governor of the Crown Colony of Newfoundland.*

Unfortunately, Walwyn would be given little time or opportunity to bask in the warm glow of this further evidence of His Majesty's confidence. Within a week, the disaster of which the Governor had warned came to pass – two ships torpedoed and sunk at Bell Island, with a combined loss of forty lives. But far worse was yet to come. Just three months after that, the Knights of Columbus Leave Centre in St. John's, operated as a rest and recreation facility for Allied military, would burn to the ground with 100 dead and as many more injured. It was clearly the work of a saboteur.

During the same period, a suspicious fire razed the Canadian Army barracks on Signal Hill, just off the Battery Road, fortunately without loss of life. Next, a similar fate befell the U.S. Army barracks at nearby George's Pond that was serving as an officers' quarters. Once again, there were no casualties. But destruction of the exclusive Old Colony Club on Portugal Cove Road, well-known to be a favourite destination of military officers for intimate dinners and dancing, caused the deaths of four young women, members of the staff who resided on the premises. The manager and his family and two other female employees were lucky to escape into a snowstorm through an upstairs window.

Nobody could tell for certain that all were further examples of sabotage, but it had become the official attitude to assume that fires in military or quasi-military locations were by the nature of the location suspicious, unless there was clear evidence to the contrary. In other words, there must be witnesses who were prepared to swear to the accidental or inadvertent nature of the fire, otherwise enemy action was taken for granted.

The newspapers took note of a flurry of meetings and inspections with regular and volunteer firefighters on the part of high public officials. Commissioner Emerson was reported to have stressed "the importance of [the work] and the assistance they would render this community in time of grave emergency" – a clear signal that grave emergencies were to be expected. Chief of Police O'Neill spoke to volunteer firemen of their critically important role "in combating any conflagration threatening the city" – a chilling signal that the threat of further major fires was very real.

In the meantime, the Civil Defence Organization and its Air Raid Precautions arm were holding and planning air-raid rehearsals and, in a "realistic test," the newspapers reported, "searchlights flashed across the sky picking up a plane which crossed and re-crossed the city at very high speed. The A.R.P. organization quickly swung into action. Intermittent explosions representing bombs were heard in all directions . . . about 20 [fire-bombs] were 'dropped' on a section of Military and Bannerman Roads but in less than a couple of minutes squads of A.R.P. workers were on the scene and had them quenched."

The alarm of "the approach of hostile aircraft" was given at 11:00 p.m., and at 11:50 the sirens sounded the all-clear.

"Immediately on the sounding of the alarm, streetcars, buses, and taxis came to a stop, and scarcely a glimmer of light was visible, except for A.R.P. vehicles and army trucks, which sped through the city picking up their men and conveying them to battle stations. At Fort Pepperrell civilians were evacuated and the roads patrolled on the watch for the enemy that might land by parachute.

"Everywhere, A.R.P. patrols were on guard and appeared to take their duties as seriously as if a real raid was in progress. The police were on the alert and wore their steel helmets."

In a press conference the next day at his headquarters in Bishop Feild College on Bond Street, the Civil Defence director, Col. Outerbridge, was very pleased.

"Everyone in the A.R.P. organization performed as they should have done if a real raid were in progress," he said, "working with smoothness and efficiency."

The blackout, he reported, was being well-observed in the extended area from Cape St. Francis to the Witless Bay Line, a distance of about fifty miles. In the Civil Defence effort "almost every citizen" was co-operating, Sir Leonard declared confidently. Little could he suspect the viciousness of the body blows that were about to be inflicted on the community.

Saturday night in St. John's, and it was freezing cold. Constable Stephen Reynolds was on duty in a primitive, unheated traffic control box on Rawlins Cross, at the intersection of Military, Queen's, and Monkstown Roads, his job to signal traffic to stop and go. Even with ankle-length greatcoat, fur cap, and leather mitts he was unable to keep warm. Every so often, with little or no traffic in sight, he would emerge from the confining structure to stamp his feet vigorously, and swinging his arms wide, bring the mitts together with a series of perceptible *whapps!* in an attempt to restore circulation in hands that he was sure were on the verge of freezing solid.

"At least twenty below," he told himself, glancing skyward. A clear winter sky, he had been taught in childhood, meant bitter weather. However, according to his late grandfather, "Clouds o'er the city a blanket make, and milder weather then will take."

There were, indeed, a few clouds moving in from the west, and heavy flakes of snow making their appearance. And something else: a red reflection in the sky that could mean only one thing.

He rushed back inside the box and grabbed the telephone.

"Reynolds, at the Cross," he shouted to the sergeant at the Central Fire Station who answered. "There's a big red glow in the sky behind the R.C. Cathedral . . . . Could be Shamrock Field!"

Only a few days earlier, the newspapers had reported on the commendation of Gunner R. E. Bragg of the Newfoundland Militia, stationed at its Carpasian Road encampment, who had discovered and extinguished a fire in one of the buildings. Officials said that, but for his quick action, the whole Shamrock Field complex would have been endangered.

Hanging up, Reynolds fished out of an inside pocket, with some difficulty given the cold of his hands, the gold Waltham pocket watch his grandfather had left him, and pressed the release to open the cover. It was 11:05 p.m.

To the west, near the corner of Pennywell and Freshwater Roads, two of his fellow constables, Blanchard Peddle and Clarence Bartlett, were doing foot patrol. They were anticipating a busy time when the crowd from the K. of C. Hostel, the name it was most often given, emerged into the frosty night in half an hour or so.

Peddle was peering at the front window of Jackman and Greene, Grocers, where, in the dim light, he could make out the prices of geese and chickens, fruit and chocolates, English biscuits, and various other items specially stocked for Christmas, hand-painted on the glass in chalky white script by someone with an artist's flair. Then, in the window, he saw something else: the reflection of a red burst of flame. At first it seemed it must be inside the store – an optical illusion. Then he turned, pointing in the direction from which they had come only minutes earlier.

"My God, Clarence – look! It's the K. of C., all ablaze!"

Bartlett had walked a few yards down Boncloddy Street to have a look around. The urgency in his partner's voice caused him to rush back to the corner, where he could get a view down to

Harvey Road. Peddle was right. Flames were shooting out through the roof of the structure that lay just east of the C.L.B. Armoury.

Peddle raced across the street to the nearest fire alarm box, smashed the glass, and pulled the handle. He knew the location was wrong but the Central firemen, coming up Harvey Road, couldn't miss the fire. The time was 11:10 p.m.

Much closer to the scene, Corporal Raymond Hoosier stood on the sidewalk, his back to the burning building, oblivious of what was already well under way inside. One minute there was nothing out of the ordinary. Then he heard crackling noises. Looking over his shoulder, the U.S. military policeman was shocked to find smoke and flame exploding out where there were none even seconds before.

She had arrived at the hostel with time to spare – a perfectly turned-out example of how women's army members were supposed to look, blond hair pulled back in a tight bun, uniform freshly pressed, mannish stride signalling that she was all business.

The big show would not start for another forty-five minutes and, when it did, she knew few people in the building would be paying attention to anything but what was taking place onstage. Showing her ticket, which merited hardly a cursory glance, she was waved inside. But, instead of heading into the auditorium which was already beginning to fill up with early arrivals determined to get seats close to the stage, she climbed the stairs to the second floor and crossed the long recreation area with its jukebox, piano, and pair of Ping-Pong tables. Two young men in undershirts and sailors' bell-bottoms, seeming hardly old enough to be out of school, let alone in the navy, inexpertly batted a ball back and forth.

She knew exactly what to look for – the two large storage closets that, just as she had seen them earlier, were packed with inflammable materials such as toilet paper, paper hand towels, and containers of furniture oil, soap, disinfectant, and other maintenance supplies. She calculated that the rooms were located directly above the auditorium and the projection room with its own storage area for highly combustible films.

Working quickly, she turned several large cartons on their sides. She broke the seals and pulled out long trails of paper extending to the floor. It took only a couple of Seadog wooden matches to ignite a blaze that would result in the worst toll of death by fire ever in Newfoundland history. The blaze set, she calmly walked downstairs and out into the night.

In common with Newfoundlanders in every walk of life, Governor Walwyn and the Commission of Government were deeply shocked by what occurred in the course of an hour or less on a busy city street in the centre of the city, within a few dozen yards of the main police and fire department facilities. They lost no time in appointing Mr. Justice Brian E. S. Dunfield of the Newfoundland Supreme Court, who had begun his career as law partner of Prime Minister Morris on the eve of the First World War, to conduct an inquiry. The first thing he did, at the opening session, was to bar the press and the public.

"This investigation will be held in camera," the jurist declared with what many – though not all – considered impeccable logic.

"To hold an inquiry in public and to have the evidence published every day is not the best way to get at the truth of a matter," he reasoned. "Everyone knows that it is the practice of the Court to send out of the room all witnesses except the one in the box at the moment. The police, too, and indeed most inquirers try to keep their witnesses apart from each other, so as to detect any discrepancies.

"Even with the best of intentions, and in good faith, a witness who has read the statements of a dozen others is apt to convince himself unconsciously that he saw the same things they saw," the judge went on.

"And again, if it should happen – I have no reason to suppose it at present, but one never knows what will turn up – that any conduct of a doubtful nature has to be investigated, we have to bear in mind the scriptural admonition that in vain is the net spread in the sight of any bird. Therefore, since we have to choose between efficiency and interesting the public, we must, in the public interest, choose efficiency.

"The public will receive the results of our labours in the form of a full report, and I shall make every effort to push on rapidly and avoid a long-drawn-out inquiry.

"Hereafter, then, only the Commission, staff, counsel, and witness of the moment will be present at the sessions."

The Evening Telegram objected, asking whether the argument might be used to exclude the press from courts in general, pointing out that coverage of trials "serves a far more important purpose" than merely satisfying public curiosity: "safeguarding that clause of the Charter of Freedom which declares that 'to no man will we sell, or deny, or delay, right or justice. We will not go against any man or send against him, save by legal justice of his peers or by the law of the land.'

"Since the recognition of the right of the press to publish proceedings in Court or in that other tribunal of the people, the Parliament, its value in ensuring integrity has outweighed any other considerations. *The Telegram* deplores the decision to exclude the press from an inquiry that touches on no matter related to the operations of the war and that concerns entirely public welfare."

The editor of *The Daily News* was somewhat more restrained, but branded the decision to exclude as being "without precedent."

Keeping "a watching brief for the public" at the courts and various inquiries was "a privilege the press has never abused and the grounds for exclusion in the present instance seem to be inadequate."

Their objections were to no avail.

* * *

Not everyone was in the auditorium for Uncle Tim's Barn Dance. For instance, in Dormitory A on the second floor, Royal Canadian Navy Signalman Maurice Weldon was preparing for bed. Four R.C.A.F. men had just "hit the hay." The same was true of a couple of Yanks on temporary duty from Argentia.

A Newfoundland Militia member in battledress, just coming off duty, entered and headed for a storage room that he supposed was a toilet. On opening the door he was met by a sheet of flame.

"Fire! Fire!" the man yelled, and ran for the stairs, leaving the door ajar.

"Shut that bloody door," Weldon shouted too late, and went to do it himself. He saw that fire filled the top of the cupboard and threatened to burst out of its confines. In that instant he read on burning cardboard cartons the words "Toilet Tissue."

"Dear God," he cried, "people are going to be burned to death in this," suddenly realizing that he himself could be among them. He succeeded on the second attempt in shutting the door. As he did flames burst out over its top, searing his arm and shoulder.

"Wake up! Get up, quick! The place is on fire!" he screamed at the sleepers, shaking a couple of them, then followed the uniformed soldier in a mad scramble down the stairs in his under-wear. Fierce heat followed him to the bottom, so hot he could hardly stand it, but he managed to fight his way out of the building. In the midst of a growing bedlam the Newfoundland Militia man was shouting over the noise to John J. St. John, the hostel's accountant, who had grabbed the telephone and was making a desperate but futile attempt to reach the fire department, precious minutes that cost the former newspaperman his life.

Dunfield would speculate that the opening of the storage-room door was the trigger that set off the larger blaze. Gases from burning materials, including highly combustible sheathing on walls and ceilings, had been bottled up because of the absence of ventilation in the roof, he reasoned, and just waiting to explode. When they did, virtually the entire structure was engulfed as if a bomb had gone off.

"At just about the time the soldier was opening the door on the flames above," he wrote, "and thereby perhaps giving them the final fillip of oxygen which started the explosions on their way, the fire burnt down to the roof of the projection booth, made a hole for itself, and began to come through with a hiss. Pressure was doubtless building up behind it above.

"We know the fire was coming into the top of the booth, because a naval man broke open the door and describes it for us. At the same time, the fire was working down into the walls at the end of the canteen and southwest corner of the kitchen which were also the walls of the right rear corner of the auditorium.

"Smoke and very soon flames began to blow out [through] the projection slots [into the auditorium]. Those near began to shuffle and move. The performers stopped, thinking there was a fight. People began to move back to see the fight. J. L. Murphy, the producer, exhorted the people from the stage to be calm, and called for music. Then the cry of 'Fire!' was raised."

THIRTY-ONE

The Knights of Columbus Fire: Horror and Heroism

THE WARTIME BLACKOUT was having the effect of keeping most people off the city's streets, which were no longer considered safe at night. To a large extent this ensured – although it hardly can have been intended – that residents were kept ignorant of much that might be going on around them after dark, even in their neighbourhoods and right next door. In imposing external darkness, the blackout required shutters and blinds on residential and other windows so internal light was unable to shine through. If householders peered outside, they saw only total darkness, so few bothered. The town could be burning down around them, and few would realize it.

Radio station VOCM had begun broadcasting Uncle Tim's Barn Dance direct from the Knights of Columbus Leave Centre beginning at 10:30 p.m., before an audience of 500 servicemen and women and civilians. Popular female vocalist Mary Bennett – stage name Biddy O'Toole – received sustained applause for her rendition of "Bonnie Blue Boy"; then master of ceremonies Barry Hope (in real life Joe Murphy) announced the next number: Canadian sailor Teddy Adams singing "Moonlight Trail."

The broadcast was suddenly interrupted. Even if listeners heard the original shouts of "Fire! Fire! Fire!" it is doubtful that many imagined what was transpiring in that crowded auditorium. It was total darkness except for flames swirling overhead. There were flimsy metal chairs to trip over. The windows were heavily shuttered, and doors which opened inward were blocked by coughing, choking, screaming people who were trying to get out. In a few tragic minutes, it became a death trap. The victims were scores of military personnel and their hosts, officials of the Knights of Columbus Canadian Huts Organization, and community volunteers.

The spectacular blaze raged for several hours. Although it completely destroyed the year-old building, and lit up the Saturday night sky, remarkably few people noticed.

It was not until they saw the shocking headline in *The Daily News* on Monday morning, a headline that was virtually a story in itself – "STARK TRAGEDY NUMBS CITY WHEN NEARLY ONE HUNDRED PEOPLE PERISH IN BLAZING INFERNO AS K. OF C. HOSTEL IS RAZED TO THE GROUND" – that hundreds and thousands realized fully what had occurred, and how many people were injured, horribly burned, and disfigured, or had perished.

At that point, authorities had released the names of only five of the dead.

"It was stated," according to *The News*, "that there will be no release of names until the bodies are definitely identified and next of kin notified. Regarding the people in hospital, the authorities took the same stand. Some are badly burned and injured, others not so badly, but it is felt that it may cause unnecessary anxiety to relatives to furnish any details just at present." For most people, then, the newspaper provided the first details, scanty though they were of the disaster, under the subheading:

500 PEOPLE PRESENT AS THE BUILDING
IS SUDDENLY ENVELOPED IN FLAMES

The greatest tragedy in the history of St. John's occurred on Saturday night when fire destroyed the Knights of Columbus Hut on Harvey Road and brought death to at least 100 persons and injury to hundreds of others. The actual figures are not yet obtainable and it may be days before the sad story is told in fullest detail. So far police place the number of dead at ninety-seven, whilst other authorities give the figure as 104, with something over 100 in the various hospitals receiving treatment for more or less serious injuries. Many more had slight burns which did not require hospital attention; indeed, there were few of the 500 or more who were in the building who escaped unscathed. St. John's has had many tragedies, but nothing in its history has been so horrifying as the holocaust of Saturday night.

How the fire occurred no one seems definitely to know, but that there was an explosion of some kind and that the flames appeared to burst from all sides at the same time is confirmed from many quarters. Radio fans who had tuned into the Saturday night programme from the Hut report hearing a noise like a detonation, then screams, then silence. Individuals who were in the building tell a similar tale. One said the noise seemed like a row outside the assembly hall, and at the next moment the devastating flames appeared.

The suddenness of the fire and the speed with which the building was enveloped in flames was startling and bewildering. Pedestrians passed the building and saw nothing amiss, yet a moment later were startled by the crackling of fire and the appearance of flames shooting hundreds of feet high. The Hut was situated only a few hundred yards away from the Central Fire Hall, and yet the firemen who were promptly on the scene and worked hero-ically, could do nothing to save the building.

The scene within can be better imagined than described. At least 500 people were in the building, the large majority of them in the auditorium listening to the "Barn Dance" programme. Some thirty were in the dormi-tories, others were scattered about the building in the canteen, writing room, etc. With the first scream of fire pandemonium reigned and there was a rush for the exit. Almost instantly the lights went out, and this added to the confusion as the doors being tightly closed and the windows shuttered because of the blackout, it was impossible to know which way to move.

Individuals near the door, however, succeeded in opening it, and others smashed some of the windows. It was through the latter than many succeeded in escaping, among them several women who owe their lives to the cool-headed men of the services and others who helped, and in some cases literally threw, them out. The auditorium was fitted with moveable chairs and over these the frightened occupants stumbled in their haste, many falling never to rise again. In the crush, men and women were trampled under foot, while others suffocated as they tried in vain to fight their way to the exit.

Eye-witnesses declare that it was apparent from the first that there would be a heavy loss of life, though there were many acts of heroism in which men risked their own lives to bring others to safety.

Outside meanwhile, crowds had gathered. Firemen, police, members of the armed forces joined in a strenuous effort not only to help the trapped but also to prevent the flames from spreading. Residents of nearby homes waited in fear and trembling, but fortunately there was no wind, and the fire was confined to the one building. A strong westerly breeze might have brought disaster to the whole easterly section of the city. Just across the street, a few yards away, were the United Church College Home, the Holloway School and St. Andrew's Presbyterian Church; if these had caught the firemen would have had a task almost beyond their ability to control. The blaze started shortly after eleven o'clock and the building was completely destroyed by midnight.

Well aware of the work of the Constabulary in dealing with the greatest military crisis since the French attacks, occupations, burnings, and threats of the same in the eighteenth century, the Governor penned a personal note to the Chief of Police:

```
Government House,
St. John's, December 22, 1942

My Dear O'Neill:

I should like to congratulate you personally, as
well as your men of the Fire Brigade and the
Constabulary, for the magnificent work of the past
number of weeks, culminating in the actions of
the last day or so. I realize that much good
effort has also been put forword by the A.R.P.,
the fighting forces and civilians. But it is in
the selfless performance of their duty of the
Brigade (as we saw in containing the K. of C.
fire, which might have become an even greater
disaster) and of the Police in their good work of
security and investigation, even this very week,
that the safety of the community rests.

With best wishes of the Season,
Yours sincerely,
(sgd) HUMPHREY WALWYN

Chief of Police O'Neill, O. B. E., J. P
```

"A spectacular success, Fräulein," Stroesser warmly congratulated Johanne when she knocked on his door on Sunday morning, "just as you promised. My sources tell me there may be at least a hundred dead, and as many more injured. To use your words, it is one of the great achievements of the Third Reich in the war in this hemisphere. You will receive due recognition, I assure you.

"You must fill me in on all the details for inclusion in my report to Berlin. I can tell you that Admiral Canaris, and the Führer himself, will be exceedingly pleased with your success."

"Thank you, Herr Stroesser," she replied, colouring slightly. "It was unbelievably easy to get access to the building – no doubt, the uniform played a big part."

Visiting her superior, she wore civilian clothes, and had altered her appearance by changing her hairstyle and wearing heavy-framed glasses.

"However, I do have a concern. It may be nothing to worry about, but on leaving the place last night, I was stopped by two local police officers on foot patrol.

"They asked to see my identification, which, of course, I could not refuse, and one of them wondered – half-joking, I think – why I was leaving the place just when the big show was getting under way. I answered that I had to go and visit a sick friend. But you know how it is – they usually write everything down, and you never know when it might come back to haunt you."

"Hmmm . . . I understand you would be upset by it," Stroesser said, hiding his concern, but realizing the matter was much more serious than he was prepared to let on. "So long as it was only a routine check, it may not amount to anything. I shouldn't worry too much about it, but let me know at once if anything else should occur."

Damn! If only she'd been more careful leaving the place. This will come back to haunt us . . . perhaps even destroy our operation here!

At the headquarters of the Newfoundland Constabulary at Fort Townshend, only a few hundred yards from the still smoldering K. of C. Leave Centre, the Chief of Police presided over a hastily called meeting of senior officers of the force, particularly the heads of the Criminal Investigation Division and the special wartime Security Division.

"Gentlemen, thank you for coming out on Sunday morning. I am sure you appreciate the urgency of the situation. I do not think I need describe to you the enormity of the disaster that has struck this community. As it now appears, we have 100 people dead and perhaps twice as many injured, some seriously. However, there is not the slightest bit of hard evidence, as yet" – he paused for effect – "notice I said 'as yet,' that this was arson, let alone sabotage.

"But I do say this. It is wartime. We have had a series of fires which I feel safe in saying were suspicious. Technically, most of them – in fact all but the Old Colony Club – have been outside of our jurisdiction, that is, in facilities under military control, and they would be quick to tell us to mind our own business were we to attempt to intervene.

"In the present case, however, that is not the situation. Even though the great majority of those killed and injured no doubt are military personnel, this fire occurred in civil jurisdiction, and I – speaking, I should say, for the Commissioner of Justice and the government – intend to keep it that way. By the way, I hope we shall have complete identifications in two or three days, as soon as Dr. Josephson can get autopsies done. It's a big job, but the military have doctors they can lend him.

"Now, here's what I really want you to consider. Assuming, we must, that this fire was deliberately set as by an enemy agent or agents, what is the most effective way we can tackle the investigation? And something else – how can we do so without causing panic, without actually telling people that there is no need to panic, that their safety is in good hands? I suggest we must be seen *doing* things rather than *saying* things. Let our actions speak for us. We need to set the tone, to show we are pursuing business as usual. That will be the most effective way."

The plan that emerged from the meeting was threefold:

1. Interview everyone known to have been in the hostel Saturday night, including all injured persons capable of being interrogated, and in the case of local people, their next of kin, plus anyone else of interest.

2. Set up a secondary group to sift through interesting information provided from first-round interviews, re-interview when necessary and pursue any leads quickly.
3. Process all reports in such a way as to provide comparisons of interesting information with that gathered by the first-line interview team. Reports of fire investigators examining the physical site would be fed daily to the primary interview team.

"There seems to be one particular gap in the plan," Inspector Cahill of the C.I.D. suggested. "People who might have been stopped or questioned in the vicinity of the fire scene. They may not have been inside, or say they hadn't, but that remains to be seen. If they were in the vicinity, we're interested and need to know who they are. A public appeal might help."

The plan was amended accordingly. During the Constabulary's morning parade on Monday, all ranks were made aware that names and pertinent data on all persons stopped or questioned in the vicinity of Harvey Road between 4:00 p.m. and midnight Saturday were to be turned in at once to Cahill, the C.I.D.'s operations deputy. Among these, inscribed in a policeman's breast-pocket notebook, should have been the name of a member of the Canadian Women's Army Corps, but cold hands and a mistaken tendency to assume that people in uniform were above suspicion lent her anonymity. Johanne's name had not been recorded.

Few may have realized it at the time, but the sinking of two ore carriers on the Bell Island anchorage on September 5 reflected the changing face of the Second World War in the Atlantic.

"The fact is," Malcolm McCommon would remind his Memorial University students in retrospect, "that Japan's surprise aerial assault on the U.S. Naval Base at Pearl Harbor caused President Franklin D. Roosevelt to abandon the fiction of United States neutrality vis-à-vis the Axis powers.

"America was now required, while continuing to support the Allies in pursuing the defeat of Hitler, to fight a war of its own and to do so with a Pacific Fleet decimated in the surprise attack of December 7, 1941, when along with many smaller vessels, eight battleships were destroyed or damaged and one capsized. The U.S. suffered over 2,200 casualties and lost nearly 200 planes, while Japan's losses to carrier-based aircraft that carried out the attack were negligible."

The picture McCommon painted was quite correct. The pressing need to both replace and increase resources in the Pacific meant diverting them from the protection of Atlantic shipping. But over and above that, Roosevelt's declaration of war meant Hitler no longer had any reason to hold back from U-boat attacks on Atlantic shipping. Grand Admiral Karl Donitz declared "the whole American coast is open for operations"[18] and launched Operation *Paukenschlag* (Drumbeat), a strategy that clearly aimed at choking off North American support for Britain and the Soviet Union.

"These combined developments," the political scientist pointed out, "created pressure on Canada to shift priorities from protection of domestic waters to convoy support. Accordingly, the waters around Newfoundland, the Grand Banks, the Cabot Strait, the Gulf of St. Lawrence, became significantly more dangerous places. The ferry SS *Caribou* became a victim of this change of emphasis – that's how come an ill-equipped minesweeper was sent as her escort, rather than a destroyer or even a corvette – and those Bell Island vessels as well."

Following the loss of the ore carriers SS *Saganaga* and SS *Lord Strathcona*, and again in the wake of the sinking of the *Caribou*, debate ensued both within official circles and among the public concerning the adequacy of protection afforded shipping in Newfoundland waters by the Royal Canadian Navy. Changes were made in escort rules for the Gulf ferry service, and improvements were made in Wabana Patrol Orders requiring patrol "to be maintained off Wabana anchorage and off the loading wharf unless no merchant shipping is in the area," and protection was to be given to the loading wharf itself.[19]

But the changes clearly were not good enough. Consequently, when a Nazi U-boat entered Conception Bay one night in November, and surfaced in darkness and light rain, it went completely undetected. Manoeuvring to escape the sweep of a searchlight, it spotted two vessels lying between the submarine and the searchlight, and then a third.

A torpedo launched against the 3,000-ton collier SS *Anna T.*, waiting off the Scotia Pier to discharge, was off the mark. It actually passed under the stern of the iron ore carrier SS *Flyingdale* which was loading at the time, and slammed into the pier inflicting great damage. The U-boat next fired two torpedoes into the 6,000-ton SS *Rose Castle*, waiting on the anchorage. The ship broke in half and sank within a minute or two with the loss of twenty-eight men out of a crew of forty-three. The submarine then trained its sights on a smaller ship, the 5,600-ton SS *PLM 27*, also at anchor, which, when the torpedo struck, sank immediately losing twelve members out of a crew of fifty.

Twice during the previous evening Newfoundland Militia lookouts had reported sightings indicating a possible submarine presence in the bay, but navy Fairmiles patrol vessels were unable to confirm anything. Early the next morning, a Newfoundland Militia lookout at Lance Cove saw a submarine surface after the attack on the *Rose Castle* and *PLM 27*; he would state for the record that it remained on the surface for eight or nine minutes. It was said that the first naval vessel to respond to the attack only appeared on the scene some fifteen or twenty minutes later.[20]

THIRTY-TWO

Scorched Earth Plans:
The Threat of Total Destruction

FIRE HAD BEEN the nemesis of the old city from the earliest days of settlement. This was particularly the case from the mid-1700s, when naturalist Sir Joseph Banks counted "returning fishermen" in St. John's in the range of 10,000, and the summer population was said to be nearly half that of Tennessee, almost twice that of Illinois, and three times that of Michigan.[21]

The Phoenix insurance company of London, in writing Newfoundland's first fire policy in 1782, expressed concern over the large number of new buildings "built in such manner . . . [that] there was a probability of the whole town being destroyed in one fire." *The Times* of London worried in 1798 that "the houses are built of wood . . . [S]hould a fire happen the consequences must be dreadful."[22]

Predictions of extreme destruction were some time coming to pass. Then in February 1816 a fire that broke out at King's Beach destroyed an area bounded by Prescott Street, Gower Street, and the harbour east to Fort William. It was prelude to "great fires": of February 1817, that wiped out virtually the entire business and commercial district; of June 1846, that devastated three-quarters of the city, everything from Springdale Street east to Hill o' Chips and on the harbour side of Water Street, east to Maggoty Cove; and of July 1892, the greatest of the "great fires," after which "almost nothing remained standing from Signal Hill to Beck's Cove, and north to LeMarchant, Harvey and Military Roads. More than two thirds of the city . . . lay in ruins."[23]

However, the so-called "great fires" and innumerable lesser conflagrations of the past would be as nothing compared with what was envisaged in a top-secret "scorched earth" plan, devised by faceless British bureaucrats, that proposed the complete destruction of twentieth-century St. John's should it be in danger of falling to the Nazis. It became a frightening but realistic prospect as the Battle of the Atlantic raged on with no assurance of an Allied victory.

No faint heart, Governor Walwyn blanched despite himself when first the "Instructions Issued to Certain Colonial Dependencies on Scorched Earth Policy" reached him by "MOST SECRET" despatch from London. The orders were to develop "denial plans" – a diabolical scheme to deny a potential invader access to strategic assets by destroying them.

In case of Nazi invasion, coastal batteries spotted around Newfoundland's capital city, few as they were, along with ammunition stores and all wharves and docking facilities, were to be demolished. It was the same for strategic structures such as landmark Cabot Tower with its key communications centre, the Newfoundland Drydock, naval repair shops, and the railway station. Torbay Airport, all military buildings, power stations, power and communications lines, bridges, hospitals, radio stations, newspapers, and vehicles both military and privately owned, were on the list for destruction. Stocks of food and other supplies were to be utterly done away with, except those the fleeing residents of St. John's could manage to take with them.

This was all to be accomplished by controlled explosions, by the use of sledgehammers, and ultimately by fire. Huge petroleum storage tanks located high on the Southside Hills contained hundreds of thousands of gallons of gasoline, kerosene, and other petroleum products. It was considered a simple matter to open the outlet valves and permit the contents to gush down to the harbour in a huge inflammable flood. Ignited, it would erupt in a mushroom cloud of flames and smoke. It was calculated that the extreme heat would set off destructive fires in the old wooden wharves and buildings that ringed the perimeter of the harbour.

And what of the people, who were to be kept absolutely in the dark about the "denial plans" until they were implemented in full? It seems they would have to get out any way they could – significantly, all boats were to be destroyed except those capable of travelling at least 100 miles. Perhaps these would be held in reserve to help the refugees to escape. At some point, two or three ships loaded with rocks and concrete would be sunk in the Narrows, blocking access in and out of the harbour.

"It is too terrible to contemplate," Walwyn told a rare nighttime emergency meeting of the Commission of Government. "But I can better appreciate now the response of Governor Davidson in 1914, when he spoke of blocking the Narrows behind the *Dresden* if she dared to invade our harbour, and of the citizens taking up arms.

"However, having said that, London awaits a reply. We have to decide how to respond to the policy – whether to accept it or not. Under the circumstances, I would say a formal vote is required. If there was an invasion today, would we be prepared to destroy everything and flee, or – knowing what we do about the brutal treatment meted out to Nazi-occupied peoples, would we, and by 'we' I mean Newfoundlanders or certainly St. John's people, be prepared to live under such a regime for God knows how long?"

A numbered copy of the policy, stamped "TOP SECRET" and required to be handed back at the end of the meeting, was in each member's place, but there was only brief opportunity to scan its contents.

"Does this apply only to Newfoundland, or are other . . . 'colonial dependencies' . . . involved? Canada, for instance?" Puddester, as so often happened, was the first to speak. Knighted by the King during the 1939 Royal Visit, the former Deputy Speaker of the House of Assembly took his seniority as vice chairman of the Commission very seriously.

"I understand," Walwyn replied, wary of the Commissioner's tone, "that it has been sent out on a top-secret basis and approved by the Canadian War Cabinet Committee which is headed by the Prime Minister, Mr. King."

"So that's it – Canada deciding that Newfoundland's capital should be burned to protect Canada? At least Davidson was for fighting on," Puddester exploded.

"No, no. It's not like that," the Governor protested, displaying obvious irritation. He had never quite appreciated Sir John's nationalistic outbursts. "As you get into the fine details you will find that the policy also applies to Canadian cities – Halifax, Sydney, and Shelburne in Nova Scotia, Saint John in New Brunswick, Québec City and the Gaspé . . . all of us on the Gulf and the St. Lawrence River. It also applies to airports on the Canadian west coast, looking to the possibility of a Japanese attack."

"Well," Puddester snorted, "I don't accept that the Canadians are prepared to burn down or blow up Halifax and Québec City. I could see them putting the torch to St. John's, though – wouldn't hesitate, and, in fact, might take great delight in doing it.

"I'm totally against this, as I believe all Newfoundlanders would be – if they were given a choice. Which apparently, by the looks of the secrecy, they won't be. I know our people. They'd rather fight and die than flee, or be slaves to Hitler and his crowd."

"Gentlemen, this represents a contingency position . . . . But it is purely speculative." Emerson, as Commissioner for Defence, found himself in a peculiar position, but was not persuaded that the policy was necessary – or wise to have on paper. "It provides, if in a most extreme way, against a situation that may never come about. We also have to be concerned about panic if this ever got out. The best advice I have from the military is that the new convoy arrangements, backed up by intensive anti-submarine activity out of Argentia – both sea and air – is having its effect; and we may well have seen the peak of U-boat operational success. If the new anti-submarine efforts continue to be successful, as I believe they will, there should be a dramatic falling-off in attacks on our shipping in the next months. We are winning the Battle of the Atlantic. I would say no to this, Your Excellency, or let us, at least, buy some time."

"This is the most awful, ridiculous, cold-blooded thing I have ever heard of." Winter, who would soon be leaving Home Affairs and Education for a Supreme Court sinecure, was surprisingly outspoken. "The very wording that is used – that the application of the policy is to be 'ruthless' and that it is to be 'rigorously applied' . . .

"And who is it that is going to do it? What would be the difference, I ask you, between Allied military forces driving our people out of their homes, herding them onto cattle boats as refugees to be shipped God knows where, and then burning the town, and the Nazis doing it? I am totally opposed."

"Is there further debate?" Walwyn asked. "Are we ready for the vote?"

The British members had not spoken. On rare occasions when votes were required, it was not unusual for the Commission to split down the middle, the three Britons voting one way and the three Newfoundlanders the other, leaving it to the Governor to decide. Before he could proceed, Ira Wild, the Cheshire-born accountant who had served as the Commission's comptroller and auditor general from its inception to 1939, then elected to return as Commissioner for Finance in 1941, intervened.

"I would like to say that I agree completely with my Newfoundland colleagues. We have a choice – either acquiesce in this wretched policy, or decide here and now to reject it, and that is my position. I have no idea who devised the policy, but I consider it a gross insult to the Newfoundland people to be considering their future – tantamount to judging their courage, their loyalty really – in secret like this. I am entirely against it. We should reject the policy and send it back without comment.

"Gentlemen, it appears to me that a vote is no longer required."

Taken somewhat aback by the unexpected vehemence of Wild's statement, the Governor smiled to himself. "Hand in your copies, if you please."

Having inspected the crash site near Musgrave Harbour on March 4, the civil Court of Inquiry to investigate "the accident which occurred . . . on or about the 20th February, 1941 to an aircraft en route from the Newfoundland Airport to Great Britain piloted by Captain Mackey with Flying officer Bird, R. A. F., as First Officer and Navigator and Wireless Operator Snailham and as passenger Sir Frederick Banting" convened at the Newfoundland Airport for four days of closed-door hearings, from March 5–8, 1941.

"Gentlemen, " Air Commodore Walsh explained at the formal opening, "this is not a statutory inquiry held under any law or regulation of the Dominion/Colony of Newfoundland. We are convened under the authority of His Excellency, the Governor in Commission, for the purpose of determining the cause of the crash of Hudson III bomber T-9449, and the manner of the deaths of three persons, two of them Canadian citizens, and a citizen of the United Kingdom.

"The Court is authorized to call upon any person in this jurisdiction in the name of His Excellency, and any other person deemed to be capable of rendering assistance to the Inquiry, in the determination of the cause of the accident and the circumstances thereof, and to render all assistance possible."

Further sittings, he announced, would be held in Montréal, head office location of Canadian Pacific Railways, and in Ottawa.

"I request you to furnish to me," Commissioner Woods had written in the Letter of Appointment, "as soon as you can conveniently do so, a full report upon the accident and upon the causes thereof, together with such recommendations as you may deem advisable with a view to remedying any conditions likely to cause any similar accident in the future, and to make such observations as you may deem advisable in connection with the accident, including an expression of your views as to whether blame for the accident is attributable to any party, and if so what party or parties."

The letter specified that Walsh and Wing Commander Adams, R.C.A.F., despite their military connections, would be "acting in a civil capacity." The third member, Stewart Graham, was a civilian employed by the Canadian Department of Transport.

The Commission of Government met on April 2, when Woods reported that he had received the report and findings. It was agreed that the report should be communicated to the Secretary of State for Dominion Affairs in London, the Secretary of State for External Affairs at Ottawa, and the Canadian Pacific Railway. But it was also agreed to keep it from the public. The Commissioner would issue a press communiqué stating that the report had been received and that its findings related to purely technical matters which it was not considered in the general interest to disclose.

In his dual role as an observer for both the British Ministry of Aircraft Production and the Canadian Pacific Railway, Capt. D. C. T. Bennett sat in at all but the Ottawa segment of the inquiry.

"I was not present in Ottawa," he explained in a secret report to his principals, "as it consisted entirely of arriving at a finding. In accordance with normal procedure, I was not informed of the nature of the finding."

Bennett reported that no specific terms of reference or rules of procedure were laid down, "but the Court was conducted at all times in accordance with normal procedure for such a Court. Strict propriety and secrecy were maintained at all times."

He said the members "extended to me fullest co-operation and gave me access as C.P.R. representative to all available evidence."

As to the cause of the crash, based on the evidence his opinion was that failure of the port engine appeared to have been due to "the fracture of a small lug to which is attached the thermostatic control spiral of the oil cooler.

"When this fractured the thermostatic control vibrated into the 'Closed' position by passing the oil direct back to the tank, cutting out all cooling. The oil temperature then rose to such a degree that scavenge failure occurred, and the oil was drawn out through the breather on the port airscrew. The pilot was then slow to feather this engine, and the failure to feather when he did press the button may be attributed either to particles of metal in the oil, jamming the feathering pump, or to the high oil temperature, causing the feathering pump to jam."

Failure of the starboard engine, he added, "appears to have been due to carburettor icing."

However, he went on to qualify this conclusion.

"This statement cannot, in my opinion, be made as a definite one. But in view of the symptoms and the lack of any evidence to the contrary, and in view of the fact that the pilot was running on hot air in temperatures where he would better have been on cold air (in accordance with instructions issued), icing in the carburettor seems the most likely cause."

In the days following the inquiry, sabotage was prominent in memoranda the Newfoundland Government's Air Advisor, Pattison, sent to his superiors:

```
18 April, 1941


"[T]he only point that concerns us would
appear to be the question of access of unau-
thorized persons to aircraft when at
Gander. This point was brought forward by
some of the witnesses and comment is made
in the covering letter of the Court of
Inquiry C 60-2-17 dated 21 March, 1941.
Personally I am of the opinion that hidden
sabotage would be impossible provided the
employees of the C.P.R. and Shell [Oil]
Company were known to be reliable. There
would appear to be no reason to suspect any
```

of these employees. However, with the
increased number of aircraft expected to
commence by 25 April . . . I have discussed
this matter with Captain Ross of the C.P.R.
Air Service [and] it is suggested that [in
addition to the Army sentries) two additional members of the Ranger Force be
posted to Gander for this purpose."

18 April, 1941

"It is not apparent as to why [proceedings
of the Court of Inquiry] would be necessary
for the [Banting] executors regarding life
insurance. It is possible that this request
may have been made owing to the question of
doubt as to the cause of the accident. Wide
publicity has been given to an unofficial
statement that the accident was caused by
sabotage. From the conclusions of the
Court, the cause of the accident was
certain technical failures in no way
connected with sabotage. Thus is brought
forward for your consideration the desir-
ability of issuing a statement to this
effect [but] it may be undesirable at this
time to reopen public interest."

15 May, 1941

"Referring to my letter NFD/106/19 of 18
April, I brought forward one point which
required attention, that is the possibility
of sabotage. This point has now been overcome by the appointment of Rangers to the

> Airport with the sole duty of safeguarding
> the aircraft and equipment. There is one
> additional point, that is the guarding of
> the petrol supply. This supply is stored in
> the open and the possibility of sabotage is
> present. It may be that the guarding of this
> petrol should be the concern of the petrol
> company. However, the Army authorities may
> regard this as coming within the scope of
> their obligations. I brought this point
> forward on the occasion of Brigadier
> Earnshaw's visit but no decision was
> reached."

As a follow-up to the Banting crash inquiry, Walsh, as president of the Court, had written Canadian Pacific about certain matters, and in a "SECRET AND CONFIDENTIAL" letter C. H. Dickens, general manager of the Air Service Department, responded. Walsh also sent a copy to Commissioner Woods.

"Without in any way making any excuses," Dickens wrote, "it has been extremely difficult under conditions prevailing to get an organization set up in Newfoundland which will function smoothly and easily . . . [but] you will note from the answers set out herein that considerable progress has been made."

Then followed a point-by-point response to the inquiry chairman's questions ranging from why Mackey had not released parachute flares before the crash (he did not think it would have done any good), to why no axe was carried in the aircraft (in future a three-pound axe, a can opener, and six small boxes of matches in a metal container would be supplied, and crewmen would be required to carry a pocket knife, a small flashlight, a waterproof match case with matches, and a couple of bars of chocolate).

Complete reorganization of the C.P.R. Air Service Department had been under way, with appointment of a Base Manager in Newfoundland and a chief clerk to assist with administration. In addition, three additional maintenance men had been sent to Newfoundland Airport with six more to come. A superintendent of maintenance had been employed, and refuelling was made a direct responsibility of C.P.R. maintenance staff.

"Well," remarked Walsh to his fellow inquiry members, "everything seems to be operating as it should. This is not for the official report, but someone – usually someone important – has to die before needed improvements are made. It was ever thus!"

Commissioner Puddester had been having trouble sleeping in the wake of the Scorched Earth Policy meeting. It was nearly midnight when he finally drifted off, only to become entrapped in nightmare images of exploding oil storage tanks, towering flames threatening St. John's from end to end, and family members, friends, and colleagues, and their homes and properties, about to be swallowed up. A figure vaguely resembling himself, rather than attempting to stanch the flow of gasoline from the hillside storage tanks, insisted that the valves be opened even wider to cause the flames to burn higher.

"John . . . John, wake up!" he heard a distant voice urging. "Chief O'Neill called – the harbour is on fire!"

When he came fully to his senses, it was to find that this nightmare was very real. His wife, Mary, was shaking him vigorously to deliver a terrifying message. The big Imperial Oil dock on the South Side of the port of St. John's harbour was burning fiercely, with blazing petroleum spreading over the harbour waters to threaten scores of warships, merchantmen, and schooners tied to the wooden jetties.

Led by His Majesty's Rescue Tug *Tenacity*, which had superb firefighting capability, military and civilian personnel managed to suppress the dangerous blaze with great difficulty but with minimum damage.

How it had started was a mystery, but sabotage could not be ruled out.

THIRTY-THREE

Search for the Arsonist:
Aftermath of the K. of C. Fire

THE PLAN DEVISED by O'Neill to bring order out of the anticipated chaos of the biggest investigation the Constabulary had ever been called upon to handle was beginning to work, as he had known it would. It just would take time. Every interview, of which there were hundreds, was given a category – interviews with survivors, the injured in hospital, hostel officials, nearby residents, casual observers, firemen, other policemen, even casual passersby. The list seemed endless, and every one had a story to tell concerning where they were and what they had seen in connection with the terrible tragedy of the Knights of Columbus fire. The first-line interviewers passed brief, written summaries to the analysis group, who decided whether to pursue or set aside each summary – or perhaps to re-interview the subject. The results of this second step went on to the third group, who also were responsible to co-ordinate the information they received with occurrence reports for the critical period.

"It's not perfect," the chief of police remarked to Mahoney of the Security Division and Whelan and Cahill of the C.I.D., when these senior officers joined him in his office for a cup of tea and an informal review of progress after days, that would soon stretch into weeks, of intense effort. O'Neill had decided to take personal charge of this aspect of the investigation to allow other senior personnel to carry on with their own regular, but these days increasingly heavy, responsibilities.

"But it's beginning to show results, and that's what we need to see. For example, there's a young naval rating named McFadden, from Nova Scotia, recovering in the hospital from severe burns. It seems he and another sailor by the name of Bowers – who, it appears, did not get out alive – were playing Ping-Pong in the rec room of the hostel when a Canadian Women's Army Corps member walked through towards the upstairs storage areas where the fire may have started.

"We also know from the manager of the hostel, Mr. Quinn, that a C.W.A.C. member, the only one to do so, apparently, picked up a ticket in advance for the barn dance. She signed for it, but unfortunately – well, you know what must have happened to those records, like everything else in the building. On top of that, two constables on foot patrol spoke to a woman in uniform leaving the club just before the fire broke out, but didn't record her name. The question, of course, is – was it the same person in all three sightings?

"Now, there's nothing wrong, or against the law, in any of this, but if it was the same person, why go to the trouble of picking up a ticket, and one that was much in demand, if you had no intention of using it? Why be upstairs in the recreation or storage area when the entertainment was going on below? Why leave the place at the very time the concert was in full swing?"

The other officers were obviously impressed, especially Whelan whose operations deputy, Cahill, had suggested various improvements when the plan was first put on the table.

"Chief, have we any idea who this person may be?" he asked.

"Not yet, but we're working on it," O'Neill replied grimly.

"I believe," wrote Mr. Justice Dunfield, "that we have clearly traced the principal place of origin and the disastrous course (of the K. of C. fire) but we have not, so far, discovered who set it. I am of the opinion, though I cannot prove it at present, that it was of incendiary origin, for these reasons:

(a) the small cupboard, full of cartons, with limited free floor space, and dark because an electric bulb was lacking, was not a place to which people who might be careless with matches or cigarettes would be likely to resort.

(b) I doubt if a match or cigarette dropped outside the cartons would have ignited them.

(c) The inflammable points were the one (or possibly two) cartons broached and in use. I judge from description that a light would have had to be inserted sidewise in these; it could hardly fall into them. They were not face up or near the floor, but on their sides some distance up in a pile.

(d) No grounds are to be found for supposing that either spontaneous combustion or ignition from electrical wiring took place in the cupboard. The point has been considered.

The inquiry commissioner noted that a single witness on the evening of the fire "saw the twin cupboard to this, which was outside the dormitory in the passage. Its door was open. Some rolls of toilet paper, or possibly of towels, were on a shelf, and the ends of the paper had been pulled out and trailed down, an unnatural and suspicious state of affairs."

He pointed out that this story was told before the public heard that subsequently "toilet paper disposed extensively and in a very suspicious manner was found in the loft over the Y.M.C.A. hostel, a building similar in origin, construction, and use" to the K. of C. hostel. He remarked that the connection was "instructive" – that a criminal often repeats a method that has been successful. Reference was also made to fires that destroyed the Old Colony Club – a building "much resorted to by the Forces," and a small fire at the American-operated United Services Organization canteen – known as the U.S.O. Building, not far from police headquarters – had been discovered and extinguished "in a place where one would not have expected to find it."

The commissioner described these coincidences as "at least remarkable" and added that at first sight, "one cannot help suspecting a concerted design against buildings frequented by the Armed Forces. Taking into account the whole situation, as well as some incidents known to the police which it would not be expedient to discuss here, I am of the opinion as stated, though the guilty party is not known and the motive is doubtful."

Therefore all persons controlling buildings of consequence, especially those frequented by the Armed Forces and such places as moving-picture theatres, "would do well to assume that attempts may be made on their buildings, and to exercise great care and watchfulness accordingly."

After digging around among accumulated papers and documents, pay books, military citations, and letters, for a frustrating two or three hours, during which time he more than once felt it might be a wasted effort, Ricketts found what he was looking for – a scrap of paper, tucked in the pocket of a road map of a section of eastern France and Belgium. On it he had written down many years earlier the names of German prisoners captured that day in a stinking enemy redoubt in the trenches of Flanders. Among them was the name of Karl Otto Stroesser.

"Well I'll be. Just imagine, that," the Victoria Cross winner said aloud, even though he was alone in the attic storage room. He found it hard to credit that he'd actually found the paper – but was taken aback even more to know that a survivor from that long-ago battlefield incident had now turned up in St. John's.

"Inspector Cahill, please," the quiet-spoken hero said into the phone, working hard to suppress the excitement he felt rising despite himself. He had thought those emotions had gone away for good.

When the detective came on the line, he said, "Mike, it's Tom Ricketts . . . . I've got it. I've found a name for you!"

But Cahill also needed a face, and Ricketts offered to supply that as well.

"I've got a pretty good memory for faces, you know, so if you'd like to send over an artist – I can't leave the shop, I'm all alone here – I can describe this Stroesser as he looks today, or at least as he looked the day he came in here for a package of Royal Blends."

Cahill said he would do so right away, and decided this was one likeness he would *not* put in the papers. If he was going to find Stroesser, who might be using the name Friedmann, secrecy and surprise rather than publicity would be the means.

Every policeman on the beat, and especially the detectives, was given a copy of the sketch. But they were also warned that the man in the drawing was armed and dangerous, that he had killed before, and no doubt would be prepared to do so again.

Since ordinary constables on patrol went about their business unarmed, they were ordered to keep their distance – to merely observe and report. As for the C.I.D. men, who carried concealed sidearms, they were given more latitude, but at morning parade there was a strong caution issued that having a gun and getting the chance to use it were not necessarily the same thing. With a man like Stroesser, as cold-blooded as they come, O'Neill was personally on hand to point out, the warning went double.

At her listening post at Civil Defence headquarters on Bond Street, Johanne Horstnagel, alias Joanne Smith, learned from the daily flow of gossip that police investigating the Knights of Columbus fire were interested in talking to a member of the Canadian Women's Army Corps. She was surprised, even though she had been half expecting, had been dreading the possibility she might be discovered.

"I don't suppose you might be the one," an attractive, blond secretary, Dianne McCarthy, laughed as she opened a package of Purity Cream Crackers and offered it to her uniformed colleague to accompany the steaming mugs of tea on their desks. However, seeing how the frivolous suggestion upset Joanne, she regretted it immediately. They had, in a short while, become good friends around the office, and this was the day Dianne had planned to invite the newest member of the team to Sunday dinner. She imagined it was no fun being on your own in a strange city, and a home-cooked meal would be great for morale.

"Oh, I'm really sorry, Joanne. I shouldn't have said that, but it was only in jest. My husband, Mike, always says I have a wonderful ability to put my foot in it."

"It's not that, really, dear," Joanne replied, her voice suddenly quivering.

"It's . . . it's about my father, in Ontario – he had a stroke, you know, just before I came here to Newfoundland, and now I've heard from home that he really isn't very well. I'm afraid he . . . he . . ."

She stopped short of completing the thought, and took out a handkerchief to make a great show of dabbing her eyes. The spy silently congratulated herself on her performance when she saw Dianne had suddenly become teary-eyed as well, and then awkwardly turned the conversation to other things.

But it was bad news so far as Joanne was concerned. She suddenly felt threatened and vulnerable, and knew she must report this latest development to Stroesser as quickly as possible. But worse was to come.

Only a short time later, one of the A.R.P. men, a big, beefy fellow with a ruddy complexion and a droopy mustache, came into the office and somewhat breathlessly announced what he had heard on the street that very morning.

"There's a rumour the C.I.D. might be on the trail of a foreign agent and circulating his picture.

"What's this bloody place coming to, anyway?" he demanded of no one in particular.

THIRTY-FOUR

The Death of Stroesser,
and the Fiery End of U-69

ON THE NORTHEAST CORNER of Water and Prescott Streets, a rookie policeman spotted a man walking quickly, and carrying a suitcase. He came up from the waterfront and turned east on Water Street. The policeman was certain the man was the one in the photograph he had in a breast pocket.

To make sure, Constable George Piercey turned his back to Water Street so he appeared to be looking in the window of Long Brothers, Printers. He slid the picture out of its envelope so as to compare it with his mind's image of the man he saw in the street moments before. As he did so, a young woman in a C.W.A.C. uniform came rushing down Prescott Street and, turning the corner, collided heavily with the policeman. They both went flying.

In the confusion Piercey dropped the sketch he was holding. Johanne picked it up and was shocked to recognize that it was a likeness of her boss, Stroesser. She got to her feet and, in her confusion, not knowing what else to do, thrust the picture back into Piercey's hand and walked hurriedly away, heading east on Water Street.

In the meantime, the man the constable had hoped to identify had disappeared. However, in response to his urgent alarm to police headquarters from a nearby call box, a squad of officers arrived in a matter of minutes. They began a systematic sweep of streets in the general area around King's Beach, the place where

Sir Humphrey Gilbert had claimed Newfoundland for the English Crown nearly 400 years ago, and where it appeared their elusive quarry must be hiding.

Fifty-nine steps above Water Street in the same vicinity and at the same time, in a converted warehouse loft overlooking Newfoundland's National War Memorial, a pair of Royal Canadian Navy skippers were meeting for a few beers and bitter conversation. The place had been formally named the Seagoing Officers Club, but was more colourfully known as the Crow's Nest, arguably the most famous wartime refuge for naval officers in the free world. The object of their anger was their own navy brass.

Lieutenant Leslie P. Denny, R.C.N.R., commanding officer of the corvette HMCS *Drumheller*, and Lieutenant John Lawrence Finlayson, R.C.N.V.R., commanding officer of the Fairmile *HMCML Q78*, had both been cited by a naval Board of Inquiry arising out of the torpedoing of a pair of merchantmen, the SS *Rose Castle* and the SS *PLM 27*, with the loss of forty lives, off Bell Island.

The board had found that Denny failed to organize the patrol to the best advantage, and to take action immediately to order all vessels in the patrol to search for the U-boat. Finlayson was found to have erred when his Fairmile proceeded at once with rescue work rather than immediately setting out to find the attacker.

"What were we supposed to do," the motor launch skipper spat the words out, "just leave those poor devils to die? We picked up twelve still alive, for God's sake – if we'd left them like *Grand'mere* left the *Caribou*'s people, that would be another story!" He signalled the waiter for another round.

"Yeah, and I don't know what the hell they mean by 'best advantage,'" Finlayson, the corvette captain, added. "You're out there in the pitch dark, three o'clock in the morning, with wreckage sticking up all over the place, doing the patrol.

You can only try to cover the ground systematically and with due caution. As far as I'm concerned, that's what we were doing!"

"Make it two more," Finlayson said, when the waiter appeared at their table. But before they could start on their seconds, the phone behind the bar rang, and the barman picked it up.

"Lieutenant Finlayson, telephone," he called out.

The officer took it, had a hurried few words, and rushed back to the table.

"C'mon, Les. Looks like we've got a chance to redeem ourselves. There's a sub right off the Narrows, and we're ordered to go and get him!"

Scrambling down the long flight of ice-encrusted wooden steps, and then beyond to street level, they piled into the lorry sent to get them quickly to the dock. They couldn't help noticing a squad of Constabulary officers who, at the same time, were jumping out of cars.

Neither party could know that they both, the navy and the police, were involved in the same effort: to nail Stroesser and foil his means of escape.

Stroesser was minutes ahead of the pursuing police, all the time he needed. The "suitcase" was his radio transmitter, with which he had made contact a short time earlier with Graf in *U-69*, requesting that he proceed immediately and urgently to Quidi Vidi Gut to take him out of Newfoundland. Since the episode with Chartwell, the *Abwehr* agent had decided it was best to have his own small boat moored in the tiny inlet against just such an emergency.

He had observed the collision between Johanne and the young constable. When she reached the corner around which he was keeping out of sight, Stroesser took the agent's arm and steered her to a car he had parked in a vacant space off St. John's Lane.

"Come with me," Stroesser commanded. "The authorities are on to us and we have to get out of here now, quickly."

"I know," she gasped, out of breath. "I was on the way to warn you." In brief moments they were en route to "the Gut" and shortly had put to sea.

Foggy conditions prevailed off Quidi Vidi, and Graf felt it was safe to surface closer to land than he otherwise might have done. Accordingly, a few hundred yards out, but still dangerously in range of coastal artillery, Stroesser and Johanne saw the submarine. Like a huge whale, it breached the surface and lay waiting for them. Stroesser breathed a sigh of relief. Admiral Canaris and his influence had come through yet again!

The conning tower hatch opened, and several sailors emerged to man deck-guns and to urge with hand signals that those in the small boat make it quick. Then suddenly, as they came closer, one of the men on the U-boat, whom Stroesser judged to be the first officer, held up his hand like a traffic policeman stopping cars. Strange that Graf had not put in an appearance.

"Just a minute," the officer said. "Nobody said anything about women coming on this boat. That is something we cannot have. It is bad luck. You may come aboard, Herr Stroesser, but the person with you may not!"

"That's crazy," Stroesser retorted as his little punt bobbed on the waves. In a matter of seconds it would be tight against the huge side of the submarine. Only a few yards remained between them and escape. "This 'person' as you call her has done more to advance the cause of the Third Reich than most people I can think of. Let me speak to Kapitainleutnant Graf, please, so we can get this straightened out."

"I have my orders, Herr Stroesser. You and you alone are to come aboard, and you had better hurry."

The words were hardly out of the man's mouth before there was a terrific *whoosh!* as a coastal artillery shell screamed close overhead to crash into the sea, sending a geyser of water thirty or forty feet into the air only a couple of dozen yards from *U-69*. The craft had been detected by Canadian Army lookouts on Signal Hill and the heights over Cuckhold's Cove. It was also likely that corvettes were on the way, the so-called "nasties" of the Royal

Canadian Navy that were on stepped-up patrols in the area since the Bell Island sinkings, and anti-submarine aircraft from the nearby Torbay R.C.A.F. Station as well.

"That's it . . . . The next shot will probably find our range," the man in the conning tower shouted. "We cannot remain here any longer. Are you coming or not, Herr Stroesser? We have to get out of here and we have to do it now."

A few more seconds and, without warning, he turned to the open conning tower hatch and shouted to the crew below, "Dive! Dive! Dive!"

He disappeared, slamming the hatch behind him. Several seamen were caught still on deck. Presumably their fate was simply to be considered "unfortunate."

Somebody has written with a great deal of truth that war is hell. Hell was about to engulf *U-69* as it had the SS *Caribou*, sent to the bottom by the submarine only a short time before. The next artillery shell did, indeed, find its mark, exploding with a roar and a sheet of flame against the side of the ship, and another and another. Stroesser's flimsy little punt disappeared in a shower of splintered wood, and he and Johanne with it.

Now the sub-chasing airplanes were overhead, and the Royal Canadian Navy closing in. They pounded the crippled submarine mercilessly, each explosion an expression of vengeance for the dead of the *Caribou*, the Bell Island ore boats, the Old Colony Club, the victims of the K. of C. Hostel fire, and the sabotage at Argentia – and, yes, for Major Sir Frederick Grant Banting and those who had perished with him.

When the bombs found her torpedo storage compartments, a mighty, flaming explosion literally tore the submarine apart. The blast shook the ancient hills nearby, caused tremors in the solid granite structure of Cabot Tower, more than a mile and a half away, and sent a smaller version of a tidal wave surging across Freshwater Bay.

Thousands of residents of the St. John's area, especially in The Battery below Signal Hill, in the Quidi Vidi area, and in Logy Bay, had a front-row seat to the destruction of the Nazi submarine, even if the fog somewhat obscured their view. However, those who looked to the next day's newspapers for confirmation of what they had seen, or thought they saw, found only this cryptic version, in which it was easy to visualize the wartime censor with very large scissors in hand:

> The Naval authorities announced that an action took place yesterday against a presumed enemy submarine in waters off eastern Newfoundland. Further details were not released.

In the meantime, the beaches from Cape Spear north to Cape St. Francis were littered for weeks with wreckage, and in the first few days bodies and body parts, many in clothing bearing the insignia of the German *kriegsmarine*. Canadian naval recovery teams made regular patrols to clear the beaches of items that might be upsetting or dangerous to the civilian population, including small arms ammunition and live shells from the U-boat's heavier deck-gun.

On Bell Island, residents couldn't help but notice an old black dog, crippled with arthritis, coming down night after night to spend the lonely hours whimpering and barking while gazing sorrow-fully out over the waters where the SS *Rose Castle* and the SS *PLM 27* had been torpedoed with heavy loss of life. It was believed the dog had belonged to one of the sailors lost in the sinkings, and a local youngster named Stephen Neary had taken to leaving food for the animal. Following the destruction of *U-69* with all hands (it was believed to carry fifty officers and men) the old dog was seen no more. But people living in the vicinity claimed that on dark and foggy nights they still could hear him, pitifully howling his sorrow over Lance Cove Beach.

POSTSCRIPT

Although extensive reference is made in this book to the Court of Inquiry, conducted under the authority of the Government of Newfoundland by a retired senior officer of the Royal Canadian Air Force, into the crash of Hudson No. T-9449 and the death of Sir Frederick Banting, the report of the inquiry is nowhere to be found.

Governor Walwyn, in a secret telegram to the Secretary of State for External Affairs of Canada and the Secretary of State for Dominion Affairs of Great Britain, advised, "We are issuing here brief communiqué to the effect that findings of Court deal exclusively with technical matters and that publication of report not in public interest."

It is clear, then, that a report did at some point exist. However, researchers, including the author of *The Banting Enigma*, have been unable to locate it in the National Archives of Canada, in the records of the Department of National Defence, or in the Canadian Pacific Archives. Nor has a search of the records of the Provincial Archives of Newfoundland and Labrador produced the desired result.

Furthermore, although it appears an autopsy on the body of Sir Frederick Banting was conducted at the Banting Institute in Toronto, the report of that procedure also seems to be missing.

The fact that official, public documents concerning the mysterious death of such a prominent Canadian are absent from public and private archives raises the suspicion of a cover-up. It lends weight to speculation of foul play, specifically of sabotage/assassination, at the Newfoundland Airport in Gander in the month of February 1941.

ACKNOWLEDGEMENTS

The author wishes to express sincere appreciation to the following for assistance and encouragement in the preparation of this book: Roland W. Abbott, Musgrave Harbour, NL; Robert Banting, Oakville, ON; Frank Bartlett, Corner Brook, NL; Jeff Blackwood, St. John's, NL; Michael Bliss, Toronto, ON; Deputy Chief (Ret'd.) Gary Browne, Royal Newfoundland Constabulary, St. John's, NL; Mark W. Callahan, St. John's, NL; William F. Case, St. John's, NL; Ann Marie and Gary Churchill, Arnprior, ON; James Dempsey, Halifax, NS; Patrick Fleming, Harbour Grace, NL; George French, Archivist, Corner Brook Museum and Archives, Corner Brook, NL; Roderick B. Goff, Gander, NL; Gary Hebbard, St. John's, NL; Bill Johnston, Historian, Directorate of History and Heritage, National Defence Headquarters, Ottawa, ON; Fabian M. Kennedy, St. John's, NL; the late James J. Lynch, Royal Newfoundland Constabulary Historical Association, St. John's, NL; Roanne Mokhtar, Reference Archivist, National Archives of Canada, Ottawa, ON; John E. Murphy, Phoenix, AR; Judith Nefsky, Archivist, Canadian Pacific Archives, Montréal, QC; Capt. Joseph Prim, St. John's, NL; Shelley Smith, Provincial Archivist, Provincial Archives of Newfoundland and Labrador, St. John's, NL; Jennifer Toews, Acting Manuscript Librarian, Thomas Fisher Rare Book Library, University of Toronto; Brian Williams, Curator, North Atlantic Aviation Museum, Gander, NL.

Also the following: Staff of the Centre for Newfoundland Studies Archives and the Queen Elizabeth II Library, Memorial University of Newfoundland, the A. C. Hunter and Michael Donovan Public Libraries, the Newfoundland and Labrador Provincial Archives, and volunteers of the Royal Newfoundland

Constabulary Historical Association, all of St. John's, NL; the Laurier-Metcalf Branch of the Ottawa Public Library (particularly Ottawa Room Archivist Brian Silcoff); the City of Ottawa Archives; and the National Archives and National Library of Canada, Ottawa, ON.

REFERENCE SOURCES/
BIBLIOGRAPHY

In the interests of contextual accuracy, the author perused the following publications, and is grateful to the authors thereof:

Benton, William, Pub. *Encyclopedia Britannica*. (Chicago, London, Toronto, 1961.)

Bliss, Michael. *Banting, A Biography*. (Toronto: McClelland & Stewart, 1984/1992.)

Bradford, Sarah. *George VI*. (London: Weidenfeld & Nicolson, 1989.)

Bruce, Harry. *Lifeline: The Story of the Atlantic Ferries and Coastal Boats*. (Toronto: Macmillan, 1977.)

Bryden, John. *Deadly Allies*. (Toronto: McClelland & Stewart, 1989.)

Buchheim, Lothar-Gunther. *The Boat*. (New York: Bantam Books, 2000.)

Concord Desk Encyclopedia. (New York, 1982.)

Butler, David. *Lusitania*. (New York: Random House, 1982.)

Butler, Rupert. *The Gestapo*. (Phoenix: Amber Books, 2004.)

Cardoulis, John N. *A Friendly Invasion II*. (St. John's: Creative Publishers, 1993.)

Christie, Carl A., with Fred Hatch. *Ocean Bridge: The History of the R.A.F. Ferry Command. (*Toronto: University of Toronto Press, 1982.)

Doyle, Richard. *Imperial 109*. (New York: Bantam Books, 1977.)

Fox, Arthur. *The Newfoundland Constabulary*. (St. John's: Robinson Blackmore, 1971.)

Harvey, Reginald. *Mackenzie King of Canada*. (Oxford: Oxford University Press, 1949.)

Hayes, Carlton J. H. *Political and Cultural History of Modern Europe, Vol.II.* (Toronto: Macmillan, 1939.)

Horwood, Harold. *Bartlett: The Great Explorer*. (Toronto: Doubleday, 1977.)

House. Jack. *Winston Churchill: His Wit and Wisdom*. (London: William Collins, Sons, 1965.)

How, Douglas. *Night of the Caribou*. (Hantsport: Lancelot Press, 1988.)

Jorgenson, Robert G. *Newfoundland Gallantry in Action*. (St. John's: Jesperson Press, 1993.)

Journal of the Canadian Aviation Historical Society. (Willowdale: The Canadian Aviation Historical Society, Spring 1987.)

Lamb, James B. *The Corvette Navy*. (Toronto: Stoddard Publishing, 2000.)

Life at the "Crossroads of the World", History of Gander, Newfoundland: A Compilation. (Gander: Gander Senior's Club, 1988.)

MacMillan, Margaret. *Paris 1919*. (New York: Random House, 2001.)

Manchester, William. *The Last Lion*. (New York: Little, Brown and Company, 1983.)

McGrath, Darrin M. *Last Dance: The Knights of Columbus Fire*. (St. John's: Flanker Press, 2004.)

Miller, Francis T. *History of World War II*. (Toronto: Dominion Book & Bible House, 1946.)

Neary, Steve. *The Enemy on our Doorstep*. (St. John's: Jesperson Press, 1994.)

Nicholson, G. W. L. *The Fighting Newfoundlandler*. Government of Newfoundland and Labrador/ Thomas Nelson, 1964.

Nicholson, G. W. L. *More Fighting Newfoundlanders*. Government of Newfoundland and Labrador. Hazell, Watson & Viney, 1969.

Noel, S. J. R. *Politics in Newfoundland*. (Toronto: University of Toronto Press, 1971.)

O'Leary, Grattan. *Recollections of People, Press and Politics*. (Toronto: Macmillan, 1977.)

O'Neill, Paul. *A Seaport Legacy*. (Erin: Press Porcepic, 1976.)

O'Neill, Paul. *The Oldest City*. (Erin: Press Porcepic, 1975.)

Parker, John. *King of Fools*. (New York: St. Martin's Press, 1988.)

Penney, A. R. *Centennial: Newfoundland Railway*, 1881-1981. (St. John's: Creative Publishers, 1981.)

Prim, Capt. Joseph and Mike McCarthy. *Those in Peril*. (St. John's: Jesperson Publishing, 1995.)

Shields, Jim. Introduction to the Military History of Newfoundland. Naval Association of Newfoundland, Eastern Division, 1998.

Smallwood, Joseph R., Ed. *Encyclopedia of Newfoundland and Labrador*. (St. John's: Newfoundland Book Publishers and Harry Cuff Publications. Vol.I, 1981; Vol. II, 1984; Vol. III, 1991; Vol. IV, 1993; Vol.V, 1994.)

Sweetenham, John. Mcnaughton, Vols. I, II and III. (Toronto: Ryerson Press, 1968-69.)

Taylor, A. J. P. *Beaverbrook*. (Markham: Simon and Schuster, 1972.)

Taylor, A. J. P. The *Origins of the Second World War*. (Toronto: Penguin Books, 1961/1963.)

Thistle, Mel, Ed. *The Mackenzie-McNaughton Wartime Letters*. (Toronto: University of Toronto Press, 1975.)

Tuchman, Barbara. *The Guns of August*. (New York: Bantam Books, 1976.)

Watt, Sholto. *I'll Take the High Road*. (Hertfordshire: Brunswick
   Press, 1960.)
Newspapers, including:

The Beacon, Gander, NL.
The Citizen, Ottawa, ON.
The Daily News, St. John's, NL.
The Daily Star, Toronto, ON.
The Evening Telegram (*The Telegram*), St. John's, NL.
The Gazette, Montréal, QC.
The Globe and Mail, Toronto, ON.
The Journal, Ottawa, ON.
The Western Star, Corner Brook, NL.

SOURCE NOTES

Prologue

1. Tuchman, Barbara. *The Guns of August*. Bantam-Macmillan, 1976

Chapter 7

2. Nicholson, G. W. L. *The Fighting Newfoundlander*. Government of Newfoundland, 1964.
3. *The Telegram*, June 1, 2003.

Chapter 8

4. Bliss, Michael. *Banting: A Biography*. University of Toronto Press, 1992.
5. Harvey, Reginald. Mackenzie King of Canada. Oxford University Press, 1949.
6. Bryden, John. *Deadly Allies*. McClellan & Stewart, 1989.
7. O'Leary, Grattan: *Recollections of People, Press and Politics*, Macmillan, 1977.
8. Ibid.
9. Bliss, Michael. *Banting: A Biography*. University of Toronto Press, 1992.

10. Thistle, Mel, Ed. *The Mackenzie-McNaughton Wartime Letter.* Toronto: University of Toronto Press, 1975.

Chapter 9

11. Parker, John. *King of Fools.* New York: St. Martin's Press, 1988.

Chapter 10

12. Nicholson, G. W. L. *More Fighting Newfoundlanders.* Government of Newfoundland/Hazell, Watson & Viney, 1969.
13. Miller, F. T. *History of World War II.* Dominion Book & Bible House, 1946.
14. Ibid.

Chapter 13

15. *Winston Churchill: His Wit and Wisdom.* William Collins, Sons, 1965.
16. Ibid.

Chapter 23

17. Carl A. Christie with Fred Hatch. *Ocean Bridge: The History of RAF Ferry Command.* Toronto University of Toronto Press, 1962.

Chapter 31

18. How, Douglas. *Night of the Caribou.* Lancelot Press, 1988.

19. Neary, Steve. *Enemy on Our Doorstep*. Jesperson Press, 1994.

20. Ibid.

Chapter 32

21. Paul O'Neill, Paul. *The Oldest City*. Press Porcepic, 1975.

22. Ibid.

23. Ibid.

WILLIAM ROGER CALLAHAN, born in St. John's November 7, 1931, is one of Newfoundland's and Canada's most senior journalists, having worked in print and broadcast media for nearly a half-century with a short time out for politics. He was natural resources minister in the final years of the last Smallwood administration of the Newfoundland government.

Callahan's interest in the Banting story was piqued by his discovery that documents relating to the investigation of the Hudson bomber crash of February 1941 in the Bonavista Bay wilderness were not to be found in any major Canadian archive, thus compounding the mystery surrounding Sir Frederick's death. *The Banting Enigma* offers a possible explanation for what happened in the context of wartime intrigue.

As editor of all three daily newspapers published in Newfoundland in the twentieth century – *The Telegram*, *The Western Star*, and the now defunct *Daily News*, Callahan set a record that will likely never be equalled. During those years he published literally thousands of commentaries on politics and public affairs.

His other books include a detailed explanation of the Smallwood era, a centennial history (as editor) of the Christian Brothers in Newfoundland, and, currently in progress, an anthology on the Viking discoverers of Newfoundland. *The Banting Enigma* is his first novel.